CAN YOU SURVIVE

THE ZOMBIE

APOCALYPSE?

CAN YOU SURVIVE
THE ZOMBIE
APOCALYPSE?

MAX BRALLIER

GALLERY BOOKS

NEW YORK
LONDON
TORONTO
SYDNEY

Gallery Books
A Division of Simon & Schuster, Inc.
1230 Avenue of the Americas
New York, NY 10020

Text Copyright © 2011 by Max Brallier
Illustrations Copyright © 2011 by Christopher Mitten

First Gallery Books trade paperback edition February 2011

GALLERY BOOKS and colophon are trademarks of Simon & Schuster, Inc.

For information about special discounts for bulk purchases, please contact Simon & Schuster Special Sales at 1-866-506-1949 or business@simonandschuster.com.

The Simon & Schuster Speakers Bureau can bring authors to your live event. For more information or to book an event contact the Simon & Schuster Speakers Bureau at 1-866-248-3049 or visit our website at www.simonspeakers.com.

Designed by Jaime Putorti

Manufactured in the United States of America

10 9 8 7 6 5

Library of Congress Cataloging-in-Publication Data

Brallier, Max.
   Can you survive the zombie apocalypse? / Max Brallier.
      p. cm.
   1. Zombies—Fiction. I. Title.
   PS3602.R344455C36 2011
   813.'6—dc22

                                                2010034649

ISBN 978-1-4516-0775-8
ISBN 978-1-4516-0880-9 (ebook)

FOR THE GUYS—

AMARU, ARDLE, BAKER, CHEWY, MANDO—

YOU KNOW WHY

ACKNOWLEDGMENTS

Boy, where to start. My wonderful agent, Jason Allen Ashlock, for believing this could be a book. My brilliant and always patient editor, Jaime Costas, for not only editing the hell out of this thing, but for editing the hell out of it while on maternity leave. Genius illustrator Christopher Mitten, who I kind of hate now because his stuff here is so damn good that it far outshines my writing. Jaime Putorti for being a constant pleasure to work with. Lily Kosner, for sending me the most important email of my life. And for their advice and guidance I must thank Katie McKim, Matthew Shear, Joe Goldschein, Michael Homler, Jill Sullivan, Tara Cibelli, Maggie Lam, Mike Amaru, Wes Ryan, Jess W. Brallier, and Nancy Trypuc. And, of course, Mom and Dad. Love ya. You too, Rube!

THE LEGEND

Every dead body that is not exterminated becomes one of them. It gets up and it kills. The people it kills get up and kill!

DAWN OF THE DEAD

In the brain and not the chest.
Headshots are the very best.

FIDO

I don't know what's going on, but I know it's not a prison break. No chemical I ever heard about can make a dead man walk. This is something that nobody has ever heard about or seen before.

This is hell on earth. This is pure hell on earth.

NIGHT OF THE LIVING DEAD

A BRIEF MESSAGE ON THE ZOMBIE APOCALYPSE AND YOU

Beyond this page lies unspeakable horror. Bone-crunching, blood-splattering, brain-impaling horror—the horror of the zombie apocalypse.

If you're reading this, you've probably read your fair share of zombie stories and watched your fair share of zombie flicks. But this time it's different. No longer do you get to sit back idle as a bunch of fools make all the wrong moves. All hell is about to break loose—and this time *you* have a say in humanity's survival.

You're twenty-five years old. You live in a crappy, overpriced studio apartment in Manhattan. You work a corporate job that you're not particularly fond of. Up until now, your day-to-day life offered few surprises.

But today, on a hot and humid July morning, zombies have come to Manhattan.

You have choices to make now—lots of them. Moral dilemmas. Strategic decisions. Weapons. Vehicles. Will you be a hero? Or will you cover your own ass at all costs? Will you survive the coming hours, days, weeks, and months? Or will you die amidst the chaos and violence of a zombie uprising?

Or, worst of all, will you become one of them . . . ?

The choice is yours. And hey, if you don't make it—you've got no one to blame but yourself.

Will this ever end? These Monday morning meetings always run long. Every damn time. God, in the history of man, has a morning meeting ever not run long?

As usual, you overslept, missed the subway, and arrived ten minutes late to work so you missed the Krispy Kremes and one of the good chairs. Now you're stuck in a tiny little plastic thing you're pretty sure you can hear bending underneath your weight—or maybe that's the sound of your stomach aching for a doughnut.

Your head's still hurting from Saturday night. Can't drink like you used to. College days: drink, puke, sleep, drink, puke, sleep, drink, puke, sleep, watch some basketball, drink, puke, sleep. Rinse. Repeat. Graduate three semesters late. Good times.

But you're a grown man now. An *ah*-dult. An *ah*-dult stuck in a miserable Monday morning meeting—with no Krispy Kreme.

All you can think about is five o'clock and getting home. Being enveloped by your well-worn but pretty-darn-comfortable-if-you-don't-say-so-yourself Craigslist couch. Ordering some Chinese. Sweet-and-sour chicken (sauce on the side), fried rice, an egg roll. Watching some *Seinfeld*. Good stuff.

Oh yes—to be home . . .

You pull out your phone. 10:40 AM. Sigh, seven more hours to—

Suddenly—violently—Angela, the cute brunette receptionist, bursts through a set of double doors and explodes into the conference room.

Everyone turns. Someone giggles. Confused looks all around.

Eyes wide, Angela stands in the doorway, silent for a moment, then: "Um—sorry to interrupt—but I think you need to turn the TV on."

Matthew Trypuc—head of marketing—glares from his usual spot at the head of the long conference table. Cool and condescending. "Angela, you're interrupting."

Prick. The poor girl just ran in here looking like she was going to wet herself—she must have a decent reason.

Angela ignores the big boss's dirty look and runs the length of the long conference room to the fat old Mitsubishi TV in the corner, a leftover from the pre-PowerPoint days. The oversize TV sits on a banged-up TV cart—you're pretty sure your middle school had the same one.

Someone asks Angela to explain. She doesn't say anything. Continues to work on the TV.

A woman at the end of the table—you recognize her from around the office but don't know her name—gets up and hurries out of the conference room. A few people follow her, headed for their computers to check CNN.com or MSNBC.com or whatever their news site of choice is.

You think terrorists. So does everyone else, most likely. You picture the word—*terrorist*—bouncing around their collective, coffee-fueled brains, along with images of explosions, crumbling buildings, and out-of-control beards.

The TV hums to life. One of the local news guys sits at a desk:

> *Again, we don't want to alarm you unnecessarily, but our early reports say these patients are exhibiting bizarre, radical, and even violent behavior.*

The broadcast cuts to an aerial view of Mount Sinai Hospital. You know Mount Sinai. It's about twenty blocks north and a few avenues east from your office. Went there a few years back when you had a hangnail that got infected and your mom convinced you that you were about two days away from needing full hand, and possible arm, amputation.

Now a shot from the ground: a pretty blond reporter, clearly not ready to be on live TV. A mass of ambulances, cop cars, fire engines, and workers stretches out behind and around her. The flashing red and blue lights strobe across her young, makeup-slathered face. You can make out the hospital about a hundred yards in the distance.

She reports:

> *Are we on? I'm on? Ahem. Yes, we've just received word that patients are rioting inside the hospital. At this moment, it's still not clear what the cause of the violence is—or how and even if hospital employees may be involved. Of course, any news we get we'll pass along immediately. Again, for those of you just tuning in, you're looking at Mount Sinai Hospital, where violence has reportedly broken out among a number of patients and possibly hospital staff.*

An aerial shot now:

A dozen police cars have formed a semicircle around the main emergency room entrance. More are arriving.

The big sliding doors beneath the EMERGENCY sign slide open and out stumbles a young doctor, bleeding from his face, neck, and shoulder. Blood pumps from his wounds, spilling out onto his scrubs. He takes a few shaky steps before collapsing onto the little green Mount Sinai carpet that lies in front of the door.

The office is silent for a split second—then a flurry of *Oh-mygods, Jesuschrists,* and *Whatthefucks.* The woman sitting next to you grabs on to your arm. It's weird.

The doctor begins convulsing. Blood streams onto the sidewalk and pools at the curb. Then, seemingly out of nowhere, a female patient in a hospital gown bursts out from the ER and dives on top of him.

The entire conference room gasps.

The patient is biting the doctor. No, not just biting. Eating him—devouring the guy. Tearing into his flesh with her teeth and hands. Clawing at his body. Ripping skin from his limbs. As she tosses her head back to chew, stringy flesh hangs from her teeth.

The screen goes black.

For a second, no one says a word; no one is quite able to process what he or she is seeing. Then a large woman (copyediting department, you think) explodes into tears, hands cupped over her face, and rushes out of the room. More follow her, reaching for cell phones as they squeeze past one another and out into the hall.

The TV picture returns. Shakily, the pretty blond reporter clutches the microphone, talking, but there's no sound.

There's action in the distance—something happening. All sorts of movement.

A mass of people begins to fill the screen behind her. What's happening? Rioting? Maybe. Thirty people. No, more. Fifty. Hospital workers, it looks like. And cops and firefighters. Running from something. No. Charging. And—Christ—what is wrong with these people? Their faces—albino white, twisted, possessed. Splashes of blood on all of them—some drenched. The reporter, oblivious to the chaos behind her, continues reporting. The cameraman sees what's coming. The screen flashes, and the camera falls to the ground, still broadcasting.

All you see now is feet—some shuffling, some running. Then suddenly a sickening close-up of the reporter's twisted face and neck as she hits the cement. Someone pounces on her. That pretty blond hair is torn from her scalp. Teeth dig in.

Behind her, the mob continues moving. A heavy work boot

tramples the reporter's face and you see her head partially implode.

More follow. Hundreds. Some stumble forward. Others run, awkward but quick.

Finally, the camera is kicked, spins wildly, and the broadcast cuts out.

Panic sets in all around you. Chairs hit the floor. A woman screams in pain as a man, quick to exit, spills his hot coffee on her lap. Crying. The conference room empties, your coworkers running for their phones and computers—desperate for news, desperate to get in touch with their loved ones.

You sit in your stupid uncomfortable chair, stunned, unable to move. Words dance around your brain along with images from comics and movies—and then finally you blurt out, to no one in particular,

"Zombies. Zombies . . . *ZOMBIES! THE LIVING FUCKING DEAD!*"

You can't believe it. You *don't* believe it. You goddamn *won't* believe it.

But you saw it. Right there on the TV.

Have to get up. Have to move.

You don't trust your legs to hold your body if you stand. For a long moment you just sit there, still. Sweat gathers on your brow. A drop crawls down your forehead and along your cheek. Finally, you force yourself to stand. You're relieved when you don't fall to the floor. You head for your cubicle.

You get to your computer and start typing. Hands are shaking. You're hitting all the wrong keys. You feel weak. Realize you're not breathing. You remind yourself, *breathe.* You sit down. Breathe in and out. Calm yourself. You bring up DrudgeReport.com. You see the red siren . . . never a good sign. Above, in giant letters, is the headline:

Zombies Take Manhattan?

A number of smaller links sit below:

Walking dead . . .
Running dead? . . .
Avian bird flu in NYC? Developing . . .
911 reporting claims of the dead returning to life . . .
Huge horror hoax?
Manhattan under siege? Developing . . .

Jesus Christ. You have to get the hell out of Manhattan ASAP.

You jog to the elevators. The hallway is packed. After the fourth or fifth time the doors open to a full car, you say fuck it, you'll hoof it. You're on the fifteenth floor. The stairs aren't much better. Dozens of people, running down. Someone trips, catches himself, and smacks face-first into the wall. He's knocked out cold. You and the others step over him as you continue your descent. The fire alarm screams, impossibly loud, along with flashing white lights—someone opened the emergency doors.

You take the stairs two at a time, going over it all in your head, trying to figure out where to go when you hit the street. Million-dollar question.

You finally get to the ground floor. Coworkers flood past you out the revolving doors. Didn't know they could spin that fast. You nearly lose a hand, pull it back just in time. You and two other guys squeeze into one slot—you being the meat in that sandwich—and a split second later you're spit out onto Eighty-fourth Street on the West Side. A street you've been on hundreds of times over the course of your short career. But this time, it's unrecognizable.

The streets are packed. Loud. Car horns blast. People yell—angry, violent screams.

And more, it's hot. Stinking hot and humid. Air so thick you could cut it with a knife. A New York City July. You think while you sweat . . .

If you think your best chance of getting out of the city is via taxi, turn to page 204.

If you want to jog the twelve blocks and two avenues to the Seventy-second Street subway and catch the next train to Brooklyn, turn to page 205.

If you want to get back to your apartment ASAP, turn to page 22.

Fuck it. You're getting on that train. You push. In front of you, a man fights to get on—only to be shoved out by the mob on board.

You bend your knees and turn yourself sideways, making yourself as small as possible, and squeeze through the sweaty mass of bodies. Two women go at it, exchanging blows with their purses—it provides you with a glimmer of space and you slip onto the cattle car.

A dozen times the doors nearly shut, each time making it partway, then opening again.

The pleasant, oh-so-calm recorded voice comes over the speaker: *Stand clear of the closing doors, please.*

Two tall black teens scream at each other, headphones blaring.

Stand clear of the closing doors, please.

A young doctor, still in scrubs, gets in the face of a Spanish woman for no reason, then shoves her in the chest. Someone sticks an arm in to break it up.

Stand clear of the closing doors, please.

You step on a man's foot. Large guy, looks homeless, but wears a gold watch. He glares at you. Type of guy looking for a fight.

Stand clear of the closing doors, please.

A large woman pushes past you. She grabs the thin man blocking the sensor, standing near the doors, and tosses him off.

Ding. The doors shut. Sarcastic cheers.

You breathe a long sigh of relief as the car pulls out of the station. The conductor says nothing about the happenings in the city. You blow by the next two stations. At each one a thick crowd—a hundred scared faces visible for one blurry moment as you whiz past.

On board, people wave their phones around, trying to get a signal. A pregnant woman cries in the corner. No one offers her a seat.

The conductor comes on and announces that, due to an accident at Houston Street, this train will make one final stop on its route and then continue running as a 7 train to Queens. You crane your neck to look at the map on the train wall. A train switching routes entirely like this—that seems unheard of. But at least Queens is far away from here, and you can get to Brooklyn from Queens, so you hang tight.

At the next stop, the train unloads and a fresh crowd eagerly takes their place. The train now continues on its new route.

You pull out your phone. Smile, for one short second, at your new background: Bruce Willis from *Die Hard*. Now there's a goddamn hero. He would have known what to do. You stick your phone up over your head like everyone else. No signal. Damn.

Sliding your phone back into your pocket, you notice for the first time the man in the seat below the map. He's at the end of the row, slouched against the metal handrail. His face is a pale, bluish white, drained of nearly all color. Blood is slowly seeping through a violent tear in the puffy New Jersey Devils jacket that covers his shivering body.

Oh shit. You can see the headline: ZOMBIE MAN AWAKENS ON SUBWAY, KILLS DOZENS.

His face is nearly see-through now. Veins visible through his translucent skin.

You look from side to side. No one else notices him.

Finally, his head flops back and rests against the Plexi-glas windowpane. Eyes wide open. Doesn't look like he's breathing . . .

If you want to shout for a doctor, turn to page 51.

Not your problem? Say fuck it and get your ass to the next car? Turn to page 86.

IT'S ELECTRIC, BOOGIE
WOOGIE WOOGIE

Desperate, you tug at the power cord on the back of some big thing with red lights on it. With three strong jerks, it rips loose. Sparks fly.

The beast launches itself over the side of the booth and onto you. Mouth open wide, saliva dripping, it goes in for the kill.

You jam the cord into its mouth and the bitch shakes violently. Almost jerks loose of it. You push it farther down its throat. The bitch's eyes light up.

But still it keeps coming. Teeth inching closer. One last chance before you're dead. You rip the cord from its mouth and jam the sparking, spitting end into its eyeball. It sizzles. You push farther, deeper into the eye socket.

Then, a split second before its teeth have a chance to sink into you, the cord pushes through to the brain. The monster shakes harder. Faster. Head jerking back and forth. Vomits all over your chest—bile and chunks of red. Then, finally, it goes limp and collapses on you.

You lie there for a moment, happy to be alive. Then the smell hits you. Burnt eyeball. Charred brain. Vomit. It's not nice. You push the thing off you and stand.

Turn to page 335.

After a long moment, you manage to squeak out "Um, I'm a Pirates fan, actually."

He laughs—then lowers the shotgun. "Pirates fan? Don't think I've ever met a Pirates fan."

"Well, there aren't a whole lot of us."

"As long as you ain't a Yankees fan, we're cool. Can't stand a Yankees fan."

Jesus—are you really talking baseball while a dead cop lies at your feet? A dead, headless zombie cop, at that.

"All you parking garage guys carry shotguns?" you ask.

Chucky hops on the hood of the SUV and takes a seat. He lights a cigarette and lazily bounces his feet off the headlight. "Nope. It was up front of the cruiser. Grabbed it out the other side of the car soon as the cop fell out."

You nod and look around. It's dark—he's got all the lights off, except for the one in the office, by the gate. The office light flickers, goes out for a second, then comes back. "Hey, there's a power line down outside," you say. "Does this place have a generator or anything? Emergency power?"

He looks at you like you just asked him the metric weight of Mars. "I just park the cars, man. I don't know about a damn power grid or whatever."

Gunshots outside. Then an explosion. The sounds echo down the ramp and through the garage.

You're sure as hell glad you're not out there—but how long will you be safe in here? You spend a moment sizing up your surroundings. Eye the entrance. "Can we lower that security gate?" you ask.

"I was about to do that when that cop came barreling down here. Then you showed up."

"So let's do it now."

Chucky hops down off the SUV and you follow him to the office. It's tiny and cluttered. There's a desk, a computer, two chairs, papers everywhere. Chucky opens a metal box on the wall and pulls a switch. There's a loud grinding noise. Through the window, you watch the metal gate slowly lower, shutting you off from the outside world.

You walk to the gate and lean against it, tired. You replay the morning's events. Started off pretty regular: woke up late, crowded subway ride, morning meeting—that's when things went a little haywire. Zombies, crazy cab ride, dead cop, general chaos and horror—

"Smoke?"

You jump. Chucky's standing beside you, holding out a cigarette.

"Shit. You scared me. Uh, yeah, sure." You take one. You're not much of a smoker, but if there was ever an occasion, this was it. You take the lighter. On the third try you get it. You wrap your fingers through the metal fence and rest against it, exhaustion tugging at your body.

Together, you smoke in silence. He finishes his. Flicks it through the metal gate. Lights another. A moment later you finish yours. You don't ask for a second, and he doesn't offer.

"Shh, shh," he says, hushing you, even though you weren't making a damn sound anyway. "Look."

A zombie staggers down the ramp. It's an old man in a short-sleeve button-down, splashed with blood. Wisps of white hair. Horn-rimmed glasses, one lens cracked. It trips over its feet, regains its balance, and continues to shuffle along. Its shoulder scrapes against the ramp wall as it stumbles forward. A streak of blood tags the wall.

More follow behind it. A dozen, you guess. You watch, aware that you're safe behind the gate, but still scared shitless. You want to run—retreat into the temporary safety of the garage. But you don't. You watch. Just a short time ago they were regular people—now they're actual living dead monsters. Their faces—almost familiar looking, despite the gashes and the gore. The same people you passed every day on the street, stood behind in line at the movies, worked with, drank with.

"C'mon," Chucky whispers, touching your shoulder.

You snap out of it and step back.

"Stay in the dark," he says. You nod and park yourself behind a large support beam. Chucky jogs over to the office. Through the window, you see him open a box on the wall full of keys. He flips through a few, turns around to look back at the garage, then flips through a few more. Finally, he takes a set of keys, shuts the box, and jogs back across the garage floor.

You follow him to a black two-door Mercedes that sits directly opposite the gate, allowing you a clear view of the entire garage. He unlocks the doors and climbs into the driver's seat. You hesitate a moment, then get in the passenger's side.

You watch the things gather at the gate. Some claw at it. Others pay it no attention and just sort of stumble about. After a while, it's simply too much to look at—you can no longer process what you're seeing. You recline the seat and before you know it, you're asleep.

You wake up confused—not sure how much time has passed. You smell something in the air—pot? No, couldn't be. Wait—yep. Next to you, Chucky is puffing on a blunt.

"Wakey-wakey," he says, grinning and waving it in your face. "You want?"

Uh-uh. You were part of the DARE generation. You know the dope on dope. Turn to page 120.

What the hell, this day can't get any weirder, right? Turn to page 196.

"I want the ax," you say.

"Why should I give you the ax? This is my bar."

"You own it?"

"No, but I'm in charge right now."

You beg with your eyes.

"Fine, take it," he says. "You getting killed don't help *me* any."

He takes the pool cue in his meaty paws.

You lift the fire ax from the table. Shit, it's heavy. Real heavy. Not what you expected. You carry it in front of you with both hands, by your waist. You're scared now—unsure. You don't think you can wield an ax like this. Especially not in the middle of any sort of battle.

Anthony unlocks the door. "You first," he says, grinning.

Son of a bitch.

Gently, you use the ax to poke open the door. It's barely halfway open when the beasts attack. You raise the ax high into the air. It nearly pulls you off your feet. You struggle to hold it.

Then, with everything you've got, you swing it. It catches the first beast in the waist. You yank it out, bringing a string of gore with it. The thing continues to come at you. You raise the ax above your head and bring it down. Thing is heavy—no accuracy. You aim for the head but instead bury it into the zombie's shoulder.

It's a sickening feeling—this weapon you're wielding, going a foot deep into this being's flesh. You struggle to jerk the ax

free from the zombie's muscular shoulder. But you're too slow. The next beast lunges at you. Puts its cold, clammy hands around your neck.

You scream. The ax falls from your hands. Pain shoots through your foot. You look down, horrified—the ax is stuck in the floor, and your foot is in two pieces. You lift your leg, leaving most of your foot on the floor. You take a step, pain shooting up your leg, and stumble back. Three more jump on you, gnawing on your face and body, and together you crash to the ground. You feel your own hot blood pooling around you. One of the things tears at your ear—there's an awful sound as it rips off. God. God help me, you think.

"Anthony," you manage to get out. "Anthony."

He kicks one beast off you. Breaks the pool cue over another one's face, sending a chunk of wood spinning down the hall. Then he reaches down, grabs the thing by its ears, and rips it up. Slams it into the wall, then tosses it down the hall, knocking the rest of the beasts back.

"Anthony, please," you beg.

He raises the pool cue. His face, unsure, goes blurry as you focus on the chalky tip of the stick. It lowers, slowly. He squeezes his hands around it, flips it over. Now you stare up at the splintered end. Blood drips off it—a drop falls into your eye and it waters up. The cue lowers, getting larger as it closes in on your eye. Just an inch from your eyeball.

Then, at once, he forces it down, ripping through your eye, blasting through your skull, and destroying your brain.

AN END

FIREWORKS

A pair of bullets whips past. A woman's pained scream erupts behind you.

You pull at the door of the Honda Civic next to you. The driver, a middle-aged man, heavy wrinkles across his face, a Titleist ball cap covering his eyes, shakes his head no. You pull. He slams his hand down on the lock.

More bullets. More screams.

You drop to the ground and bury your head in your arms. After a moment, the heavy sounds of gunfire slow. You raise your head.

A stampede of people, coming right for you. Now you know what it feels like to be a kick returner, staring down an entire special teams unit. They run, frantic, a huge group, two or three people wide.

You roll to your right, underneath the Civic.

Feet scramble past you. An elderly woman falls. She shuts her eyes. You reach out, try to help her, but there's nothing you can do. She's trampled. A hundred feet run over her. A heavy boot lands on the back of her head, pushing her face into the cement. Blood seeps from her nose. A crack as a huge man steps on her ankle, snapping it. A few horrific minutes later and the stampeding crowd has thinned. The woman is dead.

You roll out from the other side of the car, closer to the middle of the bridge. A large gap, maybe ten feet wide, runs down the center of the bridge, separating inbound and outbound traffic. Steel girders connect the two sides.

Across the gap a police officer is standing in the middle of a crowd firing into the air. His cruiser sits behind him, door open. Possible safety, you think. The cruiser is bulletproof. Probably has a shotgun inside. A radio!

You peer down the gap at the bridge's lower deck. No people. No army. Just the dead. The monsters have completely taken it over.

You climb up on the closest girder, the metal warm against your palms. You begin to inch your way across. The moans of the dead rise up.

There's a huge blast as the car ahead of you explodes. Instinctively, you reel back, trying to shield yourself. In the process you lose your balance. Your foot slips off the girder. Then your leg. Suddenly you're clinging to the edge, hanging on for dear life.

Don't look down. Don't look down. Don't look down.

You look down.

Fucking idiot. Why'd you look down?

Gnarled hands reach up—a moaning throng of the dead, begging for you.

You struggle to pull yourself up. You kick your feet—but there's just air.

Their moans get louder as the beasts sense your impending fall.

You block out everything—the angry sound of gunfire, the deathly moans, the agonizing screams. You concentrate only on making it back up. Feel your muscles tighten. Your hands grip the steel. Finally, using everything you have, you pull yourself back up onto the girder.

You stare ahead. Not going to fall again. Not going to die. You move forward—slowly, steadily.

Finally, you make it to the other side. You pass the burning car and beeline it for the cruiser. Hop the hood of a taxi, slide off like Starsky. Jump across the next car.

You dive into the cruiser and slam the door shut behind you. It's a mess inside. Dunkin' Donuts coffee cups on the floor.

Empty food bags—KFC, McDonald's, more Dunkin' Donuts. A pack of True cigarettes nestled between the dashboard and the front window.

WHAP WHAP WHAP!!!

The bulletproof glass spiderwebs. Your heart leaps up your throat as you realize the cop is shooting at you.

The officer frowns, frustrated.

You wave—mouthing "What the fuck?" You're not locking him out. He can get in the car, too. You're just looking for cover.

He pushes a citizen aside and marches toward the car.

What the fuck is this nut job doing?

He fires twice more. You lunge across the car and lock the door. The cop shakes his head and pulls the keys from his belt. Waves them at you and smiles.

Then, out of nowhere, three of the beasts tackle him. He's gone—just like that.

More zombies run past, headed toward Brooklyn. They pay no attention to you. Up ahead, you can see the Army stepping back.

Then the artillery starts. The big guns. Tanks? You're not sure. Something loud as fuck. Ahead of you a truck explodes. A giant, fiery blast. Then another. Bodies fly through the air. A man is launched wildly off the side of the bridge.

You watch, eyes wide, as the bridge lights up like the Fourth of July.

If you want to get out of the car and run, turn to page 343.

If you'd rather hang tight and pray the firing subsides, turn to page 308.

WHERE THE HEART IS

Home, you think. That's the best bet—has to be. Familiar. Safe. Secure.

You alternate between walking and jogging through streets quickly turning explosive. It's a miserable thirty-block hike to your apartment. You keep your eye open for a cab. Nothing, all full.

You get to your building a half-hour later, soaked in sweat. Up the five flights of stairs to your apartment. Through the door. Slam it shut and collapse against it, exhausted. God, it feels good not to be moving. Sweat bleeds through the back of your shirt and the fabric sticks to the door.

You close your eyes. Breathe slowly—in through your mouth, out through your nostrils. Calming.

You open your eyes. Your apartment looks strange, feels just slightly off—something about being home at a time when you weren't expecting to be. Like a stranger in your own space.

A mouse skitters across the floor. Sonofabitch—so that's what goes on while you're at work? Yeah, well, that's what you get for leaving the Ray's Famous box out with half a slice of pepperoni-and-sausage left.

You stand up and flip on the local news. A bunch of images of random chaos. No real reporting—just people blabbering, clueless. No one has any real idea what's happening, but they're paid to talk.

People loot a corner store in the West Village. Shit, you should stock up. You've got about five edible things in your apartment right now, and that's including a month-past-the-date carton of eggs and a half bottle of Black Velvet—Jack Daniel's cheaper, shittier cousin. You look over again at the half slice of pepperoni-and-sausage and quickly throw it in the fridge.

You grab your keys and head for the corner bodega.

It's packed. You realize suddenly that you're in survival mode. You have a vague sense of what to do from watching a lot of bad disaster movies. You navigate the narrow aisles, grabbing the essentials. Batteries. Frozen pizzas. A glass candle with a smiling, open-armed Jesus on the front. Ramen. Beer. Lots of beer.

It's getting ugly. People shoving. Grabbing for what they need, even if someone else already happens to be holding it. The Korean guy who runs the bodega threatens to close the doors unless the customers "form one motherfucking line!"

You grab all you can carry, pay, and leave. Outside it's only getting nastier. People rushing about. Like a great storm is on the way and everyone is racing to get to shelter.

Hands full, you take the stairs up to your apartment as quickly as you can. Your building is usually empty—more often than not you come and go without seeing anyone. Not today. People in the hallways. Some coming, most going—all moving quickly, with a frantic yet steady purpose.

You lock your apartment door behind you. Both locks.

Your phone's ringing. The *Speed* theme—*DUN DUN* DUH DUH *DAH DAH*. You walk in just in time to hear the triumphant bass finale.

You look at the display. See your mom's big smiling face. Great . . .

If you want to ignore the call and start pounding beers, turn to page 190.

If you want to answer Mom's phone call, turn to page 225.

"You can stay here if you want. You, uh, you shouldn't be alone."

You shouldn't be alone. You idiot. Who do you think you are? Could you be any more obvious?

"Yeah? I'd love to—I'm going crazy over there. And I keep hearing things—probably just my imagination—but it's scaring *the fuck* out of me."

"I can imagine. So, great, you'll stay here." *Good work!*

You're beaming. Heart swelling. Thank the Lord for this massive zombie takeover.

She walks through the foyer and into the kitchen, looking around. "I haven't been in this house in years."

"Yep, been a long time."

She turns and smiles. "It's good to see you again."

Your face feels a little flush, so you quickly turn and look around the house like some idiot prospective buyer. You don't want to embarrass yourself.

You find some still edible food in the kitchen. You make the best meal you can—peanut butter and jelly on Ritz crackers with orange soda. You apologize, and explain that most everything else seems to have gone bad.

You talk some, about what you've been doing, how she's been. She doesn't work at the flower shop anymore; she's a cashier at the local Target now.

"Nothing wrong with that," you say.

She frowns from behind her cup of soda.

"I didn't mean it like that."

"It's OK. Things don't always turn out the way we plan, huh?"

"Tell me about it."

"But you're in New York City right? I saw on Facebook. That's exciting! I've never been."

"Yeah, it's OK, I guess—my rent is like, just, absurd."

"I still live with my parents, so . . ."

"True."

You finish your meal in silence, then get the generator from the garage and get some power going. Together you go through the house. Looking for food, things that you can use. You watch old movies she's never seen before. Play the same old Nintendo games you used to play when you were kids. With the specter of death hanging over you, you grow close quick.

You're outside playing Ping-Pong when Kim suggests you go for a swim in your parents' pool. Um . . . yeah, only been waiting near twenty years to hear those words. You get to work skimming the pool.

Kim steps out of the house in just her underwear.

"I hope this is OK," she says. "My bathing suit is all the way across the street."

Ohmygodohmygodohohhgohgdoghdoghodhgd . . .

You try to get the words out. But all you can do is stare. She's stunning.

You stutter. "Sure, sure, that's fine, of course."

That night you make love on your back lawn. Then you lie on your backs, looking at the stars. It's like a movie. Nothing could be more perfect. Once again, you thank the Lord for the zombie apocalypse.

You wake up with Kim's head on your chest. A little puddle of drool has formed below her mouth. It's cute. Imperfect. Human.

You're in love.

You give her a nudge and a kiss on the forehead.

"Good morning."

She looks up at you with her big doe eyes. "Good morning, you."

You. She just called you *you*.

"I'm going to go try to find some stuff for breakfast," you say, stretching. You stand and start getting dressed.

"You're leaving?"

"I'll be back in a few," you say. "Who knows how long we'll be here, and we're low on food."

"And toilet paper," she says.

Wow. Just conjured up an image of her taking a dump. And it didn't gross you out. This truly *is* love.

"And toilet paper," you say. "I'll be back. Lock the door behind me. Keep all the gates locked."

"I will."

You take the pistol. Three bullets left.

Turn to page 270.

PLACING YOUR TRUST IN THE ARMY

The hazmat guy leads you into the military trailer. Inside, machines buzz and hum. Men work, some at computers, others with test tubes. Along the wall are four see-through Plexiglas cells like you'd find in a modern prison. Three of the four cells contain one civilian each: a child in the first, a young, normal-looking guy with a shaggy beard in the second, and an elderly black woman in the third.

The last cell is empty.

You're starting to regret your decision.

They lead you to the fourth cell. The hazmat guy types a code into a keypad on the wall, the door opens, and he shoves you inside.

In the cell next to you is the elderly black woman. You try to get her attention, but she's too busy sobbing.

After the first hour or two in the cell, you begin to bang on the glass, trying to get some attention. Nobody notices—soundproof, you guess. At one point, one of them sees you. He taps another guy on the shoulder, they chat for a second while staring at you, then go back to work.

After what feels like six or seven hours, the trailer begins to move. You travel for hours on end—a day or two, maybe.

Every time the trailer brakes, you slide into the wall. Then they pick up speed again and you go sliding back. Hit your head hard at one point. Bad headache. The headache is followed by hunger. And then the thirst—nothing compares to that. You need liquid. Water, beer, milk, piss—*anything!* You've lost all track of time—can only think about getting something wet down your throat. You wipe sweat from your brow then lick your hand. Lap your tongue around your chapped lips. Anything.

Then, finally, when you don't think you can take any more, the trailer stops—for good this time.

You're dragged out of the cell. Nobody speaks, and you're too exhausted and dehydrated to complain or ask questions. You're pushed out into a large industrial park. The sunlight stings your eyes. They bring you inside a building that, on the outside, looks a lot like a regular, civilian hospital.

The next month is hell. You're locked in a dark hospital room. They run all sorts of tests on you. Needles in your arms. Little suction cup things on your face and chest.

Then, one day, they pull you out of the locked room. A military man throws you your clothes and tells you you're free to go.

Really? That's it? Must be some mistake, you think, but you're not going to wait around to confirm your suspicions.

You get dressed and rush out of the lockdown area and down to the main floor. Then you step through the doors, out into the blinding afternoon light, not sure what to expect. Not sure where the hell you are. Not sure what the world's got in store for you.

AN END

SEND ME AN ANGEL

It's been two months, three weeks, and four days. Power went after two days. You're really, really, *really* about to lose it.

You're safe, relatively. First thing you did was board up the building's front door—then piled every damn thing you could find behind it. Thus far, no zombies inside the building. For that, you're thankful.

In the beginning, you thought you'd do some reading. The lady had some books. That had you relatively excited. But damn near all of them are religious books. And a whole bunch of issues of *Guideposts*. Like, literally, no joke, nineteen years' worth.

You try starting a diary, but there's nothing to say except "zombies galore outside, read more *Guideposts*."

Food is all but gone. The old lady doesn't have a scale, but you can tell you've lost a significant amount of weight. Your cheeks are thin. Gut has subsided some (that you won't complain about). You've looted every apartment in the building and you're still out of food. Fucking New Yorkers—they have fridges like frat boys. You're down to ketchup packets.

You need to go out. Need food. And water. The water continues to run—but who knows for how long? And if the water goes, every other holdup like you is going to hit the streets at the same time, desperate. It'll be a madhouse. There's a Duane Reade drugstore four blocks down and one avenue over. If you go slowly, move carefully, and watch your ass, you just might make it. But what you'll find there, you have no idea. Could be ransacked, empty, useless. Could be locked. Could be full of monsters. You don't know. But you can't wait any longer—soon you'll be too weak to even attempt it.

The old lady's bathroom was in the process of being redone. From the looks of it, it was probably some son of hers who never got around to finishing it. In there you find a crowbar splattered with beige paint—could be of some use.

Duane Reade it is.

Around noon you climb out onto the fire escape, just like you've done every other day since this started. Over the past month, you've observed their behavior with near obsessive detail.

They're slow as all hell—until they want to eat. When they get a whiff of food, i.e., some poor asshole, they're fast. And when they get close, they close in on a victim in a split second. They grab and don't let go.

Three days ago, you watched a woman die just like that. She had been holed up in the school across the way—around dusk, she made a run for it. Don't know why—maybe she was out of food, maybe she just couldn't stand it anymore. She didn't make it to the sidewalk before one of the monsters got her. Dragged her to the ground, tore open the back of her head, and went to town.

It's obvious they can see, smell, hear just like anyone else. No better, no worse (unless they happen to have had their eyes ripped out or their nose cut off or their ears blown away).

They seem to have grown anxious. Food has dwindled. At first, people were everywhere—plenty of food to go around. Now the herds have thinned. They're moving more—seeking out food instead of waiting for it to come across them.

Occasionally they fight one another, but nothing ever comes of it. They're like wild dogs—they'll bark and nip and scrap, but that's it. They never dine on their fellow undead.

The day is quiet. It's chilly. It was hot when everything first went to shit—now it's cold. Leaves have fallen. Streets melancholy.

The sun sets. You go over your plan one last time—down the fire escape, slowly through the playground, then the three last blocks to Duane Reade. Once you get there, you'll wing it—no way to plan for what you'll encounter.

You slip the crowbar into your belt and slowly make your way down the fire escape. As gently as possible, you lower the ladder. Still, it makes a hell of a racket. You stay there on the fire escape for a good ten minutes, making sure none of the beasts comes to check out the noise.

They don't.

You sneak through the playground, keeping your distance from the monsters that now inhabit it. Soon you're past and out.

The city is spookily quiet. You hear the occasional zombie moan, but little else. You creep down the side streets, hugging the walls.

You're close. You hop a fence, sneak down an alley, and you're directly across from Duane Reade.

And it was all for nothing . . .

Moans echo from inside the store. In the moonlight, you catch flashes of them, eerie and white. Can't tell how many, but the store looks packed.

You crouch down behind two overturned trash cans and watch. They're not going anywhere, that's for sure. Hopeless.

Goddamn it! You want to scream. Now what? More ketchup packets? Fuck that. After reading all those damn issues of *Guideposts* you've started to convince yourself there might be some hope in the afterlife . . . So you might as well just run into the store and let them kill you—at least this nightmare would be over. No—then you'd be a zombie yourself—and still starving. Best bet would be to hang yourself from the ceiling fan in the bedroom. Loop your belt around your neck. Pull it taut . . .

You sigh. Knock the thought out of your head. Not giving up

yet. Dejected, you turn to head back up over the fence, then stop dead in your tracks.

A low mechanical rumble. Then louder. Heavy machinery? Construction crew? Helicopter?

Motorcycles.

No, not just motorcycles—Harleys. A dozen headlights pierce the darkness. Heavy metal thunder.

The bikes blaze past you. On all but one of the bikes, there's a passenger on the back brandishing a weapon. The leader rides alone.

One passenger carries a huge wrench—has to be a foot and a half long. The bike buzzes by a female zombie in a wedding dress. The man with the wrench swings as they pass, taking her down. She doesn't get back up. The combination of bike speed and the weight of the wrench shatters the skull and destroys the brain in one blow.

After the first drive-by, five, six of the beasts lie dead on the ground as the bikes speed away. The roar fades as they disappear down the avenue. But no—then it grows louder. The crisscrossing headlights cut through the night again.

They fly past. The driver closest to you has a huge blade mounted on his arm. Fist closed, he slashes out. Decapitates an undead man. The pack speeds away. Six, maybe seven more zombies laid out on the street.

Then, again, they swing back around. But this time not for a fly-by. The bikes come to a halt. Kickstands drop.

The bikers go to work. Chains, bats, machetes, pipes, two-by-fours. One particularly large biker wields a piece of pipe buried in a hunk of cement. In less than a minute, every zombie in a one-block radius is dead.

You inch closer, trying to hear.

"Alright, you four, hold the perimeter!" one shouts. He's the leader. Four men sprint off, each to one corner of the street. You read the stitching on the back of his leather jacket.

HELLS ANGELS.

"Tommy, you're up," the leader says.

Tommy is aptly named. He steps off his bike and whips a tommy gun from a chain strap around his back.

One Angel turns his bike so the headlight shines on the Duane Reade. You can see the beasts clearly now—ghastly, gruesome, decomposing things. They've made it to the front of the store and they're coming through the shattered windows and the broken door.

Tommy lets loose. In the movies you always see people shooting tommy guns from their hips, spraying widely.

But not Tommy. Military stance. Legs spread. Sights up. One eye shut. Perfect form.

Three shots. Dead.

Three shots. Another dead.

Three shots. Another. Another. Another.

He takes out every single one of them—has to be twenty. And not one of the beasts gets close.

The leader slaps Tommy on the back, says something that sounds like "nice shooting," then shouts to the group, "Do it!"

The four men keep the perimeter while everyone else loots the store. In less than a minute they've wiped the store clean. A few of the bikes have sidecars—they throw their loot inside.

Damn. These guys are good. If you want to survive in this zombie-infested city, hooking up with them just might be your best bet.

But they could also just as easily shoot you and leave you dead in the street.

Ahh, fuck it.

You grab your crowbar and walk out into the street, hands up.

"Hey, uh, hey fellas," you say.

They all turn.

"The fuck?" one says.

"Hi."

"What do we got here?"

"Um. Well I'd like to come with you guys."

A chorus of laughter.

"No for real."

"Fellas, mount up," the leader says. They do.

He walks over to you. "Kid, go home."

He's two feet from you. You can see him clearly now. Head shaved bald. Thick beard. Tats running up his neck.

"Look," you say, "I don't need to be a real, like, *official* Angel. I just—I mean, I've been stuck in some old lady's apartment for months. The world seems to have ended. I'm not going to make it much longer. I need food. Shit, I need to have a goddamn conversation with someone."

The leader stares at you. You can see the wheels turning. Then he pulls out a huge revolver from a holster by his side. *Dirty Harry*–type shit.

"Whoa," you say, putting your hands up and stepping back.

"Relax, kid, I wouldn't a waste a slug on you—even if I did want you dead."

"Thanks for that."

"Limpy, get over here!" he shouts, not taking his eyes off you.

"Limpy?" you ask.

"That's right. I'm Jones."

"As in Indiana?"

"As in Jones."

"OK."

Limpy hobbles over.

"Now kid," Jones continues, "normally, I'd tell you to take a hike and that'd be that. But, you're lucky. Well—depending on if you're a half-full or a half-empty kinda guy."

He points the gun at you, then points it at the thin, gangly guy limping his way over. Does this guy really need to use his .357 Magnum like it's a goddamn laser pointer?

"That's Limpy."

You nod.

"Limpy's got a real, real serious gambling problem. Real fucking degenerate. Helluva pal, though. He liked the ponies."

"I loved the ponies," Limpy says.

"Limpy," Jones says, "I got an idea."

"Shit yeah."

You don't like where this is going.

"Kid, here's the deal. Take it or leave it. You go stand in the middle of that intersection there," Jones says, waving the gun across the way. "You stay there for five minutes—you live— and I'll let you come stay at the club. Limpy, you think he's gonna live?"

Limpy smiles. "Hell no."

"OK," Jones says, "I'll take the odds. Limpy thinks you die. I say you surprise us and live. You live, you got a place to stay. You die, you die. You understand?"

You swallow. "I understand."

"So, what's it gonna be, kid?"

Hell no! You're not dying in the middle of an intersection just because some biker asked you to! If you want to turn and leave, turn to page 334.

At this point, you've got nothing to lose, right? Turn to page 181.

THROUGH THE GLASS PAINFULLY

You turn, grab the chair next to you, and give the huge glass window two hard whacks. It cracks.

Tommy's coming for you. No time to finish clearing out the glass.

You leap.

The glass that overlooks the Garden shatters as you fall through. It's not like the movies where Bruce Willis just jumps through and keeps moving. The window explodes into a thousand tiny glass razor blades.

Blood pours over your eyes—so much that you can't see. You take one step and fall—your calf muscle is sliced to shit. You try to catch yourself, but spin awkwardly around the back of a chair and tumble down the stairs. It's a long way down—and there's nothing there to stop you. You try to grab hold of something, anything—but gravity's winning.

Your head smashes against a heavy cement step, and everything goes black.

You come to, sprawled out on the court. A gigantic zombie looms over you. Through the death mask, you recognize him. Starting center for the New York Knicks.

He leans down, rips you to your feet with his monstrous hands. Takes a chunk out of your shoulder, then lets go. You drop back onto the court.

Jesus. Five of them approach. The Knicks' starting roster. Standing over you. Ready for dinner . . .

AN END

THE BAR IT IS

Praying for good news, you forget the cab and head for the bar. Almost on cue, the crowd thins. People pour through the doorway, poking at their phones. Good sign or bad, you don't know.

You step inside—take in the heavy smell of beer and spilt liquor. With the TV crowd gone, the majority of those left are the serious drinkers, the lifers. The guys who spend early Monday afternoons in a bar, alone. There's about a dozen of them—most at the bar, a few at the tables in the back.

The bouncer, a large, mostly fat, black guy in a Joe Namath jersey types on his BlackBerry.

"What's the news?" you ask him.

Paying you as little attention as possible, he nods to the TV hanging above the door: two talking heads at the news desk. Trying to look professional, but mostly just looking confused.

The broadcast cuts away from the studio to helicopter shots of the city. Different locations. Lincoln Center. Washington Square. Columbus Circle. Everywhere the same—zombies swarming, attacking, feasting.

Christ. This can't be real.

The broadcast switches locations again. A mass of the beasts gathering around Battery Park. Jesus—that's the southern tip of Manhattan—miles from the hospital! How the hell did they get everywhere so goddamn quickly? Then the broadcast cuts again—this time zombies milling around a deserted subway station. Your stomach turns as you realize that if just one infected person gets on a subway or on a bus or in a cab—

shit, they could get anywhere. God, these things could be on a plane and off to Antigua or Timbuktu or who-knows-the-fuck-where.

You're having trouble breathing now. Chest tight.

You catch your reflection in the mirror behind the bar. You look like you just caught a sucker punch from Mike Tyson. Everyone else wears a similar look—like maybe Mike Tyson ran around the bar real quick and sucker-punched everybody. Even the old vets, the seen-everything-and-drank-their-way-through-it-all guys—just stunned looks on their rough, withered faces. Staring at the mirror, you start to zone out—hypnotizing yourself almost. Anything to not have to look at that TV or hear the news or think about what's happening outside or imagine the nightmares the future holds.

Someone bumps into you and brushes you aside, snapping you out of your trance. A bony, thin guy, late twenties, in a slick suit with slicker hair. Wall Street, all the way. You wonder what he's doing up here during work hours, everything financial is below Fifty-ninth—maybe his doorman caught him on his way out of his fancy, prewar apartment building, told him something was going down. Or maybe his coke dealer's in the neighborhood and he's chasing a Monday morning high.

He pushes past you and edges up to the bar. Raises a wad of cash in the air. "Hey—honey!" he calls, waving the cash at the bartender.

You notice the bartender for the first time. She's a knockout. Petite—five feet at the most. Natural blond hair. Tiny Derek Jeter shirt hugs a pair of gotta-be-fake tits. She walks the length of the bar and eyes Wall Street, unimpressed. "Yeah?"

He drops two crisp hundred-dollar bills onto the bar, flashes her a toothy smile, then announces loudly: "World's ending. Drinks are on me, kiddies."

If you want to stay at the bar and take Wall Street up on his offer of free drinks, turn to page 212.

If you'd rather forget the bar and try to figure out a way out of the city, turn to page 130.

You turn your back on the bar—if it's good news, you'll find out about it later. And if it's bad, you don't want to know.

After a half hour, a cab slows to a stop at the corner of Eighty-fifth and Broadway and an older woman gets out. You hear her on her phone: "Of course I heard—I'm going upstairs right now and locking the door."

You run for the cab. Three others do the same. You get there first, though, and you don't give in. Everyone argues. You tell the other three guys to take a hike and you get inside. "Brooklyn Bridge. And step on it," you say, like you've turned into some badass. But there's nowhere to go just yet, so the cab just sits there. And the three guys are right outside your window, glaring at you from the sidewalk. You flip open your phone and pretend to talk on it.

You've got a friend in Brooklyn—it's the best plan you can think of at the moment. You check your phone for his address and yell it out to the cabbie. He pulls out into a gap in the traffic—blabbing on his Bluetooth in a language that definitely wasn't available for study in high school.

"Can you put the radio on please?" you ask him.

He doesn't. Either doesn't give a damn or can't hear you over his stupid Bluetooth. You wonder if he has any idea what's happening right now in the city.

"Hey! Radio!" you shout, annoyed.

He shoots you a look through the rearview mirror, lets it linger for a second, then reaches down and turns the radio on. Top 40 stuff. Lady Gaga, you think.

"Thanks, but can you put the news on?" you ask.

Nothing.

"News station?"

He ignores you. You ask twice more, then give up. Oh well—probably better off not knowing anyway. You look out the window. Seconds later you're biting your lower lip and bobbing your head to the music. What? It's a good song.

Back to your phone. You try to send a few texts, but the connection keeps timing out. You agree to resend in digital, whatever the hell that means.

Half an hour later, you've gone maybe ten blocks. Streets are absolutely packed—unlike any other Monday, 11:30 AM you've ever seen in the city. It's Macy's Thanksgiving Day Parade status. You could walk faster than this.

You try to call your friend in Brooklyn.

Ring.

Ring.

Ring.

Then an automated voice, "I'm sorry, due to *unusually high call volume* we are unable to connect your call at the moment. Please try again later."

Goddamn it—fucking AT&T.

Traffic's still not moving. Anxious, you pick at the stickers on the back of the driver's seat. Watch the news on the little TV. It's the same cheesy clip playing over and over: Regis and Kelly talking about the wonders of New York City. All sorts of shots of landmarks and multicultural crowds and all that good shit. Just begging for tourist money.

Outside, it's nothing like that. Not the iconic city that never sleeps. Not the Manhattan from *Manhattan*. No—it's a powder keg—a city on the verge of exploding.

Finally, after an hour and a half of stop-and-stop-some-more traffic and a forty-three-dollar cab fare, you can see the entrance to the Brooklyn Bridge. And it's just what you had feared. Absolute gridlock—on the street and on the bridge. Police try to direct traffic, but it's useless.

Thousands of people are crossing the bridge on foot. A mass exodus. A guy on a ninja bike drives past you, weaves in and out of the traffic, past the police, and up onto the on-ramp. Bastard. Guys on motorcycles have all the luck.

You sit, anxious. An hour goes by. You move maybe ten feet. A cop directs traffic. Finally, he waves his hands in the air and gives up. He walks through the maze of cars, hops on his police bike, hits the siren, and drives up onto the bridge.

Again, pricks with motorcycles.

You're about to give up, pay the fare, and join the pedestrians when you hear it. The sound. You can just barely make it out over the din of horns, sirens, and angry New Yorkers. Shouting. Screaming. It's the sound of panic.

Out the window, to your left, you see it. People running. *Stampeding.* Behind them, the zombies. Hundreds. Thousands, maybe. A thick mass of the dead—stretching all the way across First Avenue. A goddamned army of the things, headed right for you . . .

Lock the door and hold tight? Turn to page 147.

Get the hell out and run for it? Turn to page 183.

THE HAMMER
AND THE DRILL

You take the hammer and the drill from the table. Hold one in each hand. Feel their weight. Two weapons are better than one, you think—even if they are close range. This gives you freedom of movement—you can wield them like twin Glocks on some John Woo shit, no prob. You forget about the *Big Buck Hunter* gun and follow Anthony out of the office. He carries the fire ax.

Standing at the door to the hall you listen to the moans. They're louder now. Anthony unlocks the door slowly. You can almost hear the click of the pins.

You breathe in, pause, breathe out. No point in waiting.

"Let's do it."

He kicks open the door and sends the two closest zombies flying back.

In front of you is a regular-looking guy—type of guy you might see around the office. You swing the hammer, catching him in the side of the head. He stumbles to the side. You follow the hammer blow with the drill, squeezing the trigger and burying it into the thing's ear and into its brain. After a second, you pull it free, blood and brain spraying off the still-spinning, squealing drill bit. The thing drops.

The next one leaps at you. You duck. Awkwardly, it falls onto your back. Before it can attack you, you stand and flip it over onto the floor. You go in with the drill—but Anthony's there first, burying the ax into its face.

You give him a thankful nod and turn your attention to the others. Behind you, you hear Anthony take care of the two on the floor.

Four down. Seven to go.

You push the drill up through the chin of the next one. Not deep enough. It thrashes at you. You kick it back and let loose with the hammer. Finally, it falls.

The next one, an old woman, lunges at you. You raise the drill to block the attack. The drill bit pierces the thing's hand. You yank it out, swing it around, and ram it through a busted pair of old-lady shades and into its eye. You swirl the drill around, scrambling its brains, while pounding its head with the hammer, and it finally goes limp.

Anthony steps ahead of you now. He swings the ax wildly and misses—the blade sticks into the wall. He tugs. It's stuck. That split second is all it takes. Two are on him.

You ram the drill into the back of the head of the closest one. After a moment, its grip on Anthony loosens, and it falls.

But it's too late. The other one has its mouth around Anthony's face. Blood pouring down both of them.

Anthony's bit. Done for.

Fuck, fuck, fuck. What now? Panicked, you turn to run back into the bar—but it's blocked. The two that Anthony had handled—he had put the ax through their chests, not their brains—it didn't do anything except leave them in a bad mood. Have to kill them all over again . . .

But then you stop—

You sense Anthony rising behind you, and you slowly turn back. He's gigantic. He fills the entire width of the hallway. His face—moments ago normal—has changed. Amazingly, just a minute after his death, the blood has clotted, dried. He rocks back and forth on his thick, trunklike legs. Stares you down— Christ, almost like he recognizes you.

Fuck that noise—peace—time to run. Turn to page 124.

Stay and fight? Turn to page 330.

Jones walks past you.

You snap out of it and work your way down, following the Angels. Weapons over their shoulders. Heads down. The job is done, but there's little rejoicing.

You board the bus. Lean over the front edge, exhausted, ready to get back into the dead man's bed.

You see it out of the corner of your eye. A flash of iron in the moonlight. A tank. U.S. military.

And too late, you realize. They were never going to give you anything. No pardons. No pats on the back. No job well done. No nothing. Just do their dirty work, and that was that.

The tank aims at the bus. You brace for death.

BOOM!!!

AN END

You stare right back at him. You should help. But your body won't move. Something down in your balls won't let you. Fear. Feels like leaning over the side of a roof twenty floors up. Like Anthony's asking you to jump. You can't.

The feeling in your balls jumps to your gut and then volcanoes up your throat—puke.

You turn away and run to the back of the bar and into the bathroom. You jiggle the handle. Vomit seeps out the side of your mouth. You ram your shoulder into the door and it opens. That's as close as you get—puke splashes the floor. Last night's pizza.

You don't feel any better—just more frightened, more incapable.

You slam the door shut behind you. Search for a lock. None. You put the toilet seat down and take a seat. Drop your head into your hands—cold and clammy. Icy sweat drips from your forehead. Your mind fades out—black spots fill your vision.

After a long, scary moment, the world comes back to you. You can hear faint screams coming from the bar—or maybe that's the street. You hope street.

You pull out your phone, hit Safari, and check the Web. Nothing will load. The whole country—hell the whole world, maybe—is online right now, checking the news, trying to figure out what's going on.

Just then, you hear a scream. A man's scream. Then more. "Oh Lord!" someone shouts.

A rush of noises from beyond the door. Bar stools hitting the floor. Glasses shattering. Chaos.

You tiptoe toward the door. You need to block it, or else you're next. You look around for something—anything.

There's a loud slamming sound from just outside the door. The hinges buck. You back into the corner, terror rushing through your body.

Banging on the door. The wood splinters. The door's top hinge pops off and it falls open, awkwardly, still attached at the bottom. It lands on the sink and cracks apart.

A rotund redheaded man collapses on top of the door, blood pumping steadily from an open wound in his back.

Standing behind him, staring directly at you, is one of them. One of those things. On TV you believed it, but you didn't understand. But now—right in front of you—it's real. A zombie. The walking dead. A beast in a business suit. Blood is spattered across its yellow power tie and the pink shirt beneath it.

Sonofabitch. It's Wall Street.

Its face is deathly white. A hole is torn in its cheek—you can see the inner workings of its mouth and jaw. It jerks forward. Fills the door.

You make a move for the bathroom stall. But it's too late. It leaps. You stick your hands out, try to toss it aside. No luck. Its teeth get a hold of your hand. It rips you forward and sinks its teeth into the bridge of your nose.

Your body goes into shock. You lose all sense of time. Minutes later, hours maybe, you regain some vague semblance of your senses. And then some. You smell flesh. Want it. Need it.

You're one of them now. And you've got a driving urge to devour that pretty young bartender . . .

❄ AN END ❄

IS THERE A DOCTOR IN THE CAR?

His eyes stare up at the ceiling, glossy and devoid of life. Then they roll back into his head—a slot machine, both wheels coming up death.

"Hey," you say, quietly, to no one in particular. You've never had to yell for a doctor and to be honest, you're feeling awkward as hell about it, despite the circumstances. "Um . . . is anyone here a doctor?"

A thirtyish woman, straight off the set of *Sex and the City*, turns and looks at you like you asked her if she wanted to swap underwear.

"Is anyone here a doctor?" you ask, louder now. "This man needs help!"

You look back down at him. He's no longer shivering. Definitely not breathing. Jesus . . .

"Is anyone in here a doctor?" you yell.

A tall, handsome woman with dark, mid-length, curly hair pushes her way over and announces herself as a neurologist.

You talk fast, stuttering. "I don't think this guy's breathing— and—and—and his eyes just rolled back in his head. And he's all bloody there—by the arm."

You half expect her to throw a stethoscope over her neck, pull out a little black bag, and play small town doctor making a house call. Instead she leans over and lifts open his left eyelid. Then his right. Nothing looking back but creamy white.

She orders the onlookers to get back. There's little room and they complain loudly—but manage to squeeze to the side and clear a small space on the bench. She lays him down and opens his coat. You see the severity of his wound now. His shirt is torn, like it's been clawed by a wolf, and there's a huge gash on his chest. Despite the size of the wound, there's no blood leaking. Dried, black blood around the gash and on his jacket—but nothing wet. The doc looks puzzled. Not a good sign.

She shoves her finger into his open mouth and clears out his throat. Gross. Then she pinches his nose and puts her lips onto his. Really gross. She performs mouth-to-mouth, then presses down repeatedly on his chest.

For a good two or three minutes, he doesn't move. She continues to perform CPR. Then you notice his left foot. It's twitching slightly. More. Jerking. After some chest compressions, she blows more air into his mouth.

"Hey, doc—"

Suddenly she lets out a blood-curdling scream and pulls back, blood pouring from her mouth and his. The man's hands shoot up like a pair of catapults and latch on to the back of her skull and pull her close. Blood pours down her face and onto her chest. The thing is devouring her face. Screams echo through the car. The passengers try to run—but there's nowhere to go. Finally, the doctor flies back, half of her face gone. Blood splashes your shirt and sprays the wall.

Panicked, you push your way to the rear of the car and slide open the door. You step onto the shaky walkway that hangs between your car and the next. Screams chase you.

Your hands grip the metal chains that link the cars and you walk across. You pound the door of the opposite car.

Through the window a man, eyes wide, shakes his head and holds the door shut. You tug. Nothing. A crowd gathers at the window—staring at you and, with horror, staring at the carnage behind you.

"Please!" you shout.

More passengers follow you, pushing you from behind, desperate to escape. They push.

"Open the fucking door!" a young woman shouts.

More people. Slamming you into the door. Your chest feels like it's going to collapse. The train takes a hard turn and you feel your feet begin to slip. The momentum of the turn tosses you to the side—only the chain railing keeps you from being thrown to the tracks below. People continue to push from behind. A man wedges beside you and tugs at the door. Nothing. There's not enough room for both of you. Your waist presses against the chain.

Either that door opens, or you're all going to die.

"Please!" you shout, locking eyes with the man on the other side of the glass. But it's too late.

The chain breaks. You reach out, trying to grab at anything. You're falling back. Everything moves in slow motion. Then you hit the tracks and the heavy metal wheels grind you into a dozen bloody pieces.

AN END

They examine the lock.

As Walter squeezes the trigger, you lunge for the gun. You get his arm and knock it into the air. The pistol fires harmlessly into the ceiling.

Voices outside. Feet slap cement as the looters scatter.

Walter stands up, fury in his eyes. "You son of a bitch."

"You were going to kill them!"

A cool, scary calm comes over him. He raises the gun.

"Oh no, please, please don't—"

BLAM!!!

You look down. A small hole in the center of your chest. Blood begins to soak through your shirt, forming a perfect maroon circle.

You fall to the floor.

Walter's gravelly voice. "Shoulda minded your own damn businessssssss . . ."

AN END

Well, might as well go around and meet the neighbors. You walk the halls, going from door to door. No answer. No answer. No answer. Down to the next floor.

You hear television coming from one apartment. Good television. Explosions.

It smells like pot outside the door. You knock again. Nothing. Harder.

You're about to give up when the door opens. Now it really stinks like pot. Smoke wafts out into the hall. It's a young guy, your age, in a bathrobe. Half a beard. Big pair of headphones around his neck. He sticks his head out and looks both ways.

"Yo."

"What's up," you say.

"I don't know, you knocked."

"Yeah, uh, I don't know, I wanted to see who was still alive around here. I've had a hell of a day."

"Huh?"

"Y'know, with all this shit."

"What shit?"

"You didn't see the news?"

"News? Nah bro. I've been sitting here for the past"—he glances over at a cheap Mets alarm clock—"shit like nine hours just getting ripped and playing *Call of Duty.*"

"You didn't hear the gunshots?"

"What gunshots?"

"All the gunshots and shooting and screaming and all that shit."

"Nah. I got a four-hundred-and-ninety-dollar pair of Sennheiser headphones. You play video games? You play videogames, you'd love it. It's like you're in the middle of friggin' Afghanistan, no joke. I spent like three grand on this *sick* surround sound system—then the old lady upstairs bitches every time I crank it."

"Oh yeah—that's the old lady next to me." The *dead old lady,* you think.

"Yeah, total bitch, right? So anyway I shut down the surround sound and went with the headphones."

You nod slowly, then "OK, so, uh, dude—fucking zombies are all over the place!"

He looks at you like you've lost your mind. Hell, maybe you have. "Bro, what the *fuck* are you talking about? You eat some bad acid or something? Mushrooms—is it mushrooms? You wanna come in, lay down, take a few pills? Chill you out?"

You shrug, nod, and walk inside. Holy shit. . . .

His apartment is out of this world. Fifty-inch flat screen mounted on the wall. Blu-ray rack with at least a hundred titles. PS3. 360. Wii. Old-school Nintendo. Old-school Super Nintendo. 64. Sega. *Sega CD!* Everything. Two bedrooms. Full kitchen.

"How do you afford this?"

"You a cop?"

"What? No."

"You sure? 'Cause if I ask if you're a cop and you say no I'm not a cop then you can't arrest me for anything I do after that."

"I'm not sure that's true, but no, I'm not a cop."

"Then follow me," he says, grinning.

As you enter one of the bedrooms you see how he makes his money. Rows and rows of marijuana plants everywhere. Bright white grow lamps.

"Holy shit—this has been going on in my building this whole time?"

"Yeah, son. You blaze?"

"Well shit . . . now I do."

"So what were you saying about zombies? Wait—yo, is that blood on your shirt? And your hands?"

"Yeah, I just killed a Nazi."

"You what—"

"Dude, this apartment is amazing! How do you turn on the TV?"

He picks up a beautiful Logitech universal remote and switches to cable. Horror in hi-def. He watches, stunned.

He shuts the TV off. Slowly, not speaking, he sits down and stuffs a good twenty dollars' worth of pot into a massive glass bong. He lights it and draws deep—exhales thick, almost green, smoke. Then, still silent, he hands it to you.

You take it. Three-piece design, all glass on glass. No rubber to muck anything up. In green letters running down the side is the word RooR—as nice a piece you've ever seen. Nearly three feet tall, probably seven pounds in your hands. Made in Germany—you remember that piece of trivia from your college days. Thick glass, ash catcher, diffused downstem to cool the smoke.

You rip the bong—feel the smoke fill your lungs—then explode in a coughing fit. You hand it back.

His name's Matty, he says, but call him the Ardle, everyone calls him the Ardle. The Ardle runs his finger over his enormous Blu-ray collection and pulls *Starship Troopers*. He pops it on. The bass rumbles.

Minutes into the movie, you're so stoned, so lost in the action, you momentarily forget about the chaos outside. "Man," you say, "this movie's not just so bad it's good, it's so bad it's amazing."

The Ardle turns his head. Through a cloud of smoke: "What, no way man—it's legitimately good."

"Dude are you watching this—it's ridiculous!"

"Nah, bro. You're missing it. It's all social commentary about mankind and war and mindless violence and shit."

"I dunno man—I think it's just an excuse for coed showers and big guns shooting bugs and getting Doogie Howser back onscreen."

"Nah dude—social commentary."

"That makes it good?"

"Yeah, I mean—yeah—social commentary automatically makes stuff good. I think. There!" he shouts, pointing at the screen. "See those tattoos they're getting—just like the Nazis, man. Just like the Nazis."

"Hunh." You take another bong hit.

You squint at the screen and nod slowly as you exhale. "I killed a Nazi today."

"Right, that's what's up." With a burst of energy he sits on the edge of the couch and faces you. "You killed a Nazi, and now here we are. Just like this. It all makes sense now. You get me, right?"

And you do. You get him.

You continue watching the film with a newfound, marijuana-induced respect for it. When it ends, you leave—but not before asking to borrow some pot. Borrow, as in smoke and never give back. The Ardle does you one better and gives you a sandwich bag of weed plus your own plant. You carry it to your apartment like a baby. You put it out on the window and name it Audrey III, then spend the next two days in a haze, smoking constantly, watching Audrey grow and trying not to think about reality.

And then the power goes. You go to the window. It shuts in large chunks, block after block going dark.

Immediately, you think about the effect this'll have. You'll have to change the way you're eating—anything that'll go bad you'll have to eat now. Snack food, cereal, that kind of stuff you'll save.

A knock at your door. You grab the hockey stick, the splintered end still stained red with the Nazi's blood, and tiptoe to the door. You peer through the peephole. Phew—the Ardle. You open the door.

"Just saw the power went," he says.

"Yep. Didn't take long, huh."

"Nope. I've got a solar hookup—keeps the pricks at Con Ed from realizing how much energy I'm drawing for my business. You want to stay by me for a while, you're welcome."

"Yeah—yeah sure. I'd love to crash on the couch. It'll be about one hundred degrees in here without the AC."

"No prob, homes."

So you stay with him. It's like college again. You spend your days smoking pot and playing video games. Weeks go by, each day running into the next. Yeah, it's actually *just* like college. You'd forgotten how quickly time passes when you're high off your ass all the time.

After a month or so, you help him carry his flat screen up onto the roof. You take extension cords from a few abandoned apartments and run cables out through the window. You find two beach chairs in the basement, haul them up there, too.

You spell out HELP in empty beer bottles—when you have to go, you piss in them, keeps them from getting blown over by the wind.

The roof is your new home. During the days, the two of you play video games and watch movies. The Ardle's got a BB gun—you alternate between blasting away at pigeons and shooting at the zombies on the street below. The zombies are surprisingly not as fun—the BBs don't register.

It's a cool, breezy afternoon when they come.

You're napping, soaking up the sun, when you hear a loud mechanical howl above you. Your eyes snap open. You're staring up at the belly of a massive military helicopter. It hovers,

kicking shit up all around you—magazine pages flip, an empty
Mountain Dew can is thrown off the ledge.

Then a ladder drops.

Rescue has come.

But do you even want it?

Do you want to ignore the helicopter and keep
hanging out—after all, this sort of is paradise . . .
If so, turn to page 283.

If you want to climb the ladder and leave with the
military, turn to page 85.

"No thanks. That's all you."

You watch him do his heroin. It's gross, unsettling. So you curl up on the floor, roll your sweatshirt up into a pillow, and close your eyes.

You wake up hungover as fuck. Louis is sprawled out on the bed, needle still in his arm.

You make your way downstairs. The place is trashed. An Angel snores underneath the pool table. Guess that's how it goes after a successful zombie-killing run.

You pass out on the couch and don't wake up until you hear the helicopter. It starts in your dream as an old muscle car, driven by a horrific undead man, chasing you. The engine turns to a roar, and then you snap to, awake.

Most of the gang members are gathered around the monitors behind the bar. You peer over their shoulders and watch. It's a military helicopter—not very heavily armed, looks more like a transport. It lands on the street outside, directly in front of the club. It's a tight fit between the two sides of the street—it takes the pilot two attempts to set down. He finally does, and two soldiers hop out, rifles up.

They give some sort of army hand signal, and a man in a pressed military suit and gray trench coat steps out. He approaches the club, the wind from the slowing blades kicking up his coat so it looks almost like a cape. Standing directly beneath the camera, he gives three hard knocks.

"Whaddya think he wants?" Whiskey says.

"Kid, get the door," Jones says. "Find out what he wants."

"Why me?"

"Because I said so."

Three doors separate the club from the outside world. The first, nothing special. The second, heavy metal. The third, more metal. You unlock all three and walk outside. You look him up and down. He wears a green and beige service uniform. Pins and medals over his left breast. Plenty of stripes, too. Under his right arm is a large manila envelope.

He scans you as well, obviously surprised to see an unshaven kid in a filthy *Point Break* T-shirt open the door.

"Hi," you say.

"Can I come inside?"

"Who are you?"

"Colonel Troficanto, United States Special Forces."

"Uh, OK sir, one second."

"Huh—"

You shut the door. Back inside.

"Colonel something. Special Forces."

"Well—what's he want?"

"I don't know."

"You didn't ask?"

"No, sorry, hold on."

Back through the three doors. "What do you want?"

"I'd like to speak to whoever is in charge here."

"What about?"

"An opportunity to help your country."

"One sec."

"Kid, let me—"

Back inside.

"He says he wants to speak to whoever's in charge and that he's got an opportunity for you to help your country."

Everyone laughs.

"Fuck we'd want to do something like that for?" one says.

"I don't know," you say.

Jones stares at you.

"Again?" You sigh.

Jones nods.

Back through the three doors.

"Sir, why would they want to help out their country?"

He doesn't quite know how to answer this one. "Because it's your goddamn country."

You frown. "I don't think they give a damn."

"It'll be mutually beneficial, believe me."

"Alright, I'm not doing this anymore. Come inside."

You lead him in. Colonel Troficanto stands at the door. "Gentlemen."

No one returns the greeting.

"Who should I be speaking to?"

"Speak to us all," Jones responds.

The Colonel frowns, but does. "We've been watching you."

"What else is new?"

"Not what I mean. To be quite honest—we're impressed. Do you know what's going on in the rest of the world?"

"I can imagine," Jones says.

"I'll be brief. Four months ago, something went very, very wrong at Mount Sinai Hospital. A virus was released. Yeah, zombies. Right now, Manhattan is the main problem," the Colonel continues. "It's a complete clusterfuck. We tried a ground assault. Got a lot of my boys dead."

"Get to the fucking point," Jones says, lighting a cigarette.

"We'd like your help."

"Our help."

"Correct. Like I said—we've been watching you, via satellite. When you go on your little, ahem, runs, you're successful. Very successful. So, we'd like you to clean out some of the, uh, *messier* parts of the city. Soften them up. Then the military can come in and finish the job."

"And get all the credit," Whiskey says.

"That's right. I'm not here to offer you a shot at glory."

You look up at that crest. *When we do right, nobody remembers. When we do wrong, nobody forgets.*

"So why do we do this?"

The Colonel now pulls the manila envelope from under his armpit. Opens the metal tabs and removes another manila envelope. He flips it open.

"Joseph 'Broadway Joe' DeStefano. Killed two men in a drug-related shootout in Kansas City, 1987."

He looks up, scans their faces, makes eye contact with Broadway Joe. "Didn't have the beard in this photo."

Broadway Joe's expression doesn't change.

The Colonel flips the page. "Samuel 'Wild Bill' Hickock. Rape. Nineteen ninety-four."

Wild Bill stands up. "Bullshit!"

"Sit down, Bill," Jones says. Not happy, he does.

"Thomas 'Tommy Gun' Baker. Assaulting an officer of the law, one count, 1999. Murder in the first, two counts, 2002."

"Wes 'Whiskey' Ryan. Operated a methamphetamine lab in southern Georgia. In 2006, it blew up, killing two men, one a United States marshal."

"And Johnny 'Jones' Amaru. Murder of a police officer. Nineteen eighty-four."

Jesus Christ, these are some serious dudes. And this Colonel—well, you hope he doesn't know about that shoplifting charge at T.J.Maxx from middle school . . .

The Colonel looks around. "Do like we ask, all this goes away."

It seems simple to you. But many of the guys, especially the old-timers, don't like the idea of, and they say this, "working for the man."

Tommy's convinced the government won't stand by their promise even if they do complete the job. Some of the Angels resent having to risk their lives to bury crimes some other guys committed two decades ago.

Finally, Jones calls for a show of hands. It comes right down the middle: 17 for yes, 17 for no.

Then Jones turns to you.

"Well," he says, "what do you think, kid?"

If you think the Angels should tell the Colonel to take a hike, turn to page 233.

If you want to accept the mission, turn to page 354.

You barely have time to think before the shooting starts up again. You press your back against the tail end of a Budget rental truck.

You concentrate on breathing—slowing your pulse rate. Calming yourself. People are rushing about, panicked, mad, and it's getting them dead fast. Some run toward the Army, confused, dying needlessly in some sort of Brooklyn Bridge Pickett's Charge. Others run away from the Army and the M16s, toward the beasts.

You poke your head around the side of the truck and nearly get it shot off. Two bullets whiz by. The young driver of the truck—poor kid was probably moving into his first apartment— is riddled with bullets as he tries to get out. The side mirror pops off, and the kid's shoulder separates from his body. He stumbles back and collapses, smearing a thick line of blood down the side of the truck.

You pull your head back.

Holy. Fuck.

Blood from the kid's body pools around the rear left tire and seeps into your sneakers.

To stay alive, you need to think. One mistake, you're history. And not the good history—not the kind that ends up in a middle school textbook—the bad kind, the forgotten kind.

You peek around the other side of the truck. You don't almost get shot—good start. Squatting down, you make your way along the side of the truck, to the next car. A convertible. The driver and his three passengers—pretty, young girls—are all riddled with bullets. The arm of the girl in the front seat hangs over the side, blood dripping down to her hand, collecting around a massive diamond ring, and trickling off her fingers. You gently push her dead arm aside and keep moving.

Still low to the ground, you work your way down the bridge, hugging the sides of the cars.

Suddenly a mass of people, twenty or thirty, you can't tell, comes tearing around the side of an SUV up ahead—stampeding right toward you. The Army catches two of them in the back, dropping them. The rest keep coming. You try to get out of the way—no luck. The first guy knocks you aside. The second, a woman, rolls you onto your back. They trample you. You use one hand to cover your face and another to protect the family jewels.

After a few brutal moments the game of doormat ends and you're left bloody and bruised. Since they were running back to the city, the Army seems to have let most of them live. Up ahead, you see the soldiers, guns up, ready to unload on anything coming their way. You slide under the SUV, wipe the blood from your eyes, catch your breath, then slip discreetly out the other side.

You're about two-thirds of the way across the bridge. Only one football field to go. You have no idea what you'll do when, *if*, you make it to the other side—but the United States Army still seems like a better bet than the army of the undead behind you.

You continue your crawl. When the firing begins again, you slide back under the nearest car. When it lets up, you move. It's slow going, but you see no other way around it.

As you near the head of the bridge, the cars are no longer in any sort of order. Some point this way, some that.

Fenders latched together, smoke pouring from hoods. Twisted metal.

Then, just beyond the mess of vehicles is the Army.

KRAK!!!

A sound like nothing you've ever heard. Loud times infinity. An earthshaking blast. Cannon fire. Coming from a tank—one of four that guard the exit to the bridge.

Another one fires. A huge explosion behind you rocks the bridge.

While the smoke clears, you try to think. You've got one chance. One chance at survival. You've got to get to one of these soldiers—hopefully not some trigger-happy fool—and plead your case.

You reach one of the tanks and crawl underneath. Make your way along the massive tread that covers the wheels.

Up ahead, you can see feet. Boots. You crawl forward and reach out. There's a scream, then the loud report of an automatic rifle, and the cement in front of you rips apart.

You yank your hand back underneath the tank. "No! No!" you shout. "No! I'm not—"

Bullets pelt the cement again. You skitter back underneath the tank and scramble out from the rear end.

Here goes nothing. Slowly, arms up to the sky, you rise.

Across from you is the biggest goddamn machine gun you've ever seen. Well, the only goddamn machine gun you've ever seen in person, but it's big as fuck. You see the soldier's eyes—wide, scared. Just about as scared as you.

"I'm not one of those things," you say.

Artillery erupts around you. The world shakes again. You shout to be heard. You can't hear a damn thing, but you can tell he's waving you back across the bridge. Back the way you came.

"Go, or I shoot," he shouts over the firing.

You shake your head like a wet dog trying to dry off. You frantically wipe the blood from your face, trying to make yourself look like less of a bloody mess. "I'm not one of those things. I'm not bit. I'm not hurt. I'm not infected. I'm not fucking dying or fucking dead or whatever *the fuck* is going on. I'm just trying to get to Brooklyn."

The soldier continues to stare at you. You can see the wheels turning. See him struggling. He's probably got orders to kill anything that looks remotely human—but to shoot a guy like you, a regular Joe . . .

"Please . . ." you say. Begging now.

Finally, he takes a few steps back. Taps the shoulder of a higher-up, someone with rank. They exchange some words. The officer looks you up down like a piece of meat. He nods. The soldier marches over to you and grabs you by the arm. "Alright, let's go."

"Thank you, thank you, thank you."

He leads you back through the maze of tanks and Humvees. Past the gunfire.

Beyond the bridge, men stand around in big yellow plastic suits—hazmat, you think they're called. The shit from that Dustin Hoffman movie with the monkey from *Friends*. *Breakout. Outbreak.* Something like that.

One of the hazmat guys, accompanied by the soldier, leads you by the arm to a large trailer that says MILITARY SCIENCE on the side.

And then a burst of fear rushes through you—your knees go weak. What if they're going to take you and do a bunch of experiments on you? You know you're not infected—but they don't know that. They probably don't know much more about what's going on than you do. You could end up some test patient—the star of some alien autopsy shit.

Your mind races.

If you want to go with the Army and the dream of safety, turn to page 28.

Forget about it—the Army's too scary—run! Turn to page 185.

A MAN'S HOME IS HIS CASTLE

You skid to a halt and hop off the bike, the things right behind you.

You run up the back of your parents' Camry, up over the top, and leap off the hood to the fence. You scramble over and fall into the backyard.

Kim comes running out of the back of the house. "What happened?"

"Back inside, back inside, go." You follow her, through the back door, into the kitchen, and then through a swinging door into the dining room. There, you look out on the front yard.

"What is that?" she asks.

"The entire high school varsity football team."

"You brought them back here?"

"Not on purpose!"

"You're right, sorry. Well, fucking now what?"

"We get to work. Lock up everything."

A man's home is his castle—in this case, quite literally. You have your princess. You've already rescued her. This isn't Super Mario Bros. Your princess isn't in another castle. She's here. In *this* castle. Now, as the king, you have to protect her.

That's right. You're the king. *Hail to the king, baby . . .*

You get to work. Lock all the doors. They scratch and claw at the big front window. Have to do something about that.

Backyard. Tool shed.

Thank God your dad retired early and went on that absurd Tim Allen, "I'm a man" kick and bought all those tools and decided to build the patio himself. It's the shittiest patio in town, sure, but he's got one hell of a tool set.

You reach the shed, throw on his tool belt, and start putting anything that might be useful inside. Hammer. Nails.

Weed Whacker? Nah. That'd only work on, like, kids.

Chainsaw? That could work.

Ooh, nail gun. Fuck it, bring both.

There's some spare wood in the rear of the shed. Just long enough to board up that window.

A scream. No. Kim. . . .

You forget the wood and dart back inside and into the dining room. Shit! They're through the window already. Three of them. Only the dining room table separates you from the beasts.

"Kim! Get in the closet." She does. You throw your mom's good chairs to either side of the table to slow their approach.

OK, chainsaw time. Now—how the hell do you turn one of these things on? You tug at the cord. C'mon, start, goddamn it!

GAROOOMMM!!!

There we go. Alright, you bastards.

The first one slithers over the dining room table. You run up and swing. It hits the floor, headless.

Next one comes over the chair. You ram the weapon into its chest. Bad move. It continues clawing at you, even as you grind up its insides. You turn the chainsaw sideways and rip it out the side of its stomach, leaving the thing slumped over. You rear back. Chainsaw, right down the middle of the head. One left.

You back up, through the swinging kitchen door. Not quick enough—it lunges for you, sending you stumbling back. You lose control of the chainsaw and it drops to the floor. The thing's on you. Going for your face. You grab for the nail gun in your tool belt, but before you can get a firm grip—

Smack.

Its head goes flying to the side. Kim stands above you

clutching a cast-iron skillet. You scramble to your feet, grab a santoku knife from the wood block, and bury it in the side of the thing's face.

"Go in my bedroom and lock the door, OK?" you tell Kim. She nods.

Before you creep back into the kitchen, you disable the safety system on the nail gun. Now it's a fine zombie-hunting weapon.

Slowly, you open the door.

The entire varsity football team is in your dining room—minus a couple of casualties from the previous skirmish. Had this been ten years ago—well, that would've been pretty cool and made for a helluva party.

Right now, not so good.

You flip the dining room table, sending the good china flying. That blocks them some. They struggle to get over it. You back against the wall, don't want anything getting you from behind.

You aim the nail gun. Pop two in the head. Third shot misses, shattering your mother's favorite mirror.

They come at you hard. Unrelenting. You fire a load of nails into the closest one. Six into its face. Finally, it drops.

From beside you, you see the whirl of glinting metal, which makes contact with a zombie and drops it immediately. You whip your head over. Kim's standing next to you, holding one of your father's golf clubs.

"Kim, back upstairs, go!"

"You need help."

"Kim, go!"

It's too late. One of the things has her by the arm. Pretty kid. Probably the quarterback. He sinks his teeth in and tears out a chunk of flesh.

"No!" you shout. Kim screams. You unload the nail gun into the QB's pretty face, leaving him all sorts of ugly.

You spin, they're everywhere. Need to retreat. You drag Kim

into the kitchen. She holds her bleeding wrist against her stomach.

You have seconds.

Cut off Kim's arm, hoping to save her? Turn to page 276.

Take her upstairs, away from the zombies, and deal with her then? Turn to page 282.

You put it out of your mind. There's nothing you can do about it anyway—you couldn't take this guy down even if you had ten guys helping you.

You scan the horizon. Hauk treads water, working his way along the fence, beneath the park. Above him, zombies roam across the grass.

Through the binoculars, you see Taft. His stomach is torn open. He stumbles across the street.

Then Hauk goes under.

"You got him?" Hammer asks.

"Looking."

"Got him?"

"Looking."

"Find him!"

"I'm trying!"

Hauk's head pops up, bobbing in the water.

"There!"

Hauk emerges from the water, scampers up the hill, and ducks down behind a truck, his back to it. He gives you a thumbs-up.

You spot two of them. From up the street, coming his way. Pair of goth girls.

"To his right, two of them," you say.

No response.

"Hammer, to the right!"

You watch as the zombies draw closer.

"Right! What the hell are you—"

You look over. The binoculars drop from your hand and clang on the floor. Hammer's undead eyes are staring right at you.

"Oh shit—"

Hammer launches himself at you. Pushes you against the ledge. Mouth wide. Teeth shimmer.

You push back, throwing him into the pillar that holds the torch. His hands dig into your throat.

You feel for his gun. Around his belt. Unclip it.

He closes in. His eyes wild.

You rip the gun free. Whip it up. Squeeze.

The flash momentarily blinds you. The bullet rips up the side of his face, tearing open his cheek. The muzzle flash burns his skin. He stumbles back, against the ledge. But he's not dead. He raises his head. Angry.

You raise the pistol. Put five shots into his bare chest. The skin explodes and blood splatters the floor. The final shot knocks him back, over the side.

You run to the edge just in time to see him bounce off the statue's base and fall to the cement, hundreds of feet below.

You catch your breath. Christ, that was close.

Shit, Hauk!

You run to the rifle and look through the scope. OK, just like the video games, you tell yourself.

You spot the two goth beasts bearing down on Hauk. You line the closest one up in your sights. Fire. The side window of the SUV explodes. Hauk spins, draws his sidearm.

Little lower, to the left.

You fire. A flash of red comes from the zombie's top and it falls. Hauk fires and blows the other one away before it gets him.

Six more immediately surround him.

With superhuman speed, Hauk pushes through the crowd and sprints down the street toward the two tanks and the Humvee, at least a dozen beasts in his path.

It takes you three shots to get the first one. Finally, you connect with its head. The she-beast's hair flies up, and it falls. Hauk runs past it.

Next one. Homeless guy. Huge jacket. Ball cap. Messy beard. You can almost smell it from here.

You put the crosshairs right on its head. Squeeze. His head jerks to the side and his ball cap flies through the air.

Hauk dives inside the overturned Humvee. The beasts gather around it.

Goddamn it—c'mon—get outta there!

You continue firing, putting them down. But there're too many. No way he's going to get out of there. You scan. Look around them. A motorcycle. Harley, overturned.

You get the gas tank in your sights.

Squeeze.

A window in a building about twenty feet beyond the bike shatters.

You adjust your aim. Fire again. The bike explodes. The blast catches the beasts in the back, hurling them forward and to the ground.

Hauk peeks his head out from under the Humvee. Momentarily clear. He books it for the water, firing as he runs, killing two.

At the fence, one of the beasts stands in his way, its back to you. A big guy. Bald head. You see Hauk aim and squeeze, then see the horror on his face as he realizes he's empty.

You train the sights on the back of that big bald head.

Then you squeeze.

The head comes apart and the thing collapses in a heap.

Hauk runs past, then leaps over the fence and dives into the water. He swims a quick fifty yards, climbs back on the Hellfire, and guns it.

OK—made it this far.

You race back down. Panting, pain in your side, you exit the statue base. Hauk is motoring across the harbor, a stream of

water kicking up behind him. He rides the Hellfire up onto the rocks, leaps off, and vaults over the fence.

"Where's Hammer?" he asks.

"Dead. He was bitten—attacked me, went over the side in the struggle."

"What?"

"You heard me. That's what happened."

Hauk doesn't say anything for a moment. Then, "Where?"

"I'll show you."

You walk to the base of the statue. There's a bloody pool on the ground, no body.

"Fuck me, where'd he go? I killed him!"

Hauk glares at you. "Forget it," he says finally.

"You get them on the radio?"

"I got some civilian—guy runs the helicopter tours off the West Side. He said he'd come when he could."

"When he could? We don't have time."

"Yeah—well, he didn't seem to care."

Then you hear the splashing. You turn. Zombies are streaming out of the water from every direction. They struggle getting over the fence as intestines and flaps of skin become caught on the tines. They slip, their decomposing skin soaking wet. But they make it over—land on the grass—and get to their feet. Then they start running.

"Fuck—inside!" Hauk shouts as he takes off running. You follow him.

And there, just inside the entrance, is Hammer. Body mangled. Bones shattered. Blood everywhere. He moans. Limps toward you.

Hauk fires. Blows undead Hammer's brains out the back of undead Hammer's skull. You sprint past.

Christ, climbing the Statue of Liberty twice in an hour—not your lucky day. The monsters follow, racing up the steps behind you.

You climb higher. And the beasts keep coming. No way to

block the doors behind you. No way to keep them from chasing.

Finally, you reach the peak—the torch. Hauk looks over the side. "How do you like heights?" he says.

"I hate them."

"Yeah, me too—that's why I joined the Marines, not the Air Force."

The beasts flood the platform. You and Hauk quickly climb over the side, hanging on the edge of the torch, three hundred feet above the ground.

You take the lead, dropping onto Lady Liberty's arm, wrapping your body around it as you slide all the way down to her sleeve. You smash against it, nearly fall off the side.

Hauk comes next, barreling down the arm, right for you. You brace yourself—it's a tight spot—if he hits you hard, you'll both be over the side and dead. He slams into you, rolling to the side and almost over. You grab him, holding tight as he steadies himself.

The beasts try to follow, unsuccessfully. They tumble over the side, free-falling to the ground.

Together you sit on the rock-hard sleeve of the Statue of Liberty, wind howling, threatening to blow you off, and you wait. Wait for the helicopter that maybe, just might, be coming . . .

AN END

Walter pulls the trigger—the loud pop of the gun echoes through the door, the glass shatters, and a man screams. Then a woman's voice: "Fuck, babe! Son of a . . ."

A pause. Then,

KRAKA KRAKA KRAKA!!!

Bullets rip through the door and into the store. You jump to the side, hands over your head. Walter's not as lucky. He screams and rolls over in pain.

Outside, the man whimpers.

You look over at Walter. "Where are you hit?"

"My goddamn leg. I'm fine."

But he's not. In an instant, blood begins to rush from the thigh wound.

More voices outside. Hushed whispers. The woman again. Then, louder, "Get back, get back, it's gonna go."

You and Walter exchange quick "oh shit" glances. Then the entire door frame explodes, sending chunks of metal and wooden shrapnel into the store. A jagged splinter gets you in the gut.

A man and a woman enter. She's tall with a whole mess of bright red hair. The man is balding, in his early fifties you guess, with a hint of Spanish or Puerto Rican to him. He has his hand on his shoulder, blood pouring through his fingers.

"Watch the door," the redhead tells the Puerto Rican. She reloads the big-ass pistol in her hand.

Alright, shit's about to escalate. You stand up, arms raised. "Hey, listen, this is a big misunderstanding."

Redhead points the gun at you. "Misunderstanding? You just shot my husband."

"Well actually *he* shot your husband," you say, nodding toward Walter.

Walter shoots you a WTF look. "Sorry," you mouth, and shrug. "You did."

"Look," the woman says. "We're here for supplies. We got kids at home. We're scared like everyone else. Let us take what we need, we won't kill you."

"Who are you giving orders to?" Walter shouts, then rolls over, groaning and clutching his leg.

You're about to launch into a grand "why can't we all just get along" speech—but it's interrupted by the zombies coming through the now nonexistent door. A teen in a red CVS one-hour-photo shirt leads the pack.

Redhead shoots the undead teen in the face, sending it falling back into the others, stalling them for a second.

"Can we all stop arguing and shooting at one another for one fucking second here and worry about those things outside?" you say.

Silence.

"Good." You grab a hatchet from the wall behind you and stand beside the door. It's the perfect choke point—they can only make it through two or three at a time. As they enter, you hack at their heads. Each one takes about two or three whacks to kill.

The redhead stands at the center aisle, steadily dropping the ones you miss.

You continue pounding away with the hatchet. Your arm grows tired. At least ten bodies lying on the floor, clogging up the doorway.

The Puerto Rican carries over a huge shelf and leans it against the door frame, completely shutting it off. Phew. You can breathe.

You turn your attention to Walter. He's bleeding heavily.

You grab a painting rag and try to make a tourniquet. It does little.

"I don't know what I'm doing; do either of you?" you ask.

"Hang on," the redhead says. She's examining her husband's wound. Looks like the bullet just grazed him.

Then she gets down on the floor and rips open Walter's jeans near the wound. The blood pumps faster. Walter appears to be unconscious. "Give me your shirt," she says.

You pull your button-down over your head, popping off the top button, and hand it to her.

Then, from around the side of the aisle, one of the beasts latches on to the redhead's legs.

She shrieks. The Puerto Rican falls back, not sure what to do. You look around for some sort of weapon.

It's a disgusting mess of a thing. Bullet wounds all over. Huge chunk of its face missing, thanks to your hatchet. But it's still going. Fucking thing—must not have been as dead as you thought.

BLAM!

Walter. Up on one elbow. Pistol smoking in his hand.

The thing collapses onto the redhead's leg. She kicks it off. "Th-thanks," she stutters.

"Anytime," Walter says, then passes back out.

You look up at the woman. "Maybe we should all go in the back and lock the door, huh?"

You and the Puerto Rican drag Walter into the back room and put him beside a lawn mower. You shut the heavy door and lock it, then the redhead gets to work finishing the tourniquet.

"OK, he should be alright," she says.

"Good. Can we all be friends now?"

She looks at her husband. He shrugs. She nods. "Friends."

A few hours later Walter comes to. He's dazed. Takes him a second to realize where he is. Then, throat dry, barely able to talk, he calls you over. "Kid," he says, sputtering out the words, "there—on the wall. Take the keys. The yellow Kawasaki has a full tank."

You look up at the redhead. "You're not gonna shoot him when I leave, are you?"

She smiles. "No. No, I'm not going to shoot him."

You pat Walter on the shoulder. "OK. You da man, Walter."

You turn to leave. "Kid," Walter says. "Take the gun."

You smile and nod. Gun in hand, you open the door to the back and silently shut it behind you. The yellow Kawasaki bike glistens in the moonlight. It's a beauty. Four hundred and fifty cc's, brand-new.

Only thing—you've never driven a dirt bike before. You hop on. Insert the keys. It roars to life. Loud as hell. Christ, have to get out of here quick.

But the sound draws one. Approaching you is the biggest, fattest motherfucking undead beast you've ever seen.

Trying to kick-start the bike. "C'mon . . ."

Shit. No time.

You pull the revolver from your waist, extend your arm, aim, and squeeze. Amateur hour. Your arm flies up. Bullet goes God knows where. This isn't the movies, you remember, as much as it may feel like it.

The fattie quits with the shuffle and runs toward you. Its body shakes, flab quivering.

You step off the bike. Take a solid stance. Raise the gun. Aim down the barrel.

It's close. Almost upon you.

You squeeze.

BLAM!!!

You blow its brains out the back of its fat head. Its momentum carries it forward and it hits the ground face-first with an earthshaking thud.

"That's right, big boy." You can't help but raise the gun and blow the smoke like Dirty Harry.

You hop back on the Kawasaki, stick the gun in your belt, and hit the road.

Turn to page 261.

You stare at the ladder, then look over at the Ardle. He shrugs. You shrug back.

"You first," you say.

He thinks for a long moment. "No. No, you go. I gotta stay with my plants."

"You sure?"

"Yeah, I'm sure."

"Definitely? This could be your only chance."

He nods. "Definitely."

"Alright then—I'll see you around."

"You bet."

You clench fists, give each other tender manhugs, and you begin climbing.

AN END

NEXT CAR, PLEASE

This man needs help. You should call for a doctor—pull the emergency cord—do *something*. But what you saw on TV was too scary. You try to help this guy, next thing you know he's eating you. Nope—not for you.

"Sorry, sorry, excuse me, thanks, sorry," you mumble, working yourself into the corner of the car, nearing the rear door.

Ignoring the RIDING OR MOVING BETWEEN CARS IS PROHIBITED sticker on the metal door, you slide it open. The roar of the subway echoes through the crowded car and the passing track below seems to nip at your feet. You step on the small, shaky walkway and cross. You open the door, catching a man by surprise. You give him a half smile and squeeze inside.

You turn and glance back at the car you just left. You can't see the man anymore—the car is too crowded. Over the rumble of the train and separated by two heavy doors, you don't hear a thing. But, minutes later, you see the chaos unfolding. The passengers at the door turn in horror, blood splattered on their faces.

No one in your car notices yet. You back away from the door, work your way to the other end, and cross over to the next car.

You squeeze your way through, gathering dirty looks like a bum begging for change. You get to the rear door. Through it you see only the dark tracks—you're in the last car.

A station whizzes past. A sign flashes VERNON BLVD. You're out of Manhattan now, in Queens.

The train continues to barrel along. You fly past Queensboro Plaza—nearing Long Island and the burbs. The train doesn't slow. Nothing from the conductor. No announcement that the train is swarming with zombies.

The car shakes and rocks. You've never been on the subway doing speeds like this. The train bounces on the tracks as you turn down a hill.

You fly past another station—just a blur of people, a flash. In the distance, you can make out the parking lot where Shea Stadium used to stand. Then the new Citi Field.

The train rocks more. Shudders. Goes down a hill and your feet lift off the floor slightly. This isn't right. Next big turn, this thing's going off the tracks. You're going to crash.

You need to secure yourself, somehow. You look around. Panicked looks on everyone's faces. Fuck it. You push a bunch of people to the side, drop to the floor, and roll underneath a row of seats. You grasp the bar by your head as tight as you can. Press your feet against the rear wall.

You play the waiting game. After a few minutes, you start to think everything might be OK. But then—

CRASH!!!

Everything goes black. You're flying through the car.

And then it all stops. For one peaceful second, there's silence as you float in zero gravity. Then screams. The piercing howl of an alarm. Shouting. Another crash.

You're on your back, on what seconds ago was the ceiling of the train. The car has completely flipped.

People on top of you. All around you. An old woman in a blue shawl lies beside you, not moving.

Everything hurts. You try to stand, but disoriented, you fall. The world spins.

You drag yourself across the car's former ceiling, clawing your way through the mass of bodies and grimacing like hell as the pain tears through you. You grab the closest metal hand pole and pull. It's a miserable, painful struggle. But it could be worse, you think, as you pass a man, twisted on his side, face wet with blood and clearly dead.

The large Plexiglas windows that run across the side of the train are broken. Not shattered, like real glass, but bent out of their casing. You pull your way up, squeeze through, and fall out.

You're lying in a large grass field. A Little League baseball diamond. The train wreckage stretches out behind you, cars smoking. Some cars are still up on the track, flipped; others lie in the field.

Thirty yards away, a grassy hill leads up to the tracks and the street. You read the sign—ROOSEVELT AVENUE. Last stop in Queens. You're out of the city. You made it.

Then they begin pouring out of the cars. So many you can't believe it. Hundreds of the monsters.

A few living people, too, make it out. Some run from the things, screaming. Others just stumble out, too disoriented to figure out what's going on—then they're pounced upon by the horde.

You scramble on all fours up the hill, hurting everywhere. You steal a glance behind you. Not good. Two of the dead have wandered over your way. They notice you. You switch from a modified crawl to a shaky, off-balance run. Ugly, but effective.

Fuck.

Need to make it up that hill—they're coming quick.

BLAM! BLAM!

You dive to the ground. A pair of cops stand on top of the hill—one heavyset, the other thinner, younger looking. You put your hands up in the air.

"C'mon!" the young one shouts to you.

You scurry up the grass like a wounded dog, the smoking wreckage of the train behind you. Then you turn, stand between the two cops, and take in the clusterfuck that surrounds you. Half the train is still on the tracks, which run down the street. The other half is down below, in the field. The two beasts that were chasing you are dead, but there are hundreds more behind them.

Then it hits you: Cops—police—authority! You're saved!

"Guys—officers—we gotta get outta here."

The heavyset cop stops to reload. Drops his clip to the ground, slides in another. Never looks up at you. "Not until backup arrives."

"Backup? There're a thousand fucking, I-don't-know what, fucking monsters down there—and more inside the train. We have to go!"

"Wait in the car."

Fine. You'll take that. You pull the rear handle. Locked.

"It's locked," you say.

"Kid, do you see what's down there—we don't have time to help you."

"Vinny, he's right," the thinner cop says. "Let's go. I don't even know what the fuck I'm shooting at!"

"We're shooting the goddamn things coming at us!"

"They're people!"

"Not anymore they ain't."

"Do you know how much paperwork we're going to have to file over this shit?"

That stops the heavyset cop. "Motherfuck, fine, let's go. This never happened." He looks at you and you nod.

The thin cop gets in the passenger seat. Heavyset one walks around to the front driver's-side door. You pull at the handle. "Hey, it's still locked, you gotta hit the button."

"Yeah, yeah, one sec—"

Time stands still.

With a thunderous crash, a minivan, two zombies clinging to the front, slams into the rear of the cruiser at near 50 mph. The two zombies on the hood are launched through the air, then hit the pavement twenty yards out.

The cruiser flies forward. The heavyset cop, halfway inside the car when it was hit, is pulled underneath. He gets caught in the rear wheel and dragged. Eventually, the cruiser rolls to a slow stop, just as its bumper hits the zombies. They don't

CAN YOU SURVIVE THE ZOMBIE APOCALYPSE? **89**

move. Nobody moves. You see the other cop now, his limbs splayed at odd angles.

The driver of the minivan, a middle-aged woman, is thrown against the airbag. You rush to help her. Then you hear their moans behind you. You spin. A half dozen, lumbering up the hill. The mass feast continues behind them.

Fuck—need to split—now.

If you want to take shelter in the nearest building, an elementary school, turn to page 286.

Take off up the street, hoping to put as much distance between you and these things as you can? Turn to page 253.

HAMMER'S TIME

You have to kill him before he turns into a zombie. You have to. Don't want to. Definitely don't want to. But if you don't—he's going to turn, and then he's going to turn you.

Slowly, you go for your knife. Feel your way along your belt. You find the handle. Gently release it. Pull it out.

You turn to Hammer. He's looking right at you.

"Not smart, friend."

In a split second he's up. He grabs you by the throat and rips you to your feet.

"You're bit," you choke out. "We have to get you help."

"Don't want no help."

He lifts you off your feet. "Wha—"

"You're about to have a very bad accident, friend."

"No, no!"

It all happens in slow motion. He lifts you higher. His massive arms flex. He throws you. Into the air. Over the side. Spinning. Down past the massive tablet in her left hand. You see her sandals, green and worn. Then the concrete closes in.

AN END

In dead heroin junkie Louis's room, you sleep. No AC—the heat is unbearable. You toss and turn throughout the night. Death chases you through your dreams.

Downstairs, the Angels continue to party. Drink. How do they keep going like this? Every once in a while one will come in, reeking of booze, and mess with you. You tell them to go to hell.

The Angels continue to do what the government asks. You don't go—you've done your part.

Then one day Jones comes in, kicks the bed. "Get up."

You wipe at your eyes. Sit up. "Why?"

"Man's here."

You climb out of the bed, still disoriented. Look around for your shirt.

"Wear something of Lou's."

"Huh?"

"It's alright—here," Jones says, tossing you a T-shirt from Lou's dresser. Reluctantly, you put it on and follow Jones out the door.

The Colonel is sitting in Jones's room, on the bed, not looking happy about being there.

"Gentlemen," he says.

You take a seat.

"Last one."

"No shit," Jones says.

"That's right. How's it felt, serving your country?"

"Fuckin' lovely. What's the job?"

"Empire State Building. Clear it out. When you get to the top, pop this," he says, handing Jones a flare. "We see that red smoke, we know you've done your job."

"The file," Jones says. "Give me the file."

"When you complete the job."

Jones stares him down. "If you fuck me . . ."

"Don't worry—you've done good. You'll get your reward."

You go back to Louis's room. Suit up. Borrow a pair of heavy black jeans. Black boots. Leather coat.

Turn to page 172.

In one motion, you drop the rifle, dive for the morning star, leap back onto your feet, whip it around your head once, and snap your arm out.

The spiked ball barrels through the three monsters. Rips the first one's head apart, carries through, shatters the second one's face, and then finishes by nearly ripping off the cabdriver's head. They all collapse.

Screams up ahead to your right. You reel. Chucky drops two of the things with a shotgun blast. Phew. It looks like your group is safe, but time is running out. Two more come at Chucky from the side—he spins with the halberd, taking off the first one's head, then jamming the sword end through the head of the second one. He pulls it out, leaving a massive, gory vertical hole in the thing's face.

Feet trampling. They besiege you from all angles. Over the wall, from the park. Down the museum steps. From up the street.

"We gotta move!" you shout. "Everybody—quick!"

Directly ahead is the bus. Through the back window, you can see a passenger inside, pacing back and forth, hungry. Must be the guy the driver mentioned—the one who went schizo; went zombie.

Chucky jogs up alongside the bus. Wesley is next to you. You toss the bloody, gore-covered morning star to him. He looks at it like you tossed him a rubber chicken. But when his wife screams, and he turns and sees her zombified form running up on him, he doesn't hesitate. He swings. The morning star hits it in the chest. Sends it sprawling back. *Whoa.* He tackles it now, raises his arm, and brings his BlackBerry crashing into its face over and over again.

You drop the assault rifle's magazine out—remove the jammed bullet—and pop it back in. You drop to one knee, turn, aim, and put a round through the forehead of one of the other charging beasts. Good—it works.

You give Chucky a thumbs-up.

He boards the bus. You stay behind, watching through the back door. The undead passenger spins. Chucky scuttles down the aisle, halberd out, and spears it. He keeps running, carrying the thing down the aisle, slamming it against the rear of the bus, and pinning it to the wall. The thing kicks wildly, waves its arms around, then clutches at the pole in its stomach.

Chucky gives you a nod, then ducks. You raise the gun and fire through the back door, blowing the monster's head to pieces.

OK, bus is safe. Your group is running past you, fast. Good. Chucky edges his way out and ushers them inside while you hold off the charging horde. The rifle pounds your shoulder—each shot more painful than the last. It's sore—hurts like hell. Finally, everyone's on board.

You and Chucky step on last.

"Alright, Wesley," you say, out of breath, "let's go check out this yacht."

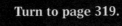

Turn to page 319.

If you have to die you'd rather be run over by a train than be eaten by a horde of the walking dead. And you can't let that kid die down there. You throw one last look down at the tracks—the train's headlights telling you if you're gonna go, you gotta go now—and with the approaching enemy behind you and probable death in front of you, you make the big Butch Cassidy leap.

You land in a mass of bodies. Your ankle twists. Standing on the tracks, frozen, is the boy. You grab him around the waist and tug him to the ground. Together you roll beneath the platform overhang.

Screams pierce the darkness as the train rushes by.

You press the kid's head against your chest and squeeze your eyes shut tight. Rats skitter over you. Your skin crawls as their disgusting little feet scamper over your arms and face.

Finally, the train passes, leaving behind a sick, disgusting mess of death. You feel like a soldier, witness to the aftermath of his first battle. You want to look away, but you can't. You just stare for a moment—shocked and horrified, but happy to be alive.

"Keep your eyes shut for now—alright, kid?" you say. He does as he's told. You take him by the hand. "I'm going to Brooklyn," you say. "You want to go for a walk?"

The kid says nothing, eyes closed. He nods his head once, short and hard.

"Alright," you say, "we walk."

The trek is slow going. It's dark. Sounds around you—some

you're probably just imagining. Feels like at any moment some monster is going to leap out from the darkness and take you.

Soon you see movement up ahead. You stop in your tracks. You squint, trying to see what it is. Relief floods over you when you realize it's another person, doing the same thing you are. There're a few people, walking up ahead. You keep your distance.

More trains pass—each time you press your body flat against the tunnel wall and keep your hand on the kid.

Your shoes are soaked. Huge, muddy puddles line the tunnel. After nearly two hours of walking, you're approaching the Fiftieth Street station. You check your iPhone. Yes, service.

"OK, kid—I don't want to leave this subway until we have to. It has to be crazy out there—"

You stop. A sound up ahead. You hug the tunnel wall and listen.

"What is it?" the kid says.

"Shh . . . I'm trying to hear."

What you hear isn't nice. Moans. Then sounds of eating. People being devoured.

Shit. You look down at the little guy. Eyes gigantic and wet. You have to get him through this.

You get down on one knee and whisper. "OK, here's the plan, buddy. We gotta keep moving. So we're gonna crawl, real quiet, right past this station. Stay under the platform. You gotta be quiet. Super quiet. You ever play the quiet game?"

"Yes I've played the quiet game. But I'm six and three-quarters. I can be quiet without the quiet game. You can just tell me to be quiet and I'll be quiet."

"Oh. OK, well, good. Be quiet. Let's go."

You walk the next few yards, sticking to the tunnel wall, then slowly get down on all fours, and begin crawling.

You crane your neck and whisper, "OK, here we go. Keep your hand around the bottom of my pants, at my ankle here. So I know you're with me. Everything's gonna be fine."

A woman moans. Not the sick, guttural moan of the dead—but the pained howl of someone still alive. The things make disgusting, throaty sounds. Someone shrieks. It sends a chill down your spine.

You're at the overhang. Can they smell you? God, you hope not, you think, as you crawl underneath the platform.

You keep crawling. Hands in rat shit. Knees in puddles of filthy water.

Brave kid. Keeps his hand on you the whole time.

You're halfway now. You're going to make it, you think. Going to fucking make it.

Then an arm swings down past you. Your heart stops. The limb hangs there. A woman's dead arm. It's been chewed all to hell—the bone visible. Flesh hangs off it like string cheese, some caught up in her silver watch.

The kid screams.

Fuck!

You turn. He has his hands over his mouth, shaking his head back and forth. His wide eyes say sorry.

The moans above you stop. Feet shuffle. Something falls down. Fuck, fuck, fuck.

A shadow stretches out across the track. One of the things. It leans over the side of the platform. Sort of sniffing, looking. You grab the kid and get as far back as possible.

Two more of the things now, down on their stomachs, reaching out, looking around.

Grab the kid and run like hell? Turn to page 104.

If you want to stay still and pray they go away, turn to page 168.

Instead of waiting for them to come to you, you run right at the mother. Take it out, then deal with the rest, you think. You launch yourself and ride it to the ground. Before it gets a chance to bite, you push the pointed edge of the crowbar up through the roof of its mouth and into its brain. You rip it out, a string of gore coming with it, and hop up over the putrid creature.

The father and daughter turn around to face you. You step back.

Footsteps behind you. You spin. Another one—quick— coming hard and fast. Fuck—you're done for.

BAM!!!

The entire side of the quick one's head blows out. In a split second, it crumples.

You look at the Angels.

"OK, I'll waste one bullet on you, kid!" Jones shouts.

Mental note: thank the asshole.

Back to the father and daughter. You crack the father in the face. Its head spins, but it comes right back. Tackles you. The crowbar skids across the cement. You're pinned. It goes in for the kill. You want to push it back—but you can't risk getting hit by those teeth.

You grab its head, lifting it. It's near unstoppable. You press your fingers into its eyes. They're dry, don't feel human. You keep going, pushing through, into the sockets. You feel the soft, mushy interior of his skull. But it feels no pain. Doesn't stop. Teeth closer. Inches from your face.

99

You push in deeper. Thumbs completely through its eyes now. You have leverage. You push up while turning your thumbs outward toward the side of its head.

A quick jerk to the side and it's off you. You stand—not a second to breathe—the girl's on your leg. You try to shake it off, but it's not going anywhere.

"Three minutes!"

You grab the girl monster by its hair and rip its head back. Pieces of your jeans hang from its teeth. Christ—close call.

You toss it as far as you can. Need to separate the father and daughter. The thing flies six, maybe seven feet. You rush over and smash it in the mouth with your sneakers. Its baby teeth, probably loose already, spill out across the sidewalk. You grab it by the hair, run with it, and toss it into a Dumpster. It hits the top of the Dumpster and falls in. The lid shuts behind it.

The father's on its feet again and coming fast. You look for the crowbar—it's a good ten feet away. And the fat, Hawaiian shirt–wearing, drool-spilling, son-of-a-bitch father stands between it and you.

"Almost there, friend!" yells one of the Angels.

"Looking fucking lovely," shouts another.

You step back. Pat yourself up and down. Looking for anything.

Your belt. You unbuckle it and rip it off.

The monster's closing in. Hands out. Mouth open. Just as it gets to you, you jump to the side, wrap the belt around its neck, cross your hands, and pull tight. You step behind it and bury your foot into the pit of its knee. It goes down. You pull the belt even tighter. If it had been breathing in the first place, it'd be out by now. But the lack of oxygen ain't doing a damn thing. It shakes, trying to jerk itself free.

You let the belt go, lift your foot, and kick it as hard as you can in the back of the head. It falls forward. You put your knees into its back, grab it by its hair, and slam its head into the sidewalk. Again. Again. Again. Until its face is nothing but mush. Finally, a piece of its skull cracks and enters its brain. The thing's done.

"Four minutes!"

Alright. One minute left. Let's do this.

You stand up.

They're coming out of the shadows like rats. Dozens. Closing in around you.

But you're not scared. Shit, if time was up—you might even be a little disappointed. You're not yourself anymore. You want every one of them. You're angry. Full of bloodlust. Plain fucking demented.

You run for the crowbar. A punk rock thing comes at you—black and white sneakers flashing in the moonlight. It lunges for you. You dive to the cement, roll, grab the crowbar, and bury the sharp end into the base of its skull as you rise. It kicks, twitches. You push it in farther.

An arm on your shoulder. You rip the crowbar free and spin. Old man. Mouth wide open. You grip the crowbar with both hands and block its bite. Its teeth clamp down. You hear them break. Bastard has some jaw on him.

You roar and push. Run, driving it backward. Farther. Screaming now. You run it right into a wall. Two solid whacks with the crowbar and its head sags.

More now. Three, four. You swing the crowbar wildly, trying to keep them at bay. Connect with one's eye socket. Makes a nasty, mushy sound. Three more behind you. You're surrounded.

Goddamn it. Wild swings. Anything to keep them away. You're not going down without a—

RATATATAT!!!!

Their heads blow apart like watermelons. Chunks of skull and brain matter and fleshy, matted pieces of hair fly through the air. Then, almost in sync, the zombies fall to the ground.

Tommy. Gun up and aimed. He grins.

"Almost made it six minutes."

"Six?!"

"You looked like you were having fun. Didn't want to interrupt."

"You son of a—"

"Don't worry, I had them in my sights."

"And what if I only made it four minutes?"

"Then you'd be dead."

"Well I fucking made it, didn't I?"

"That you did," Jones said, getting on his bike. "Now get on—any longer here and the whole neighborhood's gonna come out for our little block party."

Turn to page 115.

LET IT HAPPEN

You can only imagine what's going through her head as she watches the army unload round after round into this mass of zombies, many of them children.

She sees her daughter. Stops in her tracks—then darts into the crossfire and swoops the girl up. She turns to run, then stops. The girl is already one of them. The woman lets out a bloodcurdling cry. Her daughter's tearing at her face.

You turn your head, unable to look, and walk to the back of the store. "Walter, maybe we should head out the back, huh?"

He sits on his stool behind the counter. "Go to hell. I've owned and operated this store for twenty-seven years. I'm not running now."

You nod and take a seat. You and Walter sit in silence. Walter keeps the gun on the counter and stares at the door. You keep your eyes on your shoes. Nothing to say—the sounds of battle outside are noise enough.

After an hour, the fighting stops. Walter walks to the window and peeks out. Hesitantly, you follow. All of the military vehicles are gone. Bodies are strewn across the ground. The zombies are everywhere—many of them soldiers.

Walter goes back to the counter and turns the scanner back on. It's all frantic reports, garbled orders, and calls for help. Around dusk, the transmissions slow. They finally cut out altogether just after midnight. Then it's radio silence . . .

Turn to page 378.

You grab the kid by the wrist, scramble out from under the platform, and take off sprinting down the track.

"You OK?"

"Yeah," he squeaks out through hurried breaths.

No more low moaning from the things. Loud now. They're angry. You hear them hitting the tracks.

Then something louder. A train.

You look behind you. It's coming around the bend, lights nearly blinding you. Through the bright white beams you can see the silhouettes of damn near fifty of the things.

To your left is the third rail. If you had time, you'd carefully cross it and avoid the train. But you don't have time. You have fifty fucking zombies on your heels.

You start running, dragging the kid.

Up ahead you see a maintenance door. It's like that moment in *Stand By Me*. You're River Phoenix, obviously. (Well, you want to be River Phoenix—clearly, you're more Wil Wheaton.) Just have to outrun the train and get to that door.

You swoop the kid up in your arms and sprint. Long strides. Feet splashing in the dirty water. You trip, stumble, regain your balance, and keep going. You can feel the train bearing down on you.

Then you're safe—in the doorway—just like that.

A split second later, the train passes. Went your whole life without ever almost getting hit by a train and now that's three times in the past few hours. Not your day.

The train roars by, taking the zombies with it. Three are

stuck to the front like hood ornaments. One, a Brooklyn hipster type, reaches out at you as the train passes. You get a quick glimpse of its hands and a supertight lumberjack button-down, and it's gone. You've got your hand over the kid's eyes by now. If he makes it out alive, poor guy's going to be traumatized as all hell.

Other zombies are caught beneath the wheels. You half expect the train to grind to a halt with all the gore in the wheels, but it doesn't. The wheels keep turning, the zombies keep getting diced.

Once the train passes, you and the kid start walking again.

After a moment, though, it's clear they're not done. There's a dozen behind you still, at least. Persistent fuckers.

You pull the kid along, running like hell. You see a light in the distance. Next station. If it's swarming with monsters, you're dead. Need a little luck on your side here.

You come up on it, heart pounding.

Thank Christ—deserted. You lift the kid up and over the platform edge. Then you hoist yourself up. You finally breathe. The zombies are clawing at the platform edge, but they can't make it up. Moaning, they try with everything they've got. Dead arms slap against the platform. But nothing.

You and the kid leave the station and come up near the Lincoln Tunnel. Might as well walk that way, see if you can get through. Nothing interesting ever happens in New Jersey.

And then you come upon the Javits Convention Center—biggest convention center in Manhattan. And across the top, a huge banner: COMIC-CON 2011.

Outside is a guy dressed up as that Star Wars character in *Jedi* who watches the ship leave with the binoculars. Appropriately, he's holding a pair of binoculars, staring in your direction.

From across the avenue you can hear him shout, "They're here!"

And he's pointing at you. Huh? Quite the welcome.

Then you hear them behind you. Running for you. Hundreds.

You sprint across the street, kid's hand in yours, up the front steps and inside the convention hall. Clearly, they've been preparing. Armaments have been set up. Booths moved to block the windows.

And then you realize, and you can't help but smile. Zombies have just struck Manhattan. And inside this joint are about twenty-five thousand people who have been waiting their whole lives for exactly this to happen.

A guy dressed as Legolas from *Lord of the Rings* steps past you and out the door. He pulls an arrow from his quiver, draws back the bow, and fires.

The single arrow sails through the air—a weapon from another time, out of place inside the modern city.

But it's still deadly as all hell.

The arrow nails the zombie leading the charge—goes straight through its head and the zombie crashes to the ground. Legolas steps back inside, takes a slow look around, and says, "Alright, geeks—time to shine."

Turn to page 368.

He charges, closing in, fast.

You jump to the side, just in time. His hand swipes at your chest, but gets nothing. As he passes, you grab hold of the strap keeping the tommy gun around his shoulder and tug. It pulls him back toward you. You pull again, hard as you can, and the strap breaks.

He waves his arms around wildly. You kick him in the side, pushing him back.

Then you unload.

Bullets riddle his body and shatter the glass. Punch through his chest and send him back, through the window. He disappears over the side.

Christ. You stop. Breathe. Your hands are shaking. Your whole body shudders.

A noise at the door. Without thinking, you spin and squeeze the trigger.

It's Joe Camel. He collapses into the door frame, panting, holding his gut, then falls to the floor.

"Fuck!"

You run over.

"Came to help," he gets out. "Just came to . . ." He fades away. You killed him.

You help the woman up. She can barely stand. You try to get her attention, but she doesn't speak. You usher her into the sidecar, toss the crowbar in her lap, and drive the roaring bike out into the hall.

Moaning. Loud. Fuck. Dozens of them. Must have followed Joe Camel up. Sonofabitch.

You hit it. Cruise back down the hall. They give chase, keeping pace. At the end of the long hall is a service elevator. Big metal thing.

You point the tommy gun forward while trying to keep the bike on a straight path with your left hand.

You glance in the side mirror. They're coming fast. No time to slow down.

Bike bouncing, arm shaking, you aim for the buttons beside the elevator. You fire.

Bullets punch the wall. Sparks fly. The elevator door opens.

Nice work.

You release the throttle and slide into the elevator. Reach out and hit the bottom button, wherever that goes. It doesn't light up. You hit it again and again until the light goes on. Phew.

Your relief is short-lived. The door doesn't close.

Come on, damn it. You slam the DOOR CLOSE button with your thumb and hold it, then press it what seems like a hundred more times. You break into a cold sweat as you realize you may have broken the elevator by shooting at it. What were you thinking?

The beasts stampede toward you.

Shit. Close, door. Fucking close! You're freaking out.

They're coming fast.

Close!

The door shuts. There's a loud thud as they slam into it.

Phew . . .

The elevator starts going down.

It opens to a dark hall. Slowly, you ride out. You don't recognize anything. This isn't the way you came.

You take a right. And there, right in front of you, is the main floor of the Garden.

Directly across from you, the exit. But in between you and that exit—an entire basketball court full of the undead.

"Hey, lady—wake up," you say, pushing at her. "I need your help." Nothing. She's useless.

You eye the crowded court. No way you're making it across there. Wait—the RPG. The huge JumboTron that hangs over the arena. Bring that down, it'll clear you a path. Maybe. Hopefully. Hey, best chance you've got. You climb off the bike and assemble the small RPG. Look it over. Hold it over your shoulder and pull the trigger, right? Simple enough . . .

Then a moan. A roar, almost. You stare at the court. From around the tunnel exit comes Tommy. He leans against the wall. Blood-spattered—but not bleeding.

There are thousands of the beasts out there. You pull the trigger and miss, there's going to be a thousand of them on top of you.

You need to concentrate—must get Tommy out of the way first. You pull out the crowbar. Hold it, one hand at the top, one at the bottom. Sharp edge up.

Tommy growls.

You spit on the floor.

He runs at you. You run at him. Two trains, ready to collide. Just as you smash together, you swing up, blindly. Then, as you hit the ground, you feel the crowbar pierce something solid and wet. Your head smacks the floor. Head pounding, you look over. Tommy is sprawled out, blood pooling beneath him. The crowbar is sticking up through his chin, the sharp end peeking out the top of his head.

Slowly, you rise to your feet. Look at Tommy's dead body. Almost want to say sorry.

No time. Back to reality.

You pick the RPG up off the floor and walk to the edge of the tunnel. Any farther, they'll see you. You get on one knee and aim it at the massive video scoreboard that hangs from the rafters.

You pull the trigger. A burst of heat around your head.

WOOOMPH—**BOOM!!!**

The explosion rocks the building. Blows out the side of the JumboTron. Sparks rain down upon the arena.

For a second, it doesn't seem like it's going to fall. Then the huge thing shifts. Hangs to the side. And breaks off.

It crashes down onto the center of the Madison Square Garden floor. It crushes a whole mess of them. Others are thrown out across the court. A fire erupts.

You toss aside the smoking RPG case, hop on the bike, and hit the throttle. Out through the tunnel, onto the court, through the mess of them. Down the hall and through the concourse, past your handiwork.

Next to the door, two zombies are burning. You ride between them and down the steps. Across Seventh Avenue. Then as soon as you find a quiet spot, you stop.

You pull the key from the ignition and rest your head in your arms on the handlebars. You enjoy the silence. The peace.

And then a moan.

Christ. The woman. She's been bit!

You reel, crowbar high in the air, Tommy's gore still dripping off it. You're ready to bring it crashing down on her skull.

She moans again. Then her head flops toward you. She murmurs softly and her eyes flicker. She's peacefully asleep.

You catch your breath. Close call.

You turn the keys and make your way back to the club, wanting nothing more than a dozen ice-cold beers and maybe a good movie . . .

Turn to page 92.

You and the kid race down the Nintendo aisle.

Three of them come around the corner toward you. A ragtag group of undead geeks. A kid done up as Tintin, his trench coat torn and covered in blood, but his cowlick still perfect. A middle-aged Woody from *Toy Story*, legs gone, clawing his way down the aisle. One of the dozens of Lara Crofts at the show—this one actually gorgeous, or was moments ago. Now the thing is horrifying. Her iconic green T-shirt ripped open, one breast exposed, the flesh torn.

You spin. Fuck. The other end of the aisle is blocked. A big-nosed guy in a Kid Icarus costume, feathered wings dripping blood. Horrific, undead versions of Mario and Luigi. A woman in a cheap Samus Aran costume, helmet ripped off, half her face gone.

They all come at you.

You run into the Nintendo booth, putting the row of tables between you and them. Laid out is a display of all the company's game consoles, past and present. You raise a Super NES and throw it at Tintin's head. The plastic cracks and the thing stumbles back. Beside you, the kid chucks old NES cartridges at the approaching horde.

You whip a GameCube controller around by the cord, smacking the five things in the head like a bad Three Stooges sketch.

Then a guy done up as some bizarre-looking alien pushes forward.

You reach down, grab an original NES, and bring it flying

up into its chin. Up again, cracking its jaw. Then you bring the console crashing down on top of its head, nearly shattering it. It swipes at you, but you slam the Nintendo down again, slamming the creature's face into the table.

You whip it across his face—left, and he spits blood, back right, and his nose shatters, left again, and his eyeball pops loose, then right again, and a dozen bloody teeth go flying.

You'll give yourself a B for originality, dazing him with a Nintendo, and an A for execution.

You look again at the stuff below, select the old Zapper, and start jamming it into the empty eye socket. It pushes through, and he drops dead.

That's when you realize you just killed a zombie with the Contra code . . .

But, fuck—no time for jokes. You step back—feel the booth wall against your back. Nowhere to go.

Suddenly the kid falls to the floor, screaming. Legless Woody has him by his Keds. It pulls him underneath the table.

Shit. Barrier be damned.

You grab the table and lift it up, tossing it back against the monsters. It lands on legless Woody. The kid is freed.

But you're both trapped. You look around. Weigh your options. Have none.

Your old man always told you—do the right thing. Just do the right thing in life, and everything will work out.

You breathe deeply.

"Alright, kid—up," you say. "Run, don't stop, find the exit, and then keep running toward the river." The kid steps into your interlaced fingers and climbs the booth wall.

You feel a hand on your shoulder. One of the monsters.

You stay put, raising the kid up until he reaches the top of the wall.

Another hand on you. Rips you back. The kid hangs on the wall, halfway over. He looks at you with wide, horrified eyes.

"Go!"

You're pulled to the ground, monsters all around you. The last thing you see is the boy's foot kicking as he disappears over the side of the booth.

AN END

The Hells Angels clubhouse is on the Lower East Side. They've fenced off both ends of the street—before everything went to hell, they owned the block in a sense of the word, but now they own it quite literally.

It's a brick building—five stories like every other building on the block. No windows on the first floor. One big, black metal door with a yellow and red devil spray-painted on it. Cameras everywhere—you count six, and that's without even looking for them.

You follow Jones. He knocks hard on the door three times, waits a moment, then knocks once more. Then he unlocks the door. You go through two more doors—security's clearly high on their list of priorities—and then you enter.

The Hells Angels clubhouse is basically the greatest frat house anybody ever saw. Full bar along the side. Two flat-screen TVs hanging above. Plush leather chairs. Waist-high ashtrays. Walls completely covered with photos of the Angels.

An open entryway leads to a second room in the back with a pool table, long leather couches, and another flat screen. Above the entry way is a crest—"When we do right, nobody remembers. When we do wrong, nobody forgets."

And then you realize the TV is on. Three Stooges in HD—a Shemp episode. And a stereo is playing the Allman Brothers. And there are lights.

"Wait—you guys got power?" you ask, shocked.

"Generator," Limpy says.

You nod. A smile creeps across your face as you continue to take it all in. You made the right decision.

"Good run, boys," Jones says.

"Who's the kid?" asks a guy behind the bar.

"Whiskey, meet the kid. Kid, Whiskey."

"Fuck's he doin' here?"

"Limpy bet him he couldn't last five minutes on the street. He did."

"That right?"

"That's right," you say proudly.

The Angels celebrate—drink hard, drug hard. You do your best to keep up.

Jones introduces you around. Most of the guys are friendly enough. Jones is chapter president, he explains. But really, no one guy counts more than the next guy.

"You all live here?" you ask.

"Now we do. Thirty of us here, if I had to guess. Rooms are upstairs. Tight quarters these days. Before, just a few of us lived here. Others would come and go. Shit—Bob over there's a lawyer—got a nice apartment uptown."

Bob raises his glass. You return the gesture.

"But now we're all sticking together."

After meeting everyone, you take a seat at the bar. Watch the Stooges and bullshit with Whiskey. Before the zombie apocalypse, he owned a moving company. "Had six trucks and twenty guys on the payroll," he explains, proudly.

You get a few beers in you and ask Jones to show you how to do the two-finger whistle. He spends twenty minutes trying, but you fail miserably. Then Tommy shows you how to pack a lip—you stuff your mouth full of Kodiak tobacco, take a swig of beer, then promptly puke on the hardwood floor. Apologetically, you clean it up. They laugh plenty, but don't seem to care much. More drinks. You party into the early morning.

Finally, a skinny drunk named Louis tells you you'll be bunking with him, and you stagger up the stairs behind him.

His room is a toilet. Shit everywhere—old issues of *Barely Legal,* Pabst Blue Ribbon cans, cigarette butts stamped out on the carpeted floor.

He collapses onto the bed, then reaches for a drawer. Pulls out a cigar box.

"You want?" he says, his words slurred.

"What is it?"

"Junk."

"Huh?"

"Junk. Smack. Scat. Fuckin' heroin."

"Oh . . ."

Want to play *Trainspotting* and do a bunch of heroin with Louis? Turn to page 151.

Say no, roll over, and pass out on the floor? Turn to page 61.

PENCIL PUSHER

The she-beast lunges over the side of the wall and hits the ground. Its tiny fingers, surprisingly strong, get a hold of your leg and the thing tries to chomp down. You struggle to shake it off, but it digs its fingers into your clothes for grip. You fall back, hitting the ground, hard, and it begins crawling up your body.

You grab the she-beast's exposed breast, squeezing it, getting a grip, and then you toss her against the wall. You scramble to your feet.

You look around, frantic, and grab the first thing you see.

A pencil.

In a split second, it's up on its feet.

You lunge forward, stabbing the pencil down and aiming for the eye. But you miss. The pencil pierces its cheek, snaps in two, and you fall right into the thing, exposed. The bitch sinks its teeth into your neck.

You scream. Swing wildly with the broken pencil. You connect with the thing's ear. You jam it in again—feel the wood pierce the eardrum. Blood pours through your fingers and down your wrist.

Twice more through the eardrum, then into the brain and the bitch collapses in a bloody, naked heap. But the damage is done. Your throat is torn open. Blood pours out onto the dirty, sticky floor. This is where you're going to die—in a fucking strip club DJ booth.

You open your mouth to scream, but nothing comes out. Your head goes light. Legs weak. You go for the counter, bracing yourself.

Then you get a rush. For an instant, you can feel the blood pumping through your body—you are intently aware of every microscopic cell flowing through each of your hundred thousand veins.

Then it's gone. Everything. Mind goes blank. The pain subsides. Your conscious mind begins to fade.

Woman. She fights.

Legs. Moving. Propelled forward.

Woman.

Object in way. Past it. Over. On floor. Stand up.

Woman.

Pretty woman. Fleshy.

Wet. Wet on floor. Body. Dead. Dead meat. Good meat? Bad meat. Carrion. Useless.

Woman.

Fresh meat . . .

Legs faster. One. Two. One. Two. Pulling forward. To woman.

In front of you. Woman. Shiny thing.

Woman. Speaks. Awwwwww kiiiiiiddddd ayyymmmmmmm sorrrrrryyyyy . . .

Shiny thing.

Legs faster. Woman moves. Stop woman. Stop.

Shiny thing in hand.

Uh-oh. Woman moves fast.

Shiny thing flashes. Coming at face. In eyes. Through head. Skull. Brain.

. . .

. . . . .

⋆∴⋆ AN END ⋆∴⋆

You do enjoy the occasional hit off a nicely rolled Dutch or Philly (no wraps please)—but the timing ain't so good. Too, *too* weird. "Ah, no thanks, I'm good. You're getting high right now?"

"How the fuck else you think I make it through a twelve-hour shift?"

"What time is it?"

Chucky takes a huge hit and bursts into a coughing fit. He waves at the car's dashboard clock, trying to catch his breath. 6:17 PM.

"Jesus. I was asleep for like six hours."

You scratch at your eye. You've got a mean contact high—your brain buzzes. Bass ripples through your seat and you realize music is playing. Some hip-hop that you don't recognize.

"You had a big morning, little buddy," Chucky says.

"Yeah," you say, replaying it in your head. "What've you been doing this whole time?"

He shrugs and holds up the blunt.

You sit up and look through the car window toward the gate. Very little light makes it down the tunnel, making it hard to see exactly what's out there. Looks to be about thirty of the monsters at the gate. Some lean against it awkwardly. Others bang at it. Others just wander around the small tunnel.

There's a Gatorade bottle between the two of you. You smell vodka. Chucky puts his massive hand around the neck and shakes it around like a joystick.

"Any other way out of this place?" you ask.

"Nope. Just the gate. This is a privately owned garage—has nothing to do with the building above us, so there's no access."

"There a phone?"

"In the office. But it's out. No cell service down here, neither."

The office lights flicker.

"What happens if we lose power down here?"

Chucky shrugs.

You sit silently for a moment, thinking. "You think maybe that gate'll open up on its own—like some sort of failsafe so that if the power goes out no one gets trapped inside?"

Chucky leans forward, looking ultraserious. "I don't know. But that does make sense."

The office lights flicker again, then go dark. There's a loud "shutting down" noise—reminds you of Obi-Wan pulling the tractor beam switches on the Death Star.

"Fuck," Chucky says. "If you're right . . ."

Shit. Not good. Not good at all. "We gotta lock that down," you say, not hiding the fear in your voice.

In a second, Chucky's out of the car. You follow. He runs to the office, begins rooting through the desk drawers.

"What are you looking for—maybe I can help."

"I'll find it, I'll find it . . ." he says. Then, a moment later, he triumphantly holds up a heavy chain lock. "From my old motorcycle," he says.

There's a loud grinding noise. Fuck—you whirl. You were right.

Slowly, the gate begins to lift.

Chucky darts to the gate and drops to his knees, just inches from the feet of the monsters. He loops the long chain through the bottom rung of the gate and pulls it taut toward a thin pipe that runs along the edge of the garage floor.

He loops it around—then, violently, it jerks free.

"Motherfucker," he mutters.

The gate's nearly a foot off the ground now. Any more and

the lock won't reach. You run over to help him. The two of you tug the chain, pulling with everything you've got. Finally, you get it around the pipe, and just as the gate begins to stretch the chain to its maximum, he snaps the lock shut.

You both breathe a sigh of relief.

The gate makes a loud whining noise—then starts to click. Chucky smiles.

The zombies watch you, anxious, as they bounce back and forth on their feet. Some have dropped to the ground and are swiping their hands in the gap, trying to get at you. You and Chucky step back a few feet.

"You think it's going to hold?" you ask.

"Nope."

"Well, we gotta do something . . . we need a plan!"

"Already got one."

"Huh?"

"While you were sleeping, I was thinking about how we might get out of here. C'mon."

You follow Chucky across the garage. He grabs the shotgun from the Mercedes and carries it by the middle.

"There," Chucky says.

In front of you is some sort of large vehicle, covered by a large green tarp.

"What is it?"

"C'mon," he says.

You each take a corner of the tarp and pull.

Before you sits a big old GMC pickup truck. Mounted on the front is a red snowplow. Two big, round lights sprout out of the front corners of the hood like antennas on a grasshopper.

You look it up and down. Grab the plow and shake it. It's rusty, but solid. It's perfect, you realize.

Chucky raises the shotgun slightly. "So . . . you doing the driving," he grins, "or the shooting?"

If you want to get behind the wheel, turn to page 217.

If you'll let Chucky drive and you'll handle the dirty work, turn to page 137.

Nope. This ain't for you—not dying here. Not at this man's hands.

Anthony lunges as you run past, ducking underneath his arms. In a second, you're out the door and in the alley.

Zombies everywhere. Hands grab at you. You push through. Turn on to the street.

A taxi is up on the curb, idling, its front end crashed through a bodega window. No driver.

You book it across the street. They're behind you, closing in. One grabs at your shirt, pulls you back. You jerk free, rip open the car door, and dive inside.

Immediately the beasts surround the car. Pound the windows. One, a woman in a blood-spattered waitress's apron, is halfway through the broken rear passenger-side window.

You drop it into reverse and hit the gas. The whole storefront collapses as you pull out. You spin the cab around and kick it back into drive. You floor it—a zombie on the hood goes up and over the windshield and crashes onto the cement behind you.

You check the side mirror. The undead waitress is still trying to get in through the back window—its legs out in the air, its upper body on the rear seat.

You press harder on the pedal. Pick up speed. Swerve up onto the curb to avoid a mess of cars. You're closing in on a streetlamp. You check your side mirror. Have to line it up just right.

You floor it.

Forty mph.

Harder.

Fifty mph.

One last look in the side mirror.

You blow past the pole. The mirror smashes against the metal and rips off. The zombie waitress is torn in half. Its severed upper body falls into the backseat; its lower half drops to the street.

You hit the brakes and skid to a stop. You glance back at the thing's torso in the backseat, intestines dangling onto the taxi floor. Its arms swipe at the cab partition. A disgusting lump of flesh, sure, but harmless for the moment.

You begin driving again, headed for the bridge.

At Nineteenth Street you run into a mass of them. Too late, you brake. The car skids and spins. You slam into the side of a small used furniture store. The air bag deploys, punching you in the face. Your nose breaks, bringing a rush of tears to your eyes. Blood in your mouth.

You're seeing stars. You start to drift away, but their moans snap you back to attention. They surround the car. Smoke pours from the hood. The windshield wipers flash back and forth. You try the gas. Nothing. You're a sitting duck.

No time for hesitation. You bolt out of the car, knocking one back with the door, and tear down the street. More ahead of you. Even more behind you. Nowhere to go but up.

You pick up some speed, jump onto the back of a busted sedan, and launch yourself up to a hanging fire escape ladder.

Cold, dead hands pull at your feet. Nails claw at your ankles. You kick them away and climb.

Once you're safely on the fire escape, you yank the ladder up. You're dizzy. You stop to catch your breath. Your nose hurts like hell. Blood continues to stream from your nostrils. A slice on your forehead leaks blood down over your eyes. You take your shirt off, press it to the wound, but the bleeding doesn't stop.

You tilt your head back, just like everyone's always told you *not* to do, and after a minute your nose stops bleeding. You spit blood onto the zombies below. Hit one in the face. Its tongue darts out, tasting it.

You wrap your shirt around your head and tie it tight. That keeps the blood out of your eyes.

You want to collapse. Sleep. Don't want to move ever again.

But you need to keep moving. The longer you wait, the more those things multiply. Like fucking gremlins.

So go. Just go. Stand up. Move.

And then you're out.

When you wake, it's bright. Early morning. Sun bathes you. Takes you a second to remember where you are.

Beneath you, the zombies haven't moved. Still there, still watching you, still waiting for their next meal.

You make your way farther up the fire escape. Bars cover each window.

Finally, seven floors up, you make it to the roof. You walk to the edge and take in Union Square. In the center, a park. Store-lined streets on each side.

A woman runs out of DSW, screaming. You watch as the things go from slow, stupid stumble to deadly sprint in an instant. Six of them pounce on her. Minutes later, she rises, a bloody mess, now one of them. You turn away.

At the center of the roof is a skylight. You peer through. Books. Rows and rows of them. You must be on the roof of the Barnes & Noble. Have to get inside there. Food. Shelter. Delicious little muffins.

You look around for some way to break the window. You find a cinder block. That should work. Your body weak, you struggle to lift it and toss it against the glass.

Instead it bounces off and lands on your foot. You shriek. Sonofabitch—the stupid fucking thing just broke your toe. You go to kick it—stop yourself just in time. Don't need to make things worse.

OK, trying again.

You step farther back and throw. This time it cracks it. You toss it again. A bigger crack. OK—one more—right through.

The reinforced glass breaks. You look down. It's about a twenty-foot drop.

Here goes nothing.

You jump. The same foot that just took a beating from the cinder block rolls and snaps. Sharp pain shoots up your leg. You scream. Ankle's broken, definitely. You're a fucking mess. The pain is overwhelming. You lie back. Drift in and out of consciousness.

Suddenly the entire building shakes, jolting you awake.

You limp across the store to the large window that overlooks Union Square.

The zombies aren't alone anymore. Two tanks have rolled into the southwest corner of the square, diagonal from your position. Smoke pours from the tanks' barrels.

They fire again. The building shakes. The shell travels clear across the park and explodes against the front of a Best Buy. The front caves in, rubble pouring out into the street.

The zombies start pouring out of every corner of the square. Hundreds.

A military truck with a gunner in the back skids to a halt. The soldier manning the gun lets loose, mowing them down.

The tank turret turns. Fires a shell directly into one of the rushing crowds. The blast is tremendous. Bodies everywhere.

When the dust clears, though, it's clear the military has a major problem.

The zombies are limbless, broken, bodies shattered. But they're not brainless. They still keep coming. It's now a horde of armless things running, legless things crawling, wounded things stumbling.

It's a true war zone down there.

But when the military pulls out, if you're there, it could be your escape.

Head down to Union Square and try to escape
with the military? Turn to page 326.

Check out the Barnes & Noble, get some food, and
stay put? Turn to page 267.

You don't like Wall Street and you're not drinking what he's buying. So you sneak back out the door and begin jogging to Amsterdam Avenue with your hand out, glancing back every few seconds for a cab. No luck.

You stop jogging. Switch to walking. Sweat pours down your back. The heat. The stress. The fear. You need to sit down. Someplace dark. A movie theater, maybe. Need cool air or you're going to collapse. Any second now, you'll be sprawled out across the sidewalk.

Up ahead is a neon sign for Charlie Chan's Lady Land—a strip joint on Eighty-third and Columbus. Hmm. You pull your hand back and stop.

This could be the place. You've been to your fair share of strip clubs—about as dark and cool as the world gets.

So you step inside. You show the bouncer your ID and take in the perfume-heavy, beer-laden scent. Eau de Topless Bar.

It takes a second for your eyes to adjust. Charlie Chan's is an Asian-themed joint and laughable décor echoes that— wooden folding door panels, tapestries everywhere.

You grab a twelve-dollar Bud Light, watch the flat screen behind the bar for a moment, and head to the main room. Two samurai swords crisscross above the stage. You wonder if they're real.

Your heart stops. Your dick hardens. There, below the tacky samurai swords, working the pole, is the most jaw-droppingly beautiful stripper you've ever seen.

She looks half Asian, half European. Some sort of mix that

made for something fantastic. Topless. High, high heels. A tiny white G-string. You're entranced. Stunned. Gut-punched by her beauty.

You get a seat right up front, sip your beer, and take in the show. You're the only one near the stage, so the way-hot stripper saunters down and does her thing for you. You pull out your wallet and slide a few crumpled bills onto the stage. Wish you had something crisper, bills that didn't look like they spent the night in your gym sock, but what are you gonna do.

She has a nice smile and shows it off. Then, after three or four more highly, *highly* enjoyable moments she bends over, picks up the bills, and slips them into her G-string. She gives you a cute little wave and leaves the stage.

The DJ comes over the speaker system: "Yo Yo this is DJ Aaaron Wemrock, let's give it up for Yakumaaaaaaaaa," he says, the second *a* carrying on for about twenty obnoxious seconds. "That's right, Yakuma finishing up on the main stage. Like all of our lovely ladies here, Yakuma is available for private dances and, of course, the Champagne Room. Coming up next is our very own lovely Latina Go-Go Dawson! Don't be shy, folks, let that money fly."

The main floor is nearly empty—probably typical for a Monday afternoon. Most of the crowd is business guys, taking advantage of the ten-dollar lunch buffet. You're hungry—but not "strip club buffet hungry." Gotta draw the line somewhere.

You order another beer. Six girls cycle through, an hour or so passes, then it's Yakuma again. You're waiting with a grin and another wrinkly single.

She smiles at you and begins her dance.

You're lost in an erotic fantasy when she steps off the runway and onto your table.

"Wha—"

The small table tips—but she doesn't fall—she rides it to the floor like a surfer riding a wave. On her way down, she grabs your Rolling Rock by the neck.

"What the—"

You lean back just in time to see her smash the bottle into the face of the pretty Latina, Go-Go Dawson. The stripper falls back—Yakuma follows her to the floor and slides the bottle into the stripper's neck, which opens up like a gutted fish. Blood sprays out over Yakuma like she just popped the cap off a fire hydrant.

Yakuma stands over her, holding the empty bloody bottleneck. But Yakuma isn't quite done. She raises her leg and skewers the girl's face with the heel of her stiletto.

"Sorry, Go-Go . . ." she says.

You stand. Chair hits the ground. What the fuck is going on? Yakuma seemed totally sweet and normal a second ago, and now she's in a murderous rage. And then you look closer at the dead girl's tits (you can't resist). They're greenish and shriveled.

Holy shit, zombie tits.

You look up just as three more of the things sprint toward you. Three men. Two in suits, one the bartender. Real-life zombies. Dead as dead gets. Just like the beasts on TV.

Stunned, you watch as Yakuma dispatches the first one with the same move she used on the stripper. Kills the second one with the steak knife he was using to eat his buffet chicken. The bartender, thick and heavy, charges. She uses the thing's weight to her favor, spinning as he hits her and sending him stumbling into the stage headfirst. She buries the knife in the base of his skull. His massive legs kick. She turns the blade and he goes limp.

She leaps up onstage and rips down the two samurai swords. Hmm—maybe they are real? She'd know better than you would.

She stops. Turns her gaze on you.

"I'm, I'm not one of those—" you stutter.

"No shit. This way, tough guy."

You follow her—back through a curtain and into the dressing area.

Three strippers feast on a fourth that lies on the floor.

Holy shit. Holy shit. Holy shit. Stay calm. Breathe, breathe—**you're in a strip club dressing room!!!** Your whole life has been building up to this moment.

Yakuma bolts forward, blades low by her side. One slices through the air, cutting the first stripper straight up from the chest to the top of the skull—splits her in two. Before she hits the ground, the other two are dead—with one horizontal slash Yakuma decapitates them both. Yakuma walks past them and out a door marked EXIT. She's back inside in a moment.

"No good—too many," she says.

Yakuma stops at a locker and throws on a white tank top and tiny plaid shorts. Damn. She looks as good half clothed as she does naked.

She sticks a cell phone into her back pocket and slips out of her bloody stilettos and into a pair of jelly sandals.

She orders you back out the way you came. Good-bye strip club dressing room. I hardly knew ye.

Back on the main floor. Ten of them, at least.

In the front, two strippers. One blonde, real tits, young looking. Even dead, still cute. A chunk of flesh is torn from her gut. The other a black girl, big fake boobs. One leg half torn off—blood pouring down it. And behind the two strippers, the customers. And in the very back, the gargantuan bouncer.

Nobody moves. Bass from the speaker system pumps through the floor. Shakes you. So strong it changes your heartbeat. Fucking Nickleback.

You stare at the blonde's tits. They don't move. No rhythmic up and down. The dead things sway, but their chests don't move. They don't breathe.

Yakuma holds the sword at her side. Blood drips steadily to the floor.

She stares at the two strippers—probably friends of hers five minutes ago.

They stare back.

You just stand there, scared to death, not sure what to do.

Then they charge. You sprint to your left and clamber over the wall to the DJ booth. As you land, your head smacks the floor.

You stand up, rubbing your noggin. The DJ booth, set against the wall, offers you a degree of protection from all sides. You watch in amazement as Yakuma unleashes a furious ballet of violence unlike anything you've ever seen.

She takes down one, two, three of them. Then they all come at once. Leap on top of her. She disappears. You can't see what exactly is happening—it's like the fight for a fumble in a football game—you know some wild, awful shit is happening beneath all those bodies, but you don't know the details.

And then Yakuma bursts from the top of the pile. She swings her blades in a circle, spilling zombie guts across the floor and sending them all stumbling back. Then she goes for their heads. Splitting one down the middle. Chopping the next one at the bridge of the nose, sending the top of its head spiraling off. Cleanly decapitates the next.

One is charging from behind her. You go to shout, but before you can, she turns and throws the blade. It pierces the undead thing's chest and pins it to the wall.

She jumps back and up onto the stage. Grabs the stripper pole with one hand and swings around, second blade extended. Two more zombies headless.

She leaps from the pole and marches through the rest. Chopping. Cutting. Slicing. Killing.

You're so distracted that you don't notice the redheaded stripper crawling up the side of the booth until she grabs hold of you.

"Fuck!"

You look around for something, anything. Find a copy of *Rolling Stone* and start whacking the thing on the head. Doesn't do a whole lot—big surprise.

Fuck. Thing is almost over the wall.

Goddamn it. Death is upon you. Another moment and you're dead. Frantic, you look around for *anything* you could use as a weapon.

Go for the turntables? Turn to page 318.

Stab her with a nearby pencil? Turn to page 118.

Try to zap her with the turntable power cord? Turn to page 11.

"Get behind the wheel," you say, adrenaline pumping through you. "And toss me the gun."

You catch the shotgun and hop into the bed of the truck. Chucky heads for the truck door. You haven't shot a gun in ten years—not since you were a kid at summer camp, firing .22s at paper targets of bunnies. And nothing like this—this thing is massive.

You tap on the glass partition. "Ammo?"

Chucky slides the window open and hands you two shells, plus a small cardboard box, about the size of two cassette tapes. Inside are twelve more shells.

You examine the gun. It's about eight pounds, you guess, and close to four feet long. REMINGTON 870 engraved along the side in tiny letters. The stock and pump are a dark, fake wood. The barrel and body are tinted blue.

Now, to load it. How the hell does this work? After a little investigating, you find a loading slot on the bottom. There are two shells in there now. You fill it to the top—eight shells total.

OK—eight in the gun and eight left. Sixteen shots. Make 'em count.

Slowly, you get to your knees, rest the shotgun on the floor beside you, and watch the gate. Try to mentally prepare yourself.

There's a loud snap as the bike lock breaks and the gate begins to rise. You can barely make out the figures in the moonlight. There are at least thirty—maybe more. Hard to tell. A zombie child stumbles in as the gate passes over his head. More follow as the gate gets higher.

"How many do you see?" you whisper through the sliding glass window.

"Can't tell," he says. "But we're about to find out."

You swallow. Sweat drips from your forehead onto the roof. You lay the shotgun on the roof and stare down the length of it.

Chucky works the gears—there's a loud grinding noise and the plow lowers.

"Ready?" Chucky asks.

You breathe. Slow and steady. "As I'll ever be."

Chucky hits the headlights, flooding the dark garage with blinding fluorescent light.

Oh. Shit.

A hundred of them, at least. A whole battalion of the things.

You think about your shotgun. Sixteen shots? That's it?!

The truck jerks forward, knocking you off your knees and onto your back. You scramble back up and retake your position, setting your knees wider apart for better balance.

The truck heads into the first wave. You fire a shot over the roof of the truck. The load of buck does little but slow down a few of them.

OK. That doesn't work. Lesson learned. Close range only.

The beasts are swept up, knocked to the side, and run over. They stumble past, wounded.

One grabs hold of the rear of the truck. You drop down on your back and slide across the truck bed. You kick the tailgate—the force breaking the thing's grip and knocking it off.

The truck is slowing, allowing the beasts to gather around the bed. Sick, dead hands reach for you from all sides.

"Let's go!" you shout. "What's the fucking holdup?"

"There's too many!"

"Give it some fucking gas!"

Suddenly you feel a tug at your leg. One of the things has a hold of you and he's climbing the side.

Steady and slow, you raise the Remington, aim, and

squeeze. The thing's head explodes in a thousand pieces, a cloud of red mist filling the air. His hand drops from your pant leg and he disappears over the side.

OK. First kill. You did it. You shot one. Way to go, big guy.

You pump the Remington, ready for the next zombie that wants some.

The truck shutters, shakes, and rocks—tires spinning on the pile of bodies. The rear tires rotate, kicking up bits of gore.

They claw at you from all sides. One comes up over the back—a large Mexican woman in a bright red top. Barely aiming, you point and squeeze. The blast kicks the thing in the chest like a mule, launching it off the back of the truck.

"What's going on up there?" you yell.

"I'm trying!"

Suddenly you're flung against the truck window as it roars in reverse. The tires crunch. Chucky reverses it thirty feet, putting a little distance between you and the things. Then he drops it back into drive and floors it. You're tossed onto your back and the shotgun slides across the truck bed.

Chucky's plan works. You have some speed on your side, and you move through the rows of the dead. As you exit, you catch a glimpse of a WARNING: DO NOT BACK UP! SEVERE TIRE DAMAGE sign. Yeah . . . no shit, don't back up.

The plow does its job. It's slow going on the ramp, but the truck makes it up and out onto the street, leaving a hundred wounded beasts writhing in its wake.

Chucky cuts a hard left, nearly sending you over the side. You regain your balance and decide you're probably best off sitting down.

The main avenue is a disaster zone, like a tornado came through. Cars smoke. Storefronts burn. Bodies are scattered. Ghouls stumble around.

No police. No military. Any guilt you felt about lying on your W-4 last year vanishes.

"The bridge!" you shout, pointing.

Chucky steers that way, toward the avenue. Abandoned cars crowd the way. The plow knocks aside an overturned motorcycle. Chucky plays *Frogger* with the truck, squeezing it wherever it can fit as you zigzag across the avenue.

You get to the base of the bridge. The top level is jammed with cars, none moving. The bottom level is worse—zombies everywhere.

Chucky brings the truck to a stop. Turns back and looks at you.

"It's too crowded. Can't make it across on this. I'd say hoof it, but that doesn't look too smart, either."

You look at the scattered, shuffling dead things on the bridge. You agree.

"Well, we need to get off the island somehow."

"OK—we'll go north—to the Bronx," Chucky says. "If we can't get across the bridge—fuck it, we swim."

One of the things gets too close. A child. You kneel, aim, and fire—its chest explodes. "OK, the Bronx it is," you say, dropping in two more shells. "Hit it."

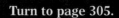

Turn to page 305.

You literally have to tell your feet: move. You bark at them like an insane drill sergeant.

Move!

Move, goddamn it!

And, unbelievably, they do.

Anthony has his shoulder against the door and his foot wedged against the bar for leverage. "That bar stool there— give it to me," he says.

The door bucks again and he's almost thrown back. You grab the stool and try to wedge it up underneath the handle. The door is kicking, making it damn near impossible.

"C'mon, goddamn it!" he barks.

Finally, the door holds still long enough for you to squeeze the seat up beneath the door handle.

"Good, now move the pool table from the back; get it up here," Anthony says.

Feeling useful now, empowered, you jog to the back of the bar. Everyone gets out of your way. You go back to the second section of the bar and into a small gaming area. Darts. *Big Buck Hunter.* Two pool tables. You tug at the table. Way too heavy. You walk back out into the bar. "Hey! Someone help me here."

No one moves. Anthony speaks up. "You, get over there and help the kid. Now." He's talking to Wall Street.

Wall Street glares. Anthony glares back, harder. Wall Street removes his suit jacket, hangs it gently over his bar stool, and grudgingly does as he's told. Together you struggle to move the

141

table. Four others come to help. Thankfully, it's a fairly cheap table. Ten sweat-soaked minutes later, you have it, lengthwise, against the door.

You step back, satisfied. No way that door's getting open now.

You take a seat at the bar and catch your breath. Wall Street continues to buy rounds, beer now, and you continue to drink them down. So does everyone else. The jukebox plays on. Time passes.

Two drunks get in a fight, arguing over the day's events. The little one shoves the big one. Anthony steps in, breaks it up. Minutes later, they get in another fight—this time about the Jets. Anthony steps in again, tells them the next person that causes a problem is getting fed to the wolves. That stops them.

The pricks on TV say sit tight, everything will be OK. There are no more shots of gore and violence. Then they stop showing the city altogether. Can't be a good sign.

You finish what must be your sixth or seventh beer. Anthony and the pretty bartender, Rachel, sit by the bar's large front window, peering through the neon beer-sign covered glass. Heavy metal bars crisscross the window, keeping you safe. You walk over.

Even in the midst of this nightmare you can't help but notice she has a rear end like a perfectly inflated basketball.

"What do you see?" you ask.

They both look at you, silent for a moment. Then Anthony says, "Those things."

"Can I get a look?"

He shrugs and steps back and you squeeze in next to Rachel. She smells like cherry Fun Dip and tequila. Yum. You give her an awkward smile, then press your face to the glass.

The mini-erection that the bartender had given you shrivels up like a worm on a hot sidewalk. Through the neon-tinted glass, you take in a scene that reminds you of Dante's *Inferno* (the SparkNotes version you read in college). Cars burn. Monsters feast on bodies. You can see clearly into a bank across the street—someone's looking out, right at you, scared shitless. Just like you.

The song on the jukebox fades. Without the music to drown everything out, the horror is amplified.

You hear the screams of a woman. You press your face against the glass and look to the right, down the street. She lies on her back, three of the things devouring her. She's still alive, screaming, as two dig at her open chest and her guts spill out across the cement. The third beast, a homeless man, claws and bites at her legs. Her dress blows in the wind.

Rachel looks away. She walks to the tip jar behind the bar, pours out a handful of quarters, and goes to the jukebox. A minute later, the music mercifully returns. Jimmy Page's heavy guitar drowns out the screams of the horror outside.

Anthony steps behind the counter and pours two drinks. You take one.

"Whole Lotta Love" ends. You can hear the jukebox working, grabbing for a new CD. Then you hear something else. A thump. Another thump. Then moaning.

You spin. The back door. Fuck.

Anthony hears it, too. He rushes around the bar, grabs you, and says "C'mon."

You walk through the bar, into the second room, and to the door. The moaning is loud. Shadows beneath the doorway.

"On the other side of this door is a hallway and at the end of that is the door to the alley—where we bring the kegs and shit in," Anthony says.

You nod and run your hand over the door. The door is hollow, the wood thin. You could probably put a fist through it.

"We have to kill them," you say. "We don't know how strong those things are. Could be strong enough to break right through. We don't want to wait around to find out."

You take a look back at the bar. Bunch of drunken bums.

Wall Street's passed out at the counter. Rachel plays with her keys. Useless, all of them.

"And I think it's just you and me," you say.

Anthony nods, then walks past the pool tables and through a door that says EMPLOYEES ONLY. He returns a second later carrying a power drill.

"You're going to kill all of them with that?" you ask.

"No. But I'm not running in there blind."

He turns the drill on. The roar of it startles you. He brushes you aside and presses the drill against the door. In a second, he's drilled a small hole at eye level. He peers through.

"What do you see?" you ask.

"Not much. Hit that light switch."

You hit the switch behind you. The bar lights go out. Rachel screams.

"Other one."

"My bad." You turn the bar lights back on and hit the switch next to it.

Anthony keeps his eye to the door for a good twenty seconds, then pulls away.

You give him a questioning look.

"See for yourself," he says.

Slowly, scared out of your mind, you press your eye to the hole.

Zombies. Lots of them. The rear door is open to the street. No action back there, though—none seem to be coming or going. You count—there are eleven of the things, milling around. The hallway is narrow. That's the one thing that works in your favor. The beasts won't be able get to you all at once. It will allow you to deal with them one and two at a time.

You pull your eye away.

"Follow me," Anthony says. The two of you walk to the employees-only room. It's a small office. A tiny green couch left over from the '80s. Lots of metal cabinets. Two lockers in the corner. A desk, papers scattered about, along with the various other junk that accumulates in a dive bar.

"We don't have no secret armory full of Uzis, AKs, and rocket launchers that's gonna help us. This is what we got."

"I don't see much."

"That's 'cause we don't got much. First, this." He lays the drill down on the desk.

"And this." He pulls the hammer from his belt and lays it on the desk. It's the hammer he killed the zombie with earlier. Small bits of flesh and hair still stick to the head—a piece of skin on the nail claw.

He walks out of the room, returns a moment later. Lays a pool cue down on the table. It rolls to the side, hits the hammer. "And this."

He messes with the padlock on one of the lockers. Pulls out a large, cherry red fire ax.

"I'll take that—"

"Nope, this one's mine," he says, laying it on the table.

"What? You're three times the size of me. Plus, you're good with the hammer. You already killed one with it. I can't even hang up a fucking poster in my apartment and I got two hammers."

He thinks for a second. "We'll see."

You look at the items scattered on the table. "Is that it?" you ask finally.

"'Fraid so."

You think for a second. "Hang on."

You grab the ax, leave the office, and walk across a small dance floor area and into the game room.

Two bright orange plastic shotguns rest in slots on the *Big Buck Hunter* arcade machine, locked on with heavy plastic ties. You raise the ax and bring it crashing down, severing the tie. You pull the toy gun out of its holster.

From the office doorway, Anthony nearly doubles over laughing. "Fuck you gonna do with a toy gun?"

You shrug. "I dunno—maybe it'll scare them. They think it's real or something. You know, learned traits. Memory. That shit."

He laughs. "OK, your funeral. So what do you want? Think carefully, kid. This could be the last decision you ever make."

Take the pool cue and the *Big Buck Hunter* shotgun? Turn to page 241.

Take the hammer and the drill? Turn to page 45.

Argue for the fire ax? Turn to page 16.

You lunge for the door and slam your palm down on the lock.

The cabbie talks rapidly into his Bluetooth, then rips it from his ear and tosses it to the floor. He grips the wheel and looks about wildly. There's a heavy crunching sound as he rear-ends the cab in front of you. Your whole body is yanked forward, and you fly into the cab's Plexiglas divider. A sharp pain shoots up your nose and through your brain. Blood pours from your nostrils. Fuck. Broken. Definitely broken. Tears fill your eyes.

No crying, jagoff. Time to think. The zombies are approaching. Fast. Like rats, filling up the cracks between cars, the sidewalks, anywhere there's room.

And devouring everything along the way.

The cabbie throws it in reverse and smashes into the car behind him. Great—a nice bit of whiplash to go along with your busted nose.

Undeterred, he throws it back into drive and jumps the sidewalk. In the short distance, he picks up speed. But he's going the wrong way. Toward the zombies, and fast. No, you idiot!

CRASH!!!

He slams into one of the things—a tall, gangly man. City sanitation worker uniform.

For a moment, time seems to stand still—and then everything moves in slow motion. You see the city-worker-cum-undead-monster lift into the air and crash up onto the hood. You can see what's coming next. The word *no* slips out from your lips. And then—

The zombie smashes through the windshield. The car slams into the side of a Duane Reade and comes to a sudden, violent halt. Blood sprays the Plexiglas partition. Completely covers it. You can't see through.

Your heart races, fear pumps through you—you're blind to whatever danger sits in the front of the taxi, just inches from you. Then the thick, crimson liquid begins to drip and clear—and you see the zombie—clothes, face, and chest absolutely shredded by the glass, staring right at you.

You scream. A loud, bloodcurdling yell.

The beast lunges for you, but smacks the Plexiglas and pulls back, confused.

Dumb and annoyed, it turns its attention to the driver. He's still alive. Trapped by his seat belt, face sliced to hell, but alive. The zombie digs in with his hands. Tears his cheek off. Follows with his mouth.

Watching the horror, you instinctively reach for the door handle. Then you stop. The car is surrounded. Ghouls everywhere.

One of the things stumbles into the passenger-side window, rocking the car. It's a big fat guy in a pin-striped shirt and ugly tie—gut pressing against the glass. He paws at the window with a bloody stump of a wrist, then moves on, leaving a thick, red smear across the window as he teeters away.

The one in the front of the car is different, his body twitching, jerking. He's finishing up with the driver. A large coil of intestine hangs from his mouth.

You look away. Double-check both rear locks. You're safe for now, but you're surrounded. Confident that the one up front won't get you through the Plexiglas, you turn, kneel on the seat, and survey the scene behind the car.

Chaos. Absolute bedlam.

Thousands of people fleeing for the bridge. The lucky ones, those already on the bridge, kick it into high gear. Worse off are the people who were still on the street when the things appeared—the ones who hadn't yet made it to the bridge. They run for shelter in stores and buildings. A few make it, but nearly every store is already on lockdown. Others see doors slammed shut in their faces. Down the block, a mother and her young son bang on the door of a bodega. A cluster of the zombies moves toward them. The mother and son flee into an alleyway. The things follow. The two have no chance.

Hundreds of the living stay in their cars, like you, afraid to leave. Not sure what the hell to do.

One of the things—what used to be a black teenager in a dirty Allen Iverson 76ers jersey and a pair of hand-me-down Jordans—feeds on a fake-tanned white guy in a slick black convertible.

Should have gone with the hardtop, asshole.

All around you, the beasts feast. Hordes of them. Killing and eating. On the sidewalks. On the streets, between cars. A fire hydrant, pierced by a crashed moving truck, sprays water high into the air. Beneath it one of the beasts, in a brown trench coat, devours an old woman. Her blood mixes with the water and a light pink liquid makes a path along the curb and down the gutter.

A man lies on the hood of the car behind you, fighting off three of the things. He loses. His chest is torn open and the three zombies gorge themselves. The poor bastard's entrails spill out onto the hood and onto the cement.

You see firsthand how everyone killed comes back to life and becomes another mindless killing thing. Some jerk to life almost immediately—others take some time and rise later.

It's then that the true horror sinks in. Each one kills two, those two kill four, those four kill eight, and on and on and on. It's like the cheesy AIDS video you had to watch in health class in middle school—only scarier. Yep, scarier than AIDS. That's scary.

It all becomes quite clear that this nightmare won't be ending anytime soon.

You dial 911. Can't connect. Fuck. Everybody in New York City is on the phone, of course. You hang up and try again. Nothing.

Again.

Again.

Again.

Nothing.

Goddamn it! The fear dissipates, replaced with fury and frustration.

"Motherfucker!!!" You punch the ceiling. Kick the back of the seats.

The beast in the front seat jumps. Takes a break from dining on the cabdriver to slap at the glass with bloody palms.

"Fuuuuck youuuuuu!" you scream. You punch the glass. You want to kill the thing. Rip it limb from limb. You pound the glass for what feels like an eternity, pouring all your anger and fear into the Plexiglas window.

Finally, you sink into the seat, out of breath. Out of energy. Out of options.

Turn to page 156.

SCAG, BROWN SUGAR, BLACK TAR, WHITE LADY, DRAGON, DOPE, MEXICAN MUD

Are you out of your fucking mind? Who do you think you are—Hunter S. Thompson? You can't hang with the Angels. But OK, hey, it's your funeral . . .

"This is my first time," you say. "I've never done anything like this before."

"Everyone's got their first," Louis says. He opens the cigar box. You catch a glimpse of a syringe, a spoon, what looks like a cotton ball, and a few other things you don't recognize. He fishes a small yellow balloon from his pocket, stretches it open, and pulls out a chunk of black stuff about the size of a marble—that's the heroin, you assume.

He places the chunk on a spoon, flips open a beat-up old Zippo, and lights it. He drops the cotton ball into the heated heroin and it puffs up like a sponge. You watch, fascinated, as he slides the tip of the syringe into the cotton and slowly pulls back the plunger.

"C'mere, gimme your arm," he says, so drunk he can barely get out the words.

"Huh?"

"Your arm—stick it out—sleeve up. Ever been to the fucking doctor?"

You do as he says.

He rubs an alcohol swab over the bend of your arm, smacks you a few times until your vein comes to the surface, then not-so-gently slips the syringe inside.

Your heart races. Anxious, excited, scared to death, halfway giddy, all at the same time.

151

He pulls back the plunger. A red cloud of blood is drawn inside. Then he injects it back inside you.

Your heart rate slows. You relax some. The deed is done. Nothing you can do about it now. No stopping it. You stretch your feet out, lean back against the wall, and wait.

Suddenly a powerful, intense rush of pleasure. Pure euphoria. You feel like a young child—just out of the shower—wrapped in a warm blanket. The gentle heat hugs you tight. All thoughts of zombies and monsters and fear and death leave your mind. Just warmth.

For a good half hour, you say nothing. Neither does Louis. You watch him intently, fascinated by this strange, weather-beaten man getting high in front of you. Your eye is drawn to the Hells Angels tattoo on his upper arm.

"Shouldn't there be an apostrophe in there—like Hell's Angels?" you ask, your mouth forming the words with concerted effort.

His eyes flitter. "Uh?"

"An apostrophe. It says Hells. H-E-L-L-S. No apostrophe."

"Apostrophe?"

"You know. A—c'mon, y'know—it's a comma, but not on the ground. A comma in the air."

"In the air."

"Yeah. In the air."

From the look on his face, he's doing some very hard thinking. After a minute, he quietly says, "Yeah, yeah, I guess there should be a comma."

"Apostrophe," you say, and giggle like a schoolgirl. Then you both go quiet again. Your head sags, and you lose track of time. Minutes, hours, all a blur. For the first time in months you're not thinking about zombies. Not thinking about death. Ghouls. The walking undead.

It's a relief.

So around noon, when Louis asks you if you want to do more, you say, "Why the hell not?"

He injects you again. You get that same rush. Then a stronger rush. Picking up speed like a runaway train.

Bam. It hits you. Everything goes black.

And there on Louis's dirty, garbage-covered floor, you overdose, death the furthest thing from your mind.

AN END

You flip the rifle over and eject the magazine. You can see the jammed bullet jutting out awkwardly. You dig your finger in to pop it free.

But it's too late.

You're knocked off your feet and carried to the ground. The shaggy hippie is on top of you. He digs his teeth into your shoulder. You howl.

You feel around for the samurai blade. You find it and rip it free from its sheath. You jam it up through the shaggy hippie's gut and cut up, spilling its insides all over you. You rip the blade up farther, into its jaw. That stops it.

You crawl to your knees, swinging the blade around wildly, trying to keep the other two at bay.

But the one beast—the middle-aged man—reaches out and grabs the blade. Squeezes it. Blood pours through its fingers, but it appears to feel nothing.

Fuck me.

You're done for.

You recover the blade and point it at your stomach. Then, like a true samurai committing seppuku, you slam it into your abdomen.

You scream.

Still holding the blade, you slice your stomach open, moving the blade from left to right. Your intestines spill out onto the ground in front of you. Completely disemboweled.

You go into shock. Your vision is foggy. Hard to see. Lights tracing.

The last thing you make out is Chucky, battling his way over to you. Then firing. Into your face. Ending it. Ensuring you don't become one of them.

AN END

You've been sitting in the cab for hours—you've seen a few cops race by on motorcycles, and that's it.

Mostly you've watched the dead multiply. Watched their numbers grow.

You wait. The thing in the front never takes its eyes off you. Hours pass.

You're not alone—other people are stuck, similar position to you. A woman in a BMW next to you sobs for damn near two hours. Didn't know someone could cry for that long.

All day the thing continues to stare at you. Every movement you make, he twitches—ready to eat. You hate it more and more with every second that ticks by. You want it dead. *Truly* dead.

As the day turns to dusk and darkness begins to settle over the city, you begin to develop a plan. On the way over you passed a construction site. It's three blocks at the most, if you remember correctly. It's big—about one square block. They're building some sort of residential tower, it looked like. The framework was up. If you get to there, you can get up to the top, try to signal for help.

But first—you're killing that bastard in the front seat.

You need some sort of weapon. You pull down the removable section in the middle of the backseat. You can't see, but you can reach through. Your hand pats around, looking for anything useful.

Bingo.

Tire iron. You pull it through. OK—you have a weapon. Now what?

Night falls. It's darker than usual. The streetlights don't come on. Then, around eleven o'clock, everything goes out. Interior lights in buildings shut off. The bridge lights go. Everything. It appears as if the city, or at least this part of the grid, has completely lost power. It's eerie—you've never seen the city so dark. It looks abandoned, deserted. You can no longer see inside any other cars. Makes you feel even more alone—it's just you, the undead thing in the front seat, and the thousands of other beasts that fill the streets.

This is your chance, under the cover of darkness.

You sit against the rear passenger-side door, tire iron in one hand. Perfectly still. For an hour, you don't move. You lull the thing into complacency.

Then slowly, oh so goddamn slowly, you bring your hand up to the door handle. Then, fast as possible, you snap the door open and jump outside onto the sidewalk. You rip open the front passenger-side door and the thing launches itself at you like it was spring-loaded.

You catch it on the side of its head with the tire iron, midair, and it falls into you. You unleash a torrent of blows. You hear its skull crack. You hear it shatter. But still it keeps coming. If the movies have taught you anything, you need to get to the brain that sits inside that skull.

It gnashes its teeth at you. You backpedal, swinging. You get lucky and it stumbles over its feet trying to get to you. While it's down on all fours, you raise the tire iron high, aim for the back of the skull, and bring it down as hard as you can. You feel it break through. The thing collapses.

Panting, splattered with blood, barely able to catch your breath, you survey your work and smile.

Then you remember the countless other zombies in the vicinity. You look up. In the moonlight, you can see them—all of them—running for you.

You book it. Head up the avenue. One lunges for you. You swing the tire iron, knocking it back, never slowing. Two more blocks.

Just run. Run like you never have in your life.

You turn the corner and see the construction site up ahead. You're close. You don't turn around, but you can hear them.

You're closing in on the fence that surrounds the site.

Close.

The sound of feet behind you—so many feet, running after you.

Closer.

C'mon!

You launch yourself at the fence. One of the things grabs your foot. Pulls you. You scramble up, shaking your leg, trying to pull free. Finally, its grip breaks. You climb higher. The top of the fence is lined with barbed wire. Your hand wraps around it and you pull yourself up. Pain, unbelievable pain. It's like arm wrestling a steak knife. Blood streaks down your arm. But you continue to climb. The barbed wire tears at your entire body. You get to the top and drop to the other side.

You hit the ground. The pain is immense, but you don't care. You smile. There're a thousand of the fucking things out there. And you just outran them all.

You lie there for a good ten minutes, catching your breath, happy to be alive. Then you stand. The construction site is a giant sort of pit, with slight hills sloping inward from every side. At the bottom is the building's foundation. And huge machines. Steamrollers. Wrecking balls. Cranes. Dump trucks. Massive things.

In the center, trailers. There's a light on in the nearest one. You can hear the rumble of a generator. Half dead, you stumble down the hill. You make it to the trailer, open the door, fall inside. You collapse onto the floor. Blood pouring out. You can taste it.

And then you hear something you very much don't want to hear.

"Its one of them! Get it!" a voice shouts.

"No, no," you manage to get out, "I'm not. The blood—from the fence."

"Bullshit. Kill him."

"Big Al, we gotta help him."

You can't see anything. Head on the floor. Too much pain. Too exhausted to lift it. Too exhausted to even open your eyes. You feel hands on you. Moving you. They tie off some of your more severe cuts.

"Thanks," you manage—then pass out.

You come to in a chair. Three men sit across from you. Construction workers.

You try to get up. You can't—you're restrained. Duct tape all around your arms and legs. The fuck?

"What is this? Why am I duct-taped to a chair?"

The one sitting in the middle—the calm-looking one—talks.

"We're waiting to see if you turn."

"Turn?"

"Into one of those things."

"Well I'm not going to. So untie me now please. Or untape me, whatever."

The big one walks over and points a ruler in your face. "Buddy, you're lucky you're not dead right now."

"You're telling me."

"What I mean is," he says, getting down and in your face until you can smell the pastrami on his breath, "you're lucky we haven't killed you."

The calm-looking one: "Big Al. Go for a smoke, huh?"

"I'm fine right here, brother," he says. He takes two steps back, leans against a counter along the wall.

"Why's everyone want to kill me? And who are you?"

"I'm Sully," says the calm"OK, Sully—why do you, Big Al, and this third guy here want to kill me?"

The third guy speaks. He has a quiet, almost timid voice. Fits his small stature. "The guys call me Fish. 'Cause they say I look like a fish."

"Yeah, you do."

Fish frowns.

Sully continues. "The reason Big Al is so eager to kill you is because we were fine here—then you showed up—and now we got this."

"Got what?"

Sully pulls the curtain aside. Through the large window you can see most of the empty construction site. And at the fence, the zombies. Clawing. Chewing on the metal. The bigger ones pound at it.

Big Al steps forward, pointing the ruler at you. "Look, fuck-head. You brought those things here. I say we give you back to them."

If you want to apologize profusely, turn to page 273.

OK, enough of this shit—tell Big Al exactly where he can stick it. Turn to page 171.

The Harley engines echo through Manhattan, the heavy roar bouncing off abandoned skyscrapers and deserted storefronts. In the sidecar, it feels like you're about two inches off the ground. The street is a blur.

Tommy follows Joe Camel. Camel rides a camo Harley with an empty sidecar. That's how you'll be taking the woman out.

Buildings flash by you. Tommy drives like a madman. Your stomach jumps with every 40-mph turn. Finally, you close your eyes, trust Tommy not to kill you, and think about the job ahead of you.

You'll ride straight into MSG, clear out the ground floor, and then you and Tommy will head to the concourse, up to the top, grab the girl from the suite, she'll squeeze in the sidecar with you, then you head back to the ground floor where you hand her off to Joe Camel and together you all ride back to the club.

You're heading for the most famous arena in the world. And it's going to be packed to the rafters with the walking dead. And it's your job—*your job*—to go inside and rescue someone. You clutch the MP5 submachine gun against your chest.

You open your eyes. White lines flash beneath you as Tommy cruises up Fifth Avenue. You come to a stop at Thirty-fourth Street, across from Penn Station and Madison Square Garden. Husks shuffle about in the moonlight, covering the stairs to the Garden entrance.

"Now what?" you whisper to Tommy.

"We wait. Colonel said they'd restore power to this grid at midnight."

Just as Tommy finishes his sentence, the building lights up and the street is bathed in white light. The large digital screen outside reads KNICKS VS CELTICS—TONIGHT, 7 PM.

The monsters turn, surprised by the light. You can see them full on now—a few dozen in the street, maybe a hundred on the ramp leading up and into the garden. You don't even want to know how many more inside.

"Ready?" Camel asks.

Tommy nods.

Camel reaches into his sidecar and hands you each a forty-ounce bottle of Olde English, filled with gasoline and dish soap. The dish soap, Tommy told you, works as a thickening agent—it'll turn the Molotov cocktails into a sort of miniature napalm bomb.

You light a match. Hold the flame to the wick. Count to five, like Tommy said. Then you let it rip.

The bombs fly through the air, across Sixth Avenue, and smack against the side of the Garden entrance, showering the stairs with fire. Yours falls short, hitting the ground, and exploding at the beasts' feet. The dish soap causes the fire to let off a thick cloud of smoke, and the beasts stumble around, smoke pouring off them.

"OK fellas—let's give 'em hell!" Camel yells.

Tommy hits it. Drives across the avenue, straight up the ramp, past the burning beasts, and into the main hall. One stands at the entrance, blocking the way. The mounted saw cuts it in half at the waist. No blood. Just dry, dead innards.

You let loose with the submachine gun. It bucks in your hand. You slow it down—three-round bursts.

You send a pair of them flying into the ticket vendor windows. As they fall, you fire again, blowing apart their heads.

Tommy pulls the tommy gun from over his shoulder and begins firing. Takes down the beasts on the stairs.

Joe Camel works more methodically. With a .357 Magnum in his hand, he fires rounds sparingly. Aims. Shoots. One in the head. Aims. Shoots. Another in the head. The blasts are impossibly loud.

Finally, the shooting stops. Empty shells litter the floor beside you. Thick smoke in the air. Two balls of wet paper towel in your ears do little—your ears ring and your head pounds.

Tommy gets off his bike and walks over to Camel. They talk for a second, and Tommy returns.

"We go to the concourse," Tommy says. "Then the elevator to the top. Camel will be waiting here, keeping things under control, then we all ride out together."

You nod.

Tommy hits the gas. Your ass smacks repeatedly against the hard seat as he takes the bike up the stairs. At the top, he slows it down. A pair of double doors ahead of you, and beyond that, the concourse.

He continues the crawl through the doors. And then you're there. It's a hall about twenty feet wide, lined with bathrooms, food vendors, ATMs, beer, and all sorts of blue and orange shit for sale. And it's packed with a mass of undead New York sports fans.

"Ready?" Tommy says.

"Not really."

"Good!" Then he guns it, headed right for them. No more MP5—time for the Vulcan. You grab the twin triggers, like holding two joysticks, press down with both thumbs, and do everything you can to hold it steady.

The Gatling gun whirls, then begins firing. Nothing could prepare you for this thing. Huge bullets tear through the monsters. Legs separate. Chests blow apart. Arms fly off. Bodies spin around. Masses of flesh burst.

Tommy picks up the speed.

You keep your thumbs on the triggers. Arms shaking. Hands hurting. It's like holding a jackhammer. Takes everything you have to keep it from shooting off to the right or left.

But you keep it forward. Keep mowing down whatever is in front of you.

The sound is beyond deafening. Chunks of tile fly off the walls. Bullets rip through an ATM machine. Money flies. A souvenir booth goes down in a mess of T-shirts and ball caps.

Finally, Tommy slows the bike—you're back where you started. The damage is tremendous. Smoke hangs in the air. Water sprays from the sprinklers.

Bodies litter the path ahead of you. Some crawl. One steps, stumbles, and falls.

"Not bad," Tommy says. "Now, we go up."

He drives to the elevator. You lean out, press the UP button, and wait. When the doors open, Tommy backs the bike in and hits the button for the tenth level.

As the elevator ascends, you sit in silence, hand on the Vulcan. It's hot. Smoke leaks out the end of the gun's six barrels, filling the elevator with the rich smell of gunpowder. You say nothing. Neither does Tommy. You hope that door never opens. You don't want to face another round of these things. Don't want to save that woman; you really don't give a damn about her right now.

But, of course, the doors open.

Right in front of you is a servicewoman. Young, maybe twenty-three. Absolutely gorgeous—or was. Her face is sunken in. Hollow looking. Nothing behind her eyes. Her left arm stops just below the elbow and her body sags to the side.

You let loose with the Vulcan. Bullets rip through her waist, propelling her into a deathly, spastic dance. The force of the shots pushes her back. As she falls, one of the massive bullets catches her in the chin and exits through the back of her skull.

The elevator doors shut behind you. You hear it begin to descend. Tommy drives. The sidecar goes up and over the dead woman. It's horrific. You feel sick—but, unfortunately, not numb. Every undead person you put back down pulls at your insides.

Tommy seems to sense it. He stops the bike. You idle in the small area outside the elevator, in front of you the long hall stretching to the left and right.

The things are coming. You can hear them running down the hall. About to come around the curved corner.

"Hey—get it out of your head," he says.

"It's gone," you say, not looking up.

"Yeah?"

"Yeah."

"OK—then shoot those things, huh? Before they eat us?"

Tommy turns the corner just as you squeeze the twin triggers and lay waste to the approaching mass. Men in suits. Business types. The type of people who can afford top-level suites.

You circle the entire upper level of the arena and make it back to the elevator. It's clear. Every zombie, dead for real.

"OK, let's find this broad," Tommy says.

There are eight large suites at the top level of Madison Square Garden. You try the first. Locked. Tommy tosses you a crowbar. You've never had to crack open a locked door, and Tommy explains it to you like you're an idiot. You wedge it in just above the handle and pop it. Tommy kicks in the door.

You peek in behind him. Tommy fires nine quick shots and drops three zombie businessmen.

It takes two more tries before you find what you're looking for. And it isn't nice.

The woman lies on the floor, barely breathing. She looks awful. She's older, mid-sixties. Emaciated. About what you'd expect for someone who spent the last three months living off what looks like nothing but water, soda, and Doritos.

Through the huge window you take in the arena for the first time. Thirty thousand undead Knicks fans. And on the floor, the entire Knicks roster—zombified.

Then a scream. You turn. Tommy. One has him pinned to the wall, teeth in his face. You can't tell where Tommy ends and the beast begins.

You lunge at them, put the crowbar up through the back of the thing's head. Arch it up and pull back, yanking it off Tommy.

You step back. Tommy's face is a mangled mess. Skin hanging down over his left eye. Blood pumping out of his neck with each beat of his heart. You can already see him turning. Changing.

You take a step back. Nearly trip over a leather couch.

He stares at you. His arms raise.

He's one of them.

Run for it? Turn to page 38.

Take on Tommy and try to finish the job? Turn to page 108.

PLEASE LEAVE, PLEASE LEAVE, PLEASE LEAVE

A long, hairy arm reaches under the platform. Its massive hand scratches at the yellow cement. It stretches, reaching farther under. Then the stupid thing falls—face-first, directly onto the gravel in front of you. It's a massive thing—looks like one of those big old '70s wrestlers.

It looks around, stunned. Then looks right at you and the boy. Eyes glazed over like there's nothing behind them.

You press yourself against the wall. Trying to stay as far in the dark as possible.

You hold the boy tight against you. Any other situation you'd be breaking about ten child-endangerment laws. You feel a drop of something on your hand. Wet. The boy's crying. You put your hand over his mouth. "Shhh."

It moans louder.

Fuck . . .

It raises its head and lets out a long, gurgling roar. Three more of the beasts fall over the sides. Down on their hands and knees, they crawl forward, closing in.

The kid cries harder. You hold him tighter.

And then they pounce.

AN END

THE GARAGE

You need to get off these streets—now. That's your only priority.

You run to the parking garage, reach the top of the ramp, and head down into the darkness. Pieces of the cop car's bumper and tail end litter the ground at the bottom of the ramp. Looks like the cruiser went right through the gate. Splintered pieces of yellow wood are scattered across the ground. Cautiously, you enter the garage.

You see the cruiser. It's come to a stop in the center of the garage floor. Smoke streams out steadily from the hood. The driver's-side door is open. The car rests gently, eerily peaceful.

Then you see the cop. He's crawling across the floor. Hand on his face, leaking blood.

You run to help him—then halfway there, you stop in your tracks. A landing strip of flesh has been torn from his cheek down to his shoulder. His injuries have nothing do with the accident. He's been bitten.

You step back.

The undead cop braces himself against the bumper of a nearby SUV and rises. He turns to you. Face pale. NYPD blues soaked in red. He sees you. You think maybe, just maybe, you see a small grin creep across his face.

He takes a step, then—

BLAM!!!

The cop's head explodes in a blast of red.

You spin—only to find yourself staring down the smoking end of a double-barrel shotgun. The gunman is a gargantuan man, some muscle, plenty of fat. Short, spiky black hair. Dark skin. Italian, you guess. Tattoos wind up from his trigger finger, spiraling up his arm.

Your ears are ringing from the shotgun blast. The man's mouth moves, but you hear nothing. Just a high-pitched buzzing.

You stutter. He barks at you.

You shake your head back and forth quickly. "I can't hear!" you shout.

He lowers the shotgun, just slightly.

You're more than a little relieved when you realize he's wearing a 24-HOUR PARKING uniform. A "Chucky" name tag hangs from his uniform. It actually says Chuck. The *y* is drawn on in green marker.

"Hey, hey," you say, panicked. You've never had a gun in your face before. "I'm not one of those things."

Chucky stares you hard in the eyes. "Who you like?"

The ringing is fading. You can begin to hear him now.

"What?"

"Who do you like? Mets or Yankees?"

"What?"

He cocks the shotgun. "I seen a whole world of crazy shit in the past fucking hour. I ain't in no *goddamn* mood to play. So . . . you a Yankees fan, motherfucker . . . or not?"

If you want to tell him the truth—you're not a huge baseball fan, but you follow the Pittsburgh Pirates some—turn to page 12.

If you want to lie to him and say you're a die-hard follower of the Bronx Bombers, turn to page 252.

YOUR BEST MIKE HAMMER IMPRESSION

"OK, listen Al—I just spent the past God knows how many hours in the back of a fucking cab, staring at the decomposing body of a guy who—despite being dead—kept staring right the fuck back at me. Then, even though he was dead, I killed him again. With a tire iron. Then I outran a thousand zombies. Topped that off by doing it missionary style with a barbed-wire fence. I'm bleeding from about a hundred different places. And, from the smell, I think I may have shit myself. Or actually, that stink just might be you, Big fuckin' Al."

Big Al doesn't like that.

"So if you want to kill me, kill me. But I'm not going down without a fight. So let me loose, let's step outside, and let's handle this like men."

Big Al smiles. "Look at this, fuckin' tough guy all of a sudden."

"It's been one helluva bad day at Black Rock, friend."

"Alright, guy, relax. I'm not going to kill you."

"Cut me loose, then.

"Yeah—you should cut him loose, Al," Fish says.

They do. You stretch. It hurts like hell. Sharp, shooting pains all over. "Thanks. Now where can I pass out?"

Turn to page 373.

"Gentlemen," Doc says, as he pulls the sheet off his workbench, "Merry Christmas."

Weapons galore. Guns. Grenades. Rocket launchers. Swords. Axes.

"Go to town, government's paying."

The men walk down the bench, taking what they want, and then head outside. You take a grenade launcher and an RCP90 submachine gun—you recognize it from *GoldenEye*.

You flip up the side mirror on Jones's Harley. Take a look at yourself. You're the beautiful bastard child of Snake Plissken and John Rambo.

It's just before midnight. Outside sits a roofless double-decker bus, glimmering in the moonlight, with the words NYC SIGHTS in big letters along the side and a huge image of an American flag next to the Statue of Liberty.

You board the bus, head for the upper deck, and take a seat in front of Jones.

Four Angels take their bikes. The rest the bus. Doc drives.

The Harleys roar to life, Doc pulls out, and your bizarre convoy hits the road. No joking. No fun and games. Men going to war. Everything at stake.

You lay the RCP90 on the seat beside you. Put the grenade launcher on your lap. Across the side it reads Milkor M32 MGL. MGL stands for Multiple Grenade Launcher, you figure. It holds six 40mm shells in a tommy-gun—style drum magazine. It can do a lot of damage. Kill a lot of people. Or whatever the hell it is you're out to kill.

You turn to Jones. "On the corner that night—would you really have let me die?"

He exhales smoke through his nose. "Absolutely."

"How could you just let a man die like that—when you could stop it? Not just a man. Me."

"I gave you a choice."

"Still."

"Choices in life, kid. Lots of them. You live with the choices you make."

"Yeah, tell me about it," you say.

You get up and walk to the front of the bus and lean against it. It's been nearly a year since that sweltering July day when the zombies came to New York—and the world. Now it's a warm May night. Type of night you should be out barbecuing. Ten years ago, you'd have been playing tag with the neighborhood kids or playing Spin the Bottle. Now you're headed to the Empire State Building to murder zombies.

One up ahead. A thin woman in a long jacket. Standing on a corner. Doc swerves to hit it and the thing bounces off the front of the bus.

The first twenty blocks are easy going. Then coming up through Union Square, things get messier. But Doc keeps his foot on the gas and powers through them. You feel a bump as one is caught in the wheel well.

At Twenty-third Street, you meet your first real chunk of trouble. An overturned SUV and a snapped streetlight block the way.

The loudspeaker, usually reserved for obnoxious tour guides, serves as Doc's way of communicating with you guys on top the bus and the bikers alongside it. Doc comes on. "Fellas, need some help here."

You drop to one knee, rest the barrel of the grenade launcher on the front wall of the double-decker bus, and flip up the sight.

THWOOMP!

The grenade spirals through the air, a trail of smoke arcing behind it. It hits the side of the historic Flatiron Building and explodes, showering the street with chunks of concrete and shards of glass.

Little lower and to the right.

You fire again.

The explosion flips the car up through the air and sends a dozen of the undead things flying. The lamppost splinters.

Doc hits the gas. The Angels circle the bus, keeping the beasts at bay.

One Angel zooms past the bus and races ahead, the twin cannons on the sides of his bike laying waste to anything in his way.

Another follows behind. He whips a bike chain around the neck of a zombie in a tight white shirt. Rips it to the ground and drags it with him. Through a sitting area, into some out-door tables and chairs, up the curb, then leaves it smashed, dead, against a streetlight.

The convoy carries on. Up ahead, through a thick fog, the Empire State Building towers over the city.

The bus slows. You pour out.

Two undead security guards stand just inside the ornate art deco entrance. Jones drops them. On the wall is a building map. Eighty-six floors to the top.

The men move out.

The Angel named Tanner carries a scythe, looking like something straight from hell. On the seventeenth floor, inside the Croatian Tourist Board office, he beheads three undead Croatian tourists.

At floor 36, the Angel named Foster uses his two-by-four spiked with rusty nails to clean out the Alitalia offices.

On 48, you open the door to the law offices of Kurland, Aiken, & Gradwohl. There are lights. A small generator hums in the corner. Mountains of food. Boxes and boxes of cereal and crackers. Music from behind one of the doors. You put your ear to it. Opera. You ready the gun and kick open the door, prepared for anything.

Blood. So much blood. Dark red, mixed with chunks of skull, caked on the wall. Beneath it is the slumped-over body of a man, his head completely gone. Shotgun in his lifeless hand.

You look around. Must have stocked up in the beginning. Planned on riding it out. But couldn't take it. You keep it in mind—then head back out.

At floor 53, the large, hairy Angel named Griz kicks open the doors to the King's College administrative offices and throws a flash bang inside. Blinds the undead professors inside and then kills them all with his ax.

On 64, you enter the offices of the National Film Board of Canada. You can smell the beast—too late, you turn. The door slams shut behind you. Your guys are locked out in the hall. Alone, you face a large man, white beard. You unload the RCP90's entire fifty-round magazine in less then a second. The monster's chest and waist are torn apart. Not a single head shot, though. Fuck. It leaps at you. Ammo spent, you jump behind a large mahogany desk, keeping it between you and the thing.

You're trapped. Frantic, you look for something, anything to use as a weapon.

Keyboard. You rip it free from the computer and smack the beast across the face. Keys fly. It does nothing.

A letter opener. You swipe at the beast. Swipe again.

Beside it, a compressed gas duster. You have one at your cubicle at work for cleaning Cheetos crumbs out of your keyboard.

You take it in your hand, holding it like a grenade, and wait. The thing sways back and forth, eyeing you, then lunges over the desk, mouth wide, ready to bite. You jam the can in its mouth. It gags. You stab the letter opener into the base of the can. There's a hiss—then the can bursts, shooting compressed air in every direction and blowing the thing's head wide open in a furious blast of red.

Your heart races. Pounds against your chest. Close one. You collapse in the desk chair. Reload the RCP90. Chunks of brain and skull on your face. You wipe yourself off and, reluctantly, head back out to the hall to rejoin your team.

The Angels continue working their way up through the building. On every floor, zombie resistance—and on every floor, that resistance is put down.

Finally, you approach the top. A sign points to the observation deck. Everyone gathers around the door, weapons high.

"Ready?" Jones says.

No one says anything. He kicks open the door. You take them in—a hundred dead tourists.

They immediately run for you. Tanner leads the way, swinging the scythe. Whiskey grabs a zombie kid—teeth snapping—and throws him up over the fence to the depths below. You back your way into a corner. Drop on one knee, trying to make yourself as small as possible. You've made it this far. Not going to die now. Anything gets close, you shoot it in the brain.

Finally, the zombie tourists are all dead.

"Head back down, men," Jones says. They do. You wait behind. Watch as Jones lights the flare, holds it high, and red smoke fills the air.

And with that, your job is complete. Jones puts his hand on your shoulder. "Let's go."

If you want to stay behind, turn to page 341.

If you'll leave with Jones and the rest of the Angels, turn to page 47.

Fuck fuck fuck.

You see Al dive into the hole after Sully. You turn, away from the hole, away from the monsters—and you run like hell. Fish follows your lead, sprinting behind you.

You tear across the lot, fast as you can. You throw a glance over your shoulder—some of the beasts go in the hole after Sully and Al. Others chase you.

Then, suddenly, you're in the dirt.

An upturned rock sent you falling. It's going to be the god-damned death of you. Unbelievable.

You look up, dirt in your eyes. Fish sprints past you.

One of the beasts lands on top of you. Buries its teeth in your ankles. You twist, ignoring the pain, and throw a useless punch. Another one lands on you—your leg twists, awkwardly, and your shin snaps. Pain radiates up your leg.

You bury your head in the dirt, grind your teeth. Goddamn it, you're going to die here.

You get a glimpse of Fish up ahead. He's climbing something. Can't tell what.

The beasts get off, take off after Fish. Blood turns the dirt around you black. You manage to roll over.

You see Fish.

And he's driving a giant motherfucking steamroller. He looks at you. His expression switches from scared to apologetic. You know you're done for. You give a woozy, defeated thumbs-up, just before one of the monsters bites the thumb off.

The stupid things don't have the sense to move. They stand in the way. Fish rolls right over them. Completely squishes them.

And then the shadow of the steamroller is upon you. You're on your back, head up, watching. You close your eyes and let it take you.

Over your feet first. Indescribable pain. Bones shatter. Muscles burst. Organs liquefy. Your body literally flattens.

Over your knees. You hear them crack and shatter.

Up your thighs. Your testicles pop. Blood floods your underwear.

Then the pain subsides and your eyes open and you watch, oddly fascinated, as the steamroller runs over your chest, and, then finally, over your face . . .

AN END

Panic flooding you, you follow the crowd. It's running with the bulls in Pamplona—new title: running from the zombies on the East Side.

You make your way through the maze of cars. You catch quick glimpses of the panicked faces of passengers. Some leave their cars. Others try to but fail—the mass of running bodies making it impossible.

Screams fill the air behind you. You just keep moving. Run up and over a car. You pass an abandoned convertible BMW Z3. Always wanted one of those, you think. Free, right there.

It's a two-level bridge. Bottom is strictly for vehicles. Top is supposed to be for pedestrians, but cars have filled the narrow pedestrian lane. Most of the zombies seem to have gone for the lower level. You run around the side, up the pedestrian path, and onto the upper level.

You're surrounded by people, all fleeing at top speed. Fuck me, I'm out of shape, you think. But you don't stop. Keep going, even when it feels like your heart is going to burst out of your chest. Four or five minutes later, you're nearly halfway across the bridge.

And then it all goes to shit.

Bullets tear through the air. The man beside you drops—his chest blasted apart. More fall to the ground, screaming.

You drop behind a car. The rear window above you shatters. You peek your head around.

It's the Army. At the opposite end of the bridge your freedom is blocked by the USFUCKINGARMY.

The firing stops. Then a loudspeaker, megaphone, some-thing:

"STOP! THIS IS THE UNITED STATES MILITARY! THIS AREA IS UNDER QUARANTINE. RETURN TO THE CITY."

Behind you, people scream—the zombies like a giant meat grinder—a wall of death—destroying every living thing in its way. Coming right for you.

Ahead of you, the Army—ready to drop anything moving—walking dead or not.

Get into the nearest car? Turn to page 19.

Keep moving forward, finding safety where you can? Turn to page 66.

Turn around, back toward the zombies and away from the Army? Turn to page 208.

"Alright, asshole, I'm in."

Limpy hoots and hollers.

Jones leads you to the middle of the closest intersection. You look up. Thirty-ninth and Eighth. The Harley headlights bathe you in blinding white light.

"Ready, kid?"

You spin the crowbar in your hands. "As I'll ever be."

Jones puts two fingers in his mouth and whistles, piercingly loud. Man, you've always wanted to be able to do the two-fingered whistle. If you live, you're gonna get him to teach you how.

Jones slaps you on the back, says good luck, and walks away laughing.

You raise the crowbar. Grip it tight with two hands. Spread your feet in a fighting stance. You take quick side steps, turning, looking in every direction.

The Angels sit on their bikes, standing, smoking, watching. Bastards . . .

A sound to your left. You spin. Heart pumping.

Here comes the first one.

A thin Asian woman. Bloody shirt, barely there. Skin rotted away to nothing. Entire rib cage visible.

Just before it reaches you, you sidestep and swing the crowbar with everything you got. Connect. Crack it square in the face. Contact reverberates down the bar and through your hands. You take the zombie clean off its feet and it lands on its back.

No hesitating.

You flip the crowbar and slam the sharp end through its face.

You don't have a chance to breathe. A cold arm tight around your neck. You swing your body down, flipping the thing up and over your back.

It hits the cement hard—but in a second it's up. Businessman. Torn suit. Entire calf muscle gone. Bone protruding from its lower leg.

"That's one minute!" one of the Angels shouts.

The businessman thing steps forward. You bring your foot down hard on the protruding bone. It snaps. The thing feels no pain—but the broken bone maims it and it falls awkwardly to the ground. You swing, nail it in the side of the head. It moans. Reaches out for you.

Three more strong swings. Chunks of skin and hair fly off. You rear back, aim, and follow through. Its head damn near comes off.

The Angels clap.

You pant. Pull a piece of the dead thing's skin off your face.

Out of the shadows come three more. A little girl, and what looks like her parents. Tourists. Probably spent a year saving up for their trip to the Big Apple—then they get there and end up as fucking zombies.

"Two minutes!"

They start out stumbling, then walking, then full out sprinting. Fuck. Three at a time?

You backpedal, mind racing.

Do you want to handle them all at once? Turn to page 367.

If you'd rather try to separate them and take them on one at a time, turn to page 99.

Before you even realize it, you're out of the cab, running. Pandemonium surrounds you. A mass evacuation to anywhere but here.

You steal a look behind you. Mayhem. More of the things coming.

You collide with a group of children—kids on a school trip or something—and crash to the ground.

A police cruiser screams by you, hopping the curb. You get a quick glimpse of the cop behind the wheel, face panic-stricken, as he flies past, plowing through a pile of curbside garbage and newspaper racks.

An ambulance swerves to avoid hitting the cop car and smashes into a streetlight with so much force that the pole snaps in half at the middle. The top falls to the street, landing on a van and sending people scattering. Sparks fly as the electrical wires dance on the streets. A zombie, curious, stumbles over to one and reaches for it. It fries. Shakes violently and falls to the ground. Then, horrifically, it rises again.

The police cruiser hops back onto the street, tires squealing. The horn honks. Too late. A man flies up over the hood, rolls over the roof, and hits the ground with a sickening thud. The cruiser doesn't stop. It swerves again, avoiding one man but hitting another. The cop loses control. The car spins on to the entrance ramp to an underground twenty-four-hour parking garage and crashes into the wall. Then, as gravity takes over, it rolls down the ramp.

You rise. Chaos all around you. Your heart races.

Don't stop, don't look back, just run? Turn to page 353.

Run down into the garage, hoping for refuge and help from the police? Turn to page 169.

Run for the bridge and hopefully Brooklyn? Turn to page 179.

UH-UH—I'M NO TEST PATIENT

You pry the officer's fingers from around your arm, jerk away, and run.

The first shot gets you in the shoulder. Goddamn it, Christ! Hot pain in your flesh—like fire. You stumble. Catch your feet. Keep running.

You don't hear the next three shots. Don't even feel them. And that's probably for the best . . .

AN END

Yakuma puts the two bloody samurai swords on the soft leather wraparound.

Rick drives like a man possessed. You watch the city fly by. The river. Thick crowds of people.

"This is a nice limousine," you say.

"Yup," Yakuma says.

"This is a nice limousine!" you shout up to Rick. He doesn't respond.

You pour yourself a Cîroc and club soda. Down it. Pour yourself another. Lean back. Try to relax. Not working.

You watch Yakuma. She has her eyes closed. She looks peaceful.

"So uh—you and [LEGAL EDIT] ever, y'know . . . back here?" you ask.

Her eyes open. "What do you think?"

Damn. You should have worked harder on fielding those grounders in Little League.

Rick cranes his neck. "Miss. We're coming up on the bridge. Doesn't look like the police are letting anyone through."

"You know the cop?"

"What cop? There're two hundred up there."

"Recognize anyone?"

He sighs, then cuts across two lanes. "Yeah, Lou, same as always."

"What time is it?" she asks Rick.

"Eleven thirty-six."

"So handle it."

Rick cuts across another lane, cutting off traffic. The partition window closes, but the intercom stays on. The car comes to a stop. You listen with bated breath. Yakuma puts her bloody hand on yours.

"Hiya Lou."

"Hey Rick. Sorry, no one through."

"I got you-know-who in the back."

"Rick, I could if I would, but I mean no one. Orders from the mayor."

"Game starts in a half hour."

"There's not gonna be a game today; you nuts?"

"It's the Sox. They're playing. He's got to get to the stadium."

"Rick—"

"Lou, it's the Sox."

"Ahh, Christ. You know I'm going to catch hell for this, right?"

"Not when [LEGAL EDIT] turns a game-ending double play to secure us a playoff spot."

"You son of a bitch. Go."

Yakuma smiles. The car begins to roll. You hear the cop telling people to move, it's an emergency.

"Holy shit, it worked," you say.

"Of course. He's the king of the city."

Twenty minutes later, you pull into the Yankee Stadium parking lot. Just as a massive horde of the dead are arriving . . .

If you want to stick with the plan and make your way inside Yankee Stadium, turn to page 345.

No way. Too many zombies out there. Keep driving. Turn to page 359.

LADY, STOP!

You barely stop to think. You claw at the mountain of chairs and cabinets you just piled against the window, bringing them crashing to the ground. You grab a chair by its legs and swing. The glass cracks.

"What the hell're you doing?" Walter shouts.

You don't know what's gotten into you, but you're impassioned and unstoppable. You give the glass two more hard whacks. Finally, it shatters. You push a cabinet aside and climb over and through. You're lucky—the heavy echo of gunfire is distracting most of the beasts. Those that do notice, you simply run past.

"Hey! Stop!" you shout.

You're running downhill—focused squarely on the woman. She's fast approaching the massacre. Up and to her left is the military—tanks, soldiers, guns galore. In front of her and to the right—more zombies.

You kick it into overdrive. Two-year-old pair of Vans smacking pavement. You close in. Leap. Tackle her from behind, just feet from the battle ahead, and together you hit the cement.

Bullets whiz past you. Over you. The woman kicks and screams.

"She's already dead. Your daughter's already dead."

The woman goes limp in your arms. Breathes heavily, near hysterical. Need to get out of here. Then the woman does something you're not expecting—punches you in the nose. Your eyes water and your grip loosens.

The woman is up. Bullets fly past her.

You see the daughter. Beneath the gray skin, the bloodshot eyes, the swollen lips, you can see the resemblance. Same hair, so blond it's white. She was a cute little six-year-old. Now she's a zombie with a huge, bloody mess of a hole where her right eye should be.

The mother sweeps up her daughter. "Oh God, oh God—Ruby, what happened? Oh God."

"Lady, get the fuck down!"

You reach up to get her. At that same moment, Ruby sinks her teeth into the side of her mother's face. The mother screams—confused, in shock at what's happening.

And then—an instant later—the next round of gunfire starts up. And bullets tear through the three of you.

AN END

You let it go to voice mail, sit down, pop open a bottle of Coors, and turn on the TV. Your mind is entering full denial mode now to combat the stress of the past hour. You quickly flip channels—can't handle any more news. Thank God for DVR—man's great contribution to society in the twenty-first century. You put on some early-season *Simpsons*. Your pacifier. Relaxing. You drink more.

The phone rings two more times. You turn it off.

You go through the beers like they're water. Well, not quite like water—you never drank seven bottles of water in an hour. Empty bottles pile up beside you. You begin playing basketball with them, tossing the empties into the sink. Violently—just asking one to shatter. Finally, one does, splashing glass across the counter and onto the floor.

Sirens outside. Nonstop. Some right out front. Some pass in the distance. It's a nightmare. You keep drinking—drink enough, maybe you'll wake up from the nightmare.

The sun is setting, casting an eerie orange light through the window and into the apartment.

You're hammered now. But the gnawing feeling—the fear—won't leave. You need something else. Not beers. Something prescribable.

You go to the bedroom. Root through your ex-girlfriend's stuff. She moved out two months ago and hasn't come back to collect it. You find a fat plastic bag stuffed with her pills—various blue and white and pink pills to deal with anxiety and depression. You grab the bottle that reads ALPRAZOLAM on the side. Unscrew the top. Dozens of little blue ones. Xanax. Bingo. Instant relaxation.

This is way out of character, you think to yourself, as you toss four into your mouth and raise the bottle of Coors. But, well, it seems like the world is falling apart—and as long as you've been alive, that's pretty out of character for the world. So, it—

BLAM!

You cough, spitting out the pills, and jump about a mile into the air. The bottle drops and the little blue guys scatter out across the wood floor. You mentally check your pants for shit. All clear.

Gunshot! That was a **FUCKING** gunshot! You try to wrap your head around that.

You tiptoe to the door. You press your head against it and listen. You can just barely make out a low moaning sound. You grab a hockey stick from your closet—an old, beat-up thing you found lying in the trash one day and figured shouldn't go to waste.

You squint out the peephole, which you realize you've never used before. Nothing there.

Stick in hand, you carefully open the creaky door and step out into the hall.

You see her immediately. A woman, lying in the corner by the stairs, on her side, face down. Blood on the wall behind her.

You recognize her. Old lady from down the hall. "That rent control bitch," you used to call her. Third day you lived in the apartment you had some friends over, went pretty hard at it late into the night. Next morning That Rent Control Bitch was knocking on your door, saying something about she's been in this building forty years, never heard such a racket, so late—how could you be so rude, blah, blah, blah. You apologized, assured her it wouldn't happen again.

Old bag. Never wanted her to die, though.

She howls with pain. You step over and kneel down. "What happened?" you ask softly. Stupid question. You heard the shot.

"Who shot you?" you ask. OK, more helpful question, but sounds pretty messed up. No response. Her eyelids flicker. She's fading fast.

You notice the door to her apartment is slightly ajar. Fuck. You should run. You *would* run—downstairs, out to the street, screaming and yelling—but there's nothing out there for you. No help. You could run back to your apartment. But then who knows—you could be next, lying on your side, bleeding out.

Fuck it. Time to man up.

You tighten your hand around the stick and gently open the door to her apartment.

CRACK! CRACK!

A bullet punches the wall behind you. Another rips through the hockey stick, splintering the top.

You're staring at the shooter—a big dude, shirtless, tats all over. Neo-Nazi type. Pistol in his hand, smoking.

No time to think. You charge at him. He fires again and you feel the bullet buzz past your head. You swing the stick wildly and miss by a long shot. Your momentum carries you forward and you stumble.

He fires another shot. Misses. Something behind you breaks.

You swing again. Connect this time with his side. Fuck—dude's in shape. Barely moved him.

He cracks you on the top of the head with the butt of the gun and drops you to the ground. Any second you expect to be shot in the back, but nothing comes. Out of bullets? Heart pumping, scared to death, you grab him by the legs and pull him to the ground with you. You roll around for a moment. Hands search. Find his crotch. Squeeze with everything you've got. You feel a ball. Left nut. You squeeze harder. He shrieks. Lashes out—lands two punches to your skull. Hurts like hell. You don't punch back, you know it won't do anything. Instead you roll away from him, grab the hockey stick, and scramble to your feet.

As he rises, you lunge forward with the stick. You're aiming for his chest—but you miss. Instead the splintered wood connects with his throat. He cries out—but his scream is cut short as you twist and push it through his flesh and into his larynx. There's a horrible cracking sound as the wood breaks his windpipe.

You let go of the stick. He falls to the floor, gurgling, blood squirting from his neck. You step back, panting like a dog, trying to catch your breath.

You just killed a man.

You.

Just.

Killed a man.

You're shaking. Weak in the stomach. Takes you a second to start thinking straight.

You go to the bedroom to make sure he was alone. He was. Then you walk back out into the hall. You check the woman's pulse—dead. You stand there, taking in the silence. Trying to wrap your head around everything.

You return to her apartment, doing your best not to look at the dead man on the ground. You search around a bit. Her kitchen is packed. Jesus—did this lady get groceries delivered by the ton or what? She's stocked. Not surprising, though—she was old as hell—couldn't do her own shopping. Probably had some delivery service set up, come once a month. Jackpot, you think. If this zombie thing plays out like the movies, you're going to need food. And there's enough stuff here to live for months, if you're careful.

But first you need to get rid of these bodies.

You stand over the old lady. Don't want to touch her. Like a dead animal in the road. You just want to keep walking.

But you can't. You close your eyes and grab the old lady by the ankles and drag her into her apartment and lock the door behind you.

You take a seat on the old lady's couch. It's covered in that weird heavy plastic, like the couch at your grandmother's place in the assisted living home. Lady has a decent new flat-screen TV and a DVD player that looks like it's never been touched. Two DVDs, still in the packaging, sit on top of the player. *The Sound of Music* and *The Best of Victor Borge*.

You flip on the TV. Every station is zombies.

> *"Unconfirmed reports."*
> *"Only been two hours, but the mayor has already declared a state of emergency."*
> *"Details are sketchy at the moment . . ."*
> *"Religious groups . . ."*
> *"Scientists . . ."*
> *"Scientologists . . ."*
> *"Secure all residences with windows locked and secured . . ."*

You turn the TV right back off.

You open the window and drag the lady over. For an old broad, she's damn heavy. You get her halfway out, then she gets stuck, folded in half, legs and arms sticking out the window straight at you. You step back and assess. You use a broom to poke at her chest, trying to push her through. You give her a good hard whack and hear her rib cage splinter. Shit, sorry lady. One more hard push and she falls through. You climb out onto the fire escape, hoist her up, and toss her over the side. She falls the six stories, then splat.

Nazi's next. You give him a kick in the side, just to let him know one last time that he's a son of a bitch and you don't appreciate him shooting at you. With great effort, you drag him out, get him through, and toss him over the side.

One last look at the bodies in the alley below, then back into the apartment. You lock the window and collapse on the couch. Jesus, and it's not even noon . . .

If you want to do some exploring and see if anyone's still in your building, turn to page 55.

If you want to buckle down and hang tight, turn to page 30.

You rub at your eyes.

Sigh. What's to lose? You take the blunt and inhale deeply, then cough loud, long, and heavy. You may have just left half a lung on the dashboard. Chucky's laughing hysterically, waving a Gatorade bottle.

You try to regain your composure. No luck—more coughing. "Drink, drink," you say, waving your hands at Chucky, feeling like you just crossed the Sahara.

"You want this?" he asks.

You nod, nearly choking. He hands you the Gatorade and you take a long swig—then you just about puke.

Chucky is cackling now. "Vodka, son. It's vodka! Vodka and red Gatorade." Like it's the funniest thing anyone ever said.

There's a fire in your throat. The surprise two shots of vodka did kill the cough in your lungs—but now you want to vomit.

"More?" Chucky says, holding the bottle out.

You wave him off. Lean back. Catch your breath. Sit there for a few minutes, just breathing.

You can't deny it—the weed and liquor has you feeling a bit numb. Good. Less scared.

For the next hour you pass the bottle back and forth, taking long, end-of-the-world swigs. Chucky plays some mixtape—"the hottest shit in the streets right now," he says—and you gently bob your head.

The high you're feeling has you talkative. You bitch about your ex-girlfriend. You bitch about work.

He complains about parking cars and living with his parents. You agree: in general, life pretty much blows.

You avoid the eight-hundred-pound gorilla in the room: the undead army at the gate. Finally, you ask him what the plan is.

"The plan? The plan is to drink."

"The bottle's done."

Chucky grins and gets out of the car, carrying the empty Gatorade bottle. You don't realize how drunk he is until you see him stagger across the lot. He watches the zombies for a few minutes; he's swaying back and forth. You can't help but think Chucky looks oddly similar to those things right now. Then he throws the bottle against the gate. The zombies perk up.

Chucky stumbles to the office, rummages around, then returns with another bottle—this one a full, unopened bottle of Belvedere vodka.

Fuck.

Chucky slides into the seat.

You drink more. Drink to the point where you forget about the zombies. Drink until you can't remember what happened thirty seconds ago.

Drink, drink, drink. Drink until you pass out.

You wake up to the sound of shotgun blasts. You're passed out on the floor of the garage. All the lights are off. It takes a moment for your eyes to adjust—when they do, you wish they hadn't.

The gate is up. Chucky is backed into the front corner of the garage by the gate, fighting for his life. A horde of zombies surrounds him. He fires a shot—the spread sending three of them stumbling back. More step up to take their place. He struggles to load the gun. Shells fall to the ground. He gives up, swings the shotgun wildly. One of the beasts digs into his shoulder. He shrieks. Another goes for his arm. He collapses against the wall, still alive as they begin to feast.

You scramble to your feet. You're drunk still, you realize. But the fear and adrenaline gives you a whole new buzz. You run for the office—your only hope. You turn the corner.

Pain shoots through your leg. One of the things, on the ground, its hands tearing at the flesh on your thigh. It's got you. It's teeth dig into your leg.

You scream. Howl. Collapse onto your back. The thing crawls up over you. You don't even attempt to fight it off. It's over. You know that.

You lie back and let it take you.

·:··: AN END ·:··:·

MAX BRALLIER

THE WAITING IS THE HARDEST PART

The claustrophobia is overwhelming, but you know your best chance of getting where you need to go is to wait for the next train, so you decide to stick it out. And you sure as shit don't feel too jealous watching everyone move from the crowded platform to the just-as-crowded train.

The train is ready to burst—you can almost see it swell. After about a dozen tries the doors shut and the train pulls out.

You take advantage of the momentary breathing room and snake your way to the side of the platform to lean against a graffiti-covered column.

People continue to pour down the stairs. You step forward, careful of the platform's edge, crane your neck, and peer down the dark tunnel. Dark as midnight. You hope to God the 2 or 3 train comes soon.

Suddenly a shriek reverberates through the station. Then another one—a man's heavy, choked cry. You look back. A fight at the top of the stairs. Jesus Christ, what is wrong with people? There's no more fucking room!

And then you see.

Two of them. On the stairs. Looking just like those things on the TV. Zombies.

Your stomach does a roller-coaster flip. Your heart punches at your rib cage—feels like it might break through. With every bone in your body you regret not fighting your way onto the train.

The two things lurch down the stairs. For the first time, you get a good look at the undead monsters. In front are the remains of a hulking Hispanic teenager. One eyeball hangs from its socket, bouncing sickly against his cheek with every awkward step he takes down the stairs. Blood covers an oversized *Scarface* shirt.

Behind it is the second beast: the undead version of a middle-aged woman who is distinctly indistinct. Could be a secretary, librarian, teacher, anything. Only distinguishing feature is the huge, gaping gash in the side of its head and the chunks of flesh and broken skull that mat its short, curly brown hair.

People tumble down the stairs like dominos. Panic sets in all around. Earsplitting screams. You can't see much of anything—just the crowd rushing around you. But you hear. Frightened moans. A child sobbing. A man squealing in agony. Violent, pained howls.

You need a way out. Against the wall are three wooden benches. You make yourself small, low to the ground, and work your way over. Then, carefully, you climb up onto the closest bench. Another man follows your lead—but tumbles down into the crowd below. He sticks his hand up, asking to be pulled up, but you turn away and brace yourself against the wall. You have a full view of the horror now.

The two ghouls continue down the stairs, tearing people limb from limb. Blood splashes the wall. Bodies tumble over the side of the railing.

The horror at the rear of the station has pushed the waiting crowd over the turnstiles and out onto the platform. A young woman screams as the stampeding crowd forces her over the ledge and onto the tracks. A dozen more follow her, crashing onto the dark tracks as the rolling mass pushes forward. It's like a sick, horrific version of the arcade game where you try to push quarters off the ledge by sending more quarters down the chute.

A young boy in a Mets cap, about to be caught up in the rush and carried over the side, grabs on to your sweatshirt.

Frantic, he tugs. You fall off the bench and onto the tiled floor. Feet trample over you. You curl into a ball. A boot slams down onto your face. A loud crack reverberates through your skull and pain shoots through your jaw.

More feet—you're pushed forward across the ground like a mop. You lunge for the leg of the bench, but it's now out of your reach. A woman's high heel lands on your hand and you yank it back—it immediately begins throbbing. Someone kicks your gut. You get pushed back, farther along the floor. You kick your feet and feel nothing but air—horrified, you realize you're next to go over. A huge fat man falls to the floor and another man tumbles over him. You wrap your arms around the fat man's leg. You look up. He's hanging on to the woman behind him. She has her arms wrapped around the bench. You struggle to hang on as bodies continue to rain over you.

BLAM!

BLAM! BLAM!

The hard report of three gunshots echoes off the underground walls.

Normally you'd be scared shitless by the sound of gunshots, but right now you're relieved. Could, *should,* mean help. The crowd thins for a short moment as another row of people falls over you onto the tracks. You grab on to the man's belt and pull yourself up. Then you slip your fingers into his collar, pulling yourself farther. He chokes as you tug, but you don't care—you want away from that goddamn ledge. You continue forward, grabbing on to the woman's leg—then, with everything you have, you pull yourself up.

Slipping your fingers into the slats you manage to get yourself to your feet and then up again onto the bench. You press your back against the cool cement wall. Standing on your toes, you catch a glimpse of a police officer. He's standing in the center of the station, by the ticket booth, firing at the beasts.

Police! Thank God!

You need to lower your center of gravity so you don't get knocked off. You sit down on the far side of the bench, wrapping your legs around the base and holding the seat tightly with your hands. Others crowd in around you, holding on to your shoulders and arms. A woman grabs at your leg, trying to pull herself up. Instinctively, you kick—nailing her square in the face. Grimacing, she falls back to the ground and disappears, swept up in the current of bodies. "Oh, God, I'm so sorry!" you yell, but she's gone. You reach up to wipe your face. Blood pours from a gash over your eye. A huge lump on the back of your head. A sharp pain in your side—cracked rib, you guess.

Two more gunshots.

You pray the cop will handle the ghouls—you just have to worry about not being pulled off the bench and landing on those tracks. To your right, the mob pushes, the beasts behind them. The lone cop, back at the ticket booth, does what he can.

There are more of the monsters now. Five or six. They're multiplying. Looks like each person bit soon joins the ranks of the undead, just like in the movies.

In front of you, a few feet away, are the tracks. Fifty or so people there, scratching and crawling, trying to get back up onto the platform. More tumble on top of them, over them. You grip the bench harder and look away, trying to ignore their calls for help.

Then, over the screams, a sound. A piercing, screeching sound—heavy iron, metal on metal.

A train. God no.

Its headlights flood the awful scene with a bright white light, making the horror on the tracks all the more clear. People climbing over one another, pushing and fighting. Bodies cook on the third rail, kicking, convulsing. You can almost taste the sick smell of burnt hair and what you can only guess is frying skin.

And then you see the boy in the Mets cap. He's down on the

tracks, scrambling to get back up onto the platform. You glance to your left. The cop is overmatched. The ghouls are pressing forward, infecting more people. A dozen of the monsters now.

And down there, the boy—his eyes wide—staring at you.

Gripped by fear, your mind races.

Is the fear too much? Do you hold tight, hope the cop can hold the beasts off, and try to save yourself once the train passes? If so, turn to page 210.

If you've got balls the size of coconuts and you want to risk your life to save the boy, turn to page 96.

TAXI?

You walk to the corner—the sounds of the pulsing city explode around you, loud enough to wake the dead. Car horns blare. A fire truck races by. People rush about. Word is spreading quickly.

You pace back and forth on the corner, arm in the air, checking both sides of the intersection. Traffic is at a standstill. You stare down the long avenue—every cab full. This is going to take forever.

Voices erupt behind you. A crowd has gathered at the corner bar, Finnerty's, an Irish pub you've walked past hundreds of times but never paid any attention to. It's packed to the gills. Outside, people hover at the windows, clamoring for a glimpse of the TV.

Hmm . . . maybe there's some amazing news on TV. Some great update—like maybe the whole thing was some sort of Orson Welles hoax dealie—and you can go home and, y'know, not worry about monsters taking over Manhattan.

If you want to investigate the bar and the hopefully good news on TV, turn to page 39.

If you'd rather wait around and try to get that cab, turn to page 42.

FUN AT THE SUBWAY STATION

Traffic is horrific—it's rush hour times twenty. No way you'll get a cab. The subway, that has to be your best bet. So you kick your feet and begin running.

The streets are buzzing, alive with the spreading news of some bizarre, unknown threat. You were a teen then, still in the burbs—but you imagine this was what the city was like on 9/11. You're separated from the immediate threat by Central Park, but there's a feeling in the air that things might never be the same again.

You catch bits and pieces of conversations as you dart your way through the crowded sidewalk—hopping onto the street to avoid one throng of people, around a car, back onto the sidewalk. You hear the emotion in the people's voices—disbelief, fear, confusion, excitement:

> *"Burn victims, gotta be—"*
> *"Gay kid at American Apparel said dead people were coming back to life . . ."*
> *"Let's get back to Hoboken—"*
> *"Girl said she saw Army trucks on the FDR—"*

Rounding Seventy-third Street onto Broadway you see the mess waiting for you: a thick line of pissed-off New Yorkers stretches up and out of the station.

Fuck.

You catch your breath, wipe the sweat out of your eyes, and get in line. You run your hand through your hair, tap your feet, sigh, anxious. A minute later and thirty people have filed in behind you. You feel slightly better—never good to be the last guy in line.

The metal grates below your feet rumble as a train pulls into the stop—then, after a longer than usual wait, the grates rumble again as it pulls away. The crowd flexes and the line moves some. Fifteen minutes later you've reached the stairs. Another ten and you're halfway down. The stairs stink like garbage, but you're happy to be out of the sun. A lone man, small and bookish, struggles to escape from the station, pushing his way up the stairs, fighting the tide.

You finally reach the bottom. The station is filled to the brim—it's like nothing you've ever seen before. You're no good at ballparking numbers of large groups of people, never have been (at a carnival, as a kid, you once guessed that an average bag of peanut M&Ms contained three hundred M&Ms. When told that was too high, you readjusted your number to seven.) But you guess there are about two hundred people in the area at the bottom of the stairs. Two hundred people, shoulder to shoulder, waiting to swipe their cards, go through the turnstiles, and get out onto the just-as-crowded platform and then board a sardine can of a train.

At the turnstile in front of you a pretty young black woman in a bright yellow, flowered dress is arguing with a business type in front of her, yelling "you stole my swipe!" He ignores her, so she squeezes into the turnstile with him. He turns, roars, and shoves her back into the crowd. No one does a damn thing but mumble.

The sound of an approaching train echoes through the station. People push harder. Little progress is made. Finally, a collective "Fuck this" echoes through the anxious crowd and damn near everyone—a mother and a son, a businesswoman, an elderly Asian man—begins jumping the turnstile, desperate to get on the train. You follow suit, then allow yourself a slight smile and mentally check off "hop turnstile" on the list of things you've wanted to do as a New Yorker.

People continue to pour down the stairs from the street,

continue to force their way in, desperate to escape the city. How many people can this place hold? You can't move forward or back. The crowd keeps coming, pushing, fighting. You wiggle your toes, trying to stay relaxed. But you can feel the claustrophobia building inside you.

You wedge yourself between two strangers, stand on the tips of your toes, and try to grab a peek of the arriving train.

Goddamn it.

It's the 1 train—headed to South Ferry. You need the 2 or the 3 train if you want to get to Brooklyn.

The train slows to a stop. The doors slide open and the crowd pitches forward. You're almost knocked off your feet. Your face smacks into the shoulder of a big guy in a blue hoodie beside you. He jerks, pushes you back. You crash into a woman who screams at the woman next to her like it was her fault. Anger builds. Small shoving matches break out.

You can't breathe. Panic building in your chest. Heat pouring over your body in waves. For the moment, you forget about getting to Brooklyn. Just need to get out. On anything, going anywhere. You don't care if it's a train or a great glass elevator that takes you to the moon—just need to get the hell out of this goddamn madhouse. Then you can collect yourself, calm down, do some thinking, and figure out what the hell to do.

But you're twenty feet from the train car, at least. And you know it'll be a nightmare on there, no better than here on the platform. And the 2 or 3 train to Brooklyn could be just a minute away . . .

If you want to stay put and wait for the train to Brooklyn, turn to page 199.

If you're going to force your way onto that subway car and come up with a plan later, turn to page 8.

Classic rock and a hard place—the rock the United States military machine, and the approaching army of the dead just about the hardest place on earth.

Bullets rip apart a woman one lane over. She jerks as the lead tears through her, then she falls back onto the hood. Uh-uh. I'm not going out like that, you think. You turn and run back for the city. About half the mass does the same. Others continue to press forward, not believing that their own military would fire on them.

Bullets scream past you. Bodies drop.

The zombies are a hundred yards ahead, moving nearly as fast as the thick crowd that runs with you. You're quite literally on a collision course with death.

You cut between two cars and scramble up the hood of an idling taxi. The cabbie, still inside, confused, scared like everyone else, shouts at you. In a second, you're up and over the cab and leaping to the next car. You continue like this—jumping from car to car—making more progress than the rest of them.

But the farther you get from the bullets, the closer you get to those monsters. Everyone knows it. Before anyone has time to think, prepare, or do anything—the army of the dead runs headlong into the running crowd. It's terror. Chaos. Bodies ripped apart. Men throw useless fists.

You continue over the cars. Dead hands swipe at you.

Then, as you leap from the roof of an SUV to an old sedan, it all goes bad. The driver of the SUV hits the gas. Your jump is thrown off—you slip and fall hard onto the concrete. You land right in the middle of a pack of zombies. You rush to your feet, try desperately to get onto the hood of the sedan.

Something pulls at your shirt. You swipe at it, feel the cold, dead arm of one of the beasts. It's an awful-looking thing—a homeless man, at one point, before he joined the ranks of the dead. Another one grabs at you. A young kid. And then another. You tug, pull, fight with everything you've got. But there's nowhere to go. You're surrounded.

Teeth dig into your skin. Pain in your shoulder. Your back. Everywhere. The kid claws at your thigh, tearing the flesh open.

You're dead. You're done for. You know it. You pray for shock to set in. Beg for God to end it.

But it never happens. Instead you feel heat all over you—a burning inside, pumping through your blood.

You swat at the beasts. They back off.

You can feel your mind going. Thoughts and emotions disappearing. You try to grab them, hang on. Things go in chunks—your name, your identity.

You have no idea how much just time has past. You're left with just the hunger. Simple, dumb bloodlust.

Something moves out of the corner of your eye. Smells good. Fresh. Your body goes that way.

AN END

Your fear of the beasts is paralyzing. As the crowd continues to push and the zombies continue to feast, you slip your hands deeper into the wooden slats of the bench.

The train roars, just seconds away.

The zombies tear through the crowd. You don't see the cop anymore. Bodies lie bruised, battered, and bloodied across the station. Limbs strewn about like yesterday's garbage.

You see that a few lucky people are able to roll underneath an overhanging section of the platform to avoid the train. Others run for the opposite side of the tracks—some successful, some not. The nots fry on the third rail.

The boy in the Mets cap stands frozen in the middle of the tracks. You give him one last look and close your eyes.

VSHOOOM!!!

The train never even slows down. Roars past, fades down the tunnel.

You don't want to, but you look. The track below you is sickening. In its wake the train has left a grisly mass grave. The tracks are slick and crimson.

The beasts have managed to negotiate the turnstiles. They'll be upon you in seconds.

You need to leave. *Now*. Onto the tracks it is, before the next train comes. You pull your hand from the bench and—

No . . .

You tug.

God no. No, no, no.

Your hand is stuck.

C'mon!

The lower knuckle on your middle finger refuses to come free—the bench like a ring that won't come off.

The ghouls approach. Five, six, maybe more. They're rising up all around you.

You push your leg against the bench and pull with everything you got.

Nothing.

The beasts come closer. You pull harder—fuck it, right now you'll lose the finger if you have to. Just want loose.

The beasts surround you. Grab at you. You squeeze your eyes shut.

You're not a religious man, but . . .

"Hail Mary, full of grace—"

· ·✦· AN END ·✦· · ·

Wall Street slides the two crisp hundred-dollar bills across the bar and tells the bartender to bring everyone a shot of tequila. Judging by the look on her face, the bartender finds this guy to be just about as charming as you do—but she takes the money. She pulls a bottle of Two Fingers tequila from beneath the bar.

"No, no—c'mon, what do I look like here? Top shelf," Wall Street says.

She shoots you a look. You smile and shrug—get a nice little warm feeling inside, goes well with the rising hell outside.

She grabs a bottle of Patrón Silver from high up on the shelf behind her, asks Wall Street if it's good enough for him, then makes her way down the bar, pouring the liquor. The drunks are quite pleased. They take their shots and knock 'em back. Some turn their attention back to the TV, others stare ahead, a few trade war stories.

You take yours. It burns. You want a lime wedge but are too afraid to ask for one. When was the last time you took a shot at noon? Well, actually, not all that long ago.

"Anthony?" the cute bartender says to the bouncer, nodding to the bottle. He lets out a low rumble that could, technically, be considered a sigh. Strides over to the bar.

"Why not," he says.

She smiles. "That's my guy."

She pours a shot for herself and a shot for him. You watch, not hiding your interest. "You?" she says, looking you in the eyes.

You stumble. "Huh?"

"Another, jackass? You want another?"

"Oh, sure, yeah."

She pours you a second shot.

"Me too, hon," Wall Street says, leaning over you, trying to push you out of the picture. You put your elbows on the bar and edge forward.

She pours him one.

"To the apocalypse," he says and takes his shot. You, the bartender, and the bouncer wait—then take yours a beat later, leaving him to drink alone. He's too caught up in himself to notice.

The liquor burns a hole in your gut. You bring your gaze back up to the TV.

The images on the television are horrific. And these are all places you know. Places you've been. And it's pure carnage. War. Police fighting, firing, sometimes seeming to win the battle, other times being overwhelmed.

The drunk to your left, huge guy, comb-over, gasps as the broadcast cuts to a horde of the beasts outside the big Gristedes supermarket on Eighty-third. "Fuck me, that's six blocks from here . . ."

You hear the chopping sound of a helicopter overhead—the same helicopter broadcasting on the TV, you realize. Yes, these things are close.

A woman's scream cuts through the air. From the street. The bouncer, Anthony, darts outside, moving quick for a big man. A minute later he returns and slams the door behind him.

"Hey, what are you—" someone says.

"Shut up," he says. "Listen! Those things are outside and they're headed this way. Anyone wants out, go now, 'cause I'm locking it up."

Before anyone answers, there's a banging noise at the door behind him. Anthony throws his back against it. Even if you wanted to leave now, you couldn't. A wall of people has gathered outside, pounding the door, screaming to be let inside.

You watch Anthony intently. He breathes heavily in and out, appears to be thinking hard. Finally, he takes his weight off the door and it flies open, sending half a dozen people spilling inside. Immediately others in the street rush for the door and the safety of the bar.

Anthony slams the door shut in the face of twenty screaming, begging voices. One, an elderly woman, pleading. He throws all his weight into the door, shuts his eyes, and pushes.

"Let them inside!" a woman behind you cries. More people gather at the window outside, tugging on the bars that cover it.

But there's no time—the creatures are now upon them. Devouring them. Teeth ripping through flesh. Hands pulling and tearing.

A drunk behind you drops his glass.

You want to move. Do something. Anything. But you don't—you just watch.

One poor bastard's face is pressed against the door's rectangular, microwave-sized window. He and Anthony make eye contact—the man beseeching him to help. Then the glass gives and the man's upper half bursts through. Shards of glass tear him to pieces. Shredded skin hangs from his face and arms. He whimpers. Then, after a long, horrific moment, he goes silent.

Anthony steps away from the door and brings his arm crashing down upon the hinged wooden divider that keeps the drunks from going behind the bar and pouring their own whiskey sours. It splinters at the hinges. He twists it off.

"Rachel, behind the bar, the toolbox!" he shouts. The pretty bartender, Rachel apparently, does as she is told. Most everyone else has moved to the back of the bar. You remain frozen in the middle.

Anthony throws his shoulder into the door and wedges his foot against the corner of the bar. The door shakes, but it holds. More creatures come. Dead hands reach through the window. One grabs his arm, tears the flesh. Anthony howls. The door bucks and bends. It won't hold for long.

He picks up the two-inch-thick piece of wood, grabs a hammer and some nails from the toolbox, and turns to work on the door.

Blocking his progress is the chunk of messy gore that was once a man. Anthony grabs the dead man by the hair, lifts him up by the head, and tries to push him back onto the sidewalk.

Suddenly the dead man's face jerks to life. His eyes light up like headlights in a graveyard. Anthony jumps back as the man, his head and shoulders trapped in the tight frame of the window, snaps his teeth. His veins pop. His eyes bulge. The blood stops dripping—it turns a dark reddish black.

It's a horrific scene. This snapping, bloodthirsty face the centerpiece—an entire street full of undead beasts the backdrop.

Anthony brings the hammer down hard upon the thing's head. No beauty to it, no precision, just heavy whacks to the thing's skull. Blow after blow after blow. Chunks of skin and skull and brain splash the wall and the floor. The head bobs, wounded, broken. Anthony raises the hammer high, pauses, then brings it down with all his might. The thing's skull shatters and it goes limp.

Anthony twirls the hammer in his hand, hooks the dead thing's nostrils with the nail claw, and lifts it up and out of the window. But there's no rest. Behind it, more of the walking dead approach.

Quickly, Anthony throws up the wood, puts two nails into the top, and begins hammering. After a few more nails, the small window is covered. But the door continues to throb and creak as the beasts press.

"Someone, get over here!" he shouts. "This ain't gonna hold for long!"

No one moves. No one says a fucking thing. Inside the bar,

all is quiet, except for the howl of Merle Haggard on the juke-box.

Anthony points at you with the hammer. "Now!"

Man up and help the bouncer barricade the door? Turn to page 141.

Run for the bathroom, lock yourself in, and pray to God that everything will be OK? Turn to page 48.

Last time you fired a gun was at overnight camp in eighth grade. Last time you drove a car was Thanksgiving, at your folks' house. You'll go with the years.

"I'll drive," you say.

Chucky tosses you the keys. You don't catch them cleanly and they clatter on the floor. Good start.

You climb into the driver's seat of the old GMC. It's a ragged old bench seat, cigarette burns and tears patched up with about ten pounds of duct tape. It's a vehicle with personality—a veteran. It's been around, you think, but it's never been on a ride like this next one.

Chucky hops into the bed of the truck and parks himself just behind the GMC's glass partition. He slides the window open, puts his elbows on the metal, and rests his head in his open hands.

"Now what?" you ask him.

"We wait for that chain to snap. If we're lucky, it never does."

"Yeah—and we just starve to death in here."

"Don't worry. I got Pringles in the office."

The mechanical *clank, clank, clank* of the struggling gate echoes through the garage, along with the moans of the hungry hoard that waits beyond it.

You fiddle with the radio but get nothing.

The little bike lock's time is almost up, you think. The clanging is growing louder and you can see the metal straining. The moans of the beasts grow louder with it, like they know what's coming. The sound sends shivers down your spine. You look at your hands on the wheel—they're shaking.

"Hey, Chucky—you got any more of that booze?" you say, not turning around, just staring at the opposition. The Gatorade bottle appears suddenly in your field of vision. You grab it. Four heavy swigs. Need all the courage you can get.

"And a cigarette," you tell him. He hands you one.

You turn the key in the ignition. The truck jumps to life. It's loud, shakes and shudders beneath you. Not a healthy automobile. You pat the dashboard like you're trying to calm a spooked horse.

You light your cigarette. Watch the chain. Focus in on it. Any moment now . . .

It snaps. The gate begins its climb. You smoke the butt, trying to enjoy every last minute before the gate rises.

You pull a large knob to your right and the headlights flash on. They flood the garage, and for the first time you can clearly see what it is you're up against. A hundred of the things, at least. A thick mass of the undead, blocking the garage's only exit.

Twisted, disfigured faces. Skin bubbling. Women in summer dresses, their strappy sandals long discarded. Kids in overalls and cute little dresses. Men in business suits. Some torn and ripped, some still ironed and pressed from this morning—a morning that now feels like it was a lifetime ago.

You pump the gas and the engine growls. You'd hoped it might scare them off. It didn't.

The gate lifts up and passes over the zombies' heads. They begin marching forward.

A large lever sticks up from behind the gearshift. You jerk it down, then to the right. With a loud mechanical churning sound, the truck's plow lowers to the ground. A few seconds later it settles against the cement.

You glance in the rearview mirror. Chucky raises the shotgun and nods.

You nod back and flick the cigarette out the window. Hands tight on the wheel. Looking straight ahead.

You hit the gas.

They charge.

There are fifty or sixty feet between you and the cavalcade of walking dead. Just enough time to pick up speed. You bear down, knuckles white on the wheel, and brace yourself as they close in.

The plow pushes through the first wave, knocking them aside like stray cows caught on an Old West train track. Some get scooped up. Others spun aside.

They shriek and howl. You're hurting them, you think. But then you realize the cries are not coming from the ones you're killing. It's the others. It's a battle cry.

You give it more gas. Bodies crunch beneath the wheels. The truck keeps moving.

You keep on the gas. Resistance. You push harder, but the truck continues to slow. Finally, the horde becomes too much for the plow. Bodies slip underneath. The wheels spin in place, turning on a pile of fleshy death.

The stopped truck makes an easy target now. One beast—an Asian teenager in a private school uniform—climbs up the side of the truck. She scratches and claws at the window. More climb onto the hood.

You pump the gas. Nothing. Hydroplaning on a bloody mess of guts and gore.

A gunshot explodes behind you. Then another. Your eyes dart up to the rearview. The beasts are scaling the back and Chucky is doing everything he can to keep them at bay.

Fuck—this ain't working.

You take your foot off the gas. The truck settles, then begins rocking and swaying on the hill of bodies.

You drop it into neutral and floor it, the engine roaring—then, after a long moment, with beasts climbing all over the truck, you drop it back into second.

It works. The truck jerks forward over the hill of bodies. The beasts clinging to the hood drop to the ground. More shotgun blasts—Chucky does his job.

The plow sweeps the next batch of beasts off their feet and you're able to steer the truck out of the garage, up the ramp, and out onto the street.

The Chambers Street you're on now is a world away from the one you escaped hours ago. The beasts are scattered in bunches. Small groups.

But the people—normal, living, everyday people—are gone. Their cars are still there. Mostly empty. Some with shattered windows, filled with living-dead drivers and passengers, now rendered too stupid to work the seat belt or door so they can leave.

A young woman on Rollerblades, her shirt ripped, face torn, rolls around. Struggles to stand—then her foot goes out from under. Turning into a zombie with a pair of Rollerblades strapped to your feet is clearly not the way to do it.

The sound of horrific carnage is gone—but the city is not quite silent. Car alarms and gunshots float over from blocks away. It's like standing outside Yankee Stadium halfway through a game—you can hear it, know something big is happening, but you're not quite a part of it.

You turn to Chucky. "You alright?"

"I'm good," he says as he reloads the shotgun.

"Good. Where to?"

"Brooklyn's out of the question. Bridge is fucked. Just head south to the bottom of the island. We'll find a way out."

"Sounds like a plan," you say, and hit the gas.

Turn to page 300.

Al and Fish sprint for the hole. You follow, sliding your way down the sandy side.

And then you're falling.

You land in a stream of disgusting water. Something lands on top of you, knocks the wind out of you. You gasp for air, but you're forced underwater. It's a body. A fucking zombie, on top of you. It thrashes in the water. You try to raise your head, but can't.

And then it's gone.

You scramble to your feet. Al has the thing. He throws it into the water, lifts his heavy work boot up, and brings it crashing down, shattering the thing's entire face against the sewer floor.

The four of you begin running.

The sewer is narrow—a dimly lit catacomb. You have to crouch to avoid hitting your head. Standing in the middle of the rounded tunnel, you could reach out and touch both sides of it at the same time.

Splash after splash behind you as the zombies hit the water. You turn and look. A dozen in the sewer already. More coming every second. They hit the water, lift their heads, and then they take off after you.

You run, splashing through the knee-deep liquid, Al, Fish, and Sully in front of you. The tunnel glows with an eerie yellow light. Water drips from cracks in the ceilings.

"Catch!" Al says.

Huh?

Al's Zippo flies through the air. You leap, grab it with one hand, and keep running.

"What's this for?" you shout, your words echoing.

"Whaddya think?"

Al comes to a halt and spins, holding a stick of dynamite. "Light!"

Your thumb, shaking, flicks at the flint-wheel ignition. On the fourth try it lights. Al holds the fuse over the flame. It catches, sparking.

The beasts are bearing down on you, splashing.

Al throws it as far as he can, straight at the one in front. It spins through the air, end over end. Then, in midair—

KRAKA-BOOM!!!

You watch as the lead zombie's chest shatters like glass and the thing's blown apart into a hundred pieces. The rest are blown back, some against the wall, others sent spiraling back into the water.

Near silence, for a moment, then the steady sound of dripping water.

And the moans.

Drip.

Plunk.

And the horrid sound of the undead. And the rough, haggard breathing of Al.

And then—a crack, a sound like skates on ice too thin.

The roof gives away, raining down heavy chunks of concrete upon the teeming horde of undead.

And then a low hum. Then louder. An echo.

Rushing water.

You can see it through the rubble—the tunnel turning back as the shadow of the tsunami approaches.

"Oh shit," Al says.

"What did you do?" Fish says, scared.

"May have blown the main line."

The tidal wave comes roaring around the corner, filling the

entire sewer. It hits the beasts, then the pile of concrete, and sweeps everything all away.

You're next.

The wave punches you in the chest. You're lost, tumbling through freezing wet darkness. Your knee bangs against cement—the top, bottom, side of the sewer, you don't know.

Through the green-black water, you see arms and legs. You hit the surface for a moment. An inch, maybe two between the water and the ceiling. Grab a mouthful of air. Then something at your feet, fingers around your ankle. Pulls you back down into the dark water.

You kick free. Feel your foot kick some sort of flesh.

Through the darkness, you can see Fish. He tumbles beside you, carried along with you. He reaches out—fear in his face. Then you turn a corner and he's thrown into the sewer wall, blood bursting from his shattered face.

Your head bursts through the water again. Grab air. And inhale water—shitty, pissy water. You vomit, lift your head to breathe in air, but only take in more water. Your hands claw at the ceiling. Find a brick. Get your finger in. You hang on—the water rushing below you, through your legs, and around your body. Your fingers bleed. Then your nails snap, rip off, and you're back under.

You see Al. His mouth is wide open. Blood pours from his throat. Undead. More monsters floating around him. You can't win. They won't drown. They'll never drown. They'll never lose like this.

Sully—you see a flash of his eyes, then he disappears, gone.

You surface again, smack your head against the brick, then go back under. You see something ahead of you. A hole. Some sort of pipe.

Then a stop. Sudden. Your shoulder blades shatter. Wedged in a hole.

You can't move—completely trapped in the water-filled pipe. Your shoulders are stuck. Something hits your feet.

Zombie. And another one. You're a fucking clog in the drain.

The sounds go first. You hear nothing. Just your own screaming inside your head.

Feels like a massive pair of hands around your neck, choking the life out of you.

Tears mix with sewer water.

And then you choke out, inhale water, and it's done.

AN END

Against your better judgment, you answer the phone.

"Hello?"

It's like the dam broke—out pours a torrent of *ohmygods whereareyous* and *areyouokays.*

Should have had that beer.

"Mom, relax. I'm OK."

Relax isn't in your mom's vocab—it disappeared the day you were born.

Your folks live outside Boston, so you don't have to worry about them ever popping in. Though they'd love to, surely. They'd be Kramer to your Seinfeld if geography allowed them.

"I'm at home, Mom."

Momtalkmomtalkmomtalk

"Yes, of course I saw the news."

Momtalkmomtalkmomtalk

"Yes, Mom, I have a flashlight."

Momtalkmomtalkmomtalk

"Mom!" you finally shout. "You—need—to—relax."

She tells you to take the ferry to your aunt Judy's house in Staten Island.

"Why? Why should I do that?"

She tells you it will be safe. She wants you to be safe.

"Mom—I'm safe here."

She tells you she'll send you a check for five hundred dollars if you go. OK, done. You hang up, grab your old backpack, same one you used to smuggle beers up to your dorm room a few years back, and fill it with the essentials—some clothes, Nintendo DS, a few issues of *Hustler*—and you hit the road.

The Staten Island ferry departs from South Ferry Station at Battery Park, the southernmost tip of Manhattan. You're about fifty blocks north. With no other choice, you begin running. Around you it's like an unofficial city marathon—full of a bunch of out-of-shape guys sweating through their work clothes and women regretting their shoe choice of the day.

The streets are crazy in all directions. Gridlock. Cars don't move. The sidewalks are jam-packed, so you work your way through the cars. You hear little pieces of news—that the zombies are uptown, on the West Side, in Brooklyn. Christ, who knows what the hell to believe?

You pass a police station. It's surrounded—people bang on the windows, yelling for protection, demanding to be let inside. Half a dozen cops stand out front, trying to keep order. Pushing. Shoving. Then a gunshot. People scatter. Some charge. A riot begins. You pick up the pace.

Farther on, a man bursts out of P.C. Richard carrying a DVD player. No one chases him. Three men beat another man mercilessly on a crowded street corner. No police around to stop it.

Twenty minutes later, seeing stars, jagged pain in your side, feet sore as all hell, you finally see South Ferry Station in the distance. A throng of thousands greets you. You push your way into the crowd.

Hours pass. You stand in the stinking heat. Miserable. Any longer, and you're going to collapse.

A Staten Island girl in a Wagner College tank top bitches about the heat. "It is *so* gross out here," she says. "I swear to *God* if that ferry doesn't get here *like now* I'm going to scream."

Her boyfriend, tall, 'roided out, and fake-tanned, tells her to "be cool, slut."

You can only shake your head.

Word starts to make it down the line. One of the ferries is stopped about two hundred yards out—right in the middle of the water. You press to the edge, along the waterline, where you can see. Yep—ferry, just sitting there.

A lightbulb goes off in your head. You inch your way through the park to the twenty-five-cent binocular viewers—the type that tourists drop a quarter in to get a sixty-second look at the Statue of Liberty. A few others follow your lead.

You fish a quarter from your pocket and drop it inside. Bend over, put your eyes to it. You spot the Statue of Liberty first—it takes you a moment to locate the ferry. There's all sorts of movement on the upper level. A fight. Then someone jumps—they don't quite make it—the body hits the lower-level railing and tumbles violently into the water. Another person jumps—this one makes it. Then more. The entire lower level. Dozens of bodies leaping into New York Harbor.

"Holeee shit."

Panicked gasps and ohmygods echo among the others looking through the viewers. Someone pushes you aside to get a look.

By now you can see the survivors with your naked eye. They swim furiously, headed for Battery Park and the ferry dock. They arrive in minutes. A man crawls up on the shore, bloodied and half dead. A group runs to help him. Bad idea. A scream erupts from the center of the group. A woman spins away, clutching her shoulders.

More screams from across the park and inside the dock. The crowd goes mad as more and more of the things make it to shore and start to attack.

You run for it. You make it a block. Fuck. More of them. The beasts are everywhere—goddamn it—how do they multiply so fast?!

Up ahead is a large warehouse, one of many. There are two trucks out front. A huge image of a cow with bright red smiling lips is painted on a perimeter gate. You sprint for the gate. Open, thank God. You enter, catch your breath, and make for the first open garage door.

It's open about two feet. You drop and roll underneath. Pitch black. You slap around at the wall next to the door. Feel around. Light switch. You hit it.

Shit!

Zombies. A hundred dead faces fill the warehouse. You let loose a bloodcurdling scream, squeeze your eyes shut, and prepare to die.

"Hey dude—chill—it's OK."

Huh?

You crack open one eye. One of the zombies is walking over to you. "We're not real zombies."

"Huh?" you squeak out. You look around the warehouse.

"Supposed to have a Zombie Walk today," the guy says as he shuts the gate.

"What?"

"Zombie Walk. Y'know, a zombie parade. We dress up like zombies and do, you know, the classic zombie shuffle. We start here, in Battery Park, and go to Midtown. It's a whole-day event. We do it to raise awareness."

"Awareness for what?"

"Zombies."

"Buddy—I think people are aware."

Most of the zombie walker folks sit along the wall on boxes and crates, eyes on a big fat guy talking up front, who looks a lot like the late, not-so-great president William Howard Taft.

It's a meatpacking warehouse. Main floor is near empty—besides the boxes and crates and zombies, just a few pallets. You take a seat and listen. The one you first met—clearly the leader—addresses the crowd. You take notice of his awful, fake-blood-splattered khaki shirt.

"It's getting worse, guys. Police presence has dwindled to nothing. The military seems to have pulled out of the city, from what we can tell. Obviously today's Zombie Walk isn't going to happen, but I'm glad we're all together for this epic experience."

Taft picks up the discussion: "Now what we're dealing with here appears to be some sort of mash-up of the classic Romero zombie and the more modern Rage virus zombie.

"As we all saw—these zombies just sort of walk around. Very slowly. Dumb. Classic Hollywood zombie. But when something gets their attention—they can run like the wind. Rage-zombie style."

"Looks like we're on our way to a classic Stage Three outbreak," Khaki says.

You speak up. "Classic Stage Three outbreak? What the hell is that?"

Taft takes over. "Yes. Stage Three can spread to Stage Four quickly. At Stage Four—well, then you're just one stage away from the end of the world. Like *A Boy and His Dog*. With zombies."

Then there's Four-Eyes, looks like Elvis Costello with a bad chin strap.

Elvis speaks. "We do have one advantage over the rest of these idiot Manhattanites."

You lean forward, deadly serious. "What's wrong with Manhattan?"

"Don't make me laugh."

"No, really."

"You waste all that rent money to live in a shoe box. What are you paying for?"

"I don't know. How about convenience? Living in the greatest city in the world. Where do you live?"

"Brooklyn," he says, leaning back and crossing his arms defiantly.

Khaki calls order. "Alright, guys. Brooklyn versus Manhattan. What killed the dinosaurs. These are questions that can be debated forever. Now isn't the time. You were saying?"

"I was saying we have one advantage over the rest of these—unprepareds," Elvis says, looking right at you. "We look like the zombies."

"You thinking what I'm thinking?" Taft says.

Then the three of them, together, big grins: *"Shaun of the Dead."*

"What that's now?"

"Hello? *Shaun of the Dead.* 2004. Simon Pegg, Nick Frost. Directed by Edgar Wright. Classic zom-com."

"But where to?" Khaki says. "What's safe?"

You've got it. You were just staring at it. "Statue of Liberty."

They exchange glances.

"He has a good point," Taft says. "In John Carpenter's *Escape From New York,* Liberty Island served as a base of operations for the military. We could use it in much the same way."

"Can zombies cross water?" someone in the crowd pipes up.

You interject. "I um, I just saw them swimming—but I mean I don't know if they were full zombies, or y'know, in transition or whatever."

Taft shoots you a look that says you're invading his zombie knowledge territory. "Well," he says, "the water issue depends on who you ask. In George Romero's *Land of the Dead,* they do cross the water—finally infiltrating Fiddler's Green. And in Lucio Fulci's *Zombie,* also known as *Zombi 2,* there's the classic zombie-versus-shark scene."

"But won't they smell us? You know, smell that we're different, when we're out there?" someone else calls out.

"Depends. Some zombie fiction, yes; some no."

"Wait—isn't this a meat storage warehouse?" you ask.

"Yeah."

"So—you get some meat. Rub it on yourself. It'll hide the smell."

They argue. Buncha dorks. They're insufferable. You stand up and go to explore on your own—can't stand much more of these guys.

In the back is a heavy metal door that leads to the freezer area.

Huge slabs of meat hang on hooks. Thick sides of beef. Jackpot. You walk back out to the group.

"Guys—if we want to go out there or not—having the meat can't hurt. So how about you quit arguing and you help?"

They shut up. Think for a second, then a few get up and follow you to the freezer. You're feeling pretty good—you came into this situation and took charge. Not common for you.

Five of you work together, lifting the slab of meat up off the hook. It hits the floor with a thud. You try to push it. Too cold. You leave the freezer, take off your shoes, put your socks on your hands, and put your shoes back on. They do the same. Together, some pushing, some pulling, you get the beef out onto the floor.

It takes nearly three full days for the meat to thaw. You and the others sleep as much as you can. When you don't sleep, you discuss the plan. Diagram the walk. You're just three blocks from the harbor—you'll drench yourselves in cow guts, shuffle over there, drawing as little attention as possible, then jump straight into the harbor and swim your asses off.

The whole time—as you talk, as you discuss the plan—you hear the moans of the beasts outside.

Finally, the meat has thawed enough that it's usable. Khaki calls everyone together.

"Alright," he tells everyone. "Wash up."

You stab your hand into the cold side of the cow. Pull an ice-cold chunk from the animal's meaty underside. You hold the fleshy pile in your hand and stare at it. Is this really what it's come to? Ahh, the twists and turns of life . . .

You wash your body with the meat, rubbing it over your face, neck, and arms. And then over your clothes. You stick a few hunks in your pocket. Can't hurt.

When you've finished lathering in beef, you try to rip your shirt for the visual effect. Man, Hulk Hogan made it look easy. After a minute, you get your collar to split. Guess that's all you'll get.

You look around at everyone rubbing chunks of dead cow over themselves. Christ, this is the most ridiculous plan ever. Are you really going to go through with this?

Hell no. You'll take your chances waiting for rescue. Turn to page 258.

New and improved Zombie Walk it is. Turn to page 290.

The Angels stare at you. The Colonel's look is penetrating.

You cough, then start. "It seems to me you've got a lot to risk here. And for what? You're a bunch of halfway outlaws anyways. What do you want that the government can give you? Privacy? You already got it. Money? Everyone here is doing OK."

The Colonel glares. "I don't think you're in any position to—"

"Hey, GI Joe—back off," Jones says. "He's with us, for now."

Wow. Have cooler words ever been spoken? The leader of the NYC Hells Angels chapter just told a United States colonel to back off, because you're with them. *You're with them.*

Whatever got you this far, you must be doing something right.

"Like I was saying," you continue, "I don't really see what they can offer that you haven't already got. So why stick your neck out?"

The Colonel steps forward. "How about this for an answer— because if you don't, I'll send a smart bomb straight up your asshole and turn this cute little clubhouse here into a smoking hole in the ground."

Jones is out of his chair in the Colonel's face in two seconds flat. "I was leaning toward yes," he says, "but now you can go fuck yourself. You want a war with the Hells Angels? Don't think you do—that's a war you ain't gonna win, boss. Not even the fucking Army. So why don't you get the fuck out the way you came?"

The Colonel glares at Jones, then abruptly spins on his heels and leaves.

Everyone looks at you. You look at the floor, not sure what to say.

"Fuck 'em all," Jones says.

Even the ones who wanted to go for it can agree with that statement.

Thankfully, the Colonel's threats never come true. You spend the next six months holed up in the club, making occasional runs for food and booze. On one run, you split one of the creatures in half with a chainsaw—a half second before it has a chance to get at Limpy. You're a hero.

Louis ODs on heroin about a month after that. Jones pulls you aside, tells you can have his room. You thank him. For the first time in months, you get to sleep in a real bed, and it's fantastic—even though Louis died in it.

The sleep is great—the waking up part, not as much. Something wet on your face. Water? No. Whiskey is standing over you, pissing on you. He raises his pecker, pissing in your face.

"What the fuck!" you scream, coughing, rolling out of the bed onto the floor and spitting out piss.

Whiskey laughs riotously as Tommy pulls you to your feet and knees you in the balls. You buckle over. Then he throws a vicious right hook, dropping you to the floor.

"What did I do?" you say, tears coming to your eyes.

Tommy grabs you, piss dripping from your face, and drags you out into the hall. He gives you a kick in the face that sends you down the stairs. Something cracks. Finger. Broken.

You hit the floor at the bottom of the stairs. You're seeing stars.

Then you look up. Jones is standing over you, smiling. He

holds a leather vest, full Hells Angels patch on the back. He drops it on you. Smiles.

"Welcome to the Hells Angels, kid," he says.

AN END

You rush back to Mrs. Henderson's room. The kids are at the windows, looking outside.

"Hey, knock it off—get in your seats. Don't look out there. Now tell me—is there a janitor's closet or something like that around here?"

"Yes but it's locked," the know-it-all girl says. "Billy can open it—he got suspended for breaking in."

Someone—Billy, you assume—tells the know-it-all to shut up.

"Billy, show me that closet."

He leads you down the hall. You forgot how cute elementary schools were. Charming little lockers. Drawings pinned to the walls.

He leads you to the closet.

"Damn, how'd you get into this thing?"

Billy crosses his arms.

"Tell me."

"Twenty bucks."

"Twenty bucks! You know what I pay each month in rent?"

Billy doesn't say a damn thing. You reach into your rear pocket, thumb through your wallet. "Little bastard, here."

He takes the twenty dollars, runs down the hall, opens his locker, and runs back. He sticks his hand out, grinning. "I copied the key," he says proudly.

Hmm. Badass. You open the door, step inside, and begin rooting through the closet. "Man, I can't find a damn—Billy, come here."

Silence.

"Billy?"

You poke your head out.

Billy's on the floor, shaking, a little monster girl on top of him.

"Fuck!"

Frantically, you search through the closet for anything of use. A roll of paper towels. You chuck it at the girl—it bounces off. Billy's screaming, fighting with everything he's got. You root through the janitor's closet. More crap. Cleaning supplies. Pile of rags.

In the back, a mop, still attached to the bucket. You grab it. The girl's about to go in for the kill. You whip the mop and bucket around like a giant hammer and smash it against the thing's head. The plastic cracks. Soapy water covers everything.

The thing rears back, stunned. Then charges at you. You swing again, into the thing's legs, sweeping it off the ground.

"Fuck me—if anyone up there is watching me now, I'm sorry."

You put your foot on the undead girl's throat, pinning it to the ground. Then you snap the mop over your knee and slam the splintered wood down through the undead girl's eye.

"Billy, you OK?"

He gets up.

"You bit anywhere? You bleeding?" you ask.

Poor kid's scared to death. But he shakes his head no. You give him a good once-over. He's OK. *Phew.* You order him back to his classroom and he goes, happy as hell to be away from his dead classmate lying on the floor.

In the very back of the closet you find what you were hoping for—a Weed Whacker. Battery powered. You rip the plastic cover off the blade, turning it into a giant circular saw on a stick. You rev it up. Give it a squeeze. The blade spins. Yeah, this should do.

You return to the gym. The zombie kids, along with a few zombie teachers, continue to attack the trailer. The door is coming off at the hinges.

OK—if you're going to do this, you have to do it now.

Oh, Lord. It's gonna take a lot of Hail Marys to shed this one. This isn't a prostitute-in-Amsterdam-during-spring-break type sin. Nope—this is a decapitating-little-kids sin.

No time to think about it.

You kick open the double doors. Rev the whacker to get the zombies' attention.

As soon as you see the kids, you don't feel bad—just fear. Twisted faces. Gray-green skin. Scary as all hell.

Stay strong, you tell yourself.

"Alright, kids—let's dance."

Half of them leave the trailer and head straight for you. One out in front, a little athletic kid, leads the pack.

As if in slow motion, you raise the weapon up, taking off the top of its head. Spin around, swing it, split the face of the next. Chop off the next at the legs. Dance your way through the moaning crowd, blood spraying with every wave of the weapon.

They've pried the door open. You have to move. You approach the trailer, a heap of bodies in your wake. Raise the Weed Whacker high and bring it down on the head of a kid who's about to slip inside the trailer door.

You whip it around, clearing away any others that are around you. Their chests slice open and they fall back.

Two loud honks. Praise the Lord. A school bus—just outside the gate.

"Let's go!" the driver shouts.

You rip open the door. Students and teachers are huddled as far away from the door as possible, scared. They look at you with horror. You realize you're still holding down the trigger to the Weed Whacker and it's spraying blood and gore all over the place. You let go and it whirs to a stop. "Sorry . . ."

You don't get the hero's welcome you were hoping for.

"C'mon—there's a bus outside, we have to go. I'll be right behind you."

They run for it. You stay beside them, swinging the Weed Whacker and keeping the little bastards at bay.

They all scramble aboard the bus—you get on last. "Alright, we're out of here," the driver says.

"Where to?" you say.

"North."

"What's north?"

"I don't know—but it's away from here."

"OK—one sec though—gotta get the other kids."

"Huh?"

"Gotta pick up Mrs. Henderson's class."

"What?"

"Hang tight—three minutes."

You rush back inside the school. The kids are in their class, staring out the windows, just like you told them not to. "C'mon, we're going, now."

"Where?"

"North."

"What's north?"

"Ice cream."

They chase you down the hall and out into the bloody schoolyard. They shriek as they see the dismembered bodies of a hundred of their classmates. You tell them not to look, just get to the bus.

You pull out your cell phone, hand it to one of them. "Kids, call your parents."

Then you turn to the driver. "Alright, let's roll."

·:·✦ AN END ·✦·:·

You take the pool cue from the table, slip it into your belt, and grab the *Big Buck Hunter* gun.

You stand at the door to the hallway. You can hear the things beyond it. "OK," Anthony says, "if your little idea about the toy gun is right—then that's a big help. So you're going first."

Anthony unlocks the door.

You let out a long, slow breath of air. For a moment you feel brave—like you've got it all under control. You know that moment and that feeling won't last, so you have to ride the wave while you can.

With everything you've got, you kick open the door. It hits one of the zombies, sending it stumbling back.

You raise the gun and cock it—then you remember it's fake, and cocking it is ridiculous. But you keep it raised—stick it right in the face of the first zombie.

Annnnd . . . it doesn't do a damn thing. You could be pointing a feather duster for all it cares.

It lunges at you. You grab the Buck Hunter gun with both hands and block its attack. It pushes you back and crashes to the ground on top of you, lashing away with vicious teeth. Fear pumps through you. Behind it, you see the others approaching.

You struggle. Fucking stupid toy gun—what the hell were you thinking?

Suddenly blood sprays out from the beast's back like it just sprouted a pair of red wings. Anthony stands above you. He wrenches the ax out of the creature's back, then yanks the zombie off you. You're barely back on your feet when another lunges. It goes for Anthony.

You drop the gun and swing the pool cue across your body, catching the beast on the side of the head, just before he has a chance to bury his teeth into Anthony's shoulder. The thing smacks into the wall. You give it four more hard hits to the head and it drops.

Anthony takes the lead now, swinging the fire ax. He decapitates one. Splits another one's head open down the middle like a coconut—has to jerk and wiggle the ax to get it free.

He catches the next one in the side, dropping it. It squirms on the floor. You go to work on its head, bashing it with the pool cue until it stops moving.

You continue down the hall like this—Anthony keeping them at a distance with long, lethal swings of the ax. Those that he maims, you finish off.

Finally, there's only one left. Tall guy, in a gray suit. Looks a bit like your old high school principal—if your old high school principal had one arm and half a throat. This one clearly hasn't learned a damn thing from any of his friends.

It charges.

Anthony swings.

And misses.

The blade goes over its head. The beast hits Anthony square in the chest. Digs his teeth into Anthony's side. Anthony howls, tries to push it off. Instead he trips and falls back.

You crack the pool cue over the beast's head. It does nothing, continues feasting.

You turn to run.

Fuck. Anthony's hand around your ankle.

"Help me," he says, blood coming from his mouth. "Help me."

Oh God. You try to shake free. Can't. His fingers squeeze. You can't move—can only watch.

The thing works its way up Anthony's body, foreplay almost,

then digs into his neck. Blood spills. Anthony's hand opens. Releases you.

Thank God. You turn to run back—you need reinforcements.

Then something tackles you from behind. Digs its teeth into your back. And just as suddenly, it's gone.

You roll over. Anthony stands over you. His eyes are milky, unfocused. They dart around, looking you over. Then he bends over, grabs you by the waist with his huge hands, and picks you up. He wraps his arms around and squeezes. All the air shoots out of your chest. You can't breathe. You kick. Struggle. Anything to get free. Don't want to die like this.

But you're going to.

Anthony squeezes tighter. You hear a crack, pain shoots through your chest.

Anthony opens his massive jaw. Brings his head forward, so it's just an inch from yours. And then he sinks his teeth into your face . . .

AN END

Alright, all or nothing. Keeping the zombie act up best you can, you stumble right through the three things. Brush past the lawyer.

You can feel their undead eyes on you. Penetrating you. But you keep your head up. Forward. One foot in front of the other. A soldier, marching with the troops.

The beasts surround the group. Their moans increase. You and Khaki exchange quick, worried looks, then go back to staring ahead.

You pass overturned cars and abandoned military vehicles. Two tanks. A Humvee.

You're getting close now. A hundred yards from the water. Up onto the curb, off the street, and into Battery Park. Across the grass.

You can make it. Just keep moving. A little farther.

The man next to you is breathing heavily. You turn your head just slightly. You can see the fear on his face. No act. His hands tremble.

He's not going to make it.

You try to whisper to him—tell him you're almost there. But it's too late.

The man shrieks, then peels off running. Motherfu—

The zombies all moan and roar at once.

"Run!" you shout.

You take off. Everyone does. You hear some of them getting it behind you, bloodcurdling screams, but there's nothing you can do. You're across the Battery Park lawn. Over a jogging path. And there's the water—just beyond the fence. And in front of you—blocking the way—is one of the things. Arms out. Waiting to embrace you in death.

You're so close. Not stopping, you barrel into the thing, hitting it square in the chest, and together you go over the fence and into the water. It lashes out at you once, then sinks like a rock. You see the Statue of Liberty in the distance and you start kicking and swimming with everything you've got.

Fifty feet out, you stop to look behind you. You see Khaki, swimming furiously. Everyone else is dead. Their bloody bodies draped over the fence, monsters all over them, devouring them.

Khaki catches up to you. You watch the scene, horrified. Then you continue on.

Two hours later, you're closing in on the island. You want to give up. Just go to sleep and sink to the floor of the bay. But you press on.

The waves smack you against the rocky Liberty Island shore. It's not easy going. After a long struggle, you make it onto the rocks. Your legs and arms are cut badly, but you're safe. You've never been so exhausted in your life.

You close your eyes and breathe—you feel like you might honestly be having a heart attack. Finally, your breathing slows, returns to something resembling normal. You calm down some and open your eyes.

Khaki crawls up next to you. He smiles. "We made it," he says.

"We made it."

You stand up. Help Khaki to his feet.

And then Khaki's head comes apart in a bloody mess. His forehead opens. Bullets rip through his head and explode out the back of his skull. The gunshots hang in the air. He sways for a second, dead on his feet, then collapses, lifeless, on the rocks.

You hit the rocks, eyes darting, frantic. It's then that you take in the fence for the first time. It's a standard metal fence, with taller posts every ten feet—it stretches out on both sides of you, wrapping around the island.

And on each metal post—a severed zombie head.

Above you, a seagull picks at the near fleshless skull of a Hasidic Jew—small pieces of flesh and beard and two curly sideburns are all that remain.

One down, a bald guy's faceless head. Most of the skin gone, pecked to nothing.

Farther down a woman, still has her long red hair. And not much else. The skin on her cheeks peels in the hot sun.

Dear Lord . . .

"Stand up!" A high-pitched, maniacal voice.

Beside you, the waves lick at Khaki's dead body. His brains are leaking out on the rocks. Fear pumps through you.

The man's voice again. "Stand the fuck up! One more second and I'm coming over there and shooting you! I done killed that one and I'll kill you, too."

Fuck. Fuck fuck fuck! No choice—you stand up, arms raised.

It's a soldier. Crazy, wild-eyed. Blood caked on his face. No shirt—dried blood covering his bare chest like war paint. His desert camo pants are torn into makeshift shorts.

He uses the assault rifle in his hands to wave you over. "Over—over—over—over the fence—over here."

"OK, OK. I'm coming." You climb the fence, ignoring the head beside you.

"Move slow. I been collecting heads, love for you to give me a reason to collect yours."

Another soldier marches across the field, out from the base of the statue. "Hammer! Put the fucking rifle down."

The madman, Hammer apparently, lowers the gun.

The other soldier runs up beside him. "What were you shooting at?"

"My friend, he shot my fucking friend," you say. "Killed him."

"He was one of them, Hauk, he was a monster!" Hammer protests. "I seen his face!"

"It was paint," you say, tired. "It was just paint . . ."

"Put your arms down," the second soldier says. "Hammer, go inside."

Hammer kicks at the ground like a little kid who has just been told recess is over. He sulks back to the statue. The other soldier walks over to you. Then leans over the fence. He sees Khaki's body.

"Fuck me. Sorry about your friend. Hammer's gone a little nuts—if you couldn't tell by all the heads. I'm First Lieutenant Hauk," he says, walking to a picnic bench halfway between the fence and the statue.

The Statue of Liberty towers above you. It's a hell of a sight—and it feels right, considering how hard you just fought to get here. You've never been to the Statue of Liberty—always figured you'd make it there someday—just not like this.

You follow Hauk. You walk past a pile of burned bodies. Just skeletons. Hundreds.

"What happened here?" you ask, taking a seat.

"Nothing good. Our unit, Twenty-second Marine, came by boat afternoon of day one. Island was deserted when we got here—at least that's what we thought. Then we went inside. Must've been four hundred people—all turned into those fucking . . . monsters. Didn't take long—our whole unit, dead. Hammer and I held up inside the little restaurant around back for a full day. Then we got up to the roof of the joint, and, well, we killed them all. Every last one. Our commander. Some children. My best friend. Everyone. That's when Hammer lost it. He started cutting off their heads, putting them on the posts as a warning to anyone else out there."

"Jesus . . ."

"Tell me about it. And now we're stuck. Our boat sunk in the beginning. So no communications. All we got is the two damn Hellfires back there."

"Hellfires?"

"Yeah, we use them for underwater diving missions. Like civilian Jet Skis—only they go underwater."

You nod.

"If I hadn't lost my goddamn radio we could call for help and get the fuck outta here. Get back in the fight."

"Don't think there's much of a fight. I passed a whole bunch of Army shit on the way here—Humvees, tanks—all abandoned."

Hauk perks up. "Shit—vehicles will have a radio—get us out of here. Where?"

"South Ferry, Battery Park—where I came from."

Hauk pulls a small pair of binoculars from one of the many pouches on his vest. He walks to the fence and peers through them. "Fuck me," he says.

"What?"

"I think you brought company."

"Whaddya mean?"

"Look," he says, handing you the binoculars. You bring them to your eyes. Smoke pours off most of the city. You focus in on the southern tip of Manhattan—same spot you escaped from. The creatures are tumbling into the water. One after the other, straight down.

"Yeah?"

"Last communication we got, before the ship went, was from a unit on Roosevelt Island saying those things—zombies, monsters, whatever—were coming up out of the water. They had walked all the way from Manhattan."

"Shit. I'd believe it. Guys I was with before—they mentioned something like that."

"Fuck me. I'm sending Hammer under."

"Under?" you ask Hauk.

"That's right. Have to know what's down there."

"Let me go with him," you say.

He frowns. "You got any idea what you're doing?"

"Not really. I went snorkeling in Aruba with my parents once."

Hauk sighs.

You continue. "But if I brought those things here—shit—let me do my part."

"Christ." He steps away, lights a cigarette. Looks up at the statue. Then back to you. "Fine. Go around back. I'll send Hammer over."

"OK. He's uhh—he's not going to shoot me, right?"

"Probably not . . ."

Turn to page 278.

You follow as Hammer races across the field, into the statue base, and through the main hall. Then, up to the second and third level.

"Where are we going?" you ask.

"To the good lady's crown."

Hammer is in military-grade shape and you sure as hell aren't. He takes the stairs two at a time the whole way. You do your best to keep up. You hit a MAINTENANCE ONLY door. He picks the lock and you keep moving.

Twenty minutes later you're inside the crown. The view is breathtaking. But scary as all hell. Smoke billows from Manhattan. Parts of Brooklyn, too.

Hammer kneels down, places a black case on the floor, flips four snaps, and opens it. It's a full-blown, real-deal sniper rifle. He assembles it.

Where were you three days ago? In a production meeting? Looking forward to watching TV and not much else? And now you're watching a madman assemble a sniper rifle. Life's got a way of messing with a guy.

Hammer assembles a mount and screws it onto the ledge. Attaches the rifle. Then he gets down on one knee, adjusts the sight, and appears satisfied.

You kneel down beside him, rest your elbows on the ledge, and watch through the binoculars. You're looking at the very tip of the island.

"Did you see all them heads on them poles?"

"I did."

"I did that."

"I heard."

"Just like I shot your friend."

"I saw."

"Didn't know he was a person."

"Understood."

"Still . . . don't feel too bad about it," he says, and grins, showing off a mess of crooked teeth. You want to punch him, but it's probably the worst move you could make now.

Instead you grind your teeth and watch through the binoculars. Hauk comes up out of the water—tiny, even with the high-powered focus. He leaves the Hellfire and swims to the shore. He flashes a red light, then looks up at you through binoculars. Hammer gives a thumbs-up.

"Alright," Hammer says. "It's time. Tell me what you see."

You look at Hammer's leg once more. His sock is soaked through with blood. You can't tell, but it sure as hell looks like he was bit . . .

Assume Hammer's going to turn, and try to kill him first? Turn to page 91.

Take his word that it's a scratch? Turn to page 74.

"Yankees," you say, after a long moment. Then, hesitantly, trying to look enthused, "Goooo Yankees."

BLAM!!!

AN END

UP THE STREET

The train tracks and the street alongside it run east-west. Atlantic Avenue runs up and away from the tracks to the north, forming a T. It's a main street sort of deal—a CVS, local grocery store, Starbucks.

A crowd is starting to gather in the middle of the street. Some stand, stunned at what they're seeing. Others rush to the van to help. Another over to the cop car.

You tear off, headed up Atlantic, running right through them. There's a scream behind you. Then another. You run faster. It's beginning.

Halfway up the street, you stop in your tracks. A store catches your attention—A&J's Hardware. A few dirt bikes and four-wheelers sit in the parking lot—a FOR SALE sign hanging on the fence.

Hmm. Could be your ticket.

A bell dings as you enter. A gruff-looking guy, sixtyish, leans against the counter. He doesn't acknowledge you. He's playing with a police scanner. It's going wild.

You lean over, hands on your knees, and try to catch your breath. God, you're out of shape. Holding your side, you walk to the counter.

"You uh . . . you selling those bikes out there?"

Without looking up, "You see the FOR SALE sign?"

Struggling for breath. "Yeah."

"There's your answer."

"OK. Well, uh. I'd like to buy one."

"Which one?"

You've never ridden a dirt bike in your life. "Oh ahh . . . I don't know—whatever's easiest. I don't need anything fancy."

For the first time he looks up at you. He's grizzled—got a face that looks like it just came off a short-order grill. Long scar running across his forehead and down his cheek. Short, stubbly white beard.

He sighs. "You have a truck? Unless you have a truck to get it out of here with, I can't sell you a bike. You can't just cruise away with it. Riding on city streets is against the law."

"You hear the train crash?"

"No, I didn't. Tell me," he says, looking at you like you're an idiot.

"I was on that train. All I want to do is get out of here. Cut me a break, huh?"

His tune changes. "You were on the train? What happened? On the news—all this horseshit?"

You take a seat on an upside-down stack of plastic paint buckets. Look around. It's a nice local hardware store—the type that's getting pushed out by the Lowe's and Home Depots of the world. A throwback. Old-fashioned, even.

You start in. "Fucking—I don't even know. The dead started coming to life. Zombies. I mean—just like the movies."

"I don't believe it."

"Go take a look outside."

He doesn't move.

"Go ahead—look."

He steps outside. Comes back in a second later, face white.

"Leave."

"What?"

"You heard me—get out. I'm locking up." He grabs you by the arm.

You look out the door. Most of the monsters seem to be hanging around the train still, feeding on the passengers that didn't already get it. But a good twenty of the things are already halfway up the block.

"I'll fucking die out there!" you say.

He thinks for a second, then goes outside, pulls the heavy outer door shut, and reappears. "Alright—if you're gonna stay, you're gonna work. Grab some wood."

"OK, where?"

He shoots you the same look that he keeps shooting you. You've seen it before. It's that "you're a kid" look. That "you weren't part of the Greatest Generation and you're not a Vietnam vet" look. You're from the cell phone generation. The iThis and iThat generation. If you didn't just return from Iraq with a bullet in your leg, you weren't impressing this guy.

"Aisle C, by the iPhone cases."

Oh.

You run to the back and grab all the wood you can carry. Fuck, pants are falling down. Of all the days not to wear a belt . . . You waddle back and drop the wood at his feet. He gets to work with a drill. "More."

You do like he says.

Two large front windows look out onto the street, the door between them. He orders you to start piling stuff in front of the right window while he goes to work covering the left.

He's got some cabinets for sale. Those seem to work pretty well. You stack them up. More stuff on top of them—chairs, shelves—anything big and halfway heavy. Screams continue to pour in from the streets. You work faster.

The guy finishes with the left window, then walks to the back of the store. You take a look at your window—pretty good. Secure. Then you go to find him. Through a tight doorway is a second room—this one full of lawn mowers, Weed Whackers, snowblowers, and other larger tools. He pulls out a set of keys and locks the heavy metal back door. You follow him back to the front of the store like his pet cat.

He goes back to his spot behind the counter and pulls out a pistol. Lays it down. Then nudges the phone toward you. "You want to call anyone, go ahead," he says.

"Oh, thanks." You pick up the phone, begin to dial your mom, then stop and hang up. You should call her. But she'll only worry. Ehh, you'll text her later.

"You?" you say, pushing the phone in his direction.

He shakes his head.

"No one?"

"No," he grunts.

"Oh, OK."

You set the old phone back down gently. "What's your name?" you ask.

"Walter," he says.

"Nice to meet you Walter, I'm—"

"Shut up. Listen."

Walter turns up the scanner. You can't make anything out—just a mishmash of voices.

"Military's on the way," Walter says. "Coming right through here, headed for the city."

"Military?"

"That's what I said—didn't you hear?"

"I couldn't hear a damn thing on there."

"There's a base about twenty miles up the road."

You walk to a small spot on the window that was left uncovered. The heavy rumble of military machines shakes the building. Tanks. Trucks. They're arriving now.

They stop in front of the wrecked train. Soldiers pour out of the truck and form a line stretching across the street. Thirty of them. Full combat gear.

One soldier—commander, general, however it works—steps forward with a megaphone.

"Don't move another fucking inch—none of you."

Clearly zombies aren't the best at following orders, because they take off running toward the Army.

In turn, the Army lets loose with a barrage of fire. Even from a hundred yards away, the sound is deafening. The beasts that get it in the head drop. But the others don't stop. Bullets rip through their bodies but they just stutter, stumble, and keep coming.

Fucking zombies . . .

Then comes something even more horrifying—children. School kids. *Zombified* school kids. Hundreds. You saw the school on the corner after you climbed the hill. Why the hell didn't they stay inside?

The children join in with the rest of the monsters—moving steadily toward the military. The firing doesn't stop.

There's a loud screech from the other direction, farther up Atlantic Avenue. A car comes racing down the street, directly toward the action, and comes to a halt about a hundred feet short of the battle.

A woman jumps out. She looks around, frantic. "Ruby! Has anyone seen my daughter Ruby?"

Then she sees what the military's firing upon. Children.

She lets out a Luke Skywalker "Nooooo!" and takes off running.

"Ruby! Ruby where are you?!"

Fuck me. You can see it coming. She's going to try to get her kid out of there—and she's going to get herself killed. And for nothing—if Ruby's one of those kids, she can already be counted among the dead.

If you want to try to stop the woman, turn to page 188.

If you want to let it happen, turn to page 103.

You walk over to Khaki, pull him aside. In a half whisper, "Hey—I can't do this."

"What? This was your plan. Mostly."

"It's insane. I'm not going out there with those things—I don't care how much I stink like raw hamburger. If I were you, I wouldn't go, either."

"I'm not backing out now."

"You're nuts."

"Maybe. But look—I'm a zombie fanatic—I mean, crazy. Nuts. I know it. And somehow—now—all the movies I've been watching, all the comics, all the books—it's actually happening!"

He has a crazed smile on his face. He's actually enjoying this.

"The chance to go out there, to walk among them," he continues, "it's too much to turn down. I'm scared shitless, for sure. But I also think it can work."

"Your funeral."

"Thanks for the vote of confidence."

You smile. "Well, I'll be watching. If you get in trouble, I'll do what I can to help."

"Alright."

You stick your bloody hand out. Khaki shakes it.

"Good luck."

"You too."

The group is ready. You get behind a crate and watch as Khaki raises the large metal gate, pulling on the chain like he's opening a stage curtain. It's fitting, 'cause they're damn good actors. They've got the zombie walk thing down perfectly. The world ever gets back to normal, it'll be the next big dance at the club—you can see it already.

They shuffle out of the warehouse. Across the parking lot, through the gate, and out into the street.

Before long the zombies—the real ones—take notice. They don't attack. They stumble over. Sniff them out, not unlike two dogs meeting on the street. One, a small boy, hovers around Khaki. Brushes against him.

The group picks up their speed a little bit, probably without even realizing it. You can only imagine how scared they are. Walking straight into the lion's den, no protection.

But it's working. The beasts moan. The group moans back. Really, a dead-on impression. Rich Little turned zombie.

They get to the end of the street and turn. Slowly, to the left. Just three blocks to go. Sonofabitch, they're going to make it!

Then a scream pierces the air. One of the men has lost it. He darts out from the group, fleeing down the street.

At once, the things come to life. Fully aware. Two of the ugly things chase down the fleeing man.

Everyone else scatters, most headed for the water. Goddamn it, they're done for. Without thinking, you run out into the street.

"Hey!" you shout, waving your arms. "Hey! Hey, you stupid brain-dead sons of bitches. Over here! Over here!"

The beasts turn.

The group disappears around the corner. You don't know if they'll make it or not, but you've done what you can.

And now you've got your own problems to deal with. A horde of the things, coming straight for you.

You bolt back inside the garage and jump for the chain. You're two inches short. Goddamn it. You stick your head out the door—they're through the gate, coming fast.

OK, plan B. You sprint to the back. You can hear their feet slapping the ground, just behind you. Moans turning to howls as they close in.

A hand grabs your shoulder. Squeezes around it. A nail pierces your skin. You turn into the freezer and slam the door. But the undead arm blocks it. Behind, their snarling faces. You pull the door back and slam it again, giving it everything you have. Once more and it shuts—the thing's arm drops to the freezer floor, severed just below the elbow.

Disgusted, you watch the arm flop on the ground. But your disgust turns to absolute horror as you realize the freezer doesn't open from the inside. You're trapped. Trapped with nothing but an undead arm and the sound of thirty monsters stumbling around outside the freezer.

Nearly two years later, when Manhattan is no longer owned by the undead, the Army finds your body, frozen to the core.

·:· AN END ·:·

It takes you twenty minutes before you find a sign for the highway. You ride up the entrance ramp.

The sight is unbelievable. Apocalypse. The real deal. Abandoned cars stretch down Interstate 95 as far as you can see.

You weave around the stalled cars and head for your folks' house in Wakefield, Massachusetts, about two hundred miles away. You work up speed, getting used to the feel of the bike.

It's been three days since the zombies arrived. You're unshaven. Starting to feel like Mad Max. Only need the dog.

You replay everything in your mind. The train station. That horrible ride. The crash. Watching that poor woman and her child die on the street. Walter. The trigger-happy couple. What a fucking nightmare.

About sixty miles in, the bike is low on gas. Need to fill up—last thing you want is to be stuck out here on foot.

Another ten minutes and you spot a Mobil station. You slow the bike down, keep your distance, and see what you can see. No walking dead. No walking living. Empty cars. All in all—deserted.

You keep the bike as slow and quiet as possible as you approach the station. Don't want to alert anyone to your presence.

Everything looks kosher. You pull in and get off the bike.

The Mobil station is one of those supermart things. Supposed to have everything. Could be a helluva lot of useful stuff in there. Could also be a hundred beasts in there, ready to eat you for breakfast. Wait—check your watch. 12:13. Ready to eat you for *lunch*.

The sun is high in the sky and bright as all hell—you can't make out much through the windows of the store.

Could be food, water, maps, and dirty magazines in there—but there could also be instant death.

Ahh, what the hell. Slowly, you open the door.

It looks like a tornado came through. Damn near everything gone. Where are the Funyuns? You walk the aisles. A lone Bud Light sits in the back of the cooler. You're more of a Rolling Rock man, but this'll do. You crack it open. Yum.

The technically important stuff like flashlights, batteries, toilet paper—that's all gone. But there's still some good stuff to be found. Slim Jims. Hostess Cup Cakes. A Marilyn Monroe knockoff Zippo. An Elvis one, too. You take both. No Sour Patch Kids—but Sour Patch Watermelons. Not the same, but they'll do.

Some cash on the floor behind the counter. You take it—you know it has little to no value at this point, but it just feels wrong to leave two hundred dollars sitting there when it's free for the taking.

Then you notice the back room. Could be all sorts of goodies back there. Drinks, still cool. Food that actually has some substance to it.

You jiggle the handle. It's locked.

You walk to the end of the aisle and aim the gun at the door handle.

First shot misses badly. Second shot is a direct hit. You walk over. A big hole through the handle. Sonofabitch, it worked.

You open the door—then you immediately realize your mistake. Twenty of them. At least. Truckers. Stranded travelers. All dead. All moaning. Poor fucks must've locked themselves in there and then let somebody else in who'd been bitten but hadn't changed over yet. Then it was just a matter of time before they all got it.

You book it through the store and back outside. Fuck—not

going anywhere without gas. You grab the nozzle and swipe your debit card. C'mon, c'mon, c'mon.

This is what you get for living check to check. Always thought, *What's the worst that could happen?* Well—here's the answer. The worst that could happen is that you don't have enough money for the minimum purchase to buy gas at a Mobil station on an abandoned highway to use as a flame-thrower to fight off the living dead.

Finally, it goes through.

You stick the nozzle in the tank and begin pumping.

The door flies open and the things rush out.

Now or never.

You rip the nozzle from the tank and begin spraying. Then, with your other hand, you spark the Marilyn Monroe lighter and toss it into the stream.

WOOOSH!!!

All twenty of them go up in flames. Yet they keep coming. A burning mass of the walking dead. You pour it on and finally, one by one, they begin to fall.

But they're not done. They writhe—not in pain: it's clear they feel no pain—but the burns have weakened them. Skin sticking to the ground. Fat melting into puddles. One takes a step—his foot looks like he stepped in gum, the way the melting skin stretches, some stuck to the pavement. The smell of burning skin and hair is overpowering.

They're not done. Everything you've seen so far says they'll be back up in seconds. Ignoring the wall of flames and the crackling, writhing bodies, you fill the tank—you have no choice.

You hop on the bike and gun it. Then, halfway down the on-ramp, you stop. The things struggle, reach for you. But they just burn. Smoke pours off their crisping bodies.

You stop and aim—then fire a single bullet into the closest gas pump. The whole thing goes up in a massive explosion. Michael Bay would be proud . . .

Then you hit the road. It's around dusk when you pull into Wakefield. You haven't been back in a year, at least. The setting sun gives the whole thing an eerie quality.

You pass your old high school. Past JK's Market—the little convenience store where you used to buy cigarettes at fourteen. The town is empty. No zombies, but you don't see any people, either. You wonder how far this mess has gone.

You pull into your driveway. Oh man—if your mom saw you riding a dirt bike with no helmet she'd have an aneurysm.

One car in the driveway. The SUV is gone.

Across the street is Kim Fine's house. High school crush—yours and everybody else's. Captain of the cheerleading team. Total knockout. You used to play together in elementary school—that all changed when you hit middle school and everyone realized how good-looking she was and how, y'know, average you were.

Can't help but wonder how she's doing. Last you heard she was still hanging around town, working for a flower distributor or something like that.

You get your key from under the fake rock key holder that sticks out like a sore thumb and walk inside.

"Mom? Dad?"

Nothing.

In the kitchen you find a note.

Went to your grandmother's in Ithaca. If you see this note, come. Hoping you're safe. Love, love, love, infinity—Mom

You drift off to sleep on the couch. A knock on the window wakes you. More than wakes you—scares the shit out of you. You fall off the couch.

It's Kim. Holy shit. You wipe the crust off the corners of your mouth and open the door. She looks amazing.

"Um. Hey Kim."

She jumps in and throws her arms around you. "Oh my God I'm so happy to see you. So happy to see anyone!"

Mmm. You're warm all over. You haven't seen her in years. Can't believe she's in front of you right now. Can't believe she just hugged you.

"Where is everyone?"

"They left. News said those things were on their way here."

"The whole town?"

"Pretty much."

"So what are you doing here?"

"No way to get out of here. Don't know where my parents went. I have no car. It's just been me over there, for like, ever."

Invite Kim to stay with you? Turn to page 24.

Tell her that's nice, good to see you, but you only have so much food, she needs to leave? Turn to page 329.

You limp to the escalator and ride it down. Explore carefully, slowly. The whole place is empty—everyone must have fled when this all started.

You head over to the opposite escalator and return to the top floor. Once there, you flip the switch so both are headed down. That should keep any of those things from coming up and catching you by surprise. You're proud of yourself for thinking of that.

Then you head for the good stuff—brownies, pastries, fancy coffee drinks. It's all Starbucks stuff—they have this banana chocolate chip cake thing that's good as all hell. You tear through the food, downing everything in sight, not even thinking about rationing food or what you might need to save for later. You've never been so hungry. Once you're stuffed, you're tired.

The sound of the battle outside is driving you nuts, so you retreat to the farthest corner of the store. Then you sleep.

It's dusk when you wake. You go to the window.

The zombies have won the battle. The tanks are still there, abandoned. The trees in the park burn. Storefronts caved in.

But the zombies are still standing. Even more now. Two or three thousand, just wandering around Union Square—waiting for their next meal.

Your stomach sinks. The fucking military, tanks, guns, and all—they were defeated?

God help us.

But then you realize—Christ—it could have been you out there among the undead. Stumbling around, mindless.

It's the long haul, then, you think. You ride the escalators down to the bottom floor and start exploring. The Union Square Barnes & Noble has *everything*. First you grab a floor lamp, snap the head off, unscrew the base, and use the pole as a makeshift cane. That allows you to get around. Then you overturn tables and push them against the doors. Make sure the revolving door is locked.

In the back corner of the top floor, you set up your home base. Barnes & Noble, for some odd reason, sells yoga mats. You stack three of those and make a half-decent bed. You make a pillow out of masking tape and a shitload of paper towels from the bathroom.

You do your best to make it feel like home. You get a globe, put it next to your yoga mat bed. Candles. A clock. Picture frames with photos of beaches and happy couples.

On the third day, you decide to start reading. You've never been much of a reader—but being trapped in a Barnes & Noble, now would probably be a good time to start.

Wandering through the store, a display catches your eye—a table with a sign over it that says UNDEAD SUMMER.

Lo and behold, it's a zombie book promotion. A whole table of them laid out.

World War Z, by Max Brooks
Patient Zero, by Jonathan Maberry
Day by Day Armageddon, by J. L. Bourne
Hater, by David Moody
The New Dead, by a whole bunch of authors
The Walking Dead, a set of beautiful-looking graphic novels

And then some that look particularly helpful:

The Zombie Survival Guide, by Max Brooks
Zombie Combat Manual, by Roger Ma

You grab one of each and limp back to your corner. You read for days. Nonstop. When the power goes, you read by a small booklight that attaches to the spine. Soaking up all the information you can. Which weapons are best against the undead. How to defend a home (or bookstore).

It's perfect. By the time your foot heals, you'll be prepared. Prepared to do battle with the bloodthirsty army of the dead that awaits you . . .

✦ AN END ✦

You speed through the side streets you know so well. You go for the supermarket first. That's where you see them. The beasts. The entire parking lot is full. And if they're there, that means they could be anywhere.

They hear the bike and begin chasing you. You're still riding the high from last night—you feel invincible, wind in your hair. You hit the throttle hard and lose them down a maze of side streets.

JK's Market. That's perfect. You know the neighborhood well, and it's way off Main Street.

Driving slowly, keeping the noise to a minimum, you make your way over. You park the bike and look around. Empty.

Slowly, gun in hand, you enter the store. Empty, too. Phew. It's been gone over pretty well, but there's still some good stuff to be found. You set the gun down on the counter and move through the store quickly, throwing everything you can in your backpack. Flashlight, drinks, soup.

You go to the last aisle—that's where they used to keep the Funyuns.

And there he is. JK himself. Fifteen years ago, you would have been happy to see him—that would have meant Marlboro Lights and copies of *Penthouse* (he charged you and your buddies double for everything, but man-oh-man was it worth it).

Not happy to see him now, though. His face is twisted and swollen. A chunk of the top of his head is missing.

You backpedal. "Hey—hey—don't—"

He charges. You turn and run. Goddamn it—why'd you have to leave the gun on the counter?

You run down the aisles, throwing anything you can find at him. Bags of potato chips. Copies of *Us Weekly*. He's between you and the counter, blocking your way to the gun.

You grab hold of a display case. You can move it. An idea forms.

"C'mon!" you shout.

Here goes nothing.

He powers toward you.

Using everything you've got, you pull the case to the side. It crashes down, pinning him.

You grab the gun and you're out the door. You're so buzzed with adrenaline, you forget to grab any supplies.

You get on the bike and start it up. Shit. The commotion has brought them out of the woodwork. The parking lot and the street begin to fill. You twist the throttle and zoom out on the street. Zombies follow.

You check the side mirror. Hundreds. As scared as you are, you can't help but feel pretty cool as you handle the terrain like Steve McQueen in *The Great Escape*.

You head for the high school. You know it like the back of your hand, and you can lose them in the woods behind it.

You head up over the old hill. Had your first and only fight here, under the tree you just whipped past. Through a small wooded area, then down onto the high school track. You open it up, leaving them in the dust.

But the faster you go, the louder the bike roars. And that draws more and more of them. From houses and yards they come. They stumble out—spot you—and begin their twisted, disgusting sprint.

You cross the track and head up over the baseball diamond. Your house is just through the woods. You kick up more and more dust as you rip across the baseball diamond, around the field house, and onto the football field.

And there they are.

The entire varsity football team. Undead. Seventeen- and eighteen-year-old kids—peak physical specimens. Strong. Fast. Hungry.

You kick it into overdrive, right through them. They reach out. One almost takes you off the bike.

You shoot down the small creek that separates the high school field from the woods, kicking up mud. Then slowly, you take the bike through the woods.

The things are gaining. They move through the woods unimpeded. Crashing through branches. Powering over bushes and chunks of rock that the dirt bike can't handle—at least not with you behind the handles.

Finally, you come out the other side. You're directly across from your house—the things right behind you.

You'll be safe at the house, possibly. But you could lead them straight to Kim.

Head for safety inside the house? Turn to page 70.

Try to lead them away from Kim? Turn to page 284.

"OK, look—I'm very, very sorry. I didn't mean to bring them here—I was just looking for someplace safe to stay."

"Well this ain't it," Al says. He pulls a knife from a drawer and cuts through the duct tape.

"Al, you're not doing this," Sully says.

"Yes I am."

"Al, listen to me!"

"Why?"

"'Cause I'm your goddamn union rep, that's why. You're a member of Local Two-fucking-Twelve, and you're damn proud of it—right?"

"Yeah—I am—proud enough to get this kid off my fucking work site."

Al drags you, kicking and screaming, out the door and across the lot. The other two follow, arguing with Al, but they don't stop him.

"Fish—fire up the crane," Al says.

"What?"

"Fish—the crane, now."

Fish slinks over to the crane and climbs inside. He turns the keys and it roars to life. Thick, black smoke pours out the back. The thing's a monster.

"Wait, what are you going—"

Big Al hits you in the gut. Hard. It shuts you up and drops you to the ground. You gasp for air.

The crane swings over. At the end of the metal line is a huge wrecking ball—and just below that, a massive metal hook.

Fish works the gears while Al directs it over your way. You try to run, but you're too weak. You start crawling, through the dirt.

"Uh-uh," Al mutters, grabbing you by your collar and yanking you to your feet. Then he takes the huge hook and puts it up through the back of your shirt. It's freezing cold against your skin.

You beg. "Please. Don't do this. Please, please. No. Don't. Just don't."

"Sorry bud," he says, then yells over to Fish, "raise 'er up!"

The hook jerks up. Your shirt gets tight around your throat. Hard to breathe. Tighter. Fuck—you're going to choke to death. You get your hand between your collar and your neck. Manage a little room. Just enough to pull in a small breath of air.

Your feet lift off the ground. You kick wildly at the air. You catch a glimpse of Fish, working the crane. "Don't do this," you squeak out. "Please."

Higher. You're even with the top of the fence. The crane swings, carrying you over it.

You can hear the moans of the zombies. You look down. Hands reaching up. So many undead faces. So many eager, hungry mouths.

Fear rips through your body. Panic like nothing you've ever known. You struggle. Anything you can do to get free.

The crane begins to lower. Your shirt, tight against your fingers. Tight against your throat. Try to breathe. Can't.

Please God, you think. Please get me out of here. Anything. Just make this stop. Anything.

The first hand at your foot. Pulls you down. Then another grabs you. The crane continues to lower. Then it stops, your feet just above the ground. Christ—they're just going to let you hang there, like a goddamn worm on a hook.

One of the beasts digs in, teeth in your shoulder. The pain is unbearable. Your screams are silenced as your throat is ripped out. Another at your cheek. Hands tear at you. Teeth all over you—in your thigh, at your waist.

The hands pull harder. Your shirt rips and you fall to the ground. And then, mercifully, you go into shock just before they tear you to pieces.

:·:·: AN END :·:·:

A FAREWELL TO ARMS

No time to waste. Not worrying about the things at your back, you take the chainsaw from the floor, start it up, and bring it down, severing Kim's arm just below the elbow. She screams. So loud. Piercing. Blood everywhere. It's awful.

Then, from behind, through the door, one gets you. Digs its teeth into your bicep.

"Kim!" you shout.

She doesn't think. Doesn't hesitate. With her good arm, she pulls a knife from the wood block on the counter. Jams it into the beast's head.

You look at each other. Blood pours from her open arm and you've just been bitten. Death is upon you both.

"Kim, get the butcher knife, my arm—now."

"I can't," she says through tears.

"You have to!"

You put your bleeding arm down on the counter.

"Now!"

She grabs the steel knife. Looks you in the eye. You nod. She brings the butcher knife down. You scream.

It takes three whacks to separate your arm from your shoulder. Pain. Unbelievable pain. Takes everything you have not to collapse.

Then a hand on your shoulder. Another one of the fucking monsters. Through the swinging door. You grab the bloody butcher knife and spin, burying the knife in its eye. More come through.

Need to leave—now.

276

And then—Kim's the strong one. She pulls you upstairs, into your parents' bedroom, and slams the door shut. You collapse on the floor.

Pain courses through you. Blood pours from your shoulder, pooling beneath. Just want this to end. Just want to die.

No. Not yet.

On your parents' dresser, a picture of your grandfather. A good guy, as far as you know. He died when you were young. Too young to remember.

He was a ladies' man. Worked as a surgeon in a Pittsburgh hospital. Bragged loudly about how he was going to date every nurse in the hospital. He never got past the first, your grandmother.

Then he went off to war. Not a war hero. But a good soldier. Did his job.

If he's up in heaven right now watching, there's no way you can let yourself die on this floor. No way you can let the woman you love die.

Using the one arm you still have, you get to your feet and push your parents' dresser in front of the door. Working together, you bandage up Kim's arm, then she does yours. The entire time, the monsters pound at the door.

You pass out on the bed. The pounding at the door continues.

Kim looks down at her severed arm. She sobs. You try to fight it—try with everything—but you can't. Together, you lie on the bed and cry . . .

AN END

Hauk summons Hammer over. They show you the basics of the Hellfire—it's just like a Jet Ski, only instead of controlling just right and left, you control up and down, too. Oh yeah—and there are twin harpoon guns on each side—they didn't have that in Aruba.

You suit up. Wet suit, oxygen, everything. Utility belt around your waist with a knife. You hop on the Hellfire.

Hammer skips the wet suit—just takes a knife and throws an oxygen tank on his back, the tube in his mouth, and hops on. He looks like an absolute fucking madman. He gives you a scary grin, then takes off. Hauk waves you off as you follow Hammer into the water.

About a half mile out, Hammer submerges.

Alright—here goes nothing. You hit the switch. The Hellfire hums beneath you, gets louder, then goes under. Water splashes over your goggles—and suddenly, you're beneath the surface, with a clear, full view of the underside of New York Harbor.

You pass over an old Buick, half buried in the sand. Fish swim around—none of them pretty.

Then you see the things.

Surreal doesn't begin to describe it. Hundreds of zombies, walking across the bay floor. They're even slower underwater than they were on solid ground.

Hammer fires. The harpoon slices through the water and embeds itself directly in the skull of the thing farthest in the front—a teenager in a black jean jacket. In slow motion, it

falls to the sand. Doesn't float. Doesn't rise. Just hits the ground and stops moving. Sand slowly kicks up around it.

You take aim and fire. The harpoon sticks harmlessly into the harbor floor.

Hammer buzzes over the zombies. You hit the gas and follow, staying a good twenty feet above them.

Hammer is lower than you. One of the dead reaches up, just barely misses his bare foot. You speed past all of them, get to the end of their ranks. A rough estimation—you put them at a thousand.

Hammer loops around, cutting through the water, and flies back. You follow. You fire a random harpoon into the mass of them, just because you can, and happen to nail one in the back of the skull. You're past it before it begins to fall.

Hammer continues to cruise low over them. Another goes for his foot. Catches it this time. A hint of red in the water.

Hammer lets go of the Hellfire and it continues on through the water unmanned. It glides along, downward, then crashes into the mass of zombies, sending them stumbling about and falling to the harbor floor. The sand kicks up, clouding the water while you watch helplessly from a safe distance. More grab at him now. He struggles. Rips his blade from its sheath and buries it in one of the things' faces.

Another one grabs him. Fuck—looks like it bit him. You can't quite tell.

You take aim and fire a harpoon at the one that has him. Catches it in the neck. It doesn't let go. Continues pulling at him, harpoon sticking out each side of it. Another shot, slightly higher. This one hits it in the head. Its hands open and it sinks to the sand. Hammer bursts up through the water. A small trail of blood leaks from his ankle.

You steer the Hellfire toward the surface and come up beside him. He grabs hold of the side and you head back for Liberty Island.

Hammer comes out of the water first and limps his way up

onto the rocky beach. You leave the glider in the water, strip off the wet suit, and race up behind him.

"One got you, I saw!" you shout after him.

"I'm fine."

You catch up to him. "I saw, one got you, you're bleeding."

"It nicked me."

"With its nails. That could be enough."

"It didn't fucking bite me."

"Are you sure?"

"Yeah."

"Still."

He spins. His dark eyes dart about wildly, looking you up and down. "Listen kid, shut the fuck up before I coldcock you, got me?"

Silently, you follow him back to Hauk. Hauk sits at a picnic table, looking over a map.

"Well?" Hauk says.

"Big bad fucking news, boss. I counted twelve hundred."

"How far?"

"Shit, one hour. Maybe hour 'n' ten."

"Never ends. Alright—we need that radio—now. Hammer, the kit. Get it. Cover me. Kid, you spot."

"What are you plannin' on?" Hammer asks.

"I'm going over there, I'm getting that radio, I'm calling for help, and we're getting the fuck outta here."

Turn to page 250.

You grab her good arm and pull her up to your parents' room. You barricade the door with a dresser.

You take good care of her. Wrap her up and lay her down gently on the closet floor. In about an hour she turns.

She howls. For two days straight, she growls and moans from inside the closet.

Finally, it's too much.

You rip open the door. Fire twice. Leave chunks of Kim's brain all over your mother's shoe collection.

Then you collapse against the door. Put the gun in your own mouth. And squeeze.

AN END

ACTUALLY, WE'RE GOOD . . .

"Guess our saviors have arrived," the Ardle says.

"Yeah, I guess so."

"Fun while it lasted."

"Yeah . . ."

"You thinking what I'm thinking?"

"I might be."

He smiles.

You stand up, walk around to get a good angle at the front of the copter. "We're good!" you shout, waving your arms. "We're good!"

No way they can hear you above the roar. After a few minutes, though, they seem to get the message. The ladder is pulled up and the helicopter flies away, headed downtown.

"Game of *Madden*?" the Ardle asks.

You return to your beach chair. "Def."

AN END

CHIVALRY ISN'T DEAD
(BUT YOU MIGHT BE)

You turn up the speed, fly down the end of the cul-de-sac, and spin around.

You kick off your left shoe and take off your sock. You spin open the cap to the gas tank and shove your sock inside.

Pull out Elvis this time. Spark it. You get the sock going. In a few seconds, it's burning well.

The football team is coming at you fast. You floor it, headed straight for them. The flame nips at your leg—stronger now. The pain is nearly unbearable. Your leg is burning, you're sure, but you don't look down.

You close in on the beasts.

Fifty feet.

Heart pounding.

Forty feet.

Undead coming right for you.

Thirty feet.

You cut the bike to the side and it goes out from underneath you. You hit the ground hard, road rash all down your already burning leg. You stop rolling and look up just as the bike slides into the approaching horde.

C'mon.

They rush over the bike. Past it.

C'mon!

Straight for you.

KA-BOOM!!!!

The whole zombie football squad goes up in flames. Those closest to the blast fly through the air, head over tail. You've taken out about half of them.

And the rest are blocking your way back to the house.

You scramble to your feet. Intense pain with every step, your leg white hot and the skin shredded. You sprint for your neighbor's house. Mrs. Cibelli. Nice woman. Babysat her kids a few times.

You pound the door. It's locked.

You look away for a second—see the monsters closing in. Then you hear the sound of the door opening—thank God!

BLAM!!!

You're knocked off your feet.

Motherfucker—Mrs. Cibelli just shot you.

She rushes out. "Oh God, oh God. It's you! I'm sorry! I thought you were one of those things!"

You lie on the grass, spitting up blood.

Their dog Champ comes over. Last time you saw that dog you were a kid. How'd he get so big?

This is what's going through your head as you lie on Mrs. Cibelli's front lawn, bleeding out, a pack of hungry zombies at your back.

⋯ AN END ⋯

You head for the closest building, Joshua Eaton Elementary School. Kids and teachers are pouring outside, eager to see what all the commotion is. You hear a siren in the distance, getting louder.

"Back inside!" you shout, waving your hands. "Get back inside! Zombies, the living dead . . . monsters!"

All at once the kids scream, "Zombies . . . awesome!"

"No, not awesome. Bad. Bad fucking news."

"He said 'fucking.'"

You take a group of kids in your arms and sweep them along. The teacher, a grumpy-looking lady in her sixties, rushes over to you.

"Get your hands off those children immediately!"

"Lady, take these kids and get them back inside. You too. C'mon, let's go—all of us."

She starts to scold you again—but then for the first time truly takes in the destruction of the train. Her eyes go wide. Looks like she's struggling to breathe. And then she wanders toward the train.

One of the kids, a little boy in a LeBron James jersey, follows her. You run and grab him.

"Hey—kid, stay here." You nudge him toward the others. "C'mon. Stay there."

You glance back at the teacher. "What's her name?"

All at once. "Mrs. Hennnnnderson."

"Mrs. Henderson! Get back here, what's the matter with you?"

But she just keeps walking toward the train. The zombies are distracted by the glut of fresh meat they're currently feasting on, and she passes them easily.

You glance down the street. The zombies have made it up the hill. One, down on his knees, feeds on the heavyset cop. Another slaps at the window of the van. Jesus—they'll be coming your way any moment.

"Mrs. Henderson. Come back here!" She is only a couple of feet from the train now.

You watch in horror as two white hands come out of the top of the overturned subway car and an old man zombie climbs out. It balances awkwardly on the edge for a second, then reaches for Mrs. Henderson. It falls violently to the ground, landing face-first. You can hear its cheekbone shatter.

"Whoa!" one of the kids says.

The old man thing rolls over. More bone-cracking noises. It rises. Its left shoulder hangs far lower then its right—dislocated—and its left leg drags behind as it stumbles along.

Mrs. Henderson stands still, in apparent shock.

"Lady, get back here—now!"

She snaps out of it. Turns to run. But it's too late. The old man thing, bum leg and all, sprints after her and drapes itself on top of her. Together they crash to the street. They roll on the ground for a moment before it pins her. Then it dives in. Straight for the jugular.

The kids go fucking nuts. Screams, tears, the whole nine.

The old man thing raises its head, strings of Mrs. Henderson's neck flesh in its teeth. It stares at you and the kids.

"Kids—inside—now."

It takes another chunk out of Mrs. Henderson and works its way to its feet. Behind it, more of the beasts exit the overturned train's busted windows and climb through the open doors, each falling flat on its face and getting up a second later.

They're drawn by the screaming kids. They stumble forward for a second, seem to lock on to the sound, and then run.

"Inside, go, move, move!"

You usher the kids inside and slam the doors shut behind you. The beasts collide with the double doors and bounce off.

"Someone—grab me a bike lock."

"Bike lock?"

"Yeah, don't you ride fucking bikes anymore?"

"We have Rollerblades in our shoes."

"Jesus Christ. A chain lock, any kind of lock!"

A kid runs off to his locker and appears a second later, lock in hand. You wrap the chain through the emergency door bars and lock it. If the things figure out how to pull open a door, they'll still only be able to get it to move an inch or two.

You turn and stare down the long elementary school corridor. It's empty.

"Where is everyone?"

A little know-it-all girl—smarter than you, probably—chirps up. "Principal Valiant called an emergency fire drill."

"Fire drill. Where's the exit?"

"By the playground."

"Alright. Who here's big, strong, and tough?"

Five boys and a girl step forward. "Are you kids brave? I need really super, super brave little kids for this."

They nod their little heads.

"OK, good. Go in groups of two and lock every outside door to the school, OK? Then go back to your classroom."

The kids run off. The others point you in the direction of the playground, then you order them back to their classroom, too.

"Lock it and stay inside, got it? When your friends come back, let them in, but nobody else, OK?"

From the gym you have a good view of the schoolyard. You see about 150 kids, separated into six lines, each with an adult at the front.

It's what you feared. A big, fenced-in area, set against the side of the building. One big open gate at the side. A death trap—the perfect killing ground.

You can hear their moans. They'll be here soon.

You open the window and yell—but it's too late. The things are already rushing in through the gate. Panic and confusion set in. And the dead begin to multiply.

At the far end of the playground is a trailer—one of those temporary classrooms a school uses when it's overcrowded or under construction. You did third grade in one.

The lucky ones make it inside. A few teachers. Forty, fifty kids.

In just minutes, the dead have multiplied by ten. The schoolyard is filled with murderous, monstrous undead children.

They're quick. They dart around, hunting down any kids that are still among the living and taking them down. They get their teachers, too—the payback the little bastards have been waiting for.

Once they've finished, they turn to the trailer. Surround it. Tear at it.

Poor people are not going to last long in there.

Be a hero and try to rescue them? Turn to page 236.

Worry about your own ass and stay put? Turn to page 299.

LONG WALK

As you all gather behind him, Khaki pulls the metal chain, hand over hand, and slowly the aluminum warehouse door opens.

Alright, here goes.

Being the only one not wearing absurdly detailed makeup, you stay in the middle of the group.

You put your arms out and put on your best "I'm a zombie" face. You let one lip hang. Head back. Eyes half open. Your "I'm a zombie" face is a whole lot like your "I'm Sylvester Stallone" face.

Slowly, everyone makes their way out of the warehouse. You shuffle across the parking lot, then out into the street. You move as slowly as you can—fighting every instinct to run.

The real zombies stumble around you. Get closer. Sniff you out, examine you.

A few join in your group. One sidles up next to you.

It's a lawyer type, late fifties. Sharp suit. His button-down has been torn open and there are long claw marks across his chest. His face is greenish. His hair is spotty and it's been ripped from his scalp in places. A huge, open wound stretches from his ear to his Adam's apple.

You avoid eye contact. Their eyes are dead—almost hollow. If they spot the life in yours, you're done for.

He continues to walk beside you. Sweat pours off your scalp, and it's not from the July heat.

You want to run. With everything in your body, you just want to take off.

The lawyer bumps into you, trips you up. You stumble. You try to regain your footing without looking overly alive. No luck. You hit the ground hard, sprawled out. The walkers around you try not to react. You lie there. Do you get up? How do zombies stand up? You've never seen one get up. Should you just lie there?

No. That's useless. Then you'll never get out of here. Slowly, moving as awkwardly as possibly, you get to your feet.

The businessman is right in front of you, staring at you. Two more stand in your way. Their moans grow louder.

Oh God . . .

The jig is up! Run! Turn to page 358.

Keep up the act. You can do it. C'mon. Turn to page 244.

"The museum—let's go for it," you say.

But before you can move, the SWAT truck door flies open and a zombie, in full SWAT gear, leaps from inside. You reel back, trip over your feet, and hit the ground. He pounces. You reach to your left and grab a dropped riot shield. You get it up just as the thing lands on top of you.

Its face is inches from yours, separated only by the riot shield. Its teeth gnaw at the heavy plastic. You look in its eyes—they're bloodshot to the point that they're pure red. Saliva drips. Its hands claw at the shield, then move down. Fingers dig into your sides.

BLAM!

Blood splatters the plastic. The zombie's head drops heavily onto the shield, cracked face squished against it, then slides off. Chucky towers above you, smoking pistol in hand.

"Jesus fucking Christ, you coulda killed me!" you shout.

"You had the shield thing up."

"Still!"

"Whatever. We gotta move, son."

You take the assault rifle for yourself and throw the dead officer's pistol to Chucky. He sprints back to the overturned plow and grabs the shotgun.

You peek your head around the side of the truck. Fuck! They're closing in. You squeeze the trigger and the assault rifle shakes violently in your hands. Bullets spray wildly. You catch the front one in the head, dropping it and tripping up the few behind it.

Chucky's already running. You follow, booking it across the avenue, then up the museum steps.

Chucky tugs at one of the three huge museum doors that line the top of the stairs. They're locked from the inside. He tugs again.

You look behind you. They're coming up the stairs, quick. "Let us in!" you shout.

A woman at the window. Wide-eyed. Scared. She shakes her head no.

You raise the rifle, point it at her. She scampers away from the door. You step back, aim the gun at the handle, and unload. It blows apart, wood splinters, and the metal handle drops to the floor. Chucky throws his shoulder into the door and it opens.

You slam it behind you, just in time. It bucks as the zombies collide with it. In a moment, they're at every door, clawing at the windows.

"Go," you say to Chucky. "Get something, anything—I'll hold this, I got it. Quick."

Chucky sprints to the center of the museum lobby. In a second he's back, pushing a huge wooden bench. You slide away from the door and Chucky slams the bench against it. It holds.

You stop. Breathe. Turn around for the first time. You've been to the Met once before, with your parents on vacation. The lobby is huge. High ceilings. A big stairway ahead of you leads to art, art, and more art. Large doorways on the lobby level lead to exhibit halls.

"Please don't shoot us." A little girl's voice. You look down into her big eyes, then at the gun by your side.

"Why would we shoot you?"

"Everybody's shooting everybody," the little girl says.

"You're telling me," Chucky says. "Why were those soldiers shooting at us?"

A woman, her mother it seems, steps up and puts her arms

on the girl's shoulder. "No one knows what's going on. Soldiers shooting the police. The police shooting at us. We were fine in here—until you led those things up."

"Sorry," you say, feeling legitimately guilty. But—nothing you can do about it now. You take a look around. There are about fifteen people in the museum lobby, a few on benches, the rest on the floor. No one talks. Some weep silently. Others look too shocked to move.

"Where's everyone else?" you ask.

A little man, mid-sixties, round glasses, steps forward. "Nearly all of our museum guests left as soon as they heard."

"Who are you?"

"The curator," Glasses responds.

You take another look out the door. One of the monsters' faces is pressed flat against it. Its jawbone protrudes, jutting through the flesh. Dozens of bloody palms slap the glass. Some pound with fists.

A wave of heat washes over your body. You feel sick. Nauseous. You rub at your face—pull your hand away and see a mixture of sweat and blood. "Where's the bathroom?" you ask the little man.

He points down the hall. You head that way, Chucky following. Once you're through the door, you nearly dive for the sink, turning the knob until the water runs cold, then splashing it over your hair and face.

The nausea subsides some. You stand. You barely recognize the man in the mirror. Despite the water, your face is caked with blood. Some yours, some not. You run warm water over your hands and scratch at your face, desperate to clean it off.

Chucky enters one of the stalls and takes a seat on the toilet. You hear him reload the shotgun and set it on the floor.

Chucky says something quietly. You can't make it out—your ears are still ringing.

"What?" you say. "Speak up. I can barely hear."

"I said now what?"

You shut the water off and take a seat on the floor. The cool tile feels good. "I don't know."

"I have seven shells left in the shotgun."

"OK."

"You?"

"What?"

"How many shots do you have left in the rifle?"

The rifle. The heavy gun you used to shoot those monsters. Fuck. Nausea returns. Your vision narrows and you get hotter. Bright white spots clear your field of vision. You feel more and more out of it. "I don't know," you mutter. "I can't think about that now."

Chucky walks out of the stall. "Fuck do you mean you can't think about that. You have to think about that. We gotta keep moving. And you gotta get your shit together."

You nod. Fuck. Here it comes—your insides are rushing up your throat. You pull yourself to your feet and over to the sink. You puke. Your eyes water. You drop to your knees and puke again. Spit out bile.

"You alright?" Chucky says.

"Yeah," you say, spitting again. "Just give me a second."

Your body cools down. The nausea fades. Hands grip the sink. You look in the mirror. Looking back at you is a scared little kid. A kid that was so frightened, so near-hysterical that he just vomited. That kid—that kid won't live another hour. You can't be that kid. You shake your head. You're not going to die like this. Not you.

Not. You.

You spit into the sink one last time and stand. You get your feet under you. You feel OK. You're going to be OK. You say it out loud, "I'm going to fucking be OK."

Chucky looks worried.

You pick up the rifle. You fool around it with for a second, then the magazine drops out. "It's almost full," you say.

"Good," Chucky says. "Um—but are you alright? Head on straight?"

"Yeah. I'm good."

"You sure?"

"I said I'm good."

You march back out into the museum lobby.

There, at the top of the stairs to the main exhibit hall—a zombie. A college kid, backpack hanging off it. About to come down. No one sees it.

You do.

And like you said, you're good.

You stop, raise the rifle, aim, and squeeze. The thing's head bursts and it falls over the rail, down onto the lobby floor. The shot echoes through the lobby. Everyone jumps up. Several people scream.

You clutch the hot rifle. "OK," you say. "Listen up. If there's one of those fuckers in here, that means there's more. We have to leave. Does anybody have any ideas on how to do that?"

Chucky looks at you and smiles. "Look who decided to take charge."

"I told you, I got my shit together."

No one says anything.

"Again, anyone got any ideas?" you say, shouting now. "C'mon, speak up."

A man stands up. He's with his wife and two girls. "I . . . I have a yacht."

Chucky's eyes light up.

"What's your name?" you ask.

"Um, Wesley. Wesley Downing." He has a cheesy, upper-class British accent. Must be visiting.

"Nice to meet you, Wesley." You stick out your hand. Timidly, he shakes it.

"How big is this yacht?"

"Ninety-footer," he says, less timid now, more proud.

"So it can take all of us?"

"Sure. It's a ninety-footer."

"Shut up, Wes," his wife says, standing up. "Yes, it can hold everyone here. But we'd have to get to it. It's docked at the Seventy-ninth Street Boat Basin."

A black woman, mid-forties, steps forward. "I drive a bus for the city. It's outside. I ran in here when some guy in the back of the bus went schizo."

"Good. Perfect." You walk to the doors. The glass has cracked on one. The monsters continue to pound at it. Won't hold forever. Through the mass of bodies, you can see the city bus. It's about seventy-five yards up the avenue.

But the steps are full with the things—and the streets, not much different. How the hell do you get to the bus?

That's when it catches your eye. A statue in the corner of the lobby. A huge thing—twenty feet tall, at least. It's a massive, three-headed dog—horrific, beastly, almost rabid faces.

You walk over. Look closer. The statue sits on a wheeled platform. A plaque along the bottom is inscribed with Εισαγωγή κειμένου (αγγλικά ή ελληνικά)—next to it, it's translated as THE THREE HEADS OF HADES.

You knock on it. Hmm, feels hollow.

"Don't touch that!" someone screams. It's Glasses—he's running over like his pants are on fire.

"That's an important piece—don't—don't ever touch."

"What is it?"

"Cerberus. According to Greek and Roman mythology, he guarded the gates to hell."

Fitting, you think, as the idea forms in your head—because you're sending this big motherfucker straight into the arms of hell. "How heavy is it?" you ask.

"Half a ton, I'd suppose."

You rub at your chin. "OK," you say, walking back to the group. "I've got an idea. We don't wait for the zombies to back off—we go down there, straight for the bus. Any objections?"

A woman stands up. "Out there? Are you crazy? In here

we're safe! We have food! Look—Christ, just look! There're hundreds of them, waiting for us!"

There's another crack at the glass.

"Lady, those doors aren't going to hold. And there's more of those things inside this museum. We're seventy-five yards from a bus that can take us straight to a boat that can get us *the fuck* off this island—we have to take the risk. *I'm* taking the risk. Chucky?"

"Yeah. I'm in. Sooner we get out of here, the better—place gives me the creeps."

The mother stares back at you. "O-OK"

"Good. Now"—you turn to Glasses, a small smile on your face—"which way to the arms and armor exhibit?"

Turn to page 310.

FAIL

You do nothing. You bum. You *loser*. What is wrong with you?
You just let those little kids die . . .

Have fun living with yourself. Asshole.

AN END

You take a jagged route downtown, crisscrossing avenues and side streets. Every time you seem to be making progress, you come upon some sort of holdup. Fire trucks, masses of people, more zombies.

The Army seems to have entered the city—but they're stuck on the outskirts—you see them in the distance as you cross Twenty-third Street.

You come to a stop at Washington Square Park, NYU buildings surrounding you. You look left and right. An overturned fire truck blocks the route to the east and a thick mass of the dead blocks the route to the west.

"Through," Chucky says, looking at the park. Zombie NYU students and zombie homeless dudes and zombie musicians are scattered across the park. As usual, you can't really tell the difference between them.

"Yep, right through."

You press down lightly on the gas. The truck rumbles forward, through the famous Washington Arch.

Then you stop.

The behavior of the beasts is odd. Slow, stupid. They stumble about, walk in circles, putter along. But you saw it in the garage—once something gets their interest, they move like goddamn hyenas. Zero to sixty like.

You roar through that park, they'll come for you right away. Take it slow, maybe they won't pay you any mind.

But damn it if you don't hate NYU students. Really, can't stand them. You applied to NYU out of college—they politely declined. Really, given the opportunity, you wouldn't mind taking a few of the artsy snobs out.

So you floor it. Three bounce off the front. One gets stuck, spins around the plow, then is dragged underneath. The truck bounces as you drive over it.

They come at you from all angles. A thick crowd of them. All you can make out is the dead.

Then—

CRUNCH!!!

You hit a heavy stone chess table. The truck bounces right. The wheels screech, lift up into the air, and come back down. There's a huge bang as one tire blows. You cut right. The plow smashes into one of the benches that surround the dry fountain at the center of the park. Chucky shrieks. The plow snaps and a piece flies up at the windshield, cracking it. Then the massive vehicle lifts, tips, and rolls down into the fountain.

Your ears ring. What the fuck just happened? You're wet. Fuck. Blood? No. Chucky's vodka Gatorade.

You're upside down. The wheels spin. Thank God for seat belts. You crane your neck—pain shoots through it. Fuck—you're definitely suing NYU. Through the shattered passenger-side window you see Chucky, lying on his back, on the grass. One of the beasts leaps onto him—then there's a bang, and like someone just pressed rewind, the beast flies off him in a cloud of smoke. Chucky crawls to his feet, holding the shotgun, and wipes his sleeve across his bloody face.

Two more of the things, each wearing a backpack covered in stickers and pins, come at him. He turns, panicked, not sure who to target.

"Hey you fucks!" you shout. "Over here!"

You lay on the horn. It works. They turn. Chucky raises the shotgun, aims, and takes both their heads off with one shot. Before they hit the ground he's running, his massive legs pumping. But not for safety—he's running toward you.

"What the hell are you doing?!" you shout.

Chucky slides, pretty well for a big guy, under the over-turned truck bed and sticks his head in the partition. "I ain't leaving you behind, little buddy."

"Thanks for the thought—but now we're both dead."

You jerk to the left as one of the beasts reaches through the window and grabs your hair. Another pushes past him and grabs your shirt.

You unbuckle your seat belt and fall to the ceiling, which is now the floor. The undead hand still clings to your hair. You grab it, twist, and rip it off—a chunk of your hair along with it. The truck cab is tight as hell—you barely manage to roll over.

No room to move.

No room to breathe.

Hands reaching in through the windows, grabbing at you. From all angles.

"Squeeze through the window," Chucky says as he reloads the double barrel.

You shove your body through the partition window. Manage to get up to your biceps, then you're stuck. Can't move forward or back. Claustrophobia chokes you—cold hands grabbing at you, beasts moaning, and you can't move. You kick your legs vi-olently, scared. You feel your Vans make solid contact with a face.

"Pull me!" you shout.

Chucky grabs hold of your shirt and pulls. Three horrific sec-onds, you pop through, the truck bed now a roof above you. Pain in your stomach—a cracked rib, you realize. One of the things makes it into the cab and you see its grisly face pop through the partition window, snapping its jaw at you. Chucky sticks the shotgun in its face, turns his head away, and squeezes. The thing explodes, blood spraying the inside of the cab.

"Yeah, let that be a lesson to the rest of you bastards," Chucky snarls.

"OK, now what?" you say, wiping the blood off your face with the back of your hand.

The two of you sit under the overturned truck bed, catching your breath. The back end is on the ground, leaving a triangle of open space on each side of you. And through that triangle of open space—nothing but zombie feet.

"I don't know," Chucky says.

"Yo, you smell that?"

You sniff at the air. "Yeah. Gas."

"OK, plan." Chucky pulls his pack of smokes from his pocket. Then a Bic—it looks like a Tic Tac in his massive hands. He lights the cigarette, then hands it to you.

"OK, the second I shoot, you drop the cigarette. We'll have like three seconds. Got it?"

"Wait, wait—what?"

"No time," Chucky says, then aims at the zombie legs. Point-blank range. Squeezes. The legs explode. Bones splinter and shatter. Three of the things fall. Chucky scrambles out and over them. They're already beginning to rise again.

You drop the cigarette and follow. Scamper through the hole on all fours, then push yourself up off the first zombie, stepping on its head as you run.

The things turn and watch you go. Then they give chase.

And then—

BOOM!!!

The truck goes up like the fucking Death Star. You're lifted off your feet and tossed to the grass. The zombies aren't so lucky. Forty of the flaming beasts fly through the air in every direction.

"Whaddya know, it worked," Chucky says, laying nearby.

Up ahead, a horn honks. A military transport. A soldier shouts, "Need help, boys?"

You scamper across the park to the transport. One beast stands in your way, blocking you. Arms out.

The soldier leans out the window. Fires two shots and drops the thing. Phew.

You leap into the back of the truck. Help Chucky up and in. Breathe. Relief floods you.

And for some reason, you just start laughing. Chucky, too. Laughing until you're howling. And together, in the back of the truck, you giggle your way out of the city.

AN END

"Are you aiming for them?" you ask Chucky after he hits his fifth zombie in as many blocks.

Chucky turns his head toward you and grins.

You can't look at these things anymore—can't take it. Too emotionally exhausting. You lie down and hug the gun across your chest. Stare up at the sky. The sun is setting. You listen to the sounds of this new version of Manhattan. Sirens. Gunfire. Screams.

You drift in and out of consciousness as Chucky drives through the city. Waking nightmares about beasts coming for you, grabbing you, pulling you under.

The truck slows to a crawl. The gunfire gets louder.

"Yo, heads up."

God. Back to your knees. You're on Eightieth Street and Fifth Avenue. Central Park to your left, then farther up, the Metropolitan Museum, looming over you.

Up ahead it's a small war zone—the police battling the Army. Bullets pierce the side of an armored police vehicle resting in front of the museum. A SWAT team takes cover behind it. Fifty yards farther, on the other side of the street, the soldiers fire from behind parked cars.

"Chucky, I think maybe we should get out of here."

The SWAT team returns fire. The sound is deafening. Grenades roll, and then a huge explosion as a taxi goes up in flames.

A soldier sprints to the sidewalk, tosses something over the wall to the park, then scrambles over. A second later, he reappears behind the wall, large weapon on his shoulder.

Oh. Shit.

It rockets toward you.

"RPG!"

You leap from the truck just as the RPG hits—the explosion throws you through the air. Chucky makes it halfway out the door as the truck blows.

You're sprawled out on Fifth Avenue. Your ears are ringing. Warm blood bubbles up and out, rendering you nearly deaf.

Chucky's behind you, on his back.

You hear the dampened sound of gunfire as the SWAT team moves up the street, firing as they run, taking cover behind cars.

One member of the SWAT team remains—sitting against the truck, blood pumping steadily from his neck. A man lies dead in front of him, head blown open. You watch the SWAT member intently. His head nods, like he's tired. Then he starts to shake. His legs kick. Then, in a second, he's on his feet.

Now among the undead, it sprints out from behind the truck and takes off down the street after its unit. It tackles the first SWAT member it comes across. Begins devouring him. And then it's up again, taking down the next one.

The soldiers continue to fire. Bullets rip through the thing. But it doesn't stop. In a minute, the entire SWAT unit is undead. The soldiers continue blasting away.

You turn to look back at Chucky. "Fuck, Chucky—we gotta move."

Chucky sits up, rubbing at his head. Blood pours from his nose. "Yeah, yeah—what else is new?"

About half of the undead SWAT unit runs for the soldiers. The others turn, survey, and lock in on you.

"Chucky! Now!"

The soldier's shots whiz past you. You get to your feet, pull Chucky up, and take shelter behind the SWAT truck.

You and Chucky look around, desperate for a way out. You

peek your head around the side. The zombie SWAT team is tearing up the street—they're close—maybe fifty feet.

"Museum?!" Chucky shouts.

The shadow of the Metropolitan Museum looms over you. "Could get trapped in there," you say.

"Park?"

No time to think. The creatures will be on you in seconds . . .

If you want to run for the safety of the museum, turn to page 292.

If you'd rather run into the park and try to lose them, turn to page 323.

You throw yourself onto the passenger seat, staying low. Explosions all around. The car windows shatter, showering you with tiny pieces of safety glass.

Screams. Horrific, frightened, excruciating screams. The tank shells and machine-gun fire take care of everyone, living and/or sorta-living. Thank God you decided to wait it out in a police cruiser.

Finally, the barrage subsides.

You raise your head.

Everything burns. Thick smoke—can't see a damn thing. Two people stumble past your window, shell-shocked. Even the live ones look like zombies.

But you're OK. You're alive.

Then . . . a different sound. You can't quite place it at first. You sit up. A helicopter, rising up from below the bridge. The rotors clear the smoke and it ascends through the darkness and flames like some deadly machine exiting hell.

It's a version of the Apache. You had a toy when you were a kid—looked just like it. This one's just more modern. Cannon underneath. Four massive rockets on each side, bookended by huge cannons that look like silver honeycomb. Four blades spin, kicking up dust and debris, along with the tail rotor.

It moves backward, rising higher into the air. You stare—watching those giant guns and those oh-so-deadly rockets. The roar dulls as it flies to the very rear of the bridge.

It hovers a hundred feet above the bridge.

Then, like a shark through water, it cuts through the air,

bringing all hell with it. Streams of missiles and machine-gun fire light up everything and everyone in sight. A chain reaction of cars and trucks blown to smithereens. People are torn apart. Zombies blown to bits.

You reach for the car door. But it's too late.

You see it in slow motion. The pilot's taut face. The blades spinning. The missile. It drops from the bottom of the chopper, hovers in the air for a second, and—

Oh no.

KA-BOOM!!!

∴∴∴ AN END ∴∴∴

Glasses leads the way, with you, Chucky, and the rest of the group following. You walk the long halls, past million-dollar paintings and beautiful statues, then turn a corner.

There it is—Arms and Armor. A huge, bright room with multicolored flags hanging from the ceiling. At the center, four model horses clad in armor, similarly protected medieval knights on top of them. Glass cases line the walls—an ode to all the effort mankind has put into destroying itself over the past two thousand years.

"Whoa," Chucky says. "I didn't know museums had this kinda shit."

"Cool right?"

You turn to the group. "Take what you need—we meet back in the hall in five minutes."

Everyone splits up. You walk the rooms, browsing the display cases. You wander past a collection of Revolutionary War swords and rifles, then Civil War uniforms—all the way up to World War II. Chucky's fascinated by the medieval stuff. There's a huge racket behind you as he knocks over one of the model horses while trying to pull the rider's jousting lance loose. "My bad," he says.

You head into the next room and something strikes your fancy. Samurai armor. You look closer—the nameplate says ARMOR (GUSOKU), 17TH AND 19TH CENTURIES; EDO PERIOD; JAPANESE.

Bingo—that's the one for you. You step back and slam the butt of the assault rifle into the case. It cracks. Once more and it shatters. Gently, you remove the armor.

You pull the yellow and blue robe over your head. You skip the baggy pants and sandals—your pants and Vans will do just fine. You tie the front thigh guard, sort of like a very thick skirt, around your waist. Then you lace up the greaves to protect your ankles. Next is the chest piece, not unlike a baseball catcher's chest protector. Then you strap on the thick, layered shoulder armor, followed by the sleeve armor. Then the helmet and neck guard. Finally, a small side katana—no more than three feet long. You ignore the larger blade, too much to carry with the rifle.

As you leave, you catch a glimpse of your reflection in one of the cases. You look patently absurd—yellow and blue Samurai gear, frayed work khakis sticking out the bottom, assault rifle in hand.

Then you see Chucky and don't feel so ridiculous—he's donned head to toe in heavy medieval jousting armor. Heavy medieval jousting armor that is *way* too small for him. His gut sticks out the bottom. He has the shotgun slung over his back. In his hands a massive, ornate halberd, five feet long—at the top, a dazzling but deadly battle ax with sword blade at the peak.

You laugh. "What the hell is all that shit?"

"It was Henry the Second's," he says.

"Who's that?"

"I dunno—some old dude from France. Badass though, huh?"

"Little tight, no?"

"Bro I'm six five—dudes were like three feet tall back then. This is the best I could do."

Behind Chucky, something catches your eye. A medieval morning star—a wooden club, about two feet long, with a length of chain at the end connecting to a spiked metal ball, slightly larger than a softball. You flash the samurai sword and break the case. You pull the morning star out and tuck the club into your waistband. The steel ball bounces gently against your thigh armor as you walk out into the hall.

There are the rest of them.

The mother, minutes ago refusing to leave, now holds an elaborate pirate sword. Beside her is her young son, with a matching dagger.

A fat man with chain mail draped across his chest holds an old British hunting crossbow.

Wesley has nothing in his hand but his BlackBerry. His wife, however, wields a long trident.

The rest of them, similar items, old armor, clubs, anything that looks like it might be protective or good in a fight. Many of them carry round wooden shields.

But strangest of all is Glasses. He has a small black satchel over his shoulder, nothing else. And he's barefoot. You don't ask.

"Looking good, guys," you say. "Now let's go check out that big dog."

You lead them to the Cerberus statue and order everyone to get behind it. They do—though Glasses looks quite conflicted.

Then, on your order, everyone pushes.

You dig your foot into the floor. Throw your shoulder into it, giving it everything you have. Beside you, the mother does the same. Chucky, a juggernaut, screams, and gives it a huge final push and the wheels begin to turn. You continue with it, guiding it across the museum lobby until it's at the far left door, closest to the bus.

The massive statue fills the entire door frame. You continue pushing—the middle hound's snout now against the glass. Then it breaks through, shattering the glass completely. Undead hands reach through and the moans turn to howls. The twin doors finally crack and open. Then the statue slides out— the front two wheels tip over the top of the stairs.

Like a bobsled team, everyone jumps on, one foot on the platform, one on the statue. You take the front left, Chucky at the front right.

The Three Heads of Hades hangs on the ledge for a second, it tips, and then—

Then goes.

CRASH!!!

The thing barrels down the stairs, crushing everything in its way. It's like riding a runaway train—it bulldozes over the beasts, never slowing. The monsters are spun around, beaten, destroyed.

The statue hits the streets with a tremendous bang. The wheels snap off and it skids across the street.

Behind you, nearly fifty zombies lie on the stairs, not moving, brains mush—crushed under half a ton of Greek architecture.

"Move!" you shout.

At once, everyone leaps off, weapons up. They form together, and you all begin jogging. The bus sits a hundred feet down the avenue, so close but so far.

You stay along the left side of the group, assault rifle up, morning star on your waist, samurai sword sheathed at your side. Chucky takes the right side, carrying the massive halberd with the shotgun slung over his back.

Six of the monsters sprint down the sidewalk, then cut through two burning cars, straight for you. The mother steps forward, slashes out with the ornate pirate sword. Slices open the face of one. Her son rams the dagger up into the chin of the next.

Chucky fires, blowing the other four back with one blast from the Remington.

Footsteps coming up behind you. You turn, too late. The beast plows into you, knocking you to the ground. It wrestles its way up on top of you.

You look up into its undead eyes.

Christ . . .

You recognize the thing. It's your fucking asshole boss, Matt

Trypuc. For a second, you're too shocked, too confused to even move. You've wanted to kill your boss a million times—but you never thought he'd actually try to kill you.

Its head lowers, its mouth open.

Then a flash of black steel. Blood.

WTF . . .

Jutting out from your undead boss's forehead is a ninja throwing star. Your boss-turned-beast rolls off you.

Glasses sticks his hand out and pulls you up. "Seven years in China, studying at the Shao-Lin temple," he says.

Glasses is a fucking ninja?? This day just keeps getting weirder . . .

His hand flashes into his satchel and then out—three more throwing stars fly through the air, each one a direct hit to the face of a charging beast.

He moves forward, reaching for more.

No time to rest. Footsteps to your left. Two zombie soldiers and a regular-looking guy. You raise the rifle, aim, and squeeze. All three shots hit the first zombie soldier in the face. Takes it off its feet. You pump six shots into the second thing. Its chest blasts apart in a bloody mess, but it barely slows. You squeeze again—*click*—out of ammo. Fuck.

The two remaining monsters draw near. You look to your right. Chucky's battling half a dozen of them. Glasses flicks another two throwing stars through the air. Wes's wife has the trident buried in the chest of a wild-eyed woman who's foaming at the mouth.

Everyone, locked in battle.

You, on your own for the moment.

You sling the assault rifle over your back and begin spinning the morning star above your head. You have no idea how to use this thing. What the hell were you thinking? Honestly, a morning star? Just 'cause it was cool-looking? You jackass.

Here goes nothing . . .

You extend your arm and lash the weapon out at the soldier.

Direct hit. The spiked ball slams into the side of its face and the soldier's head explodes like someone placed an M80 inside its skull. Its helmet flies through the air and it hits the ground. So does the morning star, as you lose your grip on it. It clatters away.

The other thing—a middle-aged guy, khakis and a denim shirt—is close behind.

You release the clip on the rifle, it hits the ground, and you pop in a new one. You aim for its head. Squeeze. You miss. It's close now. You aim lower and blow the thing apart at the knees. It crumples—a second later, it's crawling, growling, as it pulls itself forward. You put twenty bullets into the cement all around its head, a few finally making contact and leaving its skull leaking cerebral fluid.

Phew.

You spin, need to get a sense of the group. The fighting continues, but you're moving—getting closer. About halfway to the bus.

One sprints full-out at Chucky, arms swinging around maniacally. Chucky throws his heavy, steel-laden shoulder into it, knocking it to the ground. Then decapitates the next with the halberd.

A man screams. You spin. Wesley. A zombie draped over him. He slaps at it, trying to fight it off. And then next to him. Another scream. Wesley's wife.

Fuck. No time to save them both.

Women and children first, right?

But you need Wesley's yacht to get to freedom.

Sorry, Lord.

You fire, blowing the beast off Wesley. Then pivot—but his wife is already dead. Her throat is torn out and she's sinking to the ground. You kill the beast, then her. Wesley runs over, drops to his knees, sobbing.

You step over, grab his arm, and yank him to his feet. "No time. Mourn later."

You keep jogging. Getting closer. One comes from around the side of the bus, wild hair flowing. The fat man with the crossbow fires. Nails it in the chest.

"The head!" you shout. "The head!"

He fires again—the bolt goes through the thing's eye, blowing the back of its skull out.

You glance over to check on Chucky. He's wielding the halberd like a maniac, decapitating beasts left and right.

Glasses jumps out in front of the group. Does some crazy, Street Fighter Guile–style backflip kick. He nails the zombie in front of him in the chin. Its jaw snaps shut. Blood sprays as it bites off its own tongue. The tongue hits the ground a second before the body.

Wave after wave of zombies come at Glasses. And this small man, the same man that scolded you for touching a piece of art just twenty minutes earlier, deals with them all. He never stops moving. One undead arm comes at him, he spins, using the beast's momentum, and throws it to the ground. The kid jams the pirate dagger into its face.

Glasses is like some crazy, kung fu drum major, leading your caravan to safety. Everything that comes at him, he deals with it, and leaves it sprawled out on the ground behind him. Hundreds of monsters die at the hands of ancient swords and axes wielded by this ragtag group of civilians-cum-warriors.

You're close to the bus. So close.

Fuck. A loud moan. Three charging at you, all side by side. A cabdriver, you can smell him from twenty feet away. A guy about your age in flip-flops and a button down, shaggy beard. And a soldier. Looks to be the last of the military men.

You aim at the cabbie and squeeze the trigger.

Click.

You squeeze again. Nothing. The trigger won't even pull back.

Fuck! It's jammed.

You look over at Chucky—he's surrounded, doing his best to

survive. One comes at him—he punches it in the face with his heavy metal gloves and it collapses. More appear. Fuck. He's of no help.

The three things, moaning, growling, white bubbly spit all over their faces, close in. Their arms spring up, just steps away, ready to take you down.

Try to fix the jam? Turn to page 154.

Drop the rifle and go with the morning star? Turn to page 94.

THIS DJ, HE GETS DOWN

You let loose with a kick and nail the undead stripper in the chin. Her head whips back. It gives you a split second—you back up, rip the turntables loose, and bring them crashing down on her head.

It does little. She keeps coming. Over the wall. Hands on you.

You kick her again, in the crotch this time, pushing her back once more. Turntables again, across her face. This knocks her aside. You raise the tables high and bring them down as hard as you can. She drops to the floor.

You bring the tables down again. Again. Again. You feel her head break, her skull shatter. She grabs your pant leg, pulls tight.

One more heavy crash and the tables break full through the skull and crush her brain.

Phew . . .

You give her an angry kick in the gut and turn, looking for Yakuma.

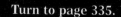

Turn to page 335.

I'M ON A BOAT!

The driver does her job well—twenty minutes later, you come up on the Seventy-ninth Street Boat Basin. As expected, it's a mess. Police walk the docks. Houseboat owners shout, demanding safe passage. Coast Guard boats are anchored two hundred yards out or so. No one coming or going.

Wesley leans over you and points at a beautiful white boat. In gold letters across the side are the words HER MAJESTY'S. "There she is," he says.

The driver parks the bus on the lawn. You go out first—leaving the rifle inside. Police presence is heavy. You've made it this far—just have to get through.

You order everyone to stay on the bus, then you and Wesley walk to the yacht. A police officer stands in your way.

"Excuse us," Wesley says.

"What?" the officer says.

"We'd like to get through, please."

"You're not going anywhere, pal."

"The hell I'm not. This is my yacht."

"No seafaring vehicles leave. I'm not even allowed to let you board."

"Not allowed to board? Are you mad? This is my yacht!"

"Hey, James Bond, I don't give a damn. Now back off."

"Wesley, calm down. Officer, this doesn't have to go down like this."

"What the fuck are you wearing?"

"Oh yeah." You remove the helmet and shoulder armor.

"Sorry, weird day," you say. "Look officer, there has to be

something you can do to let us out of here. We're not going to say anything. We won't tell anyone. Just let my friends and I board, we'll be out of your hair."

"What friends?"

"On the bus back there."

The cop leans, looks past you, and laughs. "Buddy, I told you—"

"Wesley, how much money do you have on you?"

The cop shakes his head. "If you're attempting to offer me a bribe, I'll lock you up right now."

"What bribe? I'm just asking my friend how much money he has. Wesley, how much you got?"

"What, on me, I don't know."

"On the boat."

"That's none of your business."

You turn and grab him by his upturned collar. "Goddamn it," you whisper, furious. "Do you want us all to die here? How much fucking money do you have on the boat?"

"Um—I don't know, fifty thousand American."

"Boy," you say, whistling. "Fifty thousand bucks? That's a lot."

The cop perks up, just slightly.

"You hear that, officer, he's got fifty thousand bucks on that boat."

The cop stares you down. One half of him is intrigued. The other half wants to knock your teeth out.

Finally, he caves. "Goddamn it, c'mon. Both of you."

Wesley leads the way, up the plank and onto the yacht. It's beautiful—massive, all brand-new, shiny wood, white leather everything.

The cop follows Wesley. You follow the cop. You go down a small set of stairs, through a beautiful living room area, and then into the captain's cabin. Wesley grabs a painting and swings it open. Behind it, a safe. You and the cop stare, fascinated.

"Do you mind?" Wesley says.

The cop sighs and turns. You do the same. You roll your eyes, trying to be friendly. He's not interested in being friends.

The dial spins and you hear the door creak open. Wesley sighs deeply, and you hear the door close.

You and the cop turn. Wesley stands, cash in hand.

"Fifty thousand American dollars," he says.

The cop eyes him suspiciously, then takes the cash. He flips through it. Then he pulls his radio from his belt and walks to the corner of the room. He takes a seat on the massive king bed. Wesley frowns.

"Joe, go to eleven," the cop says, then turns the dial, switching frequencies. "You there? Yeah, yeah—listen . . ."

The cop's voice drops and he begins whispering. Finally, he switches frequencies back and stands up.

"OK," he says.

"OK?"

"OK. You can go. All of you. You have five fucking minutes to board this thing and get the hell out of here, you understand?"

"You got it—five minutes—no prob."

Wesley stays behind as you run out and grab Chucky, who is anxiously hanging on to the door frame of the bus, and tell him the good news. The two of you lead everyone onto the yacht. It's about ten minutes before you get going—the cop gives you the extra five for free.

Everyone heads to the front of the boat. You hang back, staring at the city. You silently say good-bye—to your apartment, your job, your family, your friends, everything. Who knows when you'll be back? Who knows where you'll wind up?

The boat shudders and the engine starts. It pulls away.

You sigh deeply. What a day. What *the fuck* happened to the world?

You take a seat, put your feet up on the side of the boat, and watch the Manhattan skyline grow smaller. You pass the

Coast Guard boats. Pass the houseboat owners desperate to leave. Goddamn, money can get you out of just about anything, you think.

A noise behind you. Still on edge, you turn, scared. It's Chucky. He's grinning, two glasses in hand and a bottle of good whiskey. He holds up a cigar.

"Cuban?"

"Don't mind if I do."

AN END

A STROLL THROUGH CENTRAL PARK

The way your legs feel right now, the Met's massive, iconic staircase looks like Mount Everest.

"Park," you say, then take off running across the street. You hit the sidewalk and vault over the wall, landing on your back in the grass. Fortunately, the soldiers are occupied with the undead SWAT team and are no longer firing at you. You look around. Chucky's gone. Not sure which way he went.

No time to find him. You take off through the trees. Stop for a second to catch your breath. Up a small rock cliff and down the other side.

That's when you realize the park may have been the wrong choice.

They're everywhere.

An hour ago, they were lying on blankets, playing Frisbee, picnicking on prepared foods from Dean & Deluca—now they're shuffling around, hungering for human flesh.

A whistle pierces the air.

It's Chucky. The cavalry. Riding a police horse.

Alright, you've seen enough old Westerns to know how this works. One swift move. Up and onto the back.

A beast lunges at him. Chucky swings the shotgun. Catches it in the head and sends it sprawling back. Another goes right for him. The horse gallops over it, crushing it.

"C'mon buddy!" he shouts.

He sticks out his arm and hangs to the side.

Galloping closer.

You can do this.

Closer . . .

You grab hold. And up. It's not perfect, but you're on the back of the thing. And you're not dead.

Chucky rides through the things. Down a wooded path, through the hill. A bridge in the distance.

Chucky kicks the horse. It speeds up. Onto the small bridge. But there—right in the middle of the bridge—two of the beasts. The horse rears back.

Shit.

You're tossed off the horse, then over the side of the bridge. You splash down in a small pond. Chucky lands on top of you, pushing you under.

You swim up. Catch your breath and look around.

The monsters stumble toward the lake. Gathering until they surround it completely. Then, from all sides, they pour in.

You tread water. Scared to death. No idea what to do.

"The fuck, they can go in the water?" Chucky says.

You're too panicked to respond.

"Fuck this," Chucky says, and starts swimming. Then a splash, a scream, and he goes under.

"Chucky!" you shout.

He bursts up through the water. Gasping for air. You make eye contact. See the fear in his eyes. Then he's pulled back under.

Then you feel it around your leg. A hand, tight. Thick fingers. Strong. You kick.

Then you go under.

You open your eyes. Through the murky water, you see the outline of a man.

No, not one man. Dozens.

You gasp for air. Get nothing but water. It fills your lungs.

With any luck, you'll drown before they have a chance to devour and turn you.

AN END

You book it down the motionless escalators, moving as fast as you can with the busted ankle.

The revolving doors are locked. You jump up, hit the lock. Then out onto the sidewalk. Out of habit, you look both ways before stepping into the street. The things are everywhere.

You limp across the street and up a small set of stairs and into the park. You duck down behind a tree, catch your breath, and watch. The zombies seem drawn by the sound of the gunfire and they're all headed in that direction.

You make your way from tree to tree. Up over a fence. Bullets whip over your head. You take cover behind a bench. The things are all around you. No safety anywhere. The gunfire lets up for a moment, just long enough for you to hear a low moan behind you. You turn just in time. A tall, lanky thing—head tilted to the side—lunges for you.

You leap onto the bench and over the fence. Hit the ground. Ankle throbbing. Sand in your mouth. You spit it out, look around. A dozen small dogs around you, yapping away. Goddamn it, the dog run.

You get to your feet. You can see the tanks through the trees. You're halfway there, halfway to your goal. Halfway home.

CRACK!!!

The world shakes as a tank shell slams into a massive oak tree behind you. The entire tree explodes, raining down splinters of wood.

Eyes wide, you watch as a huge branch crashes down. You try to jump out of the way. Too late.

A blast of pain blows through your body. Your chest shatters. You're pinned, a heavy hunk of branch lying on top of you. Sharp pains when you breathe. Ribs are shattered.

The little Manhattanite toy dogs yap away. One licks your face.

And then you feel something at your feet. Please be a dog. Please . . .

No. You hear the moan. You do your best not to move. Maybe if you just lie there, it will go away.

You feel something pressing against your pants. Then into your skin. Teeth. It's slow, tentative—like the thing can't tell if you're living or dead and wants to know before it starts eating.

Once the teeth get into your flesh, though, that changes. You scream as it bites down.

Then it rips its teeth free from your leg.

Then, suddenly, it appears over the top of the branch. A teenager. Short, spiky hair.

It looks you in your eyes. Looking through you. You stare back, horrified.

Then its head bursts open and blood rains down upon you. The thing sways for a moment, then falls to the side.

Had that bullet come a moment earlier, you might not have zombie saliva pumping through your veins right now.

You're stuck. You're going to turn into of those things. And you can't move. Can't kill yourself. Can't do anything to stop it. Just have to lie there and take it.

After a long while, the tanks rumble away. The zombies' moans surround you from all sides.

Soon you feel it taking you over. A living death, creeping through your body.

The hunger. It tears through your body. And then everything goes dark . . .

You don't wake.

Another you wakes.

An undead you.

An undead you that smells meat. Meat in the form of a small, yapping Yorkie with a small heart collar around its neck.

You reach for it. Grab it by its neck. It yelps.

You eat.

❧ AN END ❧

NO, DREAMGIRL,
PLEASE LEAVE

You jackass! What's the matter with you!?

Put the book down. No, no. Throw it out the window. Or burn it. You don't deserve it.

This was the hottest girl in high school! This was Melissa Lefevre in *Angus*. That whipped-cream chick in *Varsity Blues*. What's-her-name in *Fast Times at Ridgemont High*.

Just . . . just die, jackass.

AN END

You should try to run right past Anthony. Try to dodge him. Then out into the street. You figure that's your best chance of survival.

But then you picture Rachel. Breathtakingly beautiful bartender Rachel. If you leave, undead Anthony is going to shuffle into that bar and kill everyone, including her.

She's too pretty to die like that.

Hammer in your left hand, drill in the right, you run at the two undead things and swing with both arms. The drill gets one through the temple. The hammer bounces the other one's head off the wall.

You pull the drill from the one and bury it into the other one's face.

You can hear Anthony behind you. You have to make it back into the bar.

Then he hits you. You see stars and stumble forward. You spin around, through the doorway and into the bar. You get your footing and lunge forward to shut the door. But Anthony's already through. It's like he has no intention of devouring you until he's finished murdering you.

Johnny Cash on the jukebox. *Don't bring your guns to town.* Christ, what you'd do for a pair of guns right now.

Anthony swings his arm around and sends you flying. The drill and hammer slide across the floor.

You hear Rachel scream. Hear the bar patrons scatter. But no one comes to help. It's just you and him.

He buries a punch in your chest, sending you flying back

and sprawled out on the sawdust-covered floor. It's like fighting the Incredible Hulk.

He stands over you. He raises his massive fist and brings it crashing down toward your head. You roll. His fist crashes into the ground. You hear his hand shatter. But he doesn't flinch. You're back up, running for the game room, keeping him away from Rachel.

Anthony charges after you like a goddamned juggernaut. You leap across the pool table, trying to put something between the two of you. You pick up a few pool balls. Whip them at him. They bounce off his face, do nothing. The eight ball hits the table and rolls into the corner pocket.

Anthony launches himself across the table, shattering the lamp that hangs above it. You fall back—shove your legs up in the air. He lands, his chest falling on the soles of your Vans. Sharp pain runs up your legs as you keep him away in some bizarre, fucked-up game of airplane. You reach out, grab two pool balls. Your hands soar up and you slam the balls against his head. Twice more. Into his ears. Has to rattle his brain. Has to. Once more, hard as you can, and he rolls off you.

Thank God. You scramble to your feet. Look around—desperate for anything.

Darts. You rip three from the dartboard.

Anthony's up. Mad. Foaming at the mouth.

You whip one. The dart spins through the air and sticks into his forehead.

Anthony lowers his shoulder and sprints toward you.

He hits you square in the chest. The wind rushes out of you.

He's about to leap forward—finish you.

You've got one shot.

Clutching one dart in each hand, you bring your firsts smashing down.

And you connect.

Bull's-eye.

One dart through each one of his wide, bloodshot eyes.

He falls forward, on top of you. The darts stay embedded in his eyes even as your hands come loose, trying to break your fall.

You hit the floor. The weight of his body damn near crushes you. His head comes down—the tails of the darts hit your chest, and they're pushed through his eyes and into his brain. Thick blood leaks out of the sockets and pools on your chest.

He twitches, kicks, then stops moving.

"Hello?" you say. "Anyone want to get him off me?"

You hear someone. Then the body moves slightly. It's Rachel. She has her shoulder against Anthony, pushing with everything she's got. Finally, he slides some, and you make your way out from under him.

Rachel stares at Anthony. Her friend. Dead.

In that split second, she looks at you differently. Something in her eyes. She needs you. He's not around anymore.

She.

Needs.

You.

Feels damn good.

"Are you alright?" you ask her.

She smiles. "I am, actually. I probably shouldn't be—but I am. I just can't even process it all anymore. Whole thing has me feeling—I don't know—hard to explain."

Then she gets up. Gives you a smile. A sort of—did you read that right?—naughty smile. "I have to pee," she says.

"Yeah—I need to clean all this shit off me," you respond.

"I'll go first," she says, and walks to the bathroom. Then stops and turns. "Hey, toss me your phone."

"No service."

"Just gimme it," she says.

"Alright," you shrug, and throw it over. She catches it and steps inside the bathroom. A minute later, she comes back out.

You go in. Run the water. Clean Anthony's blood and gore off you.

Reaching for a paper towel, you see your phone, sitting on the edge of the sink.

You unlock it. It clicks.

And there's a picture of Rachel.

With a big grin.

Flipping you off.

And no shirt on . . .

⁘ AN END ⁘

You shake your head. "No—no I can't do that."

Limpy curses.

"OK," Jones says, "your life."

They climb on their bikes and roar away. You watch the blur of taillights as the Angels disappear into the night.

You work your way through the quiet streets back to your apartment. Climb the fire escape. Through the window. You kick off your pants, nearly trip, and lie on the couch.

Time passes. Months. You lose track. You talk to yourself. Scold yourself. Scream at yourself. You had an opportunity. It was a risk, sure. A gamble. But you didn't even play—never gave yourself a chance to lose.

And now you're stuck here—alone—a coward.

You close your eyes and sleep, thinking it'd be just fine if you never woke up.

AN END

You scan the club. Yakuma is finishing up. All that's left is the bouncer and the thing pinned to the wall.

She sprints toward the bouncer, blade by her side, and flashes past. She turns around, blood dripping from the blade.

The bouncer stands strong, arms out, frozen still.

Then the upper half of its body slides off and falls to the floor with a wet thud. Its legs stay upright. Yakuma spins on her jellies, and plants the blade through the bouncer's head and into the floor.

Then its legs fall.

God. Damn.

Yakuma looks at you, up in the booth. "What, no sweaty singles for that?" she says, pulling the blade from the floor.

"Um."

She walks to the wall and pulls the second blade from the zombie's gut. It lunges for her. She swings and leaves it minus one head.

"C'mon tough guy, let's split," she says.

You tiptoe through the disgusting mess of bodies.

"Very masculine. You've got me hot right now."

"Shaddup . . ."

You follow her to the front door. She opens, peers outside, and shuts it.

"Nope."

"Shit," you say, running your hands through your hair. "Now what?"

"Champagne Room."

"Champagne Room?"

"No sex. Follow me."

You follow her alright. You stare at her rear end, entranced. The sway of it. The way it moves from side to—

Out of nowhere, you're lying prone on the floor, head completely and totally inside some guy's open torso. Instantly, you're retching into the half-empty stomach cavity. Try to breathe. Blood in your mouth. Drowning in blood.

Yakuma grabs you by your hair and pulls you up, your face covered in vomit and gore. You puke again on the headless body, gagging. Gasping for air. Blood covers your eyes. You use the back of your hand to wipe off your face, then realize you just covered yourself in even more gunk.

You can't see—too much blood in your eyes. "Help," you squeak out.

Something cold and wet splashes over your face. Tastes like—gin? You open your eyes, which are now burning. Yakuma's holding an empty glass.

"Better?" she says.

"Yeah, thanks." You lift up your shirt and use the bottom to wipe off your face. The smell is wretched. You have to steady yourself to keep from puking again.

"Watch where you're walking, OK, moneybags?" Yakuma says, heading up the stairs.

"Yeah—I got distracted."

"It happens. You've got intestine on your head."

"Thanks." You pull off a noodle-like section of the guy's gut and fling it to the floor.

At the top of the stairs is a heavy red velvet curtain. Yakuma walks through. You use it to wipe your hands and face, trying to get the rest of the gore off. You can already feel the blood beginning to harden.

Through a second velvet curtain, and you're in the Champagne Room. It's dark, a tiny room with a few tables and couches running along the walls.

"This is it?" you say. "This is the Champagne Room?"

How disappointing . . .

Beyond the Champagne Room, you enter a small hall that leads to the bathrooms. Ahead of you Yakuma opens the bathroom window and climbs out onto the fire escape. You stay right behind her. Undead moans float up from below—along with screams, honking horns, sirens, and the sharp bark of gunfire.

Up on the roof, you get the sights to match the sounds. Buildings burn. People writhe on the streets. Monsters stumble around.

You grimace. Christ—your skin is tight with a dead man's drying blood. Claustrophobia choking you. You sit down. Spit in your hand. Wipe it over your face, desperate to get clean.

Yakuma slips the two blades into her belt behind her back so they crisscross above her butt. She pulls her phone from her back pocket and casually walks along the roof ledge as she talks. She gets loud. Then laughs. Then hangs up, hops off the ledge, and walks over.

"OK—I got a ride."

"What do you mean you got a ride?" you ask.

"A ride, out of the city."

"Huh? How?"

"Listen—I'm telling you, you can come if you want."

"Well yeah, duh, I'll take the ride—but take a look out there," you say, waving at the streets below. "It's a complete shitstorm."

She puts her finger to her lips. "Shh."

"Look—you were impressive with the sword. It was amazing. Way hot. But did you see the TV? There's absolutely no way we're getting out of the city."

"We're not. But [LEGAL EDIT] is."

"What? [LEGAL EDIT]? What does he have to do with this?"

"He's my boyfriend."

"[LEGAL EDIT] is your boyfriend?"

"We'll not really my boyfriend, but . . ."

"You're fucking [LEGAL EDIT]? [LEGAL EDIT] as in the starting shortstop for the New York Yankees?"

"Yeah. So what?"

"Nothing. I mean, yeah, sure why not. Hell, I'd probably fuck him, too. And I'm a guy. And I'm a guy who doesn't even like the Yankees. But wait—how does you doing him get us out of the city?"

"His driver—I can use him whenever I want. Right now I'm using him to get us the hell outta here. His driver comes, gets us, takes us to Yankee Stadium, we leave with the team. Trust me—that team's getting out of the city."

"There's a game today?"

"Yup, twelve-oh-five."

"Wait—how'd you even get cell service? My phone hasn't worked in hours."

"Satellite phone."

"What?"

"Gift. He's [LEGAL] fucking [EDIT]."

"So when's this ride coming?"

A car horn interrupts your thought. Three sharp beeps.

"That'd be him," she grins.

You walk to the edge. A limo has come to a stop up on the curb. The undead creatures take notice and descend upon it. Rocking, shaking it. Clawing at the windows.

The horn blasts twice more.

"Shall we?"

"Huh?"

Yakuma leaps off the building. Her hair flows, wild, as she falls two stories onto the roof of the car. She lands perfectly, blades out, on one knee.

She spins. Heads roll.

Goddamn it. Heights. Even twenty feet has your stomach doing flips. Zombies on the ground doesn't help any. But you throw your leg over the side and begin to work your way down the fire escape.

You get down to the first level—no more climbing from here. Have to jump.

"What should I do?!" you shout down.

Yakuma's a little too busy to talk. One of the monsters has climbed up onto the hood. A high school kid probably—tight jeans, tight T-shirt, trucker cap. Yakuma slides down the windshield and slams both swords through its head, lifts it up with a brutal Mortal Kombat move, and tosses it into a second one that was getting too close. One claws at the passenger-side door. Yakuma leaps off the hood, over the thing, and lands behind it. One sword flashes through the air and cuts clear through the thing's head, exposing the wet, pink brain. It falls.

Yakuma climbs into the passenger side.

"Wait!" you shout. "Don't leave without me!"

The sunroof opens. You see Yakuma's smiling face. "Jump!"

"Are you kidding me?"

"You got two seconds."

Sonofabitch.

You leap. Crash onto the roof, half your body inside through the sunroof, the other half out. Your wrist snaps against something hard. Intense pain. A feeling like fire rips through your thigh. You want to cry. No. Don't cry. Not in front of the pretty stripper.

Yakuma pulls you inside. You collapse onto the leather seats. Massage your wrist.

"Hit it, Rick," Yakuma says to the driver, and the car takes off.

You introduce yourself to the driver, but he doesn't seem too interested. Too busy driving like a madman.

"Lady, you're gonna get me in so much trouble," he says as he swerves up onto the curb, smashes into something, and cuts back onto the street. Copies of *The Onion* and the *Village Voice* splash over the window. Rick hits the wipers.

"Rick, how long have I known you?"

"I don't know. While."

"Have I gotten you in trouble yet?"

"No . . ."

"So stop worrying."

He sighs deeply. "To the stadium?"

"Yep. Stop for nothing."

Turn to page 186.

You look out at the abandoned city. "I'm gonna stay," you say.

"Huh?"

"There was a law office a few floors down. Had power. Had food. Like the military said, this is the last job—now they're coming to take the city back. I never did shit like you guys—I have no record that needs to be wiped clean. I want my reward for all this work. Apartment in the Empire State Building? How can I resist? Hey—maybe I can claim squatters' rights."

You stick out your hand.

Jones looks you in the eyes. Then grips your hand. "Good luck, kid."

"You too. And try not to kill any more cops, huh?"

Jones smiles, turns, and disappears out the door.

Down there, nearly one hundred stories below you, they look like roaches boarding the bus. It pulls back out onto Fifth Avenue, taillights glowing in the pitch-black night. You can't even hear the roar of the Harleys from this height.

But you do hear the blast from the Abrams tank.

The huge machine comes around the corner of Twenty-eight Street. The cannon fires and blows the bus apart. Soldiers running alongside it unload.

The bullets tear through the Angels. Rip them off their bikes.

Jones is lifted off his bike, hangs in the air for a second, then crashes to the ground, not moving. The soldiers walk through the street, executing any men that are still breathing.

You should have seen it coming. No way they'd let them get away with it.

When we do right, nobody remembers. When we do wrong, nobody forgets.

The tank reverses and disappears down the alleyway. The soldiers follow.

You choke back a tear as you lean against the fence and stare at the smoldering remains of the Angels. And you wait— wait for the city that never sleeps to rebuild itself.

✦✦ AN END ✦✦

You hop out. Another car in front of you explodes in a colossal ball of fire. The heat is extraordinary. Eyebrows—gone.

You turn to run but slam right into one of the things. A girl. College aged. Pretty.

It throws itself into you, sending you both flying back. Your back hits the bridge wall. The beast whips its head forward, its teeth aiming for your neck. You counter with a head butt, meeting it in the middle.

It pushes harder against you. Your upper half is hanging over the bridge. You feel nothing but air behind you. Its teeth are at your shirt. Through it. You're pushing back as hard as you can, hands on its shoulders, desperately trying to get it away. But it's got you.

KRAK-KOW!!!

A rocket slams into the car beside you—fiery, white-hot chunks of shrapnel slice through the air. The monster at your chest is thrown to the side. The explosion lifts you off your feet, and your whole world is turned upside down. Intense heat. Flames at your face. Then you're falling. Spiraling. Spiraling down into the East River.

. . .

. . . . .

Your eyes flitter. It's nighttime.

It's silent. No gunfire. No explosion. No tremendous banging sounds that make your head want to implode.

Your body is broken. Arms, legs, everything. But you're alive. How? You should have drowned. Confused, you try to move.

Garbage. You're tangled up in some sort of netting. Plastic trash bags, torn open, lay about. You're the centerpiece of a massive floating pile of garbage. And is that a syringe on your chest?

Ahh, the East River . . .

You drift for hours. Any sort of movement is impossible. The pain is too strong.

Fuck me, just let me die here, I don't care.

Then a bright light flashes over your eyelids. You struggle to open them. Can't turn your head. Feels like you're about to be abducted by a UFO.

A man's voice, shouting. "Hold up! Over there, in that hunk of shit!"

The light flashes over you again. A searchlight. The sound of a boat. Two splashes. Bodies in the water next to you. Hands on you. Ever so slightly, you tilt your head. Make out the words COAST GUARD on their chests.

A man's voice. "Hang on pal, we got you, you're going to be alright."

AN END

PEANUTS AND CRACKED BATS

The undead drift into the parking lot, moving toward the stadium, drawn by the smell of fifty-two thousand fresh, live bodies and a pennant race.

The limo stops just in front of the main entrance. Yakuma's out of the car in a flash, Rick yelling after her to be careful. You wave good-bye to Rick as you hurry to catch up with her.

You race trough the parking lot, over a track of perfectly trimmed trees, planted at perfectly measured ten-foot intervals, and around the side of the stadium. The blue walls become a blur as you race pass.

Yakuma slides to a stop in front of a set of large twin doors. In big letters: PLAYERS' ENTRANCE.

She bangs twice. A heavy metal door slides open. Slim man, suit, funny cap.

"Yakuma! How are you?"

"Fine, Freddy, move it, gotta talk to you-know-who."

"Oh c'mon, you know I can't—"

His eyes glaze over. He stares beyond you.

"Wha—"

"Exactly," Yakuma says.

"On the walkie—they said something was happening—but don't interrupt the game, don't alarm the fans."

"I think the fans are about to be alarmed, hon."

Yakuma brushes past him and you follow. As you turn the corner, Freddy shouts "Wait—are those samurai swords?"

"It's been a crazy day."

You follow her through the guts of the stadium. Down pipelined halls that are still clean. "New" Yankee Stadium. What a joke. In other countries, they hang on to their landmarks, their important buildings, their places of worship. Here they tear them down, go across the street and build crappy replicas, and slap "New" on the front.

Shit, even before zombies invaded the island, New York City was already half dead . . .

You come out in a more normal-looking hallway. Two lefts, and you're standing inside the Yankees home locker room. It's empty.

"Shit," Yakuma says. "Too late."

A beautiful flat screen mounted on the wall shows the game under way, first inning, someone you don't recognize at bat.

"Hey," you ask, "so, what's the plan? What the hell am I doing in the Yankees locker room?"

"I'm getting [LEGAL EDIT]—and he's getting us out of the city, now. C'mon, to the field," she says.

To the field. Yankee Stadium field? You watch Yakuma go, hair long and thick, ass perfect, samurai swords gleaming— yeah, you'll follow.

On your way out the door, you pass a tall glass display case. A plaque reads NEW YORK YANKEES. PRIDE. POWER. PINSTRIPES. Inside the glass—the Louisville Slugger that Babe Ruth used to hit his first homerun at Yankee Stadium. Dark wood. Worn handle. A number of gunslinger-style notches are etched into the grain—one for each home run he hit with it.

Yeah, you gotta have that.

You grab a stool and smash it against the case. You reach inside and take the bat from its stand. You feel like King Arthur clutching Excalibur for the first time. Babe Ruth's bat, in your hands . . .

An alarm sounds. Out in the hall, a security guard stops you. Yakuma flashes the blade. He shuts up and steps back.

At the end of the hall, through the dugout door, you see the bright green field. You follow Yakuma—right through the door and into the Yankees dugout. You haven't been to a baseball game all season, forgot that feel of taking in the field for the first time. The boys of summer.

The Yankees are in the field, Red Sox at bat. A few players sit around, bullshitting. The manager leans against the dugout fence, spitting sunflower seeds. The cheer of the fans is loud, overpowering. Hard to hear anything.

After a minute or so, [LEGAL EDIT] glances at the dugout and his eyes go wide. You can only imagine what's going through his mind—"is that my stripper girlfriend, splattered with blood, holding two samurai swords, in the fucking dugout? ESPN is going to shit a brick."

Without hesitation, Yakuma marches out onto the field.

Just beside the dugout stands a New York City cop. He glances over, does a double take. He shouts at her to freeze. She ignores it. He rips his Taser from his belt, trains it on Yakuma's back, takes two steps forward, and fires.

Two tiny, dartlike electrodes fly from the Taser and stick in Yakuma's neck, just above her tank top. She immediately shrieks, begins shaking violently, then hits the grass just short of the pitcher's mound. After a moment, she stops convulsing.

Shit. You tighten your fingers around the bat. OK, in for all or in for nothing, right? You sprint out onto the field and bury the bat into the back of the cop's legs. He crumples. The Taser falls to the grass. He scrambles for it, but not fast enough. You grab it and point it at him. Your heart is pounding—you can't believe you're doing this.

"Officer, look, I'm really, really sorry about this," you say softly. "But you'll understand in a second."

And that second is now. A maniacal scream. A flurry of movement in the stands. The chaos is under way.

In the seat behind first base, one of the things dines on some poor father. A gorgeous woman in the front row leaps onto the field, blood pouring down her side. She takes a few shaky steps, then falls. Fans scramble over seats. Rush for exits. Complete madness—anything to get out of there. A man in a Gehrig jersey shoves a cotton candy vendor, sending him somersaulting down the stairs, backward, gravity pulling him at a deadly speed. Bodies tumble from the upper decks, crashing to the seats below, dead on impact. A frat-boy type, already turned, is knocked over the side and lands in the netting behind home plate. Confused, the frat-boy zombie kicks, lashes out, only to get himself more entangled.

The whole time, the stadium stereo never stops—*dun dun da duh, duh dun da duh.*

[LEGAL EDIT] helps Yakuma to her feet and rips the Taser electrodes free. She glances over at you, sees the cop on the ground, and throws you a nod. She's not hurt—just pissed.

As the players take in the 360 degrees of madness that surrounds them, they slowly begin moving to the center of the field.

Bodies litter the stands. The lucky ones make it out. You can only imagine the horror in the halls, in the parking lot.

As the crowd thins, the sound of fear and panic is replaced with the hideous moans of the dead.

You, Yakuma, a handful of cops, and the entire roster of the Yankees and Red Sox are huddled together in the Yankee Stadium infield.

The monsters start coming over the walls. Slowly at first, a trickle. Then more. Crashing onto the field. Hitting the grass, then rising.

The players form a circle, bats up. You stay in the middle of the herd, like a weakling lamb. Just because you've already encountered these monsters doesn't mean you're not still shitting your pants.

All at once, the beasts charge—a huge mass of them,

coming in. Yakuma's already out there, slaying the things two and three at a time.

"Oh man, Selig's definitely fining me for this," an outfielder says to you. Then he winks, runs forward, and buries his bat in the side of the undead fan leading the charge.

And with that, the battle is under way.

The umpire gets it first. Three fans on him, tearing at his flesh. His mask is ripped off and it spins across the ground. Teeth sink into his neck. He shakes. Begins to turn. Shit. You recognize him, even as his face goes white—Jim Joyce. A player swings his bat wildly, clearing out the undead fans. Then he raises the bat high, says, "This one's for Galarraga," and caves in the zombie ump's head.

A tall, entitled-looking Yankees third baseman gets it in the leg from a young kid who happens to be wearing his jersey. He shrieks and pushes the brat away. Blood pours from his open wound.

He pulls his bat back and swings. The kid goes flying. Two more fans tackle the third baseman from behind. Teeth sink into his shoulder and neck.

A large, Dominican batter for the Red Sox runs over, does away with the two fans, and then kills the downed Yankee for good with a powerful whack. Then spits on him.

A tall, mustached, Italian-looking guy in a Joe DiMaggio jersey has his eyes on you. His lower lip has been torn open and hangs, sickeningly, against his chin. He starts in. His lip flops. You raise the bat. The power of the Babe flows through you. You point the bat directly at the man. Yep—you're calling your shot. Just like Ruth.

And then you swing.

CRACK!!!

You can almost hear Michael Kay's obnoxious home run call. "Seeee ya!"

The man's head rips to the side. His neck snaps. He falls, blood splashing the beautifully trimmed infield grass.

An older player, classy looking, grabs a bag of balls. He gets to work. Fastballs. Two-seamers. All strikes, right between the eyes. Two or three to the head, and it's a kill. The zombies drop.

The bodies pile up as the players give it everything they've got.

Yakuma and you-know-who are now standing back to back, holding their ground, she with her blades and him with his bat. The things surround them.

His bat splinters against a zombie skull. He takes another one from a Red Sox player at his feet. Must have been on deck, because there are metal batting doughnuts at the end of it. He wields it like the weapon it is.

One thing gets close. He swings, shattering its face. Two more. Same deal, one swing, takes them down.

He beats them into submission—Yakuma carves them up. Helluva couple.

Then a chopping roar from the sky.

A dust cloud kicks up around you. Debris and trash whips across the field. Five huge police choppers hover above the field. And in the passenger seat of one of them—is that? Christ, it is. Hank goddamn Steinbrenner—the old man's son—the new guy in charge.

Ladders drop from the copters. Sway over the field.

Steinbrenner yells into a megaphone. "New York Yankees, begin boarding! Long-term contracts first. Boston, you wait your turn, if there's room, you can board."

[LEGAL EDIT] lets Yakuma go first. You follow, climbing the ladder, bat stuffed down your pant leg and in your sock. You're not losing that. When you get to the top, Steinbrenner gives you the stinkeye, but as he climbs aboard [LEGAL EDIT] says, "He's with me." You feel incredibly cool.

You pull the bat free and you take a seat next to Yakuma, across from her man. The chopper fills up and takes off.

You look down at the Babe's bat, rested across your legs. Helluva thing. You pull your keys from your pocket, mark one last notch in the wood, and watch as Yankee Stadium shrinks to nothing beneath you.

❃❃ AN END ❃❃

DON'T STOP, DON'T LOOK BACK, JUST RUN!

You dart through the crowd, across Chambers Street. Feet tiring, heart pumping. Then, out of nowhere

SLAM!!!

You roll up over the hood of the car. The car brakes and sends you flying. Everything goes black. Pain racks your entire body.

No dizzying, spinning view of the world as you fly through the air—just black. You don't feel yourself hit the ground. Don't hear the wet crack as your head splatters across the cement.

AN END

"First of all, let me say how frankly fucking horrified I am by the things you guys have done. Jones, you killed a cop?"

"Prove it."

Jesus. You knew these were bad guys—but not on this level. You're surprised, though—surprised at how much it doesn't bother you. The shit you've seen over the past few months—either you've gained some perspective or you've completely lost perspective, but either way . . .

"Well, if I killed a cop, I'd want that erased," you say. "So yeah, I'd take them up on the offer."

Jones looks around at the group. Some are pleased, some aren't. But like he said before—he has final say.

"OK," Jones says, "we're in."

The Colonel smiles. "Good. I'll have your first target in seventy-two hours."

"Fine. Go with Doc to the garage," Jones says, nodding to a round, Santa Claus–looking guy in the corner. "He'll get you a list of what we need."

The next day the helicopter returns. You step outside, crack open a beer, and watch. The zombies are gathered at the fences. They moan, unhappy, hungry.

As you stand there next to Tommy, you decide to give his Kodiak another shot. You get the hang of it, not to the point of finding it less than miserable, but you're not puking. A pool of thick black spit gathers on the sidewalk below you, running into the cracks.

Three soldiers, working together, carry a large wooden crate out of the helicopter toward the club.

You hear the jangle of keys and then the grating sound of a garage door being pulled open. Doc steps out, puffing a cigar. He meets the soldiers halfway and examines the crate, then directs them to the garage. Inside, you hear him curse one, saying, "No, numbnuts, over there in the corner."

The soldiers carry in a total of nine crates, then take off in the helicopter.

For the next two days, Doc works. Comes out of the garage just to eat and get water. Each time he comes dirtier and greasier.

Then, finally, three days after the Colonel first arrived, just before midnight, Doc comes out and collapses on the couch. He nods at Jones.

"OK," Jones says, "let's take a look."

You step into the garage and your jaw drops. In front of you is the most badass collection of death on wheels since *Twisted Metal 2*. Ten Harleys. Each one armed to the teeth. Doc gives the guys the tour, but you're barely listening. Just staring at the beauties.

Doc goes over each Harley one by one. Guns. Missile launchers. Blades. Saws. Did he just say flamethrower?

"Kid!" Doc says, snapping you out of it.

"Oh, sorry. Yeah?"

"This one's yours."

"Uh, I can't ride."

"No—the sidecar. You're with Tommy."

Tommy grins and slaps you on the back.

Two pipes stick out of the chassis, parallel to the ground. At the end, about two feet in front of the tire, is a large horizontal circular saw. "Now Tommy, this blade here—this runs on the bike," Doc says. "You give it gas, the saw spins. Anything in your way—cut it right in half."

"And kid, this is my pride and joy here," he says, indicating the sidecar.

You nod, awestruck.

"This sidecar is your new home. This big bastard mounted on the front is the M61 Vulcan minigun."

"Shit yeah, the gun from *Predator*."

"Dunno, never saw it. The Vulcan's serious—shoots bullets the size of my fist. Two wires run from the main trigger down under the hood," he says, pointing to the interior of the sidecar. "Twin triggers—gotta hold down both to make it shoot. Now under here, along the side, I've got a Heckler & Koch MP5 submachine gun. Kickback ain't too bad—should be good for a little guy like you. And, ahem, at your request—a red Vitamin Water."

The Angels roll their eyes.

"What? It's refreshing," you say.

"Almost forgot," Doc says, walking around the back of the bike. "On the sidecar here, you've got an RMG multipurpose disposable rocket-propelled grenade launcher. Use it once, then it's done. Who knows what you'll run into out there, so it could prove useful. Tommy's got some experience with the things."

Tommy laughs. "Sure have—remember when we had to go to war with those fuckin'—"

Tommy is interrupted by Jones at the door. "Colonel just phoned. He's got tonight's target."

"What is it?" you ask.

"Madison Square Garden. We're rescuing a woman. Wife of some congressman."

"How do we know she's there?" Tommy asks.

"Man didn't say much. They picked her up on radio—she got a hold of some security guard's walkie-talkie. Everyone thought she was dead. She's not."

"Who's going?" someone asks.

"Tommy, Joe Camel, and the Kid."

"What, why me?"

"You're the one that cast the last vote. So now you ride. Get dressed—meet Tommy outside in ten."

Sigh—how'd the hell did you get yourself into this . . .

Turn to page 161.

THE JIG IS UP!

George Costanza running from that fire at the kid's birthday party? That's you. Pushing anyone and anything in your way aside.

You break away from the crowd. Long strides. This is your life—the whole thing—and it all comes down to how fast your out-of-shape legs can run.

You've never moved this fast before. Speedy Gonzalez meets Sonic the Hedgehog.

You're going to make it.

You hear them behind you.

No. You're faster. You want it more. You want to live.

Horrific moans.

Run. Run. Run. *Run!*

You throw a glance back over your shoulder. No . . . The lawyer leaps. Cold, dead hands wrap around you and pull you to the ground.

More hands on you. One rips into your arm. The lawyer buries its face in your belly and begins ripping through you.

You go into shock. The pain subsides. Your head rolls to the side.

As you begin to fade out, you see the rest of the group. They're all suffering the same fate. You've incited a massacre.

You've gotten every single one of them killed . . .

AN END

Yakuma goes for the door. You grab her shoulder. "Don't. There're too many out there—it's suicide."

"You got a better idea?"

"Yeah, I do. Drive. Don't stop. Let's just get away from here. I live—I mean, my parents live, outside Boston. We could go there."

Yakuma's not happy. But she takes a look out the window at the thousand beasts approaching, and acquiesces.

"Goddamn it. Fine. Rick," she yells up to the front, "keep driving."

"Yakuma . . ."

"Rick—I like you. Don't make me your cut your fucking head off."

Rick slams his hand down on the wheel, furious, but he does as she says. He peels out of the parking lot and takes off up the avenue then up the on-ramp onto the parkway. It's complete gridlock. Every lane packed.

Hours pass. You sip from the glass bottle of Cîroc. It calms you some.

And then, like a tsunami, they come. Out of nowhere. Ravaging everything. Some people, bitten, stumble out of their cars. They swarm up the highway, moving through the traffic.

Rick floors it and smacks into the car in front of you. Then, screaming, he gets out and runs. A moment later, he goes down. Tackled by a monster in a Windbreaker.

The things surround the limo. Dead, disgusting faces press against the glass. Three of them gather at the door, slobbering on it. Your heart pounds.

Yakuma goes for the door.

"No!" you scream, terrified. "Let's wait, maybe they'll leave."

"I'm not a 'let's wait' kind of girl," Yakuma says, then kicks open the door, sending the three sprawling back. She leaps out and slashes them.

Oh shit, here we go again. You take the bottle of Cîroc and follow her out the door. One gets close. You whack it across the head with the heavy glass bottle.

You cross the lanes and jump the guardrail. A wooden fence stretches along the side of the highway.

"Help me," Yakuma says, looking up.

You interlace your fingers and give her a boost. She grasps at the fence. Your eyes are drawn to her rear.

"Knock it off," she says.

How'd she know? "How'd you know?"

She wiggles her butt at you in response before making her way up. A second later, she appears over the side, hand out, and helps you up. You get one leg over. The second one's harder. Christ, like gym class all over again. Finally, Yakuma grabs you by your belt and pulls you up.

You're on the roof of a small building. You look out over the sprawling land in front of you. A monorail hangs above you. Perfectly laid out little streets. Huge trees.

"I—I think we just jumped the fence into the Bronx Zoo."

Yakuma takes it in. "No way," she says. "I've never been to the zoo. It's so empty."

"We'll find out . . ." You climb down over the side of the building. It's a little restaurant—the Dancing Crane Café. Empty. Like everything else. You grab a zoo map. Try to locate the Dancing Crane Café on the map, but you give up. Too hungry. So you hop the counter and go for food.

You've got half a chicken tender in your mouth when you hear the squeal of tires. A Bronx Zoo van rips around the corner.

"Uh-oh," Yakuma says.

Coming around the corner after the van are hundreds of them. Every visitor to the zoo on this particular late summer Monday—now a zombie.

The van flies past you, the driver's eyes wide with fear. He takes a turn and the van goes up on two wheels and bursts through a heavy metal fence. The van flips and rolls down a hill, coming to a stop against a tree. Electric sparks fly around the gaping hole in the fence.

You turn. The army of the undead has its eyes on you.

You grab Yakuma by the wrist and run down through the hole. She passes you, making her way downhill. You lose your footing and tumble. But you're back up in a second, running. You pass the overturned van. Catch a glimpse of the driver, blood pouring down his face. Unconscious.

You don't stop. You race through a small wooded area and come out in a massive field. Giraffes in the distance. Tall grass, up to your waist.

"What did we just run into?" Yakuma says, taking it in.

"I think the T. rex exhibit."

She doesn't laugh.

You glance behind you. The zombies have stopped for a moment to dine on the poor driver.

Yakuma takes off through the grass. Still running, you pull the map up. It flies up in your face. You try to hold it down, get your bearings, without stopping.

You find the café. See the line that indicates the fence.

"Yakuma," you say, through sharp breaths. "You're not going to like this. But we're in the middle of the Wild African Safari."

"Great," she says, sounding legitimately excited.

"Sixty acres of wild Africa, it says. Oh cool. Water buffalo."

Behind you, the beasts blast through the trees. The grass catches at your arms and waist as you continue through the field.

Then a roar. You turn to look. In the back of the mass, a zombie body flies up in the air. Then another.

And then a massive lion bursts through the front of the group, sending the zombies sprawling to the ground. It roars, sandy hair shining in the sunlight. Two come at it—it slaps a massive paw, sending the zombies stumbling back. It gets one in its powerful jaws and shakes it back and forth.

It rips another in half, right at the midsection.

Twenty of the undead jump on top of the lion. It roars, rises. More leap on top of it. Dig their teeth in. Two hang on to its front leg, chewing it up. Together, the beasts and the animal fall into the tall grass.

Yakuma yanks your wrist. "C'mon."

You continue through the plains. Through the tall grass, then into a wooded area. Massive trees. Monkeys swing from vines. It gets thicker. Yakuma hands you one of the blades. Together, you hack your way through.

Up ahead is a swamp. Beyond that, one of the monorail's many elevated towers. If you can climb that, you can get the hell out of this jungle . . .

A crashing behind you. Then a rush of sounds—branches breaking.

"They're back," you say.

The swamp stretches out wide to the left and to the right. With the beasts so close behind you, the only way forward is through the swamp.

You take a step into the water. Then there's a violent splash from the center of the swamp. You rip your foot out, your heart pounding.

A huge tail whips up. Two eyes come out of the water.

"Fucking Christ, is that an alligator?!"

"Crocodile, I think," she says. "But yeah. Let's go."

The horde continues through the woods behind you. You've got no choice. Yakuma steps into the muddy water, blade out, and begins wading through. You follow her, close behind.

You're about halfway across when, in a flash, a huge snout bursts from the water, tremendous mouth open. Massive, jagged teeth.

You scream like a little girl.

Yakuma stabs the sword up. The blade slices through the crocodile's armored scales, through its lower jaw, pierces its tongue, and then bursts through the roof of its mouth. Its eyes go wide, but it makes no sound. It struggles to open its mouth, but only cuts itself further.

Yakuma rips the sword out and begins swimming. You hear splashes behind you as the zombies enter the water. You dive in, swim madly.

You and Yakuma come out at the other end of the swamp. You sprint for the tower. You begin climbing. Yakuma follows. Halfway up, you stop. Clinging to the ladder, you pull the map out.

Through jagged breaths: "If we catch the monorail, we can hitch a ride to the aquarium. From there, we can walk to the Zoo Center."

Yakuma grunts. "Just keep climbing."

You make it to the top, nearly five stories. The monorail track runs across most of the zoo. You see one coming around, minutes away.

Below you, the crocodiles tear a group of the zombies to pieces. Body parts float in the water. The brown-green swamp water mixes with the blood, turning the water black.

The monorail approaches. You crouch on top of the tower, not looking down. The train car approaches. You steady yourself. Ready. Do this wrong, and you'll plummet to your death.

You dive inside. Phew. Safe, for the moment. Below you, giraffes graze. Zebras, close by, mill about. Through a canopy of leaves, gorillas bask in the sun. And then the zombies—they're everywhere. They pay no attention to the animals.

The monorail passes over a polar bear exhibit, then closes in on the aquarium.

"Ready?" you ask her.

"Ready," she says.

As it passes over the aquarium roof, you toss the swords out. Then you leap. It's only ten feet and you make it fairly effortlessly—skinned palms, but nothing broken. You collect your sword, Yakuma does the same, and she follows you into the dark aquarium.

You gasp. There, directly in front of you, a zoo worker. Trainer or something. Green shorts. Green T-shirt. Poor attempt at looking like he just stepped out of a savannah.

His face is torn to shreds.

He leaps at you. You reel back, turn your head away, and thrust out the sword. He skewers himself, sliding up to the blade's hilt. Blood spills out on your shoes. The thing grabs you by the shirt. Teeth gnash. You try to raise the sword and lift the beast up, but the blade just cuts up through its chest.

Yakuma lunges over, grabs the beast, and rips it off the sword. She has its hands pinned behind its back. You grab its legs and together you lift the beast up and throw it over the side. It drops into the tank, thrashing. Water splashes over the side. The thing sticks a dead arm out at you, stretching its fingers, moans once, then goes under.

You catch your breath, then follow Yakuma down the spiraling ramp, past the glass tank. The undead zoo worker sinks, moving along with you. It continues to thrash as it sinks farther.

Then from the bottom of the tank come a rush of tiny fish—each one no more than half a foot long. Hundreds of them.

You see the sign on the tank: RED-BELLIED PIRANHAS.

The entire school swarms. In a moment you can no longer see the zoo worker's body—just the fish, completely covering it. Hundreds of little black and red fins. Blood fills the water. Then, twenty seconds later, the fish split, swimming off in different directions.

All that remains of the zoo worker is a meatless skeleton.

One piranha continues to pick at one last piece of its brain, then scurries away.

Dear Lord . . .

You look away and continue down the spiraling path. You come to the bottom and step outside into the bright sunlight. A perfectly paved path stretches out in front of you, a fence running along the side. At the end is the visitor center.

And there, blocking your path, is the massive female lion. Its fur slick with blood. It paces back and forth. Shakes. Twitches. Its eyes wild and red.

A goddamn zombie lion.

Yakuma spins the sword. You do the same—spraying the dead zoo thing's blood on the ground.

The lion paws at the ground, then charges, hurtling toward you.

Yakuma charges the animal and just before it pounces, drops to her knees and slides across the ground. She swings the sword, cleanly slicing off the animal's front right leg. It takes its next step with a bloody stump and crashes to the ground. It whimpers. Lashes out at you with a hairy paw.

Yakuma stands over it, knees bloodied, and chops the animal's head off.

Then a tremendous roar.

You look up. At the end of the path are three more massive lions. And behind it, a wall of zombies. The animals are bloodied, ravenous. Just like their zombie friends.

You and Yakuma look at each other. Sad. Defeated.

And then they all charge . . .

·:·:· AN END ·:·:·

ALL TOGETHER NOW

You wait to see which one jumps first. But they all come at once.

The kid leaps, throws its arms around your waist. It's like a goddamned Chucky doll. You rip it free before it gets its teeth in you.

You feel your arm flesh tear. You scream. The mother zombie has its nails in you. It digs deeper, pushing them into your arm. You try to shake it loose.

But the dad creature looms over you. It jumps, throwing all of its weight on you, taking you and its family down to the ground. Your head whacks against the cement and your eyes tear up. Through the mist, you see the father's face, hovering over you. Sick, rotted teeth. Disgusting smell of death on his breath

A drop of saliva falls from his decaying lips, lands on your tongue, sending a cold shiver through your body. Then his mouth opens wide, ready to eat . . .

AN END

You went to Comic-Con International the summer you interned in San Diego. You remember the craziness. A hundred thousand people packing the showroom floor, many in costume. And not just costumes—staggeringly detailed outfits, complete with metal helmets, thousand-dollar chunks of armor, and real-deal weapons.

You grip the boy's hand and push through the thick crowd. Need to find the back exit—now. Their defenses won't hold long.

The boy looks around in awe at the convention attendees. A middle-aged Wonder Woman. An ugly version of the Bride from *Kill Bill*. Most of the crew from the Watchmen. Frank Miller's depiction of the Joker. A puffed-up Bender. A so-real-you-can-hardly-believe-it Guts Man. Edward Scissorhands, his blades shimmering, sharp.

Glass shatters behind you. People scream. It won't take long for the beasts to flood the convention hall floor and overrun the entire place. Bodies push past you. You get swept up in the crowd, carried onto the main floor, and spit out into one of the convention hall's long aisles. Somehow the kid has managed to hold on.

Behind you echo the sounds of battle as the zombies clash with the cosplay crowd.

You drag the kid down long aisles lined with tables and booths, stocked with action figures, comic books, T-shirts. Huge banners hang from the ceiling: DC COMICS, MARVEL, NICKELODEON, CAPCOM. Great—all sorts of cool shit—but where's the goddamn banner that says EMERGENCY EXIT?

It's like a hedge maze, only it's packed with people, all in full-on panic mode. You pass the remnants of the Mattel booth, slipping on Matchbox cars as you run. Transformers toys scatter the floor in front of the Hasbro booth. A sign promises a Shia LaBeouf signing.

You take a left turn. Then a right. Fuck—zombies at the end of that aisle. You turn, back the way you came. Another left.

Goddamn it! You're back where you started.

And in front of you is an epic, full-on *Night of the Living Dead* meets *Braveheart* battle. Thousands of undead New Yorkers trying to devour thousands of costumed geeks.

The battle pushes them back, onto the show floor. Fighting in the aisles. You turn to run—then realize, horrified, that your hand is empty. The boy is gone.

You look around, frantic. "Kid! Where are you?"

You sprint down the closest aisle, searching for him.

A fat man in a Freddy Krueger costume sends a case of Super Mario figurines crashing down on an approaching beast, which slows it momentarily. Fat Freddy slashes the thing in the face, splitting open four parallel slices of flesh.

Then Fat Freddy swings his open hand in a roundhouse, slamming the four blades into the thing, the steel piercing its skull. The monster drops. The next one gets Freddy, tackling him. Freddy swipes, tearing its shirt, but it's useless. The monster rips into his face, tearing at his mask, and then sinking its teeth into the flesh beneath it.

In front of you, a mock Doc Brown gets his ear ripped off by a wounded zombie, sending him falling back, screaming. He crashes into a table, sending a ten-foot statue of Bart Simpson tumbling over, pinning a young, freshly turned female zombie. Her teeth snap, biting at the air.

"Kid!" you shout. "Where the hell'd you go?"

You leap over a guy in a plush Snoopy costume, laid on his back. Costume shredded, pieces of polyester stuffing and fabric spilled out on the floor, along with his guts.

What appears to be the entire crew of the *Battlestar Galactica* is trapped in the large Warner Bros. booth. An undead Dominican woman closes in, chunks of flesh in her thick black hair. A young guy dressed as the old Doc Cottle shrieks and faints.

Boba Fetts—*why are there so many goddamn Boba Fetts??*—are dying all around you.

You turn down the next aisle, desperate to find the boy. Trekkies are littered about—either dead, dying, or rising. One gets to its feet. A goateed man, looking nearly identical to *Half-Life's* Gordon Freeman, bashes it in the head with his crowbar.

A massive Hispanic man dressed as Alex from *A Clockwork Orange* sends one of the zombies flying across the room. The rest of his droogs get it right quick in a stunning bit of the ol' ultraviolence on the undead.

Three zombie firemen stumble down the aisle toward you. A cute little blond thing done up as Buffy jumps in front of you swinging a frighteningly realistic version of the famous Vampire Slaying Scythe. But the zombie firefighters don't burst into bad CGI dust—they spill blood as they're cut to pieces. Fucking hot, Buffy.

Next aisle. You freeze.

In front of you, four guys done up as the Ghostbusters—zombified. Blood and flesh drips from their lips. Egon, missing part of his shoulder, runs at you.

Fuck.

You run.

They tear down the aisle, crashing after you.

Suddenly, in your face, a flash of wood. You drop, sliding to the ground under the swing. Above you, the wood crashes into monster Egon's face. Its nose splits.

You're on your back, staring up at one helluva authentic Donatello costume. A fat green hand pulls you up. Red headband. Raphael.

"Close call," Raphael says behind his mask. He's got a thick Irish accent.

Irish Raphael spins his twin golden sais in his hands.

He whips the first sai through the air, nails undead Venkman in the head, killing it.

Leonardo comes out of nowhere, spinning his blade and chopping off Winston at the legs. Then the sword through its head.

Stantz closes in on Irish Raphael. Irish Raphael spins, sending the thing stumbling forward—right into Michelangelo. Michelangelo whips his nunchucks out and around undead Stantz's throat. It swipes at him. Irish Raphael buries the other sai into its throat, then up through the brain. The zombie gargles, spits up blood, and falls.

You mumble thanks and keep running. Ahead is the food court.

And then you see him. Across the food court at the center of the show floor. The boy, hiding beneath a table.

To your left, the glint of steel. A massive blade in the hand of a towering, shirtless, black man.

Conan the Barbarian.

"What is best in life?" Black Conan shouts. "Killing fucking zombies!"

Black Conan swings the gigantic blade around. Chops off the head of an undead Cobra Commander. Its headless body drops to the floor, red cape draping over it like a funeral shroud. The helmeted head rolls across the floor.

A security guard, belly torn open, runs at Black Conan. Conan unleashes a massive forward kick, sending the thing flying back into a life-size Darth Vader made of Legos. Vader crashes down, scattering thousands of black Lego pieces across the floor.

Four zombies drape themselves over a dude in a nearly perfect Predator costume. Thing must have cost five grand, at least. And right now—shit—it was worth every penny. The beasts can't break through it.

Perfect Predator knocks them back. Whips around his bronze telescoping spear and pierces one through the face. The others stumble back. One falls, and Predator brings the spear crashing down into the back of its head.

But the monsters don't stop. There're too goddamn many.

One beast climbs up Black Conan's back. Another, ignoring the massive sword buried in its chest, sinks its teeth into Conan's arm.

The tide is turning. Chaos and death all around you.

A rail-thin Captain America holds two beasts off with his shield while an obese Wolverine slashes wildly in some sort of half-assed attempt at a berserker attack.

A kid in a Tusken Raider costume takes down two of them with his gaffi stick before getting it himself.

A bunch of Asian girls in Pokémon gear get massacred.

A pretty-boy vampire, covered in sparkles, is torn to shreds by Dracula.

Against the wall sits a man in an extremely authentic Iron Man suit, head in his hands, shaking. The beasts crowd about him, but can't get through the armor.

You sprint across the floor and through the food court. You grab the kid and pull.

You look up at the banners a couple of aisles away from you. One reads NINTENDO. The other LUCASFILM.

Run for the Nintendo booth? Turn to page 112.

Down the Lucasfilm aisle? Turn to page 380.

You wake to the smell of barbecue. It can't be. Can it? Barbecue?? Your stomach tugs at you. Your body lifts you, like Garfield chasing a lasagna, and you're carried out.

At the center of the site, Al stands over a grill, flipping dogs. Nearby is Sully, at a plastic folding table, examining what looks to be a map laid out in front of him. Fish sits across from him, playing with his thumbs.

You drag your feet over, still half asleep, but beckoned by the sweet smell of meat.

Al looks up. "Hey, it's the tough guy. How'd you sleep, sunshine?"

"Hey. Fine."

"Burger, dog, or both?" he asks.

"Uh—both, if you've got it."

Al nods and throws another patty on. A few dogs cook, blackened.

Everyone seems awful calm, awful relaxed, considering the army amassing at the fences. So you say, "You guys seem awful calm, awful relaxed, considering the army amassing at the fences."

"That's 'cause we figured a way out of this mess, college boy," Al says, taking a long drink from a Heineken.

You perk up. "For real?"

"For real."

You take a seat at the table next to Sully. He writes on the map with a black Sharpie. He does an equation on the side—then crosses it out. Scribbles some more. Complicated math.

"What is that?" you ask.

"Map."

"Of what?"

"City sewer system."

The sewer! Bingo. You can Ninja Turtle your way right the fuck outta here.

Al drops a plastic plate in front of you. Cheeseburger. Hot dog. You dig in. Not stopping to chew, you manage to say, "So we escape through the sewer, huh?"

"That's the idea," Sully says.

"Where's the manhole or whatever?"

Sully looks up at you, annoyed. Then points to a huge pump not far across the site. "Right there."

"Huh?"

"Pump leads to a water tank, which leads directly to the sewer."

"So how do we get down there?"

"You'll see," he says, standing up. "Fish, mount up."

Fish nods, looking nervous. He stands up slowly and walks to a huge truck crane with a wrecking ball attached. He climbs onto the metal tank-style tread and into the driver's seat of the enormous vehicle. There's a rumble and it starts up. The tracks move slowly and the crane begins to turn. The huge wrecking ball hangs from the end of a steel rope, swaying.

"So what—you just knock it over?" you ask.

"Basically," Sully says. "Fish clears out the pump, Al blows the tank, and we—"

"Blows?"

Al slams the grill shut, then holds up a stick of dynamite. "Blows."

You nod, impressed—and just a little scared.

"Right," Sully continues. "Then we head underground."

Sully calls Al over and they go over the math. Then Al grabs a duffel bag and places the dynamite inside.

"When do we go?" you ask.

Sully folds up the plans and puts them in his back pocket and looks up at you, sun in his eyes. "Now."

He waves at Fish. Fish waves back. Sully gives a thumbs-up, then there's a loud cranking sound as a secondary steel rope pulls the ball toward the crane cab. Then it stops. Locked and loaded.

"Here we go," Al says.

Fish works three large gears. Then he reaches over and slams his hand down.

The massive ball unloads, flying toward the pump. It smashes into it, breaking it to pieces. A geyser of water shoots up out of the ground.

Perfect.

And then—

Fuck . . .

Then it swings back.

You can see it coming. So can Sully—he reaches out, grabs your arm, and squeezes.

The wrecking ball swings back over the pump and into the fence, smashing through and carrying directly into the monsters. One cartwheels through the air and smashes into the side of an apartment building across the street. Another slams into the side of an SUV, setting off the alarm. The rest land on the street.

The wrecking ball swings back, sending another five monsters flying in the other direction.

The fence is torn open. The zombies pour in. "Al, blow it, now!" Sully shouts.

Al drops the duffel bag and pulls out three sticks of dynamite. Fish leaps down from the crane cab and begins sprinting toward you—at the same time, the beasts begin pouring through the open fencing and down the hill. You've got thirty seconds, maybe, before they're upon you.

"Fuck, fuck, fuck," Al mutters. He holds up the three sticks and intertwines the fuses. He eyes the bomb for a split second, wheels in his head turning, then bites off a chunk of the fuse.

Then he rips a Zippo from his shirt pocket, lights the fuse, and tosses it next to the geyser. "Get back!" he shouts, running

alongside Sully. You follow him around the side of a huge Caterpillar dump truck. Fish catches up.

"How long?" Sully asks, catching his breath.

"I tried for ten," Al says.

"Tried?"

"I had to rip it with my fucking teeth."

You peek your head around the side of the truck. The beasts are down the hill. They're coming in your direction. They're almost at the dynamite.

Then at it.

Then.

BOOM!!!

You're thrown to the ground. Your ears ring. Dust fills the air and rocks rain down around you like hail.

A hand on you. Al. He pulls you up. You see him mouth the words "come on," but you don't hear him. He pulls you around the side of the truck. A hundred zombie bodies are scattered across the construction site. Twisted and destroyed. Some dead. Some crawling. Scraping at the dirt.

Al has just blown a massive hole in the earth—at least sixty feet in circumference. It slants down from all sides to a smaller hole at the bottom. Sully leaps in. He slides down the hill, and then disappears.

You look up. Monsters just as far from the hole as you are. It'll be a race.

Are you fast enough?

To head down into the pit and go for the sewer, turn to page 221.

To turn and run like hell, turn to page 177.

On the third day, the looters come.

You and Walter are talking *Hogan's Heroes.* You've pretty much run out of topics that interest both of you. You know those bad relationships where the boyfriend and girlfriend are hanging on to just one thing? Well that's you and Walter—and that one thing is Colonel Klink. You're about to ask him if he likes *F Troop,* in hopes of widening your conversation options, when Walter cuts you off.

"Shhh. You hear that?"

"I hear the same thing I've been hearing for three days straight. Your busted AC rumbling and those fucking things moaning and groaning out there."

"No. Something else."

You both go to the window. He's right. Two people. Across the street trying to break into the CVS. You look down at Walter's hand. He grips the large metallic revolver. You can read his mind.

"Don't," you say. "They're just looking for supplies to survive."

"They cross this street, they're dead."

"And then what? You shoot them—let every one of those fucking things know we're in here?"

"Maybe. I don't give a damn. They touch my store, they die."

The pair, dressed in all black, creep across the street. They move carefully between abandoned cars. The zombies don't take notice.

They approach the store.

Walter raises the gun and slips it between two planks of wood, aimed directly at the outside door.

"Walter, don't do it."

Walter's finger curls around the trigger as the pair step closer.

Mind your own damn business and let him shoot? Turn to page 80.

If you want to physically stop Walter, turn to page 54.

EPISODE VII:
THE COSPLAY WARS

You and the kid dart down the Lucasfilm aisle. Grab a mock Luke Skywalker lightsaber out of a freshly dead man's hand.

Up ahead, you can see an exit sign, just above the top of a gigantic, near life-size model of the Imperial AT-ST chicken walkers from *Return of the Jedi*.

An undead Harry Potter and Hermione sprint around the corner. You swing the saber, knocking Hermione into Harry. But another dozen of the monsters follow.

Above you towers the massive AT-ST model. You look at the legs. You think like an Ewok.

"Push!" you shout. The kid throws his weight into the legs. You do the same. You feel it move. One final push, and it tips, bringing the entire wall down with it.

A clear path.

In front of you, the signing booths. Deserted. Empty chairs, some knocked over. Every booth abandoned.

Except for one.

He sits there. Calm. Giant black horn-rimmed glasses. A green fishing vest. White beard. Pen still in his hand.

George.

Fucking.

Romero.

And behind him, the exit.

You sprint across the floor, covering the distance in seconds. You put your hand on the door, then you stop. Turn around. What the hell is Romero doing?

"Let's goooo," the kid says, tugging at your shirt.

You nod. But you don't move.

Slowly, as if he has all the time in the world, as if an onslaught of zombies isn't facing him, Romero puts his pen down, pushes his chair back, and stands.

"Stop!" Romero shouts. Then, in some bizarre language, "*Finjt!*"

And, amazingly, they do. Every single zombie. They shuffle into a semicircle stretching the entire length of the exhibit hall. Those on the ground, eating, raise their heads, flesh dangling from their chins like a baby eating spaghetti. The wreckage of the battle stretches out behind them.

Footsteps to your left. A man comes around the corner booth, clutching his shoulder. He's bit. But not yet turned. He makes eye contact with you, then stumbles over.

You recognize him. He's an actor, maybe? Something. You've definitely seen him. *Sex Machine*?

He stumbles into you, hits the wall, and sinks to the floor.

"Hey, aren't you?" you whisper.

"Yes," he chokes out.

Good lord—it's Tom Savini. The sultan of splatter. The godfather of gore. The makeup artist that for decades made George Romero's monsters come to life onscreen.

"I never thought this day would come," Savini says. His words are raspy. He can barely speak.

"What are you talking about?"

He looks up at you. His face has gone white. He's going to turn soon.

"George did this."

"George Romero?"

"Fuck do you think I'm talking about?" he says, then coughs up blood.

"What—"

"Years ago. Nineteen seventy-seven probably. We were shooting *Dawn of the Dead*. I was"—Savini stops to wipe the blood from his chin—"I was doing makeup. We had these extras on set—just a handful, that George would never let me touch. Only George was allowed to work with them. There were these rumors—rumors that they weren't actors at all. That they were zombies. The real fucking thing. And that only George could communicate with them."

"Get the fuck out of here." But you look up, and George is in complete control of the monsters. He continues to bark at them in this strange, foreign language.

Savini nods, his eyes beginning to glaze over. "It's all true. So one night, we had just wrapped shooting and we were celebrating in this local Pittsburgh bar. I got George drunk—just kept feeding him can after can of Iron City. And that's when he started talking."

"What are you talking about?"

"Nineteen fifty-eight. George was eighteen—had just moved to Pittsburgh to study art at Carnegie Mellon. He had this best friend—a local guy, townie. He was a coal miner, like every guy over eighteen in rural PA back then. So this one night—it's his buddy's birthday, so George and his girlfriend drive out to the mine. They're going to pick his buddy up when he gets off work, surprise him. But he never comes out of the mine. No one does. Finally, it's like two A.M., and George decides to go down there looking for him."

Savini rolls over, vomits. He grabs your arm, twists. Just minutes until he turns.

"Something had happened—some gas had escaped. I'm not sure. Only George knows for sure. But down there—the whole crew, zombified. Monsters. Turned into a fucking monster. George runs like hell, gets back to the car just in time to see his best friend tear his girlfriend's throat out.

"The mining company covered it all up, caved in the mine, wrote it off as an accident. Wasn't uncommon back then.

"But George went back, two days later. Into the woods. And he found them. His girlfriend and his best friend—these mad, snarling zombies. He got a hold of them, locked them up in this shack, way deep in the woods.

"That's when George lost it. This woman—this woman that was going to be the love of his life—she was a fucking zombie. He developed this hatred for the world. You'd never know it—he buried it down so deep inside him.

"Nineteen seventy-two. Made a film called *Season of the Witch*. Then he disappeared—for five years, no one saw him. He just stayed out by that shack, studying the two of them. Doing tests. Taking blood. He wanted to figure out what had made them into these monsters—and he wanted to re-create it."

"All of his films—all shot in rural Pennsylvania. Never shot a scene more than a hundred miles from that shack. He couldn't stand to be away from them for more than a day or two.

"We never spoke about it again after that night. Though I'd hear him—in his trailer—speaking this language. This shit he's speaking now."

"Wait—so you're saying?"

"What I'm saying is, George has done it. He's re-created it. He's unleashed it. George Romero is the fucking lord, leader, and king of the undead."

Romero continues to speak to the crowd. "*Reech nargh tan sein renchhhh!*"

"What is he saying?" you ask.

Savini manages a few words at a time. "Something like 'My children, our time is now.'"

Romero continues: "*En vest nass rane ciptola. Roark thu masse. Roark san tremen. Tremen vuye DEAD!*"

Savini translates: "Here, in New York City, not five miles from where I was born, you were birthed today. Birthed to become an army. My army of the dead!"

In unison the zombies moan.

Savini begins to turn. You can see him trying to fight it off. "Go—go now," he says. "Far away from here. Just go."

Savini hobbles to his feet. "George, George old friend. This is madness."

George turns.

He shakes his head. "Tom, Tom, Tom . . . Please, don't interfere."

Then George points at Savini and barks out *"Vast minch. Enreark!"*

Six of the zombies step forward. George points at Savini.

Savini doesn't resist. He stands, ready for it. The monsters tackle him. Devour him.

"Enziet!"

The monsters stop. Slowly, they return to where they were.

"Farich!"

The zombies turn. Begin marching out the door. All of them. Back through the maze of overturned booths.

George walks behind them, letting them lead the way. Finally, they reach the exit. George barks an order, and they leave, out into the streets.

And George follows.

The place is silent. Just you and the kid. Your head is spinning. Can't believe what you just heard—what you just saw.

"What was that?" the kid asks.

"Kid, if I told you, you'd never believe me," you say, and you push open the exit door, grab him by his hand, and take off running.

THE END